BLACK

THE BURDEN

D. B. HALBERT

For information contact :

D.B.HalbertAuthor@gmail.com

Or on Tritter @DBHalbertAuthor

Book and Cover design by D. B. Halbert

ISBN : 978-0-578-45207-4

First Edition : January 2019

10 9 8 7 6 5 4 3 2 1

CONTENTS

1

It's Alright to Cry

The cold silence of the night sits gently on the secret island palace, broken by the cascading of small waves against the rocky beaches where the island's mountainous cliffs meet the sea. The stars above shine bright in an orchestra of colored nebulas broken by the radiant imposing full moon that drifts ever slowly through the sky. The mist from the lapping waves fills the air with a light freshness that cools the magically warmed air of the secret island.

From a stone balcony that extends from the rising flat cliff face, which grows from the stony beach at the rear of the island, a single glass test tube falls and in the silence between crashing waves, the fragile tube shatters ringing like a pin drop in a soundless room. A moment settles the sound far below the balcony and the open windowed doors that lead into the fourth story room, before through the peace that rests in the night's air, pierces, with unnatural intensity, Eliza's voice crying out, "Aldrin!"

The island itself shakes with the sudden burst of the painful echoing wail. From the back balcony, visible sonic waves press out over the open ocean from Eliza's mouth, with tears of sorrow and pain that form and begin to trickle from her eyes. The name trails off from her voice, which becomes a pressing high pitch wordless scream expelling the last of her breath. The weight of the sadness leaving her without air, Eliza falls forward to hold herself up on the banister.

With the ominous rumble coming to an end with the bottom of Eliza's lungs, Pearl's eyes open as her mind connects the scream with her young friend. Leaping from the water where she fell asleep, Pearl lands on the marble dock in a worried defensive stance. In the same moment, in a large room within the palace's expanse, a small orb of eyes lifts from the bag it was resting on and attempts to get its bearings through a frightened panic. Steadying himself, Boop looks at the closed double doors of the room's entrance. He closes his eyes and pushes for the wood barrier with as much force as he can apply.

Gasping through wheezing breaths, Eliza sobs for several seconds without air entering her lungs, but straightening her stance and looking to the heavens, she feels them expand before releasing again in a scream, "You weren't supposed to leave me!" The powerful echoing supernaturally loud voice washes out filling the air once more with Eliza's suffering as her voice again fades from her words into an unintelligible sound.

Running into the palace through the monolithic front doors, Pearl slips on the marble floor with her wet boots failing to maintain traction as the hypersonic sound returns, ear piercing and rattling the floor underfoot. Attempting to cover her ears in hopes of protecting them from the terrible painful sound, Pearl slips rolling against the wall, opposite the front doors, past the entry hall. With a groan to herself, gritting at the unheavenly loud noise that vaguely retains the feel of Eliza's voice, Pearl rubs the fin she rolled over, which flares out from the back of her calf through the slit she made for it in her trousers. Hearing the sound of the painful grief filled scream fade with Eliza's distant breath running thin, Pearly is reaffirmed in her desire to protect her young friend, and she begins again in a sprint down one of the halls.

Reeling away from the strong wooden doors, which stand unmoved from the full force slam of his body striking their seam, Boop shakes, dizzily remembering how the doors opened when he and Eliza entered the room. Slowly the floating orb drifts down to the doorknob, and with anxious want to escape the room to find his master, he bites onto the cold metal handle and turns, pulling the door only slightly into the room. With a way out, Boop whips into the hall rushing to find where Eliza has hidden in the vast palace.

Eliza continues sobbing as she struggles to fill her lungs again, feeling the lining of her throat throb with the sore inflammation of exertion far exceeding what could be considered normal screaming, and she wants to stop but is unable to, in sadness and chemically induced compulsion. Heaving for air and looking out to the crashing ocean, black with the night, Eliza sees on the back of her hands which hold her upon the banister, black veins showing through her skin which extend from up her arms. Worry fills her movements as she looks at them and is panicked, but her mind focuses again on her sorrow. Balling a fist and bringing it down like a hammer onto the sturdy banister Eliza's lungs fill again with air. Lifting both arms up and throwing them down and back on her sides, she lets forth another earth-shaking wail, crying, "I wanted to be stronger for you and Pearl, I wanted to be beautiful enough!"

Pearl has to brace herself against the wall as the palace once again shakes under her feet as she climbs the set of stairs to the second floor. Still, she pushes on, driven to find and protect young Eliza. Reaching the top of the stairs she is climbing, Pearl's path crosses with Boop's, and with both of them unconsciously focused on the same goal in their actions, they continue to move quickly for their suffering friend as the piercing sound suffocates with Eliza's waning breath.

Eliza more easily finds her breath through the sobbing as the words almost instantly fill her lungs to continue her demanding cry to the heavens. Looking to the stars above as her lungs fill with air, Eliza stomps a foot in anger at her grief. A torrent of wind surges around her, undoing her enormous braid, and throwing her beautiful soft sixty feet of hair back, and away from her into the room. Her voice booms with a power that dwarfs the terrifyingly loud cries she has released, as she screams, "I could have been stronger for you, Aldrin!" The words leave behind a gritting, angry, yet sorrowful taste in her mouth. In that moment, when Eliza clenches her fist ever tighter, the black veins that have spread across her body begin to glow, radiating a black and purple energy that magically lifts Eliza from the marble floor.

Pearl drops to the wall desperately trying to cover her ears, as Eliza's voice rings ever more powerfully through the halls. Boop continues only a few feet before seeing Pearl struggling to stand and drifting to her side he lifts her and helps her move ever closer to the epicenter of the sound. When the breath that carries Eliza's tremendous scream fades, Pearl's stride quickens again pushing her to find the next staircase up, underfoot.

Levitating slowly upward, but too entrenched in her weeping to notice, Eliza sniffles another breath into her lungs continuing in her angry grieving, yelling, "Why wasn't I strong enough! Why couldn't I stop you! Why can't I be perfect! Why!" Thirty or more feet above the balcony, Eliza's last words release a wave of power that washes out over the island as a visible wall of purple magic that rushes out radially. The water the falls against the rocky base of the island suddenly breaks, pulling away with the magical burst revealing the barren seafloor.

The wave casts out, passing through the stone of the palace and island unaffected by their presence, and washing over Pearl and Boop, it throws the two to the side against the staircase's wall. Pearl grabs again at her ears which from the painful proximity to the piercing wail begin to bleed. Boop again finds his way to Pearl's side and uses his body to help her to her feet and push ever closer to the scream's source which to this point has been muffled by the stone walls.

The magic surging from her pulls Eliza's appendages, outstretching them to their fullest extent, almost painfully, and releasing from her back the behemoth pair of black skeletal wings that were magically hidden within her, as she sobs, wanting to curl into a ball, before releasing a final crying yell that sends another wave of magic, "I wasn't enough!" The words fade into a final unintelligible scream. The wave that lashes out from Eliza's form is far more intense than the one before instantly creating large, menacing cracks in the side of the palace and destroying the balcony that was below her.

Pearl and Boop watch the second terrifying wave of magic, blast the door of a room in the hall they are moving through from its hinges with frightening ferocity, breaking it into splinters against the far wall. The two don't have even a second to prepare themselves for the incoming wave after they see the door break from its hold before they are slammed painfully into the wall with the force that shattered the door. Still undeterred panic fills Pearl and Boop's hearts pressing them still forward. The sound fades and they look into the room to see the balcony over the jagged rocky shore missing, broken free from its hold on the palace's outer wall.

Crossing the room in a fraction of a second, catching herself on the side of the doorway out, Pearl looks down to the rocks below fearing the worst for her young friend. In that same moment, Eliza loses consciousness and begins to fall. Boop joins Pearl at the door out of a cliff face, and in that instant one of his eyes catches sight of the falling image of a rose-pink dress and long sky-blue hair, and in a moment of instinct the small orb shoots out of the opening in the wall, turns to face the falling Eliza, and blasts his telekinetic energy into her.

Pearl feels her heartbeat in the ringing of her ears. A single deep thump reverberates as the only muffled sound in Pearl's head when the waves of force form between Boop and a target above the opening. Another slow beat flashes life into Pearl's bloodshot eyes as strands of sky-blue fall into her view against the glowing starry horizon. Turning to look for her descending friend Pearl feels another strong heartbeat behind her breaths, heavy from running. An instinct takes over with the next beat of Pearl's heart sending out one of her arms in a wanting attempt to catch the falling form. Contact is made with Eliza's form, as Pearl's hand grabs to cling to something but panic again strikes her as the dress' image passes formless over her hand. Another heartbeat, and worry fills Pearl, as her arm reaches out again in a flailing, final attempt, which finds success with her hand locking onto Eliza's wrist.

The world almost seems to return to a normal speed when Eliza falls the rest of the way past the opening in the wall. Pearl drops to the floor with Eliza's weight pulling hard on both of their shoulders. She feels a pop from her shoulder when the weight comes to a sudden stop slamming into the palace's wall. With a gritting painful pull, she heaves Eliza's heavy motionless body slowly up into the room. The spurred black bones that comprise Eliza's wings snag on the floor's edge for a second before a push from below frees them to scratch and grind against the marble with Pearl pulling their bearer into the small room.

Laying Eliza on her side, which leaves a good portion of the skeletal wings protruding from the opening, Pearl rests against the wall looking over the unconscious form of her sad young friend, on whose face tears still dry. No sign of the black veins remains visible for Pearl to witness as she presses her hand into her own shoulder rubbing it, seeing both it, and the shoulder of the arm which she grabbed to save Eliza, have dislocated. Rolling her eyes almost, apparently annoyed by the injuries presence, Pearl stands and steps to the doorway that leads to the hall. Gritting her teeth, she performs an action she has only done once before. Thrusting herself against the door frame she feels the pop and almost screams as she forces her arm back into its socket.

Boop drifts back into the room, visibly exhausted from his attempt to slow Eliza's decent, and sees Pearl stood over Eliza, the dislocated arm in hand. Flying to Pearl's side Boop's five eyes fill with a concern which stops Pearl, who explains, "Hey, buddy, Lizzy's arm came out of its socket and we have to put it back in or it will end up hurting even more in the long run. Ok? I am not trying to hurt her, but the pain might wake her back up. You need to trust me on this, we can't leave her arm like this."

Drifting away to give pearl space Boop responds in a voice like a pug's growl, "Ok."

With a nod Pearl looks back to Eliza's arm saying, "Alright, Lizzy, this might hurt, but it would hurt a lot more if you were conscious," and with a single forceful push, that ends with a pop, a sigh escapes from Pearl, who slumps back down having successfully relocated the shoulder in its socket. With a deep breath Pearl looks at Eliza, still unconscious, asking, "Wow, you really are out of it. What happened? Why did you come this far into the palace?"

"Is she alright now," Boop asks floating down to look at Eliza's gently closed eyes.

Pearl pulls Eliza closer, putting the unconscious girl's head in her lap, and she begins to stroke the soft blue hair, responding, "Her wings are still extended, and we know how much they hurt her when they retract but she's strong, she'll be alright."

2

The Palace

Stepping over the puddle as the four get down the stairs, Pearl takes the lead through the palace for Eliza, Auburn and Aldrin following. Reaching the front door, however, stops Pearl in her tracks, as out on the marble slab dock Rev and Lorm sit eating as they watch Esmerelda pace angrily in front of them. Pulling around behind Aldrin, Pearl pushes the metal braced man forward saying, "Alright, I got us here, you tell her about what happened."

Unamused Aldrin rolls his eyes and steps forward onto the marble path toward Esmerelda. He raises his hands defensively in front of himself when she sees him leading the group toward her, in turn she begins to stomp in their direction. Meeting them at the overgrown fountain halfway between the now docked ship and the monolithic front door of the palace, Esmerelda's hand sternly finds hold of Aldrin's collar. Pulling the leather of his under vest, she brings his eyes in line with hers demanding, "Alright, you four have some explaining to do, so for starters, mind sharing with me why the sun has fallen hours back in the sky?"

"There was an incident with a very powerful magic device," Aldrin responds, keeping his hands up and open to the sides of his head, "which transported the island and everything in it from near the broken isle to the coast of port Dru'heim."

Esmerelda recoils from shock at Aldrin's response, "You mean we went from being two days from Blackgate to the freaking Dwarf content? Do you know how many days that puts between us and Blackgate, between me and my family?"

Stepping to Aldrin's side Eliza reaches out for Esmerelda's shoulder explaining, "We couldn't have known what was going to happen."

"Twenty-four days," Esmerelda says releasing Aldrin with a downtrodden look on her face, continuing, "One hour to look around, turned into twenty-two days added onto the two we had left!" Esmerelda turns to Pearl who hides behind the group. With a furious glare, she takes a step in that direction to find Aldrin restraining her from further aggression. Pulling against the man wrapped in metal Esmerelda screams at Pearl, "We were only two days away, and you wanting one hour to explore, which has put us basically back at the beginning of the voyage!"

Eliza moves between Esmerelda and Pearl, raising her hands to the angry captain she explains, "Wait, wait, calm down, we can transport back tomorrow."

Confusion strikes Esmerelda still, causing her to ask in response, "Wait, back tomorrow? If you can use the same thing to take us back why can't you do it now?"

Pearl leans over Eliza's side explaining, "Magic doesn't work like that."

"Alright then explain it," Esmerelda responds, changing her stance, crossing her arms disapprovingly.

Rolling her eyes with a sigh Pearl explains, "When something is enchanted there are two forms that the enchantment can be expressed in, either consistent or surging effects. An item with a consistent effect is one that uses less magic than the structure of the item could potentially use, like my satchel, and boots, which maintain certain magical properties for me to use on my whim. The other form, the surging effect, on the other hand, uses more magic than the item should be able to manifest, causing a onetime or instantaneous effect before either destroying the object or leaving it inert. The best magical objects are created in the median area of these two options using exactly the amount of magic an object could possibly withstand having stored within it, allowing it to release surges that over time, recharge."

"And the device that transported us has to recharge?"

"Right, the big talking stone head said it should only take twenty-four hours."

"Big stone head?"

Auburn breaks into the conversation, placing a hand on Esmerelda's shoulder, "Look captain, I'm as irked by all o' this as ye are, bit thae to are trying ta git back ta their hooms in Blackgate as weel, sae thay wouldn't ha intentionally changed th' idiotic course we ur set on. Tell ye whit when they're dane wasting time in this ruin I'll buy ye a drank in Dru'heim."

With a sigh, Esmerelda puts a hand to her head responding, "I could use a drink. Don't go cheapin' out on me later, you got that?"

Pearl turns and steps back toward the palace responding, "Don't worry about that we'll take good care of your liver."

An angry look returns to Esmerelda's face before Aldrin steps again between her and Pearl saying, "I promise you that Pearl and I understand what you are going through we will do what we can for you. You have my word."

Returning to her crew Esmerelda looks back to the group, who reenter the strange excessively large palace, and sees Eliza running in her direction. Several quick clicks of boot bottoms clapping against the marble path lead the young girl into a jump that turns into a meager tackle that pushes into a deep soft embrace before the caring musical voice mutters for only Esmerelda to hear, "We will find your family, and we will make things right, ok? This is only a small delay."

Releasing Esmerelda, Eliza runs back to join the others. Two steps from the silence-stricken captain, she extends a hand up toward the palace door. From her room on the ship, where he has been sleeping, Boop vanishes, reappearing a few feet in front of his young creator, startled awake. Getting to his side, and continuing in a run past, Eliza smiles as she passes him, challenging him to a race, that he accepts. In a surprising burst of speed Boop reaches the door in half the time it takes Eliza, who joins the waiting three, and the five continue in to search the rest of the palace, their palace, in hopes of finding something magical that might help them when they get to Blackgate.

Turning a corner to step up a staircase to the second story, Pearl turns to Eliza who still struggles to catch her breath from the short sprint. With an inquisitive smile, Pearl asks, "How are you so chipper?"

"How are you?"

"Uh, well, I just can't stop thinking about what Negmor said. I have lived for so long not knowing who my father was. I thought that I grew to a point where I didn't care, but knowing now that he is alive, and that he has the same name as the man in the books my mom would read to me when I was young, I don't know, I just can't stop thinking that I will be able to meet him."

"Well, then, that will be my reason."

"But me having a father I might actually one day be able to meet doesn't affect you. I mean you just learned the people you wanted to be dead aren't, and still had the strength to bear the weight of a deal with that strange woman, so we wouldn't have to, and you are standing here, smiling, having given Esmerelda, who is furious with us, an unrequested hug, and challenged Boop to a race to return to us, after all you have been through."

"Esmerelda needed a hug, to let her really know that there is still compassion in the world, even as it feels to be falling down around her. Boop has been locked up for so long he was going to start going stir crazy if I didn't let him stretch his eyestalks. I know what Negmor said, and it sits heavy on me, but if everyone shows their suffering on their sleeve the world would never be filled with joy. I am smiling, and I am overflowing with joy because there is a chance that everything will turn out alright, because if there is even the smallest inkling of hope that even with all the things that are going wrong we might be able to come out better in the end, for what we are going through."

"Wow," Pearl breaths, stopping with Eliza's words, falling slightly behind the moving group, stunned by the young girl's perspective.

Turning to Pearl, Aldrin also stops and steps to her to explain, in a way that Eliza is unable to hear, "What did you think? That a kid who has been through what she has, been at the brink of death like when I found her, seen the worst of people, and still hasn't been accepted as even human by someone she travels with, would be able to continue with accepting the weight of all the bad that happens to her? Either she knows how to let her suffering go better than any of us, or she is stronger than any of us could ever be."

"There's a good chance that both are true," Pearl responds watching Eliza send a smile to Boop, who has flown for an open door and turned back as though asking for permission.

The five continue in near silence through the halls of the palace. Each room they peer into as barren as the last, empty of any furniture or decoration. After what feels like an hour, which only permits the group to explore a very small number of the rooms within the palace's walls, Auburn growls to the others as they open another door that leads into another empty room, saying, "Look at tha', anither empty room, whin will ye all admit it, th' palace is empty, a guid steid tae build up maybe bit thare is nothin 'ere that is aff tae help us."

"Perhaps he is right Pearl," Aldrin adds stretching with a yawn.

Rolling her eyes Pearl shrugs agreeing, "Yea, seems like you may be right. Come on Lizzy, let's go see if we can find a tailor in Dru'heim."

With a soft smile Eliza joins the others ushering Boop to follow, and they begin their way down a different set of stairs back to the first floor. There, the group step into the large unkept park of a garden that fills the center acre of the regal structure and they weave through the overgrown path that leads them back into a final hall between them and the front entrance. Walking in silence along the hall Eliza and Pearl stop as Boop breaks the quiet and begins to growl at a spot on one of the walls.

Looking closely to where Boop growls, Pearl pushes against a seam in the bricks calling to the other two, "Hey guys wait! There's a secret room here."

Auburn audibly groans when he is stopped by Aldrin's hand falling on his shoulder. Turning to face Pearl both men feel a cold breeze as the wall she pushes against slides slowly, swinging like a door into a hidden space with a staircase that leads down. Going to step away from the new opening Auburn says to the others behind him, "Great, mair empty space fur ye tae fill, efter I'm home."

"Oh, come on, it's not even noon yet your booze can wait one more area, even if it is empty. The rooms hidden behind a secret door it's more likely to have stuff in them, if there is anything in this palace at all," Pearl's voice calls to Auburn's back, unable to turn him.

Looking to Pearl to see her face expressing a determination to explore the hidden basement with or without anyone else, Aldrin rolls his eyes and lets his feet carry him quickly to Auburn. Placing a hand again on the crimson man's shoulder they stop as he says, "Look, you said it yourself, we need everyone in this group if we are going to have a chance in three days, and if anywhere in a dead wizard's home is going to be trapped, the secret rooms hidden in the wall are going to be those places."

Auburn stands still for a second, releasing a deep, angry breath before in a single powerful motion he returns to and storms through the secret door. Holding his hand to his side, he lets it ignite into a glowing orange flame that illuminates a short distance down the descending tunnel. The others join him and they venture into the darkness down a staircase that curves gently and stretches deeper into the earth than any of the other staircases they have crossed stretched up. More than a minute of walking down the tight staircase finally brings an end into view with another waiting marble floor.

The waiting room sits, not to Auburn's surprise, barren of any sign of possession, connected to another room by a ten-foot arch in the center of the wall opposite the stairs. In the left wall of the room looking from the base of the stairs is a thin hall that leads away, further than the light of Auburn's flickering fire engulfed hand can illuminate. In the conjoined empty room's walls sit two doorways. One, a set of double doors that appear to have been burnt to black coal. The other a single metal door that somehow holds on its surface a thick layer of frost. Facing the group Auburn asks in a frustrated growl, "Thare, nothin, kin we please go now?"

Pearl sighs as Aldrin turns to her with a shrug but she is confused, as worry takes his face. Pushing past Pearl, Aldrin runs to Eliza, who steps quickly down the thin hall after Boop. Stopping the young companion, he asks, "Where are you going? We are headed back up."

"Boop feels something this way, we have to check it out," Eliza responds with a look in her eyes that hits Aldrin like Pearl's determination, but with a soft young curiosity added.

Slowly raising his arm Aldrin gestures for Eliza to continue on, before saying to Pearl and Auburn, "Let's just check down this hallway and then we will head back."

Spinning with a pointed finger aimed to Auburn over her shoulder, Pearl laughs a simple, "Ha," before hustling to Eliza's side in the dark path.

Closing her eyes as the four walk behind the focused floating Boop, Eliza clenches a fist and with a soft breath lets it open slowly as it ignites in a radiant golden, flameless, heatless light that illuminates the path with the same intensity as Auburn's flame. A short distance further brings the five to a massive chamber that is three times as long as it is wide, softly glowing with blue light that pulses from glyphic divots dug into the marble of the floor that fills the first third of the room. Beyond the glowing pattern on the floor, the middle third of the room is a black square tile flanked by statues at its corners that stand armed with rusted halberds.

At the far end sits alone, on the far side of the last third of the room, a large jade table carved to appear to have jade chains wrapping around its base. On the jade slab's top is a golden stand that holds on it a single rod of black and gold folded or carved in a way to have a complex pattern of ridges along its shaft. At one end of the rod is a smooth platinum cap, which sits in juxtaposition of the chaotic, rose sculpture, made of rose gold, holding a large jagged blue gem, that caps the other end.

All five of his eyes focused on the short two or three-foot-long pole at the far end of the room, Boop doesn't notice the glyphs on the ground brighten as he drifts closer to being over them. The instant the edge of his form crosses the vertical axis of the divot in the ground, a loud pop sounds through the air and he is thrown away, struck by a sheet of magic that springs from the glyphs like an invisible wall. Falling into Eliza's arms, the floating creature shakes himself free of the daze the magic instills in him, and leaps back to head height, growling at the air before him.

Stepping to the edge of the blue markings, Pearl squats onto her heels staring at the magical barrier's base. Tilting her head in observation of the intensifying light, she approaches flipping a copper coin toward the space above the glyph. The instant the metal leaves her hand the power in the pulsing symbols on the ground flashes sending the coin shooting away in the same way as Boop. Looking to the wall the coin leapt to, Pearl mumbles contemplatively as she sees it smoking and cracked. Stepping to and grabbing it Pearl looks to Aldrin asking, "Any ideas?"

Baffled, Aldrin looks to Auburn and Eliza, before returning his wide-eyed gaze to Pearl responding, "You expect me know anything about this? You and Eliza are the magic buffs, and Auburn hates the stuff enough that he might know how to break it, but me? I don't use magic, haven't studied magic, and only know as much about it as I have learned out of necessity traveling with you."

"I just wanted to hear you say that," Pearl smiles before giving a wave over her shoulder turning back to the symbol, "Lizzy, you should get a closer look at this, if you are going to be any help breaking it or at least in getting past it."

Eliza looks to Pearl in surprise before stepping forward stammering in response, "O-ok. What am I looking for?"

"If I knew that we wouldn't be stopped on this side of the magic floor glyphs, now would we? Alright try to see if you can recognize anything about the magic, or the glyph, that would allow us to revert or subvert its effects."

"OK, I'll try," Eliza responds stepping to the other side of the pattern in the floor, before, like Pearl, she squats down and starts looking at the strange crystalline substance that radiates blue. With Eliza moving into the room so does the gold glowing light that dances with the movements of her hand.

Pearl goes to poke the blue divot in the marble expecting to have her arm thrown back from a magical attack but finds no such displeasure with her finger landing amongst the crystal structures. With a proud accomplished smug grin painting itself onto her face, Pearl looks up only to have her joy crushed as she sees standing in the middle of the web of blue lines Auburn, unamused, looking to the other end of the room. Rising Pearl looks angrily at Auburn before yelling at him, "Now how is it that you hate magic so much but found your way through that warding sigil so easily?"

Looking with a blank stare into Pearl's eyes Auburn shrugs before looking to Aldrin, "Aldrin, do ye mind taking mah spot 'ere?"

Not sure what he is agreeing to, Aldrin responds hesitatively, "Sure," before stepping forward and putting himself in the center of the magic ward placed in the floor. Free from the task, Auburn steps to Eliza, still watching from her squat position on the pattern's edge.

Gently grabbing Eliza's wrist, who out of curiosity doesn't resist, and pulling it up slightly Auburn turns to Pearl and points at the wall behind her, continuing, "A'richt, Aldrin, shift fur a seicont."

Moving from his spot Aldrin nearly jumps as the strange pattern on the floor erupts to life once more with a low thrum ringing out with the blue light returning to the room. Auburn gestures toward the wall behind Pearl who watches the gold of Eliza's light intertwine with the blue of the glowing runes, becoming green across all of the surface except for a single thin column. Pearl gasps stepping to the phenomenon unconsciously asking, "How did you even know to look for this?"

"Ah didn't, but instead o' talking, ah was paying attention to the unnatural, ower than befriending it," Auburn responds stepping to a wall and falling into a lean against it.

"Alright well this is obviously a multi-stage magical protective trial for whatever that rod is, so any idea of the next stage smarty?" Pearl demands with her hands grumpily crossing in front of her while she turns away.

"Na, I think I will watch, I got ye thro' the first third already, I did my part 'n' I didn't even wantae come back here," Auburn laughs back, crossing his arms in anticipation of impending floundering with the next two thirds.

While Auburn and Pearl snap at each other, quibbling about Auburn participating in the room's magical protection of the distant rod, Boop hesitatively floats to the point where the magical barrier struck him away. Tilting with curious distrust of the space between himself and Aldrin, Boop drifts forward slowly closing the distance. Crossing through the point that was filling him with worry the floating orb switches his attention back to the rod, letting a grin form. Slow becomes fast and Boop darts almost like a blur past Aldrin's head into the second third of the room.

The instant the levitating form crosses over the change of white marble to black, the flanking figures vanish. Reappearing within striking range of Boop, the statues move with speed that would be unnatural for them to possess if they were flesh and blood, and in a synchronized succession of strikes their rusty blades are only barely avoided by Boop who dodges in what looks from the outside to be a strange dance. Seeing the sudden aggression directed toward her small friend Eliza leaps to her feet calling, "Boop! What did you do? Don't worry we'll get you out of there."

Auburn's voice barks from the hall silencing Eliza, "Are ye serious, I don't like ye or that thing bit ye can't be so dumb. It's distracting those guardians perfectly, even with their speed they haven't landed a blow, this is yer chance to git past them 'n' grab that thing so we kin git out o' 'ere."

Eliza is stunned by Auburn's sudden interest and she can only turn to Aldrin in her panic for direction. Looking to her Aldrin reciprocates the panic calling, "You won't like it but he's right. Hurry up, before Boop tires out."

With a quick nod Eliza looks back to Boop, and seeing his breathing slowly become heavier she steels herself. Leaping forward into a run, Eliza sees Pearl mirror the movement as both of them quickly stride across the middle of the room, past the spinning statues striking at Boop, and back onto white marble where the only thing still in front of them becomes the jade table. Not wanting to spend any more time with Boop being chased by rusty blades than necessary, Eliza steps to the edge of table and reaches to grab the waiting rod.

Before Eliza's can grab the black and gold folds of the unknown object the sound of whipping chains cracks through the air and she freezes in panic. Whipping from around the base of the table before her, a jade chain leaps out striking her wrist and wraps itself tightly around her forearm. The chain becomes taught and begins to pull toward the tables base. Eliza stands, pulling against the animated chain. The rattle of a second chain cracks from beneath the table and lashing out from the knot of jade links, it finds Eliza's other arm and also begins to pull.

Pearl watches from the side, in stunned shock of the sudden motion springing from the table at her young friend. With Eliza struggling against the chains, Pearl shakes herself out of the haze that had come over her, and lunges for the rod. From the base of the table a third chain jumps out grabbing the reaching wrist and stopping it. It pulls her to the tables edge. Dropping her to her knees.

Pulling against the chains around her wrists Eliza feels the smooth, compressing links begin to warm with an unnatural heat. Seeing Pearl visibly succumbing to a magically forced sleep, and hearing the squeal of Boop crying from one of the blades making contact with him, Eliza yells at her disoriented friend saying, "Pearl I need you to stay with me for just a little longer. I need you to grab the yellow elixir from your bag, the one with pink bubbles that shrink instead of expand, and need you to feed it to me. It's supposed to shrink the drinker temporarily and shrinking might give me just enough time to grab the rod."

Looking up to Eliza Pearl asks through blurry vision, "What about me?"

"Pearl, you are obviously not well, you look like you are about to pass out. Please, you know I won't leave you here I just have the best chance of getting the rod out of the two of us and once we have it we can figure out a way to get you out."

"I trust you," Pearl says barely able to breath the words, and with her eyelids becoming too heavy for her to even keep them open, but a very small amount, she reaches with her free hand into her bag. She pulls out a small test tube filled with a liquid matching the description given to her and meagerly tries to offer it to Eliza.

Eliza lets the chains pull her to her knees, bending herself over under the end of the glass tube. The chains surge with heat becoming burning hot, in the same moments Aldrin yells from across the room, "You still had more of those things?" Through the pain and distant scolding, Eliza holds her mouth open and Pearl pours out the strange bubbling liquid, which slides quickly down Eliza's throat. Eliza straightens herself and watches Pearl slump exhausted against jade table. Only at that moment does Eliza see the jade chain wrapped around Pearl's arm releasing from under it a black smoke of burning fabric, and she hesitates to look to the chains around her arms.

A moment passes with no change instilling itself on Eliza's form, as the chains increase their temperature ever more, now guaranteeing Eliza will have sustained burns by the point she is free of their grasp. A smile grows onto Eliza's face when she feels her stomach gurgle and growl, with the potion mixing into stomach acid and begin being absorbed into her blood stream. Eliza feels her limbs become suddenly stiff, and falling back to sit she pushes out her legs and arms in an attempt to stretch. The act of stretching brings her no relief, as instead of reaching out to their absolute limit, her limbs push and stretch and continue beyond where they should stop, growing.

Eliza looks in confused panic exclaiming, "What's happening I should be shrinking," at her hands, as her point of view begins to rise and become distant from them. Her feet contact and begin pushing against the jade table sliding her away across the marble floor. The chains wrapped around her wrists remain tight but shift on the surface of Eliza's expanding arms. The fabric of Eliza's dress feels like it is shrinking on her as her body rapidly grows in size, becoming far too to large for the fabric in a very short time. Straining against Eliza's contours, the pink fabric rips and falls to her sides as the chains, unable to maintain a hold on her now much larger and still growing arms, release, returning back into the coil around the base of the jade table.

Free, Eliza feels the sting of blisters forming on her arms where the jade chains seared her flesh but wincing to hide the pain she stands and continues trying to stretch. Difficulty comes when fully stood Eliza finds herself more than three times as tall as Aldrin, with only two feet of space remaining between the crown of her head and the chamber's ceiling, limiting her range of motion and preventing her from stretching her arms upward. The growing comes to an end, leaving Eliza not misshapen or disfigured from the elixir induced expansion, instead she retains her proportions with exact detail of every curve. Confused by the withdraw of the chains from her arms, Eliza doesn't hesitate in bending over to grab the waiting rod.

Lifted from its stand the rod, tiny in Eliza's hand, releases a series of three quick flashes with an airy popping sound from its crystal which with each flash a similar flash appears in the air above each third of the room. With the first flash, the blue imbedded into the floor under Aldrin fades and disappears leaving the small crevasses dug into the marble free of any of the crystals that were present. The second flash, happening less than a split moment after the first, while the crystals still fill the divots under Aldrin, freezes the four statues in place before causing them to vanish and reappear in their corners, releasing Boop from their chase. The third and final flash, happening even still before the crystals fade from reality, brings with it freedom for Pearl from the chain burning through her jacket, and the air becomes suddenly filled with a thin fog that begins to disperse becoming nothing around Pearl and Eliza.

Standing back up Eliza turns to see the stages of the protective gauntlet revert to an inert state. She looks to Pearl who groggily moans, waking from the magically induced sleep. Looking back again to Aldrin, Eliza holds forward the rod, like a toothpick in her hand, for him to see saying with her voice booming with her increased size, "Got it!"

Immediately seeing Aldrin cast his gaze away from her, Eliza realizes for the first time fully that she grew past the point her dress could hold her, leaving her unclothed, with the amulet that Bartholomeus gave her tightly holding like a choker around her throat, and with her face becoming flush with embarrassment, Eliza shifts desperately attempting to cover herself. In the movement, the black growth on the talisman to Archangel flares and a deep loud sound like that of a large thick sheet of fabric being thrown and unfolded bellows out. A black magic wave ripples from the amulet over Eliza's towering form leaving in its wake the appearance of a perfectly fitted copy of the outfit Pearl bought for her.

Looking up through blurry vision, and releasing a yawn, Pearl quickly rubs her eyes and lets her mouth fall open slack jawed. Feeling sudden pain in her arm she looks to the holes burnt through her jacket and the growing blisters that form beneath, and hesitatively putting her other hand to the heat wound, asks Eliza, "Lizzy? How did you get so large? Weren't you supposed to become smaller? And how did you get that outfit?"

Hearing Pearl's groggy voice, Eliza's eyes open, having slammed closed in embarrassment, and looking down to herself turns to Pearl with a baffled look responding in a way that vibrates the air around Pearl, "I don't know, but hey as soon as I picked up this thing the magic that was protecting it turned off. I will also say that this outfit doesn't feel real," and with that Eliza swings her hips side to side, sending to her surprise the weightless visual of fabric swaying with her movements.

From the other side of the room Aldrin keeps his eyes averted from Eliza's position while he calls over, "Not to ruin the conversation, but did I hear that you're clothed again Eliza?"

"Looks like it I guess," Eliza responds before grabbing at the fabric. In her hand as she speaks Eliza does not feel anything when she should feel cloth, but the image moves to her touch as it would if it were real.

Returning his eyes to the direction of his female companions Aldrin's feet move beneath him pushing him in their direction and he raises his voice demanding, "Now which one of you would like to explain why in this world you still have any of those potions?"

"Hey, cool it, that potion is probably the reason that I still have my arm," Pearl exclaims thrusting her arm toward him close enough for him to almost feel the heat of her palms on his face.

"I get that, but we know for a fact that some of those potions have long lasting side effects and if you didn't notice, at the moment Eliza is too big to fit out the way we came in, and I don't see an extra sized person exit anywhere to leave through. Do you?" Aldrin asks gesturing angrily around the room

Eliza's large hands lift into the air to her chest as she looks down bashfully responding, "It was supposed to make me smaller."

"Well who would have guessed the experimental potions would not do exactly what they were intended to?"

"Well it shouldn't last too long."

"How long?"

Eliza mumbles her response with her voice still carrying loud to her small companions, "An hour."

"Hey that's not bad," Pearl interrupts the scolding, not allowing Aldrin to silently make angry gesture to Eliza's response.

Instead Aldrin angrily stomps away into Auburn's direction as Boop, feeling it safe to, whips around Eliza examining his now huge master. Leaning back down, bringing her face to Pearl's, Eliza whispers, "Hey you want to really see Aldrin freak?"

"What are you thinking," Pearl asks with a devilish grin.

"Give me the test tube with the thin brown liquid in it."

Pearl looks shocked with confusion responding, "Wait we were told to not have more than one every three days."

Eliza's face shifts to a pout as she explains, "Alfredo gave me that potion as an extra one to test and it is supposed to be used to duplicate a recently drunk potions effects."

"Wait so you'd be even bigger? Lizzy there is barely enough room for you to stand as it is."

"I don't need to stand up for an hour while we wait for the effects to revert."

"I guess you have a point there but what about the time it takes to where off?"

"What about it?"

"Won't it take longer to wear off? I mean you know I am all for pressing Aldrin's buttons and this sounds like a great idea but I don't want him leaving you down here thinking that it won't wear off at all."

"I don't know. It shouldn't make it last any longer, size adjustments become more unstable the greater the affect, so if anything, it should last a shorter time."

Reaching down into her satchel Pearl pulls out the test tube filled with the thin brown liquid, only just missing Eliza's eyes widen wantonly as it emerges from the bag. Uncorking the glass tube Pearl smiles and putting herself between Aldrin and the transaction she pours the brown liquid into Eliza's mouth saying, "This is going to be hilarious."

Aldrin paces back in the direction of the women, and seeing Pearl's back turned to him he is filled with suspicion asking, "What are you two doing?"

Turning around Pearl feigns a confused expression responding, "What? Lizzy was just telling me that she doesn't understand why you're so angry."

Putting his fingers to the bridge of his nose Aldrin explains, "Look I just don't think that you should be risking yourself for a mad man's progress you are still very young and have so much ahead of you. I don't want to see you waste away because of the empty promises of chemical remedies."

As he finishes speaking, Aldrin glances up to Eliza who straightens herself before grabbing at her stomach feeling it fill with fluid and gurgle with the replicator taking effect. Feeling her limbs stiffen again, she goes to stretch, forgetting how low the ceiling is for her forcing her to push against it. Quickly the little space that was open between her and the ceiling closes forcing her to bend forward before pushing her to her hands and knees as she continues to grow, and through a sound like stretching rubber against leather a small pop sounds, followed shortly by the clink of the medallion breaking from around her neck and falling to the ground.

Aldrin recoils away from Eliza as she expands to a gargantuan size, leaving him stammering, "Eliza, you're growing again!"

In the same moment Auburn growls from the other side of the room, "You're honestly doilt aboot this? Ah hae bin telling ye this entire time that she insae natural. Noo yer aff tae wantae wait th' oor she said it wid tak' fur her tae shrink back doon, that is o' coorse if she doesn't outgrow th' walls o' this basement room first."

"An hour isn't long to wait," Aldrin responds defending Eliza as he looks to her filling most of the room before the growing slows to a stop.

"Weel, ye don't need tae git ye nickers in a twist. Ah wis juist stated mah case afore ah let ye dae ye," Auburn says sitting down in the hall and closing his eyes.

Stepping to Eliza's side and moving to grab the edge of the enormous skirt, which drapes from Eliza's hips appearing to have, with the rest of the outfit, grown with their wearer, Pearl asks, "Wow, what are these clothes, to still be able to fit you," but reaching the point her hand should touch the giant flowing fabric it instead passes through. With a laughing surprised expression Pearl looks at her hand exclaiming, "They're not even real. Lizzy, you just won't stop surprising me, will you?"

Shifting to lay down, Eliza's very movement causes the ground beneath and around her and her group to shake. Aldrin visibly struggles to keep his footing while Eliza shifts onto her side, unable to take his eyes from her, and blushing he asks, "Those clothes aren't real?"

Pearl springs across the room picking up the rod, they have obtained, from the ground where it fell when Eliza began to grow this second time, and then to Aldrin who she turns form Eliza saying, "Hey, don't you two get down, we don't have to sit here waiting for an hour, Lizzy will be alright if we go look into one of those other rooms while we wait."

"Yea, I think that would be a good idea," Aldrin responds slowly

27

turning away from Eliza.

Standing and igniting his hand once more into a glowing fire Auburn smiles leading the way down the tunnel saying, "Leave tha' in, soonds good to meh."

Focusing on Boop's forehead Eliza places upon him her third eye saying to him, her voice carrying even more powerfully than it had before, booming into the hall with the others shaking them to their cores, "Go with them Boop, help them if they need it. I'll be fine here."

3

Consequences

Back in the room at the base of the stairs that lead down into the basement, Pearl, Aldrin, Auburn and Boop, stare contemplatively at the other two doorways that lead out of the two connected rooms. Shrugging as the others don't make movement to either the options set before them, Pearl steps to the frost coated metal door, and puts her hand to its latch. With a pull Pearl finds the door stuck in its frame, and rolling her eyes she turns to the others, asking, "So would you two men like to go wait with Eliza or are you going to come help me?"

Aldrin, still red in the cheeks responds, "Maybe we should head back."

"Go ahead then," Pearl responds with a shrug adding under her breath, just audible for Aldrin, "Who am I to get in the way of you being a creep." Not letting Aldrin respond to the accusation Pearl turns to Auburn asking, "You have made it clear that you would prefer to be pretty much anywhere but in the same room as our sweet lovable Lizzy. So, would you mind defrosting the door frame for us?"

Auburn steps to the door, pushing his fire engulfed hand to the metal he begins trying to melt the ice seal. In that time Aldrin yells at Pearl in defense of himself, "I am not a creep! I just am concerned about leaving her alone. What if something were to happen? She wouldn't be able to protect herself."

"Lizzy will be fine, remember every room in this place is empty."

"Quit th' yammering ye two, th' doors, open, 'n' guess whit it's a snaw cupboard," Auburn interjects drawing attention back to the metal doorway, from which blows a frigid breeze.

In the doorway beside Auburn a knee-high mound of snowy frost sits as a wall blocking the small room. From the ceiling, large icicles spear down connecting to shelves that stand incased in solid blocks of ice. Pearl shrugs pointing with her thumb to the thick ice slabs in the darkness saying with a laugh, "Yup only empty rooms," before hopping into the deep cold powder.

Stepping behind Pearl but not entering the room that continues to release a chilling fog from it Aldrin asks, "What are you doing now?"

"Relax, I'm hungry and I think I saw some bread and berries in here," Pearl responds waving off Aldrin's concerns. When she turns back into the cold room, she stops her movement as a figure darts through her vision in the dark. Taking a single step forward Pearl leans around one of the shelves asking the air, "Hey, who's there?"

Aldrin watches Pearl slip deeper into the room and from the door he calls to her, "Who are you talking to?"

"Quiet, I think there is something alive in here," Pearl responds to

Aldrin poking her head back to look at the door. Moving back to the small space around the first set of shelves, Pearl reaches out to a small blue-white impish figure that pulls away from her. Trying to appear non-hostile Pearl says to the creature, "Hey, don't be afraid, I'm not going to hurt you. Do you live here?"

Looking up to Pearl the small creature, a small frail being with tiny bat-like wings that do not appear as if they should be able to allow it to fly, tilts its head taking a step onto the icy floor. The creature's large nose, nearly the size of a medium sized cucumber that holds small icicles at its end, over a small mouth that opens saying in a squeaky airy voice, "You friend of maker?"

From the other side of the small room another voice almost identical to the first draws Pearl's attention, adding, "Yes, you already spoke with him."

The first then continues a smile forming on its face, "Yes, you have his binding rod."

The second voice then continues, revealing from around the other corner of the room, another creature like the one Pearl started the conversation with, which says, "You talk to Bully yet?"

"No, she not talks to Bully, still too healthy."

"None of them talk to Bully," the second creature says turning to face out the door, to Aldrin, Auburn, and Boop.

"Negmor not back, you now house masters."

"You hungry?" the creature asks as it turns back to Pearl.

Pearl, having moved her head between the two creatures turning between them as they trade which of them is speaking seamlessly and answering each other, lands with her head focused on the creature in the doorway and thinking for a moment turns with her response directing it toward the other, saying, "Actually that is why I came in here, I thought I saw some berries and bread in the ice, if it is still good I would love to have some, and I am sure that Lizzy is probably hungry too," she finishes turning to Aldrin with her comment about Eliza.

"Good, we give you," the first ice creature, responds as the second steps to one of the blocks of ice with shelves contained within. The creature's talon like hands pass into solid ice as though it were air and wrap around small containers of spring berries, and a loaf of bread, before handing everything to Pearl who awkwardly tries to take it not having a place to put the rod.

"Is this stuff any good," Pearl asks feeling the icy chill that keeps the food rock hard.

The second frost creature tilts its head at Pearl's question responding, "All food here good."

The first adds in to the second's response, saying, "Creator, Negmor enchanted home to stay full of food good for him."

Aldrin puts a hand out to the creature he can see asking, "Wait, if this storage room is magically filled and the food is magically kept fresh, why are there terraces for farming outside?"

"Food made not enough for all inhabitants," one of the creatures quickly responds.

"Plus, home too inconvenient place for all food to be stored," the other adds continuing their explanation.

"Master's favorites always here."

"No matter the harvest."

Stepping from the room Pearl nods lifting the loaf of bread to the creatures, saying, "Well, thanks for the bread, and berries. Keep up the good work I guess and try not to let that door freeze shut."

Aldrin stops Pearl as she goes to step past him toward the hall to Eliza, and he asks, "What are you doing?"

"Taking this food to Lizzy I mean it's still frozen, but she can probably swallow it whole as a nice snack."

"What about you?"

"Me, eat this stuff? Ew, gross. No, way! Ever since we got to The Cove I haven't been able to stomach anything but raw fish."

Auburn looks at the two conversing and with a look of confusion on his face asks, "Whit ur baith o' ye talking aboot? How come urr ye worried aboot feeding that thing? Th' amount o' food ye hae thare wouldn't even be a munchies fur it." Boop begins to growl with this comment at Auburn, who turns to the frost creatures, and asks, "Wha is this Bully?"

Ignoring Boop growling, one of the cold creatures responds pointing to the black doors, saying, "He summoned by master."

The other then continues, "To protect that room and beyond."

Turning to the two creatures again Pearl asks, "So like you?"

"No, we created for our job by master," the first responds.

"Bully summoned and bound to contract," the other continues.

"Doesn't like visitors."

"Will try to kill you if you meet him."

With the two creatures finishing their response Pearl puts a finger to them asking, "How do we not let him try to kill us."

One of the creatures points to the rod, still awkwardly in Pearl's grasp, while the other explains, "End contract and Bully no longer."

The one pointing continues as the other raises its hand to point, "Allowed to be on this plane."

"And you two wouldn't have a problem with that," Pearl asks pointing inquisitively at the small winged creatures.

"We have lived all our lives in this room," one of the two responds.

The second continues explaining, "And we still call him the word Bully."

The two then say in unison, "Him not being here would not be a loss to us."

Aldrin steps to the side of Pearl asking, "So wait, all we have to do is hold this thing toward whoever this Bully is, tell them we end the contract, and he is gone?"

Both ice covered creatures shrug with one of them starting, "We don't know."

"We haven't ever left this room," the other finishes.

The glowing flicker of Auburn's flame covered hand begins to dim drawing Aldrin and Pearl's attention to where their red companion had been standing only a moment before, finding him stepping away, toward the hall back to Eliza. Pearl, confused by the movement, runs form Aldrin's side to Auburn's asking, "Where are you going? I thought you didn't like Lizzy."

"I don't," Auburn responds in a growl, "Bit that'n seems tae care aboot her safety 'n' seems tae wantae keep her involved. Nae tae mention those things wur making mah head hurt. Sae, thought ah micht as weel head back 'n' tak' a nap while we wait."

"Really, I thought you were the one that wanted to just leave Lizzy behind."

"Weel neither o' ye seem tae be in a rush tae dae anythin' important, 'n' a'm follaein him sae why shuid I be?"

"Well I am glad you are coming to your senses," Pearl laughs patting Auburn's shoulder, to which he simply growls for being touched. Turning back to Aldrin who closes the door into the ice box, she calls back, "Hey we are going to go wait for Lizzy to shrink back down now, Auburn thinks he could use a nap."

Joining Pearl and Auburn, Aldrin and Boop follow the two back down the five-foot-wide tunnel back to the large chamber where Eliza lays, still nearly filling half the room, looking down at the ground where she traces the symbol engraved in the marble floor with her finger. Seeing the others return Eliza's eyes widen with a smile, and Boop rushes to her now miniscule in comparison to her. Curiosity overtakes her, forcing her to ask, "You're back, did you find anything else," her voice thrumming tremendously powerful, shaking her friends to their cores and nearly dropping them from their feet.

Rolling his eyes Auburn steps to the corner of the room furthest from Eliza and sits. In the same moment Pearl gives a smile and a thumb up expression in Eliza's direction responding, "Yea we found some food, I thought you might be hungry, and we talked to these two ice creatures that Negmor created." Letting Aldrin step to the wall near Auburn and sit, Pearl begins to explain the ice box, the two creatures, and the things they explained about the being they referred to as Bully.

After Pearl ends her explanation of everything that Eliza saw through her third eye on Boop, the air of the room rests into a quite pulse of Eliza's titanic breaths and they wait in wordless silences for some sign of the potion's effect waning. Time feels to drag on for the waiting group in the first hour as they sit doing nothing until, in her boredom, Pearl draws a dagger from a sheath on her side and throws it, for Boop who gives chase and retrieves it for her. Quickly arriving at the blade Boop lifts it and returns to Pearl, beginning a game of fetch. The game quickly ends though when Boop tires and floats down to find the black and gold rod in his maw, chewing on it like he had to the javelin of lightning, and pulling the rod free from the winded orb's mouth, Pearl nearly drops when Eliza yawns and asks, "You think I am any smaller yet Pearl?"

Not letting Pearl have a chance to respond, Aldrin interjects asking, "How is it supposed to work, are you supposed morph back as quickly as you went into that form, or is it something that is going to be gradual?"

Eliza, looks to Aldrin, and batting her eyes as she thinks of an answer responds, "I don't know, actually, I assumed like most potions with non-permanent effects that it would fade as quickly as it activated, but I might be wrong."

"You know this is entirely your fault, right?"

"Yea," Eliza responds showing her age again as she looks down and away.

"So maybe now you will choose to not take any more of those experimental potions?"

"You really think it was a mistake for me to take any of the potions," Eliza asks, her face shifting into a fat lower lipped, puppy dog eyed pout, as the earth quakes for the others with her shifting to lean toward Aldrin.

Aldrin's face flushes red, leaving him only able to stammer, "Uh, uh," before taking a deep swallow to clear his throat.

With Aldrin not responding, a smile begins to form on Eliza's face, but is broken by Auburn inserting his voice into the air of the room saying simply, "Yes."

Pearl steps over to Auburn and striking an angry stance, demands, "What are you saying mister red skin and fiery hand?"

Auburn raises a single eye brow and standing to look down at Pearl asks, "Hae we ever shook hauns?"

Pearl nearly falls back with Auburn imposing himself over her and at the strange question. Thinking to herself Pearl hesitates in responding, "No, you've kept your distance from me well enough."

In a strong aggressive movement Auburn's hand shoots out grabbing Pearl's unburnt wrist, hand he lifts it into view asking, "Whit dae ye feel?"

Pearl looks in surprise at the hand grasping her wrist, and pulling away exclaims, "Ow that's hot!"

"Nothin' magical aboot mah haun igniting th' air aroond it. Hers though," Auburn releases the wrist and gestures to the giant Eliza continuing, "is purely magical, 'n' completely unnatural. Magic isn't tae be trusted. It perverts reality tae th' will o' th' corruptible."

The ground trembles as Eliza shifts, and pushes herself, on the opposite long side of the room, in the direction of the hall out. The others in the room fall to the wall away from her looking in confused unease at her movements, noticing only then the extra space around the huge girl which was not present only moments before. Leaning against the wall Aldrin calls out to Eliza as she moves, "Eliza, what are you doing?"

Dragging herself across the room's floor, Eliza gets herself to the entrance of the tall thin hall, and hearing Aldrin she responds in a flustered tone, "I am tired of laying here and waiting, so I am going to push through this hall so we can move on."

Running between Eliza and the hall Pearl throws up her hands saying, "Wait."

"Why?"

"Let us leave first that way if you get stuck we aren't stuck behind you."

"I think I have actually shrunk so I might be able to fit."

"I agree and you might keep shrinking, which could free you if you do get stuck, but you might not. If you do get stuck still shrinking or not it would be better if we are on the other side so that we can get you food and work on freeing you that way."

With a knowing nod Eliza waits and watches as Auburn, Aldrin and Pearl leave the room, and with a head bob she ushers Boop to follow. Before she moves into the hall Eliza's hand goes to her neck, feeling for the talisman remembering that it had snapped free with her second growth spurt, and she calls Pearl, "Pearl, could you come back real quick?"

A moment later Pearl is back in the room asking, "What's wrong?"

"The amulet of Archangel, it snapped free from my throat earlier. It's real important to me, could you help me find it?"

"Sure," Pearl responds, and after a short search her eyes fall upon the gold symbol, and lifting it up, she presents the talisman to Eliza asking, "This?"

Eliza looks in confusion at the small trinket, a clean gold symbol of the church of Archangel on a broken rope with no sign of the black crystal or the corruption it had dealt to the precious metal. Through the confusion of seeing the small thing free of the ugly evil black veins for the first time since losing Bartholomeus, Eliza responds, "Yea that's it. Thanks."

With that Pearl steps back to the hall and returning her glance to Eliza for just a moment reasserts, "We will just be down the hall waiting. You don't have to push yourself, if you get stuck just breath and try to wiggle back into here. See you soon."

Pearl, dipping around the curve of the hall toward Aldrin's orange flickering light, leaves Eliza on her own, staring at the hall, maybe five feet wide and just about more than double that in height. Turning onto her side, she uncomfortably pushes her arms into the tunnel and pushes herself forward. The space is tight, pressing against the young girl as she forces her mountainous yet shapely mass into the curving rectangle of freedom. The cold of the basement's stone walls compresses her, and she feels the sensation through the magic facade of clothing that covers her visually. Pushing forward she struggles, wiggling, and slowly inching her way deeper into the hall, unaware of the complete panic the others have been struck with as with each motion Eliza makes to move a small portion of herself free before pushing it once again into being confined only making short crawling progress, the earth trembles around them.

Moments become minutes of the earth quaking with Eliza forcing herself forward. Each movement becomes imperceptibly easier for her as she continues inching onward feeling her skin uncomfortably pulling tight along the wall, only just fitting into the hall at all. Her flesh feels meager relief as it slides free for a few inches before snagging again against the rough stone signaling to her the very slight change in her size that has occurred since she started her crawl. An hour passing brings with it the fading of Eliza's hand's glow in the same moment that she feels the very edge of the halls end.

"Almost there Lizzy, we can see your hands," Pearl calls into the tunnel, putting an unseen smile on Eliza's face as her fingers wrap onto the exit's edge.

Pulling and wiggling forward inch by inch the finger tips become whole fingers and then freedom for both hands which cling to the corners, white knuckled with Eliza straining to pull herself out. Slowly over the course of a final marathon of earth shaking struggling pulls Eliza's arms, head, and shoulders finally become free of the hall. Blowing a single strand of hair from her face she smiles as she sees the others against the far wall, and with a grunt as her arms plant firmly against the walls on either side of the hall, and press to slide her several more inches she apologizes, "Sorry, for taking so long."

With Eliza releasing a tremendous breath as the mountainous plethora of flesh that is her chest slips finally into freedom, the other three stand and step to the charred black door. Pearl nods to the door explaining, "Well you definitely are shrinking, slowly and surely, but definitely shrinking. We are just going to go in here and talk to this Bully person. You should be able to see in soon enough now that you are this far." Returning a smile and a nod, Eliza returns to pushing and wiggling herself free, watching in the corner of her vision the others swing open the door.

The door creaks, ushering a voice that scratches out in response to the intruders of a waiting being's home. Like a deep horn bellow intertwined with a cacophony of nails scraping across a chalk board the voice assaults the unexpecting ears of the group, "You finally return Negmor, to be honest I didn't think it would take you quite this long to escape the prison of being trapped in another plane of reality. So, now that you know my suffering, will you still refuse to release me from my contract? Wait," a dark silhouette of a winged creature, with a long, pointed, tail, whose entire form holds protruding from it long needle like spikes, perches on a platform in the center of the waiting chamber sniffing the air detecting an unfamiliar scent.

Turning around the creature reveals in the orange flickering of the burning hand's fiery glow, a smooth round face with long black razor teeth interlocking like those of a wrangler fish. The leathery black wings connect to the creature's back and unfurl as it turns causing Pearl to shout pointing in its direction, "What in the worlds, is that!"

Seeing the strangers stood in its door way the creature releases a demonic scream and with a thrust of its wings lifts into the air away from the unknown individuals yelling, "You are not Negmor. You are seekers of his treasure that means I get to kill you." Suddenly a gust pulls Pearl, Aldrin, Auburn and Boop into the room with the winged man-sized creature leaving Eliza, alone, still trying to escape the hall that still gently clings to her hips.

The room around the stumbling group expands with its four walls nearly stretching to the length of the long walls of the gauntlet that held the rod that rests in Pearl's hand. The ceiling only dimly is visible overhead nearly twice as high as the raised ceiling of the gauntlet. In the center of the massive space, between the group and the red spiked creature, sits a raised platform as wide as the room the four were pulled from, holding a large dark iron brazier that looks to lift up in relief several inches when the being known as Bully takes flight.

A click sounds behind the group and turning to the doors Auburn finds them locked and unmoving when he attempts to reopen them. A second sound, one of stone shifting against stone, grinds in the air as, visible in the glow of Auburn's flame's, a thick green fog begins to pillow slowly out from beneath the empty fire stand. The strange vapors sit heavy against the floor inching outward, not like a gas but instead like sludge oozing out onto the raised platform in the middle of the room.

Across from them, Aldrin and Pearl watch the threatening creature lift one of its hands, and with an extended crimson index finger tipped with a black sharp nail, it produces a small condensed orb of fire barely the size of a chicken's egg. Splitting into two, the orbs shoot from the creature, each flying with blinding speed directed toward Aldrin and Pearl. Impacting with Pearl's shoulder the first orb bursts into a spherical vortex that swallows nearly a third of her for a split second before vanishing, leaving her almost dry of the slime that secretes from her skin, and filling the air with smell of seared fish. A similar burst erupts from the second orb on Aldrin's chest who, leaning back, is thrown away instead of being engulfed, leaving only a small trail of smoke rising from one of the laces of his shirt.

Standing confused by the sudden flash of fire around her, Pearl looks at the form hovering across the room on flapping wings. Only a fraction of a second passes, before she yells at it, "Hey you jerk, what was that for?"

"How are you alive," the creature exclaims in shock of Pearl's exclamation, continuing, "No normal thief could survive that blast."

"Well if you would have let us speak, before attacking us we could have told you, we want to relieve you of your contract," Pearl calls back angrily.

The green fog continues growing, pillowing further from the central metal construct filling the room more with each passing moment. With squinting eyes, the fiend, keeping its distance from Pearl and the others as they move around the room toward it, asks, "And what arrogance fills you to believe that you have such right?"

"The one who contracted you has transferred ownership of this island and everything within to our group," Aldrin interjects as he and Pearl step to the central platform before they turn to follow the demonic creature, who in an attempt to keep his distance, turns and lands on all fours and scurries away like a thorn covered red lizard.

Aldrin and Pearl step back down from the raised area with the slow crawling thick gas just spilling over the edge behind them. In the same time, the two try to converse with the monster that struck them, Auburn instead lights a torch on the wall, lets the fire on his hand extinguish itself, and draws his bow keeping his own distance from the unknown creature. Boop chooses to stare intently at the green, expanding cloud. Holding forward the black and gold rod Pearl raises a brow with a smile explaining, "See, we have this so we can end your contract. No need to fight."

Leaping down in a terrifyingly fast movement the demon grabs the rod, not pulling it from Pearl's hand and with a look of anger, and desperation, its voice curls out saying, "Then say it. Say you release me from my contract."

"Your service is no longer needed, return to your plane of creation," Pearl says grasping tightly to the rod watching the creature's face turn to panic.

"What? You can't do this to me. You were supposed to let me go not send me home," the creature exclaims looking to its hands as a thrum cracks from behind it, where a red twisting orb forms releasing into the room an intense heat and a smell of sulfur. The creature takes a step toward Pearl as it begins to struggle against a force pulling it to the orb that is unfelt by Pearl or Aldrin, and he snarls, "At least you're still going to die. You don't have time now to stop the toxin's spread."

With the pop of an object being propelled by a tube too small for it to pass through, and a thunderous clap the burning red orb swallows the demon Bully, and collapses on itself, vanishing and casting the room back into the darkness of the single torch to Auburn's side. Boop pulls quickly up and away from the rolling green fog, as Aldrin turns to the spreading substance exclaiming, "Toxin? So that's what that stuff is."

"Ony ideas oan how tae nae die tae whitevur that stuff is," Auburn asks returning his bow to his shoulder.

Grabbing Pearl's shoulder and pulling her to the wall Aldrin responds, "Well, whatever that stuff is it is coming from there," and he point with his free hand to the iron object at the rooms center.

The green fog continues to creep on the marble floor inching for the ground bound trio, and with no plan coming to their minds, their strong confident demeanor breaks, as the likely hood of their demise becomes almost inevitable in their minds, with Auburn getting to the door and pulling, only to find it still locked. Boop growls and barks at Auburn gesturing with powerful movements to the edge of the expanding gas carpet. Looking across the room to Boop, Pearl's eyes trace with his movements down to the green cloud on the ground. Where he is pointing the green gas crests and is building in height around the glow of the torch's light, and recognizing Boop's intent Pearl calls to Auburn, "The torches, light the torches!"

Spinning to Pearl and then to the lit torch, seeing Boop gesturing frantically at the strange interaction between the smoke and the light Auburn gives a knowing nod to the floating orb. Igniting his hand once more, he throws the flame in a projected bolt of fire at another one of the torches hung on the wall and hitting the blackened tip causes it to burst to life illuminating another section of the large chamber, and forcing back the smoke that had grown into the circle of bright light beneath it. Sending several more bolts flying through the air of the chamber to light each of the torches on the walls, Auburn lights the final one by simply grabbing its top.

The green smoke towers in a column in the center of the chamber held up, against its want to flood over the group, who now move about the lit chamber freely. Looking up and down the walls Pearl looks to be getting annoyed before slamming her fist against one saying loudly to herself, "Where is it? That thing said this was where Negmor kept his treasure, and there is nothing here."

"So what? We have been functioning as if every room would be empty since before we got down here," Aldrin explains not knowing the reason for Pearl's frustration.

"I know that, but I wanted to find something more than a stick so that I didn't have to feel his judgmental stares when we get to the bar, for wasting so much time in having us come down here."

"Hey, now we can just head out, and get some dwarven ale. I'm sure if you buy the first round Auburn will forgive you," Aldrin laughs pressing a playful slap into Pearl's shoulder, not noticing Auburn get pulled to the wall of still thickening green fog by Boop who gestures repeatedly, as he had at the anomaly between the first torch's light and the green gas.

Looking with skeptical curiosity at Boop, who insists Auburn toward, the gas, which now is forming precipitation within it from the pressure building as it is held back by the magics of the chamber's torches. Igniting his hand Auburn knows what Boop is asking as he sees the floating aberration smile and nod at the ignition of the orange glowing flame. With a shrug, having just been saved by the creature catching the effect the torches had on the gas, Auburn steps to the still locked black doors, and winding up, releases another bolt of flame toward the column of green.

Boop watches in glee as the cluster of embers dances through the air past him and into the gas before, in a blinding explosive display the entire volume of the column combusts becoming a short-lived pillar of fire that fades after releasing a deafening crash. Boop remains staring, starry eyes at where the fire erupted, almost laughing after it fades, leaving the metal brazier filled with a flame without the need for fuel. In unexpected movement the metal construct, raised above the already lifted section of floor, sinks back into its place releasing the sound again of stone hitting stone.

Auburn, Aldrin, and Pearl all flinch from the explosion, and hearing the click of stones Auburn turns to the doors once more and giving them a gentle tug finds them unlocked and easily opens them. Auburn jumps when the gap between the doors becomes large enough for him to see through, and find, waiting, Eliza, still enormous, patiently folded into the conjoined rooms. Scanning the room, as it becomes available for her to do so, she raises a finger and points beyond Pearl and Aldrin asking, "What's back there?"

Following the point of Eliza's finger, to the back corner, the group sees, for the first time, a door where there wasn't one when they had entered, at least that they could see. With a smile taking her face, Pearl runs to the door and without a second thought grabs the doorknob, twists and pulls. The smile is broken when her attempt to pull the door finds no success, and she instead tries to push, but also finds the door unwilling to move. Realizing the door to be locked, Pearl shrugs and sighs, asking sarcastically, "None of you would happen to have the key, would you?"

Tapping his chin Aldrin contemplates for a moment where the key may be hidden. Looking to the point of the room from where the demon was banished, he sees just barely the glitter of several metallic objects laying on the floor. Stepping to the sparkling answer, not having expected the search to be quite so easy Aldrin picks up what looks to be three differently designed keys all affixed to a single gold keyring. Releasing the keys with a toss for Pearl, Aldrin asks in response, "I don't know, are these them?"

The light of glee returning to her eyes, Pearl swipes the keys from the air and immediately presses one of the toothy metal slivers to the key hole just above the nob of the reinforced wooden door. With the first key not working, because why would it, Pearl grabs a second from the remaining two, and putting it to the hole, slides the small, strangely warm, object in and with a turn she hears the click of a latch being freed from its hold. Withdrawing the key with her victorious smirk pulling up one corner of her mouth into her cheek, Pearl gently pulls to test which way it opens without revealing her test to Aldrin, and swings the door away from her, open. Beyond though, does not wait treasure, instead an empty cavity about ten feet in width and length with a second door, waiting as the first, tightly closed.

Aldrin nearly lets free a laugh at Pearl's dismay, as she sighs and steps into the next room rolling her eyes. While Aldrin joins Pearl as she attempts to open the second door that leads to another room with a third waiting door, Auburn looks back out of the room, to Eliza who looks in with a young innocent patient curiosity for what Pearl may find. Boop flies past Auburn and gives Eliza's still enormous face a lick before zipping back in the direction of Pearl and Aldrin. In a soft growl only audible to himself and the giant girl, Auburn turns away saying, "Thanks."

Eliza smiles asking, "For what?"

Auburn only lifts one finger, pointing it toward Boop, and trying to not show much gratitude, he continues, "Yer pet saved oor lives. I'm not above recognizing that."

With his piece said Auburn steps to join the others, leaving Eliza once again on her own. With no one looking in her direction Eliza, rubs at the top of her sternum, which, behind the illusion of clothing that dresses her, is red and inflamed with a web of black veins that hold at their center a miniscule black crystal imbedded in her flesh. Panic suddenly takes the young giant, as she feels under her finger the crystal slightly grow but her worries fade when she looks up to the realization that she is simply experiencing another episode of her size reducing.

The worry returns though, when like each episode before, the reversion of the growth potion's effects stops, leaving the young Eliza, at a titanic size, still unable to even sit up in the conjoined rooms, but more pressingly as she feels the stone fade from her touch. Looking down Eliza watches through the façade of clothing the black tendrils pulse and wiggle on the surface of her skin for a moment before they fade becoming invisible. The main source of Eliza's fear comes from the knowledge that the crystal, an object known to her to be a foreign entity to her body, did not fall free from the place it had imbedded itself, but had been drawn into her. The black crystal she had seen, and felt worry for its corrupting the amulet Bartholomeus had given her, has found its way into her, near to her heart.

Finally, through the third door, Pearl, having prepared herself to be disappointed by another locked door, leaps forward with glee as her eyes fall upon a room twice the size of the two before it, teeming with mounds of golden coins stamped with the mints of several varying nations, glowing with a white light that radiates from an orb floating near the ceiling. Past the coins, along the walls several marble stands sit as display cases for several strange items. Stepping through the door, Aldrin laughs as he crosses his arms, "So, it was a good choice to come down here after all. I hate to say this but good job Pearl."

Pearl spins with an insulted look on her face asking, "Hate to say it?"

"Doesn't change what I said," Aldrin responds raising his hands defensively.

Stepping into the room and to one of the display cases Auburn raises a brow, as before him in a glass covered case, laying on a red silk pillow is a gold bow crafted in the form of a bird of prey with its wings spread forming the limbs of the weapon connected by a single taught strand of a transparent red-orange material. Auburn looks to the others, while his hands reach down opening the case. Lifting the bow he is surprised as he finds its weight balanced perfectly for his grip feeling natural in his hand as it magically radiates as a source of heat.

In a second case, rising from the piles of coins, on a purple pillow is a short foot long object only the width of a medium sized coin. Made of a polished gray substance, it is capped at one end with a small smoky white quartz ornamented with a figurine of a large black spider that holds the crystal with four of its legs and the shaft of gray with the other four. Along the gray is wrapped a smooth matted material shaped into a spider's web to a comfortable handle grip.

A third case holds in it on a white silk pillow a long thin sword, resting by a decorated scabbard. The hilt of the sword is not overly garish, having a simple curved hand guard of, untarnished by the time it has sat unmaintained, silvery steel. The blade almost sparkles in the light as Pearl's hands land on the sides of the case for her to look in at the weapon, before looking down to the rapier at her side. With a shrug Pearl turns to Auburn who slings the golden bow over his shoulder, and says to herself, "Well, I mean it is our stuff now, and that wand might be nice for Lizzy. Sorry it doesn't look like there really was anything down here for you Aldrin."

Aldrin rolls his eyes responding, "How long have we been traveling together? You really think I would be jealous about you finding stuff in an old dwarf wizard's collection of nick knacks that you think might be useful? I have plenty of ideas I have been tinkering with in my head that the gold in this room would go a long way in helping me make into a reality."

"Glad you don't feel like you are getting stiffed then if I give Lizzy that wand thing and this rod," Pearl says tapping the black and gold rod as she ties the new rapier's sheath to the opposite hip of her sword.

"Why would you give Eliza the rod? Isn't it useless now that creature's contract has been ended?"

"Maybe, but it may still have some magic in it, and Boop hasn't stopped eyeing it since he saw it in the other room. I think he wants it as a chew toy."

With a shrug Aldrin turns to leave the room saying, "Whatever. I think it is safe to say we can go get some rest in town now, without any more detours, I'm exhausted."

"Yea, I am satisfied with the treasure we found. Anything else in our palace can wait. Our palace. That's nice to say, don't you think?"

4

Dur'heim

After two hours of helping Eliza squeeze awkwardly up the staircase, the group finally emerge again on the ground floor. Pulling the stone door back into place concealing the path down once more, Pearl joins the others and they continue their way to the palaces front doors. The constant slow return to her normal size brings Eliza the ability to walk upright in the exceptionally tall halls of the first floor, but reaching the massive front door she finds herself still needing to duck through.

The sky is filled with the warm darkening light of the late afternoon sun, and drifting overhead, orange cotton clouds glow casting gentle shadows over the path between the door and the marble dock. Esmerelda, leaning against a tree, again becomes visibly angry as her eyes catch the group walking in her direction. The anger becomes terror as her gaze lifts up almost thirty-feet to find Eliza's eyes, and the shaking of the ground becomes stronger, with each of Eliza's strides being the very obvious source of the gentle quaking. A pointed finger aimed up to Eliza and eyes looking down to Pearl, Esmerelda yells, "What in the ever loving!"

Sprinting to Esmerelda, Pearl stops her saying, "Hey, don't worry about it she is steadily shrinking she was at least twice this large a few hours ago."

"T-t-twice?"

"Well, maybe three, four times. Come to think of it we couldn't get a good scale of her largest size, the chamber was so small compared to her."

Esmerelda looks to almost break with Pearl's words before Eliza steps to her asking, "It wouldn't be a problem to take us to Dur'heim now would it?"

Turning and pointing to the ship Esmerelda, nods mumbling, "Sure," and she follows the group as they step to the dock.

The black ship waits, bobbing to the gentle crests of short waves, with Rev and Lorm staring bewildered at the towering form of Eliza approaching them. Pearl, Aldrin, and Auburn climb up onto the ship's deck and Esmerelda watches in terror as Eliza goes to join them. The marble slab creaks under Eliza's mass as she steps onto it, threatening to break from beneath her, but it holds as she turns and using the ship's mast to stabilize herself, she slides onto the deck causing it to rock violently, and sink more than a foot deeper into the bay.

Joining her crew and passengers Esmerelda, still foggy from having a more than twenty-foot-tall, exceptionally well figured, young teenager, taking up most of the space available on her ship's main deck, addresses the urn calling forth the ghostly crew who begin their tasks of pulling the vessel from the private lake. Going about their tasks the ghostly crew continue to not acknowledge anyone beyond the captain, simply passing through the barrier that is Eliza's form as they need, and the ship quickly makes its way back out to sea. Sailing in a southward heading Esmerelda keeps enough of her senses to very precisely chart down the necessary information she needs to return to the island in the morning.

Two hours pass and Eliza becomes visibly smaller in that time and the deck of the ship slowly regains its free space. The ghostly crew is dismissed when in the distance the cliff face port city of Dur'heim comes into view on the horizon. Rev, Lorm, and Esmerelda take about the remainder of the tasks for the ship to drift into the dock. Getting within range to do so, Esmerelda leaps from the deck of her ship and to the wood planks of the pier.

A short stout man, with a broad chest and shoulders, wearing plain clothes with a tight faded black suit jacket, that strains to contain his thick muscular build, with a large bushy brown beard swaying with his steps, addresses Esmerelda as he approaches, "Hello there, welcome to Dur'heim if yer goin te be keepin yer ship there, then ye need te be payin yer docking fee."

Pulling a rope into a tight knot to hold the ship mostly in place, Esmerelda turns to the man responding, "Sure, how much for the day we ship out in the morning."

"Oh, if ye are only goin te be here till the mornin we only need a shill from ye."

Digging into a side bag, Esmerelda pulls out a single silver coin and tosses it to the man saying, "The names Esmerelda, for your ledger." The man quickly pockets the coin before pulling out a small leather-bound book that he writes in with a chunk of charcoal. Closing the book, the dock worker gives a nod, and turns walking back into the town. Gesturing up to her ship, Esmerelda catches the base of the gang plank as it falls to her from above.

Finally, at a port, the group on the black ship trod slowly down to the dock. Esmerelda helps each down before turning to with an open-handed gesture to the cliff port. Eliza looks up at the many levels of civilization dug into the side of the mountainous cliff, and unconsciously mutters, "Wow."

Auburn steps forward and gives Esmerelda a gentle pat on the shoulder, grunting, "Ye git us 'ere noo let's git ye that drink."

With Auburn leading the group through the busy streets Aldrin, Pearl and Eliza look about the city around them. Bore into the cliff the docks feed directly into a dark lower section of the city with large stone pillars scattered throughout holding up the weight of the levels above. Dirty, dark and damp, the sea level rests as the obvious slums, and are quickly navigated through. Auburn brings the group to a set of cranes a short way from the docks where, stepping into a basket, they are lifted quickly to the second of the city's levels. Large old iron lamps protrude from the city segment's ceiling illuminating the sturdy rigid architecture of the buildings below. Finally, Auburn stops at a door with, engraved above the frame its name and he smiles to the group, "Eigenbrew if yer looking fur guid ale 'n' a good time this is th' place tae be."

Through the heavy curtain that hangs in the doorway the smell of ale and dust fills the air. Eliza almost coughs as the bar smog fills her lungs. A pressure like that of a hand grabbing the back of her neck rests on her after she ducks into the large room with a for her, low ceiling, forcing her to remain bent over. The untrusting eyes of the dwarven patrons continue to hold themselves locked on, as she stands just over twice the height of anyone in her group, and the seven step to an empty table.

A moment passes, and a dwarven woman steps to them, gowned in a purple apron and a cream-colored linen dress. Leaning her heavy-set, shapely figure onto one of her hips, her thick brown locks sway with the motion, braided intricately together holding within, small beads of metal and stone. Pulling a small pad of paper and a piece of charcoal from a pocket in her apron the woman asks in a deep mature but distinctly feminine voice, "Hey thare tall rid 'n' hansom it's bin a while sin ye'v bin aroond, whit kin ah git ye 'n' yer friends?"

Standing and giving the nearly four-foot woman a hug Auburn responds, holding the smile from the door, "Tis guid tae see ye again Jess! A round o' th' hoose special fur th' buird, and plate o' mud boar."

"I'll git that fur ye real quick."

Auburn sits back into his seat. In the same moment, Eliza leans to Pearl, asking, "Why is everyone staring at us?"

"Because ye draw attention," Auburn laughs leaning back in his chair, "Ah mean yer two times th' size o' ony o' us, 'n' nearly three times th' size o' some o' th' locals."

"You're in a good mood."

"I'm in a guid mood most o' th' time, ah juist don't normally trust ye, bit a'm happy tae be sae claise tae hame."

"Why don't you trust us?"

"Ah trust him, thaim 'n' her, ye two, ur th' two ah don't lik', 'n' i've tellt ye why before," Auburn explains pointing to Auburn, Rev and Lorm, and Esmerelda, before pointing to Pearl and Eliza, continuing to lean in his chair.

The barmaid returns, impressively carrying seven flagons of ale, all overflowing with their head, and a large plater piled high with a mound of shredded meat that oozes gravy. With each sat person getting one of the mugs, the platter is set in the tables center. Not having removed her eyes from Auburn, Eliza stands saying to the table, "You know, I'm not hungry, good night."

Aldrin looks in confused worry as Eliza grabs a bag and steps from the table to the counter. Conversing for a short moment with the man behind the bar Eliza is handed a key in exchange for a coin she pulls from the bag and she steps up the stairs. The eyes of the tavern follow her as she leaves only turning to the group she stepped from after she ducks fully out of sight, casting a strange mixture of suspicion, and jealousy their way. A moment later and the eyes of the room return to their conversations leaving the group in piece.

Aldrin rolls his eyes and asks Auburn, "Now why did you have to say that?"

Auburn shrugs and goes to respond but doesn't have a chance as Pearl takes a big swig of the dwarven stout placed in front of her, and says, "Haters gonna hate. Don't worry about it, Lizzy is strong. She ate a lot of berries and bread, and she might actually be feeling that seemingly grow inside her as she shrinks. So, she probably isn't hungry."

"You are closer to her than I can be, so, I guess you're probably right."

In a room on the second floor of the tavern, alone, Eliza looks at the door and mutters, "Jerk. Who are you to call Pearl a freak, to call me a freak, and to be so flippant about it. Alfredo hasn't made us freaks. You have red skin, and you think Pearl is weird for having blue? Your jealous, we are becoming better than you, beautiful, precious, protected, perfect." Eliza's muttering begins to radiate from her and almost echo within the small room. The dark emotions driving her actions take visible hold on her. Black veins twist and throb into existence around her eyes. Placing the bag forcefully on the room's bed, and with a single hand thrust into it, a single potion is drawn from within.

A clear liquid with the consistency of syrup fills the glass test tube. A single sliver of a fingernail or toenail, and a single twisted strand of hair both sit, suspended in the viscous concoction. Uncorked by Eliza's free hand the elixir releases a pungent soapy smell, and it's consumed in a single swig bearing a similar taste. The slime slides slowly down its imbiber's esophagus carrying with it the nail and hair.

Eliza can't help contorting her face to the taste and texture of the potion. She releases a sigh after a moment when she feels the fluid reach her stomach, after which she sits on the bed by Pearl's bag. Patiently patting the bed's side she waits for the impending affect.

The plate of meat and gravy mostly cleared, and a pile of empty mugs on the side of the table sit with the full bellied and alcohol sodden group. The six laugh, sharing stories from their past and making jokes with each other. The jovial mood vanishes when one of the barmaids, looking at the ceiling, exclaims, "What is that!"

The group look to where the barmaid points. Pearl's eyes become wide when they witness, coming through the cracks of the ceiling boards from the floor above, clusters of hair like roots through a ceiling of dirt. Slamming her feet down from on the table to the floor, Pearl asks in panic, "Lizzy?" Leaping from her seat Pearl bounds up the stairs, and getting to the second floor she finds the hallway covered with the same outstretching tuberous locks of sky-blue hair, which fold from beneath one of the closed doors.

Eliza's voice, panicked calls out, muffled through the door, barely audible, "Someone please help!"

Pearl heaves against the door, pushing it barely open enough to see in. Through the small crack, the light coming from the room's window, reveals mounds of the hair piled against the walls of the room. A second call comes from within emanating from one of the piles, which shacks and squirms in place. Pushing again on the door Pearl calls in, "I'm here Lizzy, hold on!"

The door opens wide enough for Pearl to enter and squeezing into the room she gasps as she takes in the excessive amount of Eliza's hair that surrounds her. Mounds of sky-blue fill the room's corners, and a layer is spread across the ground. The source, struggling on the bed, Eliza, is tangled within a thick sheet of her own curls, trapped by the sudden onset of hair growth. From the large knot of hair only the young girl's fingers are visible with painfully long, twisted nails extending from them.

Pearl doesn't hesitate before striding across the room to the restrained Eliza, before grabbing handfuls of hair. Pulling and shifting the mop in her hands Pearl tries to untangle the seemingly impossible knot explaining to Eliza who struggles and moans within, "Look calm down I'm here, I'm going to get you out of this."

Eliza becomes still with Pearl's instruction, and the two work slowly over the course of an hour. Finally free, the young scared teen embraces Pearl exclaiming, "Thank you."

Pushing Eliza gently from the embrace by her shoulders, and looking into her eyes, which hold no sign of the black veins, Pearl asks, "What happened? Is that my bag?"

"Yes," Eliza responds looking ashamedly down and away, continuing, "I drank one of the potions."

"What! You had one earlier."

"Yea."

"What were you thinking?"

Eliza's eyes water, and her face falls into her hands, crying, "I wasn't, I just wanted to! I don't know what came over me."

Pearl embraces Eliza once more. Having forgotten the outfit covering Eliza to be only an illusion, Pearl is surprised when she fells flesh under her slime covered fingers, as she rubs the weeping girl's back to console her. With a deep breath Pearl sighs, "Hey, it's alright, it doesn't seem like much harm has been done. Let's just take care of those claws of yours real quick, and get the rest of your hair into as manageable of form as we can, as I am guessing you are still going to want to keep it?"

Sniffling and wiping hear nose with her arm, Eliza nods, "Yea, I think it's pretty even at this length."

"Well then," Pearl stands pulling a dagger from her side, "Those nails," and Pearl trims Eliza's extreme fingernails to short untroublesome points. Nearly another hour more passes of handling Eliza's hair, pulling if from the floorboards, folding it into a nice but massive braid, and filling it unintentionally with Pearl's slime. After the matter is settled and Eliza heart is set again to ease, Pearl leaves her young companion to sleep, and returns to the tavern below to obtain her own room, with her bag once more in her possession.

5

The Black Isles

Knocks on the doors of the tavern's halls wake the patrons, with the friendly voices of the barmaids calling into the rooms, "Th' sun is oan th' horizon, ye kin wake, or keep sleeping juist letting ye know."

The sound of movement shuffles through the tavern as the residents of the many rooms wake. The sound follows the crowd as it moves from their rooms to the hall and down the small flight of stairs, that fills tight with a shoulder to shoulder sea of hurried individuals. The river of people pulls with it the six foreigners down into the bar area where they find freedom from the almost mechanical procession of natives heading out to their days work.

Auburn sits at a table smiling and shaking his head as he sees the confusion on the faces of his traveling companions while they are moved into the open space. With the six obviously out of place individuals getting to his table Auburn laughs saying, "A'richt, noo ilka minute ah hae traveled wi' ye haes bin made worth it."

Pearl squints asking, "What do you mean?"

"T's juist hilarious tae see ye, especially, sae oot o' steid."

Ending the conversation before Pearl can respond again, Esmerelda leans onto the table saying, "We don't have time for this. Rev, Lorm and I are going to go buy some more rations for the ship, we will meet you there in less than an hour. Please, we are so close, please don't make me wait any more to get back to my family."

Aldrin simply rests his hand on Esmerelda's shoulder explaining, "We won't."

With a nod to Aldrin, Esmerelda gestures to her two friends and the three of them leave Eigenbrew. With a deep breath, Aldrin joins Auburn sitting at the table, and as Pearl pulls a chair back to follow suit she and Aldrin happen to look in the direction of the stairs. A soft smile forms on both of their faces, as stepping slowly down, having let the crowd pass before leaving her room, Eliza moves bashfully in their direction.

Nearly half as tall as she was when she went to her room the night before, Eliza approaches the table holding the enormous braid of hair over one of her shoulders, with no sign that Pearl's fishy excretion had ever touched a single strand. When she gets to the table she looks directly at Auburn and with the full-hearted innocence of ignorant youth she breaths, "I'm sorry."

Auburn looks at Eliza with surprise asking in response, "Fur whit?"

"I was too easily upset last night, you were happy to be home and I took your comment of distaste for Pearl and me too personally."

"Ye think ah cared aboot yer reaction? Yer tantrum didn't impact mah nicht. Noo afore ye gied the pitch tae yer room again howfur aboot we heid tae th' ship foremaist," Auburn explains standing and turning to the door. Before taking a step away from the table and before Pearl or Eliza can respond to his remark Auburn continues saying over his shoulder, "It's guid tae see ye nearly back tae yer normal size though."

The compliment coming from Auburn stops Pearl immediately before she can say anything, and the three move to follow him into the street. Eliza walks on Pearl's side and before they step onto the crane to descend to the sea level of the city, she asks, "Pearl, can I get my amulet back?"

"Oh, yea, sure," Pearl responds, before she begins digging in her satchel. Pulling out the metal symbol of archangel and ties it around Eliza's neck. They begin to descend.

Watching Pearl tie the amulet for Eliza, Auburn explains, "Weel don't let fowk see that wull ye, thair serious aboot thair worship of Mountain King here."

The amulet disappears under the illusion of clothes covering Eliza as she responds, "I don't evangelize, you can at least recognize that."

"Juist letting ye ken. Ye draw enough attention bein' th' tallest among us," Auburn responds pointing out the nearly half a foot of height she still stands above him.

Pearl laughs to herself, mumbling, "There it is."

The rest of the journey to the dock is quiet among the group, with the sound of the city rumbling around them. The hour doesn't even toll over when Esmerelda calls up to the deck where Aldrin sits tightening the joints of his suit, "Hey, we're going to need some help with these supplies, mind lending a hand?"

"Sure thing, Pearl get up here," Aldrin responds slamming his boot on the deck.

"Yea this seems like it could be a wand of some kind, based on the spider I am guessing one of a poison incantation, one of spider climbing or one dealing with web, I saw it in the vault in our palace and thought if any of the four of us would be able to use it, it would be you. Oh, and this thing served its purpose, it was what held the contract for the vault guardian, with him gone, I don't see a use for it, but it might have some latent magic still in it. Boop might like it as a chew toy replacement for the lightning javelin,"

Pearl explains presenting the two intricately designed rods to Eliza before the ceiling above slams with Aldrin's voice muffled through the wood becoming unintelligible. Leaving Eliza with the magically infused objects Pearl jogs to the deck and seeing Esmerelda, Rev, and Lorm, boarding with crates in their hands, she joins in loading the supplies that were purchased.

Shifting the ship from the docks back into open waters of the Southern Sea, the group sail again for the island of Negmor's palace. The short two hours of the trip pass and the group step to the waiting marble path and into the quiet structure. They continue through the dark quiet halls with the clack of their boots and the pat of Eliza's feet carrying them up the tall set of stairs to the observatory. The arrow sits raised above the black stone and turning it to point eastward the group feel the island jolt as a blur takes their vision and fades leaving the sun above them having shifted several hours across the sky.

The five, Aldrin, Auburn, Pearl, Eliza, and Boop return again to the ship and Esmerelda commands the ghostly crew setting the ship on a course for Blackgate, still two days of sailing away. The tension sits heavy on the ship as the realization of the daunting task set before them embraces the group. They were told in E'ar Falmar that the town was taken by force, Aldrin especially knows how hard that would have been, bearing with him the crest of the Blackguard, the militia that defended Blackgate's walls.

The two days pass in almost silence, with the small interactions between the group's members being limited to Eliza and Boop, who keep occupied with small games of fetch, and hide and go seek, not allowing their minds to drift into the melancholy that appears to have taken the others. Several times Pearl and Aldrin look at the two playing in the midst of the on-setting reality, and nearly in the small giggles and barks, hear Boop speak in a voice wholly his own. The worry for their own safety and the safety of those they are looking to help casts the suspicion from their minds, before they can investigate the voice's source further.

On the second day Aldrin approaches Esmerelda, before the horizon has a chance to hold upon it a sign of land, saying, "Hey, I know you want to get back to your family, but Blackgate is currently under the control of an unknown military force, I think it would be best if we didn't let them see the ship."

Esmerelda lets out a sigh, and nods, responding, "Your probably right. Crew pull portside, and the secondary sail, we need avoid being seen on our approach, and wait until night fall."

The crew follow the instructions and the ship leans to one side as it changes direction, and one of the sails is closed slowing the ship's speed. Several more hours pass bringing the darkening orange of the evening's sky, and on the horizon, grows in view a thick cloud of green that sits over the distant coasts of the Black Isles. Eliza sees for the first time the blackened twisted landscape as it rises under the cloud of smog when night finally sets in. The ship slows and comes to a stop, with the anchor being lowered. Esmerelda helps prepare the landing boat to be lowered into the water.

Aldrin, Auburn, Eliza, and Pearl, climb into the small rowboat, and to their surprise Esmerelda joins them. Before Aldrin can say anything, she puts a finger to him and without facing his direction explains, "You can tell me not to sail to Blackgate's docks, you can even let my crew stay and guard the ship, but that is where it stops you are not going to keep me from my family any longer than you already have."

"Fine," Aldrin responds looking to Eliza who holds Boop in her arms.

Releasing her friend Eliza looks into inquisitive central eye explaining to him, "I need you to stay here Boop, help make sure that this ship isn't discovered."

"Ok master. You be safe. Call if trouble," Boop responds, striking the others on the boat with surprise as they fully hear his scratchy high-pitched voice for the first time.

Pearl nearly falls back with her surprise asking, "Wait, Boop you talk?"

"Now," the small orb responds facing Pearl.

"I don't know how it happened he just started talking on our way here," Eliza explains before Pearl can follow up her question.

Pulling from his bag a small statue Auburn almost reluctantly adds to the conversation, "Here," and tossing the statue up, a name leaves his mouth, "Felix." The statue glows white as it flies up to the deck and releasing a popping sound it generates a gusting wind that spirals around it. The wind calms to a still, and the group once again find the ability to look to where the statue was tossed. In the place where it landed, instead stands a creature, seemingly the amalgamation of an eagle and a lion, which releases a screeching combination of a mighty roar and majestic call. Gesturing to the beast Auburn explains, "Found that in the palace under the case that held this bow, might as well put it to use sooner rather than later."

No response comes for Auburn's actions, and the ghosts on the ship begin to lower the dingy with a commanding whistle from Esmerelda. Grabbing the paddles Pearl begins to row and the soft waves push the boat toward the shore. The wooden wedge grinds into the pebble beach after a short minute, they disembark, pulling their vessel deeper inland. Hiding it from discovery under nearby bushes that seem almost as though their leaves are covered in a thin layer of tar.

Stepping to the lead Aldrin, calls to the others with a hand wave over his shoulder, "That's good enough, Blackgate is this way right?"

"Yea, we turned to port which is sailing speak for left," Pearl explains jogging to Aldrin's side.

"Let's do this," Eliza exclaims gritting as she grins, with the stones of the shore stabbing the bottoms of her feet.

They walk. The dark of the night around them more intense with the strange green ozone completely obscuring the stars. As they continue down the coast, Eliza notices, the little bit of life that grows from the dark cracked, stony earth resting consistently covered in a thin layer of the strange tar-like substance.

After walking for some time, the group see on the horizon, a tall reinforced stone wall begin to grow with their approach. With the walls of the waiting town growing Pearl stops and grabs her side grunting in pain, "Crud."

The other four turn to her and before them, they see her bent over with thin streaks of the black tar-like substance seeping from her eyes. Where her hand grasps on her side, the same substance oozes through the fabric of her shirt and jacket like a thick puss seeping from a hidden wound. Eliza drops to Pearl's side asking, "Pearl what's happening? What's wrong?"

"Corruption, we need to hurry and get into Blackgate, Silvermist acolytes can stop this," Pearl grunts through a blackened grin to Eliza.

6

Sisters of the Silvermist

Two guards stand above the gate as a group of five approach. One of them calls down in a growling raspy deep voice, "Stop there!"

The hooded figures obey, stopping their progress to the town's entrance raising their hands above their heads, and keeping their heads down, submissive. After a moment, a voice calls from one of the figures, a soft feminine voice with a scratchiness that fills it with the sound of age, saying, "What is this? Are we not allowed back into the town? We were doing research for the Blackgaurd, further into the isle, but our escort perished, so we have returned and need medical attention for one of our companions immediately from the sisters of Silvermist."

"Research huh? For the Blackguard you say. How unfortunate that your guard passed. This city is now under the protection of the Stormrider. A curfew is in effect."

Another voice, one of a gruff worldly man calls back nearly lifting his head, but he keeps his composure, and his head remains hidden, "Would you have us stay out here in the wastes, the corruption is already setting into one of our companions, would you doom us all to suffer that fate?"

One of the guards on the wall throws his torch down in suspicion of the strange hooded figures hiding their faces in the dim light of the night. The torch fades and nearly is extinguished with the fall. Striking the ground, it releases a spray of sparks. The fire returns and illuminates the hooded figures, more clearly revealing their forms for the skeptical guards. In the glow of the torch the guards see the hand of one of the five figures, blackened, covered in a filmy substance. Looking to each other one of the guards calls down responding to the man's question, "Stay where you are, we are letting you in, you will be escorted to the temple and then to your place of living."

One of the guards remains on top of the gatehouse as the other descends down behind the wall. A moment later the gate grinds open and the second guard stands in the opening. With a single gesture to follow him and grabbing another torch that he lights, he growls with the same deep, growling voice, "Come with me."

The group shuffles to the guard's side getting their first full look of the large form. An elongated maw, covered in blue scales, with a tan horn protruding from the tip of his nose, the man snarls down at the hooded figures as they advert their faces from his gaze once more. The muscular male figure of the guard stands nearly eight-feet-tall, with a muscular blue scaled tail protruding from his back that drags nearly a foot behind him, and he leads the five into the streets.

The town is dark, and oppressively rundown. The smell of burnt wood, and mildew fills the air. No activity breaks the dead stillness in the streets, and the windows of the structures that flank the roads are black and boarded, lightless. Turning a corner, the hooded figures recoil, as above them rushes through the air a monstrous creature with bat-like wings and an oversized scorpion's tail at least six feet long, and nearly a foot in width at its thickest point. The guard leading them is undeterred snarling wordlessly to get them to move again.

The group turn to find in their path, a large structure built with the obvious purpose of being a temple. The yards on either side of the path are dug up, leaving freshly overturned dirt where there should be grass and trees. When this comes into view, the hooded man who spoke at the gate asks, "You dug up the garden?"

"Why do you care," the large stormrider asks glaring down at the stranger, while crossing his arms in disapproving intimidation toward the seemingly frail traveler.

"We have been gone for a long time I was simply surprised."

The large reptilian man squints his golden yellow eyes at the hooded man before pushing the group forward again along the path. Stepping to the temple's doors, the guard raises a fist and slams it against the old, but well-kept wood. A second passes and the sound of the wood barring on the other side being removed slides and becomes audible to the waiting group as the doors are opened. Another large blue scaled reptilian man looks out angrily from the doorway, asking, "What?"

The guard which lead the group to this point responds, "We've got an infected one here."

"It's after curfew handle it the other way."

"Look, they were out before we got here."

"Is there a scourge among them?"

"Their scourge died before they returned, apparently."

"Fine. Bring them in, I'll wake the woman," the man within the temple growls, gesturing to be followed.

The once beautiful temple waits in disrepair through the doorway, with the space that would have once held pews instead holding mix matched wooden tables on which more blue humanoids lay wrapped in blood dirtied bandages. The man who answered the door, ducks into a back side room and a moment later reappears dragging a woman by the shoulder. Throwing her forward, the beast of a man growls, "They have corruption, fix them."

Falling to her knees, the woman visibly shakes, as she keeps her focus trained on the floor. Standing and nodding she responds in a trembling voice, "I've expended the blessings that Silvermist allots me in a day."

A swift strike from behind, slaps into the woman's head throwing her down to the side, and the deep voice growls back, "Did I ask you a question? I don't care about your fake god's rules, do your job."

The acolyte falls into the arms of one of the hooded figures, and looking up with terrified, tired eyes, she is suddenly uplifted seeing a face she remembers. With sudden almost panicked energy, the woman feigns worry, exclaiming, "Oh dear this one is suffering from a great deal of corruption."

The man who escorted the hooded figures to the temple pulls the grey robed woman up by her wrist, asking aggressively, "Are you as blind as you are stupid? This one is the one that is corrupted," and he points a beefy clawed finger at the hooded figure whose hand is coated in black.

Turning with a determination, that surpasses the trembling terror that had filled her, the woman responds almost scolding the large imposing man, "And you have dealt with corruption of the Broken Isles for most of your adult life? Do you remember the men who transformed into the monsters that killed so many and did this to so many of even your band of mercenaries? None of them had visible signs of corruption, and that made the outburst much more devastating. Now she is suffering the effects of corruption and the sisters and I should cure her but, that one needs immediate attention."

Worry takes the eyes of the two large individuals with the words of the feisty holy person. The one from the wall looks to the other before returning his eyes to the human woman, who stares at him with determination in her eyes, and he asks with panic taking his gruff voice, "What do you need, to cleanse them?"

"Get my sisters, and let us take these two into the back room. Alone."

"That isn't going to happen," the second growls, becoming clear in the distinct differences from the one that escorted the group from the gate, with the horn that protrudes from his nose splitting into two points, instead of remaining one.

The woman's eyes get wide almost in anger when she turns to the intimidating form explaining, "You have our champion in your custody, do you really think any of her sisters would do anything to risk her safety?"

With a snarl, only made more distinct with the elongated maw, the man responds, "You have a point. Fine. I'll go get your sisters."

"I'm going back to my post, these five need escort to their abodes when you are done with those two," the first large man explains stepping to the door.

Following five more women out of the side room, the split horned man growls to the door before it closes behind the other, "Whatever," and turning to the woman and hooded figures he continues, pointing to a door at the back of the building that leads into a basement saying, "Alright take the two you say are corrupted, you three stay where I can see you."

The grey robed women rubbing their eyes to remove the sleep they were woke from, lead the two hooded individuals down into the private area. The black of the windowless room is cast aside when a torch is struck into burning life, revealing the small cool cellar. Two tables stand against walls across from each other, with the one on the wall of the door holding several strange objects. Closing and locking the door behind them one of the acolytes of Silvermist asks, "Sister Helena, you know we've all expended what the mist allows us. What is the meaning of this."

The initial woman, Sister Helena, steps to one end of the room and looks to the hooded figures, and gesturing with open hands toward them she says to the room, "We must perform the cleansing ritually, for we know these two. Aldrin is that you? Pearl?"

Pulling back his hood Aldrin nods to the vested individuals, asking, "Yes. Helena, what did you mean by men transforming into monsters?"

Another one of the gowned women grabs Aldrin's arm saying in an airy whine, "Oh, Aldrin, it was horrible, all of the Blackguard succumb to their corruption blocker. The blockers transformed them into horrible monsters."

"Come to think of it how have you not transformed, Aldrin, you went through the ritual too," another of the women asks walking around Aldrin looking him up and down.

Obviously out of sorts with the attention Aldrin hesitates, responding, "Well, Pearl and I were on a different plane of existence for some time. When did this happen?"

"A different plane of existence," another one of the women asks, as the group seems to be ignoring the other hooded figure who slinks to the side, falling into a lean against the wall.

"The Blackguard went bad, well, nearly five months ago," a third holy woman responds.

"Well that explains the incident almost immediately after we got back to this plane. Whatever is causing the corruption to be so much more aggressive must still be active," Aldrin responds.

"Wait! You experienced the breakdown of your corruption barrier? How are you here, how are you alive," Helena responds in surprise.

"There was a community of elves that saved me," Aldrin responds before the other hooded figure moans sliding down the wall, leaving a trail of the black tar-like substance behind. Aldrin pushes the women aside, and drops to the hooded figure's side. Looking back to the clerics of Silvermist he says, "Enough talk, Pearl is actually suffering from corruption help her, then we can talk."

Helena shakes her head trying to focus on the second figure, with something unnatural making the normally simple act difficult. Forcing herself to Aldrin's side, Helena lifts the other form and pulls her to the table at the back of the room. With the figure placed on the table, the other women begin moving around the room relocating items from the other table around the sickly individual. Within the chaotic movement one of the women stops Sister Helena asking with concern, "Sister, what are we doing, we've never ritually cleansed someone without Lady Tristalia."

Grabbing the worried sister by the shoulders, Sister Helena stares into her eyes explaining, "I know, but those monsters are expecting us to cleanse Pearl, and if we can't, they'll kill her."

With an understanding nod, the worried woman, steps to the item covered table, and she grabs a large polished stone bowl with a thick wand of the same polished stone sat within. With the sisters stepping back from the moaning hooded form, having each placed an item next to the suffering individual, Sister Helena removes the figures hood, and is suddenly stunned when the face of the individual revealed is not Pearl's. Turning to Aldrin, Sister Helena points at the woman on the table and asks, "You said this was Pearl."

With a sigh, Aldrin looks at the wrinkled pale face of the woman lying on the table, and he goes to explain, placing a hand to the crown of his nose and gestures with the other hand at the woman, "That is Pearl. Her appearance is being masked by a spell a new companion of ours cast before we got to the wall."

"Why?" Sister Helena asks confused, but before Aldrin can attempt to respond she puts a hand to him continuing, "You know what, don't tell me, or any of us. The mere fact that we are helping a member of the Blackguard would get us flogged. Sister Iva please begin the ritual."

Lighting a single coal, the acolyte siting with the bowl places the glowing black chunk into the vessel, before covering it in a thin layer of powdered incense. Smoke begins to rise in a thin pillar to the ceiling. With a strike of the thick wand, held in her finger tips, a loud ringing begins to reverberate in the air. Slowly and methodically Sister Iva draws the side of the wand against the edge of the bowl intensifying the piercing sound that sends visible ripples up the column of smoke. With her free hand she grabs a small bottle that was set next to her by one of the other acolytes, and sprinkles a liquid from it into the bowl.

The contents of the bowl pop with the liquid's addition, and the smoke rising from it begins to change from the thin grey to a thick silvery white that carries up in it specks of twinkling glitter. As the thrumming continues the column becomes wider and grows, thickening as a cloud forms across the ceiling. The smoke's change prompts the acolytes to begin singing, and a soft hymn fills the room.

With the song leaving their lips, the women smile to each other, as they witness the cloud overhead, begin to shift and turn like a forming storm. The spinning of the mist continues for several moments before twisting down in a gentle spiraling cone toward the form on the table who is struggling to breathe. Barely touching its edge to the woman on the table, the cloud suddenly cascades down from the ceiling jacketing her, and becoming dense, almost solid.

With a nod, Helena turns from the group that continues to sing letting her voice fall from chorus, and looking to Auburn she asks him, "So what's your plan?"

"I thought you didn't want to know anything."

"That was before I was sure we would be able to clean the corruption from your bodies."

"Well to be honest, we didn't think much into this plan. You're sure all of the Blackguard are dead?"

"Every member of the Blackguard was horribly mutated simultaneously, at least every member that had made it to the trial. Any others that stood against the monsters or the raiders were killed."

"What about 'A' 'R' 'G', please tell me their resources haven't fallen into the hands of these Stormriders."

"No, shortly after the mutations began ravaging the city there was an explosion at their location, nothing remains."

"That's good, what about the Red Tide? Any major activity from them?"

"Now Aldrin, you know I would never knowingly help such lowlifes, and would be less likely to keep tabs on them. But crime has been low with martial law in place and enforced by the dragon men."

"They would have been made an example of. They're in hiding. We'll have to talk with them. You said that these Stormriders have Lady Tristalia. Where are they holding her?"

"Where else? The keep and they have men posted at the top of our tower, where she embedded her sword in the stone before handing herself over."

"We'll have to free her as well. How much longer on fixing up Pearl?"

"Just another few minutes."

7

Aldrin's Home

In the main room of the church, the three other hooded figures wait with the dragon man, as he becomes impatient, and begins pacing. The ringing thrum that bellows through the door comes to an end just before his pacing. He steps to the door with an impatient anger. With a balled fist the man hammers the wood calling in, "Hey, how long does it take to clear a little corruption?"

Before the large gloved fist can strike the door in a second series of impatient knocks, the old hinges creek revealing the robed women and the two hooded figures. Keeping their faces hidden with their hoods, the two step past the large armored man to join the other three, and the women bow responding, "We had to perform the ritual casting, it takes more time, by they are now cleansed."

"Get back to your chambers," the man growls pointing to the room he pulled them from. Turning to the hooded cluster of five he continues,

"You lot with me, if you leave my side I will have you killed. Now lead me to your place of bedding."

Under the large man's skeptical watch, Aldrin leads the way from the temple back onto the large main street. Turning the way opposite the gate they came from, he continues deeper into the town. They pass through another wall, within the city, and into a distinctly different district.

Eliza looks under the edge of her illusory hood to see the rundown distraught disrepair of Blackgate's slums. All around them the city holds the scars of recent military conflict in the collapsed burned ruins of poorly constructed homes and stores. Stepping from the slums, the group crosses over a river that splits the city in two and they continue to follow the same large street southward.

On a hill to the group's left, rises an imposing black silhouette of an imposing keep, against the deep green glowing of the smog filled night sky. Glancing to the structure, Eliza is taken by its presence expressing under her breath, "Wow."

Leaning close to Eliza, while trying to not draw attention from their escort, Pearl responds to her expression of aw, "Yea, it's less impressive on the inside, trust me."

With the attention she was hoping to avoid, Pearl stands straight again, hearing the deep growling from the burly dragon man behind her, "Stop talking. You, hurry this up."

To the command, Aldrin continues forward, stepping quickly along the large empty road. The forward progress stops though, when a marching group of more dragon men turns from one of the side roads and into the group's direction. The approaching squadron stare at the gathering of hooded individuals, before shifting their untrusting gaze to the one of their kin. A powerful shove in Aldrin's back starts the group's motion again, and they pass the dragon men, before continuing along the same path.

Another several minutes of walking bring the group to the front door of a small white house. Like the other buildings of the district they have been walking through, the one that waits for the group at the end of their journey, is a higher quality construction of the same haphazard architecture as the buildings that they passed by in what appeared as the slums. A common theme through the structures of the city remains in the black scorching of their outer walls, signs of a military conflict with unnatural forces on one of the sides. Unlike the structures of the slums, however, the buildings of this district appear as to have received some level of repair to the damage that became them, with the only exception being the building whose door Aldrin steps to which waits with one of its roof's corners collapsed in, opening an upper room.

Pulling a key from his bag, Aldrin unlocks the door, and turns to the group gesturing for them to enter. The armored man watches as they file into the unlit abode and growling, "Don't leave this building until morning," he leaves.

The small house is dark, with only a single room for the group to file into through the front door. A single table sits at the room's center three feet from an unlit fireplace. In the back corner, away from the door, on the floor and ceiling are two wooden trapdoors, with a ladder on the back wall that leads to both of them. Casting his cloak from his shoulders onto the empty table Aldrin steps to the fireplace and moving a log from its side into the stone arch, he ignites it with a small device on his wrist, that produces a small flame. Without facing his companions Aldrin steps to the corner with the trapdoors saying, "Don't be shy, make your selves at home. My home is your home, at least as long as we're alive," and climbing the ladder, his fist slams into the upper barrier before he calls through it, "Hey, there. Delira, you up there it's Aldrin."

With Aldrin's call, the sound of shifting motion quickly passes from the upper floor, preceding the sound of a metal latch clicking from above. A relieved smile takes his face as the hatch opens revealing a young woman with short brown hair and pale freckled skin that is smudged with the black of coal dust. A smile takes her face and she throws herself through the hatch into the second floor and around the man on the ladder. Pushing herself back from the embrace, Delira looks at Aldrin asking, her voice, filled with obvious youth, is scratchy and damaged when it fills the air removing the stagnant silence of the room, "Aldrin! Where have you been? You said it would take you two weeks. It's been more than four months."

Looking down and away Aldrin responds, "I know. How about you come down and I tell you where we've been, and you tell us what is going on here?"

Looking down to the table and seeing the four other hooded figures standing in the ground floor area, Delira pulls away hiding herself from their view. Her voice meagerly squeaks back, "You didn't say there were others."

"They're good people. You can trust them. Come on down."

"Ok," Delira responds, before slowly following Aldrin down the ladder.

The thin small woman, is dressed in a deep brown linen dress with a sturdy metal collar around her neck, and she hides behind Aldrin when she gets to the bottom of the ladder. Avoiding as much of the curious looks coming from the strangers in hoods as she can. Pearl laughs at Delira's shy nature while taking off her hood, forgetting that she does not look like herself saying, "You are always too cute Dee. Take it easy."

"Pearl," Delira asks, poking out from behind Aldrin.

"Yea, who else would I be?"

"You don't look like Pearl."

"What? Oh, yea about that, hey, Lizzy anything on that page about how long I am stuck with this look, or if it can be ended early?"

The tallest of the hooded figures shifts as Pearl turns in her direction, and removing her hood, reveals her youth filled beautiful pale soft face, and pulled back sky-blue hair, responding in a voice that is musical to Delira as she hears it for the first time, "I don't know let me check." The motion of the hood falling to the beautiful woman's shoulders doesn't stop instead continuing, with the illusion being revealed as her shoulders pass through the fabric which begins to fade as if being unraveled. With it falling from her, never touching the ground instead becoming nothingness, the illusion morphs into the short outfit Pearl had purchased her in E'ar Falmar. Dropping her bag on the table Eliza digs in it and avoiding the blade of the evil dagger that holds a spot in its base, she pulls out a small, ancient, folded piece of parchment, on one side of which are strange alien symbols that fill the page, in what appears to be two distinct sections. Scanning over the ink which almost magically has not been faded or damaged with the ages the parchment has held it, she looks to Pearl, she shrugs and states, "I don't know this language, it's weird, it seems almost like it changes each time I look at it."

"Wait, you cast a spell on me that changed my appearance, and we don't even know how long it will last or how to end it," Pearl asks in surprised exasperation.

"I told you I wasn't sure about it when I brought it up, but it was either make you magically draw less attention to yourself or leave you in a state that would have drawn a lot more of attention," Eliza responds in a raised defensive tone.

Pearl sighs recognizing Eliza to be right, saying, "Yea, well how about we both try to focus on it fading."

Before Pearl finishes speaking, the blurry magic that has altered her appearance ripples and fades returning her skin to the glistening sea-foam-blue and her hair back to its thick locks of ocean blue. Watching the change happen to Pearl, Delira rubs her eyes in disbelief, asking, "What just happened?"

Eliza, shrugs responding, "I guess the spell wore off."

Pearl looks at her hands laughing, "Hey I guess it did. Cool."

Her hands leaving her eyes, Delira stares at Pearl, who wasn't blue, and didn't have a cat tail the last time they had seen each other, and her eyes go wide with the question leaving her mouth, "Pearl, why are you blue?"

Before Pearl can respond though, Aldrin makes his presence known as the thing Delira is hiding behind, interjecting, "Delira please, it's late, and we need to know what happened to the city before we can make plans for the morning."

"Oh right, sorry, sorry, let me make you some water," Delira responds stepping to a bucket filled with water, and filling a small metal pot with it she steps to the fireplace, and hangs it to heat.

Watching the very shy woman step from Aldrin's side, Eliza leans into whisper in Pearl's ear asking, "Pearl, who is that woman?"

"That's Delira."

"I know that, you and Aldrin have said it several times. I mean how do you two know her?"

"Are you jealous, Lizzy?"

"No."

"Thought you were the only shy cutie Aldrin and I have saved and taken under our wings, did you?"

"I'm not."

"Well, Delira is Aldrin's, so you can be mine, all mine," Pearl exclaims throwing an arm around Eliza's shoulder with a smile.

"I am not jealous," Eliza lashes back throwing Pearl's arm from her.

"Relax, I'm only kidding, she's his slave."

"His what?" Eliza turns to Aldrin with confused concerned fury in her eyes.

Watching Auburn remove his hood and share in Eliza's expression Aldrin responds, "Hey, she is not my slave, I am protecting her from slavery."

"Is she or is she not, bound to serve you against her will?"

"I would let her leave, if that was possible, but that band around her neck is dwarven make and I haven't been able to remove it, and as long as it is on her she can't live a free life. I hate the idea of slavery, and would love for it to just not exist, but I have no control over the practice of the dwarves, and where their practice of it is accepted."

"Wait, if that is true why is it that you own a slave."

Stepping from the gathering as Eliza interrogates Aldrin, Pearl looks back from half-way up the ladder responding, "He won her in a poker game."

Aldrin sighs and puts his hand to his head explaining, "Look I was drunk, it was late, I didn't even realize what the document was that was bet."

"Well if there is a document that exists that says that she is your slave why don't you destroy it," Eliza responds in a flustered tone.

Before Aldrin can respond the shaky raspy soft voice of Delira returns to the room's air, "He did, but this collar as he pointed out means that I will never be free as long as it is attached to me, and I need documents to be out in public. If I am caught without them by a dwarf they have liberty to beat me until I tell them who my master is."

"Oh," Eliza's breath escapes her as she is taken by Delira's words.

Delira goes to respond but ducks to hide with Aldrin as a shield between her and a sudden thump that crashes across the wooden floor. A pair of boots falls from the room above. Sticking her head down from the second story Pearl points to the old pair of footwear saying, "Hey, Lizzy you can have those, they were mine a while back, should still be good," and with that she flips through the hole landing with the others.

With a deep breath Aldrin recollects the group's attention saying, "Alright this has all gone a bit strange, let's start over. Eliza, Auburn, Esmerelda, this is Delira, a freed person, who is under my protection, Delira this is Eliza, Esmerelda and Auburn, each of whom I have become exceptional friends with and who have each been a reason for me getting back here."

Standing by the fire, fidgeting with her hands, Delira raises one and gives a quick, still shy wave, "Hello."

"Now Delira, we do need to know what is going on here. So, we aren't repeating things, I can tell you we already know that the Blackguard suffered deaths to the corruption of the trial, you don't have to worry about me, a group of elves helped cleanse me of it a while back, and we have also been informed that there is martial law in place, enforced by this group, these Stormriders, and that the Red Tide seem to have gone underground."

"Well that is pretty much all that has happened, a loud boom from the north shook the very ground, and every one of the blackguard became monsters that went into a rampage, there was a ball of fire that erupted from where 'A' 'R' 'G' was located, and eventually we were saved by the Stormriders. Well we thought we were saved until they announced the martial law, and before they started taking men from their families out of the city. The poor sisters of Silvermist, have been worked ragged trying to save the sick returning with corruption wounds."

"We know, we were taken there. That is how we knew about the curfew and the deaths of the blackguard."

"I don't have any idea what they're looking for beyond the wall though."

Pearl looks through the corner of her eyes to the Eliza muttering, "We might have an idea."

"Really what are they looking for? If we could tell the men what to keep an eye out for, they might be more likely to find it."

"Trust me, what the dragon men are looking for is not something you want them to find."

"What do you mean?"

"Look Dee just trust me on this one."

Before anyone can say anything else the trapdoor on the floor in the back of the room creaks open. In a reflex with the speed of a lightning strike Aldrin spins to the open door, and draws back his fist which releases a familiar whirring sound of it charging for an electric burst. In the hole a young man with dark, dirt smudged skin wearing an old leather cap, looks up at Aldrin wide eyed with panic. Recognizing the young man Aldrin releases his fist, and the energy discharges into the air as he exclaims, "Ben?"

The young man sighs when Aldrin recognizing him, and he responds still uneasy, "Hey Aldrin. Longtime no see."

A skeptical look returns to Aldrin's eyes and he asks, "What are you doing in my tunnel?"

Delira jumps, grabbing Aldrin's shoulder, crying to him, "Don't be mad at him, he's here for me."

"Yea, sorry about not getting your permission man, but you've been gone for a while and I remembered you telling me about Delira, and I was worried about her. I've been using the tunnels to bring her food, after curfew."

"Wait, so the tunnels haven't been discovered?"

"No man. At least they're not being used."

"All the better."

"What are you talking about man?"

Pearl doesn't let Aldrin have a chance to respond as she extends a hand to Ben to aid his ascent saying, "Well Ben, It is Ben right? I didn't hear that incorrectly did I? Well we are going to take the city back from these Stormriders."

Grabbing Pearl's hand, Ben climbs up and dusting himself off he points to the blue woman with his index fingers asking, "Pearl right," and turning to Aldrin asks, "Why is she blue? You never said she was blue."

Again, before Aldrin can respond Pearl spins to him slapping his shoulder's exclaiming, "That's how you moved around so fast. Secret tunnels, really? You had me pushing through crowded streets, and you were using secret tunnels?"

Looking at the young man referred to as Ben, Aldrin finally gets a chance to speak explaining, "She wasn't always blue," and turning to Pearl he continues, "Non-blackguard members were forbidden from entering, or even knowing about the tunnels. Why do you think I didn't even let you look through that trapdoor?"

Pearl turns away with a sarcastic pout, muttering, "Ben isn't a blackguard."

"He was as close as someone could be without going through the trial, which turns out was a good thing. Now you said you brought Delira some food, don't let us get in the way. In fact, we have some rations with us we'll join you. Delira, where are the chairs?"

Ben places a bag from his back onto the table and scratching his head responds, "Well, we had to sell most of your furniture. And, I'm not the only one that has been coming to help out here."

Almost on queue with Ben's statement the hatch in the corner once again opens. From the basement, another man emerges, freezing as he sees more figures than he expected standing in the room flickering with the fireplace's light. A quiet moment sits in the air before Pearl recognizes the man exclaiming, "Alex? Hey, it's Alex!"

The man in what looks to be his late forties, with light, dirty brown hair, and a weak jawline ducks almost to hide back in the basement in the instant that there is silence, but with Pearl addressing him he reemerges sighing, "Hey, Pearl. When did you get back?"

Pearl ignores the obvious insincerity in the man's question, pulling him from the hole responding, "Come on don't be a stranger."

With the man called Alex joining the rest of the gathering in the ground floor room, his eyes immediately lock onto Eliza. Stepping past Pearl and giving her no more attention, he raises a flirtatious smirk to the blue haired stranger who looks at him with cautious distrust, and he extends a hand to her saying, "You heard Pearl, let's not be strangers. The name is Alex, what might yours be?"

Hesitatively extending her hand, Eliza shakes Alex's and responds, almost pulling away from him, "Eliza."

"And beautiful Eliza, how is it that you came into the company of a ruffian such as Pearl Sarya," the man continues, kissing Eliza's hand that pulls from his grasp as she is filled with a worried confusion of his actions.

"How did you," Eliza asks, unintentionally sounding panicked in her voice.

Pearl's hand finds purchase on Alex's shoulder sending him forward from the sudden impact, and in a laugh, she intercepts the questions, saying, "I met her after getting a cursed knife out of my chest, and he has done work for me in the past."

Straightening himself, Alex adjusts his shirt, and clears his throat as Eliza reacts to his advance, adding to Pearl's comment, "Indeed, Pearl invested in a new concoction of mine that is showing great progress. It isn't marketable yet, but I am coming really close to perfecting the formula."

"Oh, come on, you have been saying that for nearly a year know," Pearl moans leaning on the middle-aged man.

"And I have been making progress, but you can understand that our last few months have resulted in my work being slowed."

"Yea."

Eliza breaks back into the conversation as Pearl rolls her eyes and turns away, "Wait, you said it is a concoction you two are talking about?"

"Oh yea, your trying to learn alchemy, aren't you Lizzy? Alex is an alchemist."

"Really? Perhaps you could teach me some, once your home is liberated that is."

Running his hand through his hair, he groans, "Alchemy isn't something to be taken lightly."

"Yea, Alfredo made as much clear."

An angry panic takes Alex's eyes as they intensify into a stare at Eliza's and he asks with the calm of his voice breaking, "Alfredo, you can't mean Alfredo Jap, lives in E'ar Falmar?"

"That's him. Why? Do you know him?"

"He was my instructor."

"That's great," Eliza exclaims with a smile.

"No," Alex's voice halts Eliza's joy, with a cold return to being stern.

"No what?"

"I won't teach you."

"What, why?"

"Tell me, have you been part of one of Alfredo's experiments," Alex asks, and without giving Eliza a chance to respond, continues, "Don't answer that, you wouldn't have been able to grow your hair to that length, without chemical aid, not by your age. The question is how bad it is. It makes sense now, your stunning looks are chemically induced as well. Tell me in mutating yourself, did you consume a thin light brown potion, it would have had a faint iron and minty taste?"

Pearl pulls away from the two as Alex questions Eliza, and she joins the others at the table all silently munching on the small portions of food they have produced from their bags. Scrunching her eye brows with worried concern of what Alex is about to say, Eliza responds, "Yea, why?"

Both his hands finding his forehead Alex spins walking away, and back exasperating, "Oh dang it, that monster, doesn't have any remorse, does he?"

"What are you talking about?"

Grabbing Eliza's shoulders Alex looks into her eyes, instilling in her an overbearing sense of severity, explaining, "Look, Alfredo has been working on that concoction for longer than I have been alive, and rather than test it on himself, he has the poor fools that ask to be his students act as the test subjects. The major problem is that he has for the entire time I have known of him, been unable to suspend or even isolate the source ingredient reaction that causes the mixture's most prominent side effect."

Worry fills Eliza's eyes as she asks, "What side effect? I haven't observed anything, more than being constantly hungry, and I thought that was from a different potion I took."

"Chances are you wouldn't notice it, not if you only had it introduced to your system recently. If left uncontrolled though, you will begin to rapidly age exponentially, months of your life span will become weeks. Weeks will become days, days hours, hours seconds. I'm twenty-five."

Eliza's eyes water and she grabs Alex's shoulder's shaking him frantically, "No, no, no."

"Take it easy, your even younger than I was, and still look it. It takes time for the effect to really get going."

"You don't understand! I had two of them!"

Alex recoils from Eliza, who falls with her back against the nearby wall not even noticing the gathering staring in her direction silently watching, not knowing what they could do, unable to do anything, for the youngest among them in a legitimate personal crisis. As he pulls away from Eliza Alex instinctively asks, "You what? If you are a student of his why didn't you run any tests on your blood after ingesting an experimental concoction?"

"He hasn't taught me anything yet," Eliza responds her tear filled eyes finally having too much stress, and she lets her head fall into her hands sobbing, "I only have read two of the books he has required me to read before he would take me as a student."

Pearl drops to Eliza's side and wraps a consoling hug over her, and in the same moment Alex drops to a knee and grabs Eliza's knee not noticing the touch of her skin through the Illusion of her clothes in the stress of the moment, he says, "Hey, hey, no need for that, I said Alfredo never took the time to isolate the issue. Out of my personal need, I have been able to create a serum that doesn't revert the issue, but staves off the progression of the effect. I could formulate it for your biology."

Eliza looks up into Alex's eyes, with a sniffle, asking, "What do I need to do?"

Unrequested, Auburn's voice growls into the moment as he steps from the table to sit with his back against the wall of the fireplace, "Weel, if ye didn't wantae risk yer leefe tae poisons o' a madman ye shouldn't hae drank his concoctions."

Alex grabs Eliza's face pulling her to look at him, forcing her to not focus on Auburn's words, and he responds to her, "I need to take a blood sample and concentrate a few compounds, come, I left my bundle in the basement. I can take that sample and start some of the process, tonight."

"Ok," Eliza responds and standing she joins Alex in stepping to and climbing down the ladder into the small, cold basement. Drawing little more than twenty ounces of blood the two eventually rejoin the others in the ground floor room. Each of the eight finish their scraps of dried meats, and stale bread, and they find their own portion of the space's walls and drift into a night's sleep.

8

Getting a Plan

The dismal dim brown-green light of the morning sun, piercing through the strange smog that sits in the air, pokes into the ground floor room past the boarded windows and through the upper floor's hatch that was left open. Movement in the street beyond the door wakes the sleeping group within the distraught building. Pulling their bags onto their shoulders Alex and Ben, drop into the basement and begin to move into the tunnel that leads away. Stopping before the subterranean passageway's entrance, Alex turns calling up to the group, "I will have a dose for you this evening Eliza. I can promise you that."

Before anything else can be shared between the people in the building a knock on the door sounds, cracking with three strong impacts. A growling snarl of a voice commands in through the wood, "Residents of abode, Ironskin, open this door. This is a mandatory inspection."

Panicked Delira's eyes go wide as she pushes Aldrin and Auburn toward the basement calling to the door in response, "Coming," and in the same moment she removes her top. Closing the trapdoor behind the two men she pulls a rug from the second floor, and lays it at the base of the ladder, before stepping to the front door simultaneously putting her top back on. While that is happening, Eliza pulls out the old, strange parchment again, and with gesturing in the air, imparts the magic that concealed Pearl's appearance on their way into the town.

Un-latching the door Delira has to jump out of the way as it slams open revealing another blue scaled dragon man covered in chainmail, draped with a tunic bearing a grey crest in the shape of a single cloud releasing a fork bolt of lightning. The man squints into the room growling, "Did you refuge, anyone for the curfew?"

Delira looks down and away from the large man's eyes and responds, "Yes sir. Three sir. All women sir."

"I appreciate your honesty, but I'm just going to take quick look around if you don't mind."

"I don't mind at all sir."

The man turns squinting with untrusting eyes, looking Eliza, Pearl, and Esmerelda, up and down. Turning from them and to the ladder, he steps over, onto and up it, scanning the second floor. He returns first and to the door growling, "You're clean. Have a nice day, ladies."

Waiting a few seconds after the door closes behind the man's tail Delira returns to the hidden trap door, removes the rug covering it and opens it saying to Aldrin, "Sorry, they check for men hiding from the search each morning. Those who aren't taken by noon are assumed to have been let to stay in town for the day. Their gift to those they are enslaving."

Aldrin stretches leaving his gear in the basement asking, "So if we wait for a little, it won't be a problem for Auburn and I to go out?"

"You yes, but, I mean, he's, uh, red."

Auburn hops up to the second floor in two strong bounds, "Don't worry ah git it, i'll stick aroond 'ere, ye go play general."

"I didn't mean any offense."

"Ah didn't tak' ony. You're nae allowed tae walk th' streets oan yer ain either, richt? how aboot we play cards?"

Delira looks up to the hole to the second floor confused, and then to the others, and Aldrin shrugs, "We will be out all day probably. Don't draw attention to this place."

By noon, the door closes behind Aldrin and the four step again into the street, the sun still bright through the sickening film that sits above them, and with a gesture of gratitude to each of the others, Esmerelda steps from their company explaining, "Look I have a husband, and a child who is probably in a house alone, I have to get to them. I can't be part of an uprising, I got you here, that is as much as I can risk, I'm sorry."

"So, what? You're done?" Pearl asks in disgust, "What about Rev? What about Lorm?"

"They knew about this. You think I would have not told my best friends, but I would tell you," Esmerelda asks in response in exasperation.

"Fine, so you're done. Well thanks for the ride, we'll let the other two know that you didn't have a plan retrieving them."

"Look I have to go to my child ok? I have to make sure they are alright before I can do anything else. I'm sorry."

Aldrin pulls Pearl away interjecting, "Come on Pearl. This isn't a fight we need to have."

The streets are not busy, after the men of the city are shepherded from its walls. The raised conversation between Pearl and Esmerelda rings through the still air, but doesn't draw attention, with the city remaining still around them. Esmerelda turns and with a final nod to Aldrin, and a hug for Eliza, she walks away.

The path the group walks, laid before them as Aldrin takes the leads, directs them in a different direction than they walked the night before. Another bridge, closer to the rivers end, carries them to a chain of islands that splits the river, which becomes one again on the other side, far before reaching the ocean. The bit of stone and dirt the bridge brings them to holds on it, only roads that lead to two more bridges both which path toward the other side of the sludge river they are crossing. One leads deeper inland, and the other, paths closer to the shore, but first to an island that holds a tall light house.

At the point where the road forks, rises a single pillar of wood, a man-made tree with no branches or leaves. Swinging from the top rattling against the wood with the breeze, a single chain passes through a loop bolted to the pole. At the wood's base sits a bowl through which the pillar rises, empty, but coated in the powder of burnt wood.

Aldrin and Pearl keep their heads down as they pass the pillar, stepping to the bridge leading inland. An unguarded gate raised at the end of a third bridge separates the squalor of more slums from the merchant's and guard's district the three left behind, and again around them rise, in great disrepair, constructs that hold scars of tragedy in broken and charred roofs and walls.

After almost half an hour's time of walking, the tall outer wall of the town comes into view. The road splits running parallel with the barrier, a gathering of buildings wait, pressed on the far end. Directly at the point where the road splits, a building, in better repair than those around it, rises nearly triple the size of the small single-story hovels on its flanks.

Stepping to the door Aldrin turns to Eliza, and Pearl explaining, "Look, these aren't good people. Let me do the talking."

Before he can turn around, Pearl crosses her arms asking, "Do you mind explaining what we are doing here?"

"What do you mean?"

"Well for starters how about you tell us why, when we should be talking to people about mounting an uprising, you brought us to the brothel?"

"Look. Do you remember when I asked about the Red Tide in the temple to the Silvermist?" Aldrin sighs letting his head fall into one of his hands.

"Yea the town's boogie men, supposedly a crime syndicate that operates here."

"They're real. I've done work for them before. I know a guy still inside, with the Blackguard gone, there isn't much option for a fighting force, beside talking to them."

"So, you're going to talk to criminals, and ask them to help reestablish a system that made them criminals?"

"Look, I know it is a long shot and trust me I won't have us stick around if I don't like what I hear from them, but we have to try Pearl."

"Fine, lead away," Pearl responds, gesturing to the quiet brothel's door, with distaste for Aldrin's leadership in the moment.

Turning back to the door and stepping through it, Aldrin continues to lead the way ushering the trio into a large but cramped room with a small bar on one side lit by small beams of light piercing through boarded windows with its floor space taken mostly by very sturdy tables scattered within. A single person stands in the room behind the bar cleaning an empty glass, and Aldrin steps to him. With a squinted gaze the man waits for a moment looking cautiously at the hooded three that approach him before Aldrin breaks the silence saying, "You shouldn't go swimming today."

The man sets down the mostly clean, smudged glass, responding still with a skeptical gaze, "Really, are the guards chumming the water again?"

"I think it's just tide," Aldrin continues, placing three fingers on the bar.

Looking again to the woman behind the hood man, and then to the door, ensuring that the establishment is empty, he nods, opening the side gate in the bar, and gestures for the group to join him. With Aldrin leading the others through, the barkeep opens a trap door and gestures toward it. Aldrin returns the nod and begins climbing down through the stone floor, quickly followed by Eliza and Pearl, before the trap door is closed above them.

The climb isn't long, only about twice that of the drop into Aldrin's basement, bringing the three into a small unlit tunnel that radiates the necessary glimmers that allow Pearl and Eliza's eyes to adjust with their innate abilities to see without light. Only a second after though, without being asked, Eliza creates a source of golden light within her hand, that illuminates the hall for Aldrin, and they begin walking. The path is short before a second tunnel connects with it, but with Aldrin continuing straight, so too do his out of place companions. Further still the tunnel continues, and for several minutes the three remain walking straight, past tunnels that connect with their path. With each connection they pass, Pearl asks to Aldrin's annoyance, "Are sure you are going the right way?"

Each time receiving the same response, "Yes, Pearl, I know where I am going."

Finally, after nearly the same time it took them to get to the brothel from the river the tunnel ends at a strong reinforced door with an iron slit at eye level. Stepping to the barrier Aldrin looks to Pearl, and gesturing with a finger over his lips, he raises a fist and brings it to contact the door in a series of strikes, first two, then after a pause, a third, another pause, and a final knock. Finally, after a short moment, the slit opens revealing from within, a pair of weary brown eyes peering out. A fatty man's voice growls, "End of the stream."

Putting his face to have his eyes appear the same for the man on the other side of the door, as his appear to them, Aldrin responds, "But the tide doesn't worry about how the river flows."

The slit closes and the sound of several latches clacks through the wood, before the door swings open. A man just shorter than Aldrin but easily twice the weight stands with open arms in the open passage exclaiming, "Why I'll be, Aldrin Ironskin. Last we heard of you, you were flying out to take care of a dagger in someone's chest. Fancy timing to have you back."

"What? You didn't hear? The blackguard are dead. You shouldn't have come back," a much older voice of an in-shape man filled with from gravel of years of damage, adds before Aldrin can respond to the greeting.

"We've come to talk, that's it," Aldrin calls looking past the hefty man in front of him giving a pat to the man's shoulders, to accept the warmer of the welcomes.

"Ah, if talking is all you wanted you should have stayed home with your mother. You need to give me a very good reason right now why I shouldn't have you killed this instant," an elderly man asks from upon an ornate, gold plated chair with a red velvet seat and backing, which rests at the far end of a cramped room filled with a crowd of shady individuals packed shoulder to shoulder, every one of them staring angrily at the three in the door way.

"Look we need your help."

"Well that puts you in a predicament. We don't want to help you. Now get out of our side of town, man in black."

Aldrin goes to turn, but Eliza's voice stops him, as she calls to the man in the chair, "So you are fine having no control then?"

Aldrin's head snaps to Eliza, as he exclaims in a whisper to her, "Eliza, no!"

Looking at Aldrin, almost shocked at his reaction to her, she continues to the distant man, "This room is full. You are sitting on a golden chair. You want the occupying force out of the city as much if not more than Aldrin, you just haven't done it yet. Why?"

"Eliza, stop, these are people you can't talk to like that."

The older man leans forward stopping the packed room from moving for her by raising a single hand. Shifting to sit upright to display an air of regality, and tapping his fingertips together, he responds, "I like this one. She's got spunk. Alright, speak."

Aldrin turns back to the chamber with an expression of surprise on his face, and Eliza continues after receiving a friendly, almost congratulatory pat on her shoulder from Pearl, "I don't know this city. We got here last night, and I had never been here before, but from what I have heard, between getting here, and being in this spot, is that you are not the good guys. Not in the general sense of the word. You are the crime of this city, whether you see yourselves as the expressers of true freedom or are just in it for your own personal gain doesn't matter. You have an idea of hierarchy, obviously. You know this city far better than your occupiers, and you have man power. Why haven't you taken back your city yet?"

Pearl and Aldrin look at their companion in astonishment, as the man from across the room responds, "How would you suggest we should have done that."

"I, I don't know. Like I said, I don't know this city, I just know that a group, no matter their nature, can accomplish things far beyond what a band of individuals can, if they have direction and purpose," Eliza responds watching a memory of the cult of her birth parents functioning as a unit with terrifying power behind their actions.

"My companion might not be able to provide you with a way to extricate our mutually disliked occupants, but I can," Aldrin interjects stepping between Eliza and the distant man.

"Alright then Ironskin, your friend earned you my attention, speak. What do you propose?" the man responds leaning in with his attention set on Aldrin.

First turning to Eliza, Aldrin mouths, "Thank you," causing her to smile proud to have been a help, and returning his gaze to the man at the room's back he continues, "If we are going to have any chance we will have to free the champion, Lady Tristalia."

The man spits at the mention of the Silvermist champion, "What use would that be, she's already lost to them once."

"Tell me, and I don't mean this as an earnest threat, simply a hypothetical, but what would happen if you were to die, right now? Who would be the next Tide Caster?"

With Aldrin's question the room descends in clamor, and loud conversation of different individuals making claims, as to why they would deserve the title more than the others in the room. Silence returns though, slowly, with the crack of a handless gavel, being slammed onto the arm of the gold-plated chair. The old thin man squints at Aldrin as his underlings return to respecting his conversation and authority, and he asks, "What is your point in presenting discordance in the ranks of my men with such a question?"

"The point is that this group that calls themselves the Stormriders, is little more than a glorified group of mercenaries. They probably have even less hierarchical structure than you do here. You asked why worry about the champion? I would like any of your men to step forward who honestly thinks they could take Lady Tristalia in a one-on-one brawl," Aldrin pauses, looking at the room that remains silent with none of the burly men speaking up. After a moment Aldrin continues, "Our best chance is to take the assault directly to their leader."

The old leader of the Red Tide gang breaks into laughter for a moment before becoming deftly serious with a paralyzing stare directed at Aldrin, explaining his outburst, "You must be crazy. Even the high and mighty Silvermist champion has no chance against their leader. The beast is taller than a two-story building, and while the elemental breath dragon men possess is normally formidable, and even frightening to see for those who have never witnessed it, his is horrifying in its power, the lightning of a storm is only a spark compared to his air splitting breath."

"Oh, sounds almost like you would prefer to have the streets run by these people."

"How dare you?"

Aldrin looks to Eliza, and back at the old man continuing, "Well if you have another plan for taking the city back why haven't you? Criminal organization or not, and let's not get into semantics of your dealings in this city, each and every one of you is a Blackgatian, and every Blackgatian needs to work together to drive away our occupiers," Aldrin's gaze begins to pan across the room as his words begin to shape into a rallying cry, "I know that the Blackguard failed, it was our job to defend this town's people, everyone, including you, was supposed to be able to rely on the Blackguard for protection. You couldn't, and I have a feeling nothing would have changed if I had been here to be at my post when whatever happened, occurred, but trying to stick to your own will not solve the problem that now exists. Our hope, our only hope, to be our own ruling people again is to cut off the head of the snake that has coiled itself in the Black Keep, and our best option for that would be a multi part uprising."

"Now I know you are serious. What's the plan general?" the leader responds leaning back into his chair.

"Well, as I said, our best chance of removing the parasite that is the Stormriders is to take the fight to their leader. The keep is the most defensible spot in the city so I am assuming he has made his nest there. I have already been informed that Lady Tristalia is being kept in the dungeon below the keep. What will need to happen is something to draw the majority of the forces from there. I am sure you can figure that out. After that happens though, the soldiers will amass at two places. Where ever you create this distraction, and either at the temple, or the gates to the keep. That second spot depends on how powerful their leader believes himself. We don't believe them to have discovered the Black guard tunnel system on the south bank so we will be able to use those to get to the river, but trying to cross any of the bridges will end up being a problem."

The hefty man that still stands behind the group at the door interjects, out of turn, saying, "Well you can use our tunnels then, they go under both sides of the city, including the bridges."

The leader rests his head in his hand at the out of turn out burst, and Aldrin looks his way, raising a brow continuing, "Well, once we get the champion to the artifact of her faith, then we can march on the keep, and challenge this mercenary band's leader. This is the only plan I have been able to think of, I would happily consider others, because once a plan like this is set in motion, we either will succeed or we will not see the light of tomorrow's sun."

Standing for the first time, the old man gathers the attention of the room as he steps down with a stern look in his eyes, piercing into Aldrin's own unwavering glare. Getting to be within an arm's reach the man extends an open hand, saying, "Aldrin Ironskin, you said it at the beginning, those who call Blackgate home must be willing to die for it if we are to take it back from those who would enslave us, the Red Tide will stand with you. You will know when the time has come to act when the night sky becomes ours."

Keeping his eyes locked with the old man, Aldrin extends a hand accepting the one offered to him, and they shake. A gesture signals for them to be taken out, to which Aldrin asks, "If we are going to be allowed to use your tunnels to get the Silvermist champion to the Temple with as little conflict as possible, perhaps we should be shown where the different points of importance are so we know which angle we are coming from."

The man groans reluctantly turning back from his chair, and with a wave he responds, "Fine. Vect, take them to the way."

The heavy-set man gives a nod and giving a tug on Aldrin's arm, he turns back to the door and opening it, he leads the three into the tunnel. Several turns and twists in the dark pathway lit by Eliza's glowing hand, bring the group, after an unknown but tiringly long walk, to a path's end where a ladder leads up. Above them is a dilapidated building across the street from the path that leads through the overturned dirt yard of the temple. Backing into the tunnel system, the man named Vect continues in the passage way gesturing to be followed. Shortly thereafter a door appears at the end of their path and Vect explains, "Now I will try to be here to lead you, but try to remember the path I just showed you, in case I can't. As to not draw attention from people up above, the under-bridge path requires you to crawl on this," and he pats a thin peculiarly suspended path, of individual metal rods hung with only a few inches between each. Turning back to the door, decorated on the side that faces out toward the river to look like the stones around it, the man nods, "See you around Aldrin, and you too Little Miss Attitude."

The door closes leaving the three hooded individuals standing outside of the tunnel, perched over the slowly undulating almost tar like river below. Climbing up to the road above, and crossing the bridge, they find their way, by Aldrin's lead, into another structure, and down into another series of tunnels. When the three finally arrive once more in Aldrin's basement they are greeted by Delira, with a smile as she presents a hand of cards exclaiming from the second floor, "Aldrin! I'm winning!"

Worries

"Sae ye'v made a' o' th' arrangements fur how we ur all tae die then,"
Auburn asks from behind Delira hearing the hatch from the basement into
the main floor close.

"Well, our hope is to not die, but the plan is to free Lady Tristalia
from the keep, take her through the hidden tunnels to her temple, for her to
reclaim her sword, an artifact of her religion, and return to the keep to
challenge the leader of the occupying force," Aldrin responds setting his
cloak on the table.

"Great, sae oor livess hae an expiration date o' a single nicht,"
Auburn groans dropping to join the other three.

Looking in disgust at Auburn after his statement, Eliza almost yells
at him saying in a raised voice, "What's your problem?"

"Excuse me?"

"You have been a jerk the entire journey here, even after you had the opportunity to leave. We get it you don't think we have even a slight chance of succeeding. Why though, if that is true did you even come? Why can't you even for a moment stop the moody, you three are going to kill me, routine, and get on board with the plan at hand?"

Auburn raises a skeptical eye brow with Eliza's passionate berating of him, asking, "Why dae ye think ah even care whit ye think?"

"I don't care if you care about me. I know that if it were up to you I would already be dead. I do care though, about Aldrin and Pearl, and your constant pessimism about the chances we might succeed, makes me doubt that you can be trusted to be there if they need you."

"A'm ainlie saying that it's mair than likely that we ur a' aff tae die, wi' this plan o' yours."

"You had every opportunity to not come along, now we are here, and we need to know that if you are going to be with us that you won't just get in the way. Either get in line with the plan, or go away."

Pearl, having watched this exchange from the side, in silence, gasps at the finality of Eliza's comment, "Lizzy."

Auburn continues, "I've nae gotten in yer wey tae this point, ah won't git in yer wey noo. Och, 'n', ye shouldn't rely oan me, a'm repaying his kindness, nae yers," ending with a nod in Aldrin's direction.

Pressing her hands forward angrily feigning the act of squeezing Auburn's head Eliza, turns back to the corner and throws the hatch down open, climbing through in flustered anger. The room with the others is quiet for a moment, and Pearl steps to join Eliza, with the hope of calming her young friend, but before she can reach the ladder she is stopped. Aldrin's hand lands on Pearl's shoulder, pulling her back into the center of the ground floor room, and looking into her eyes saying, "Let me talk to her, she needs to understand what we are looking to do here."

Pearl gives a knowing nod to Aldrin, responding, "I can do that."

"Look, Pearl, I know you could, but I think this time I may be better to relay just how serious this is."

"Fine," Pearl shrugs stepping to the side and gesturing to the hatch down for Aldrin.

Dropping down, Aldrin immediately raises his hands defensively as Eliza turns, from angrily pacing. With her hands rolled into fists at her sides, Eliza's eyes lock onto Aldrin as she points to the floor above saying in exasperation, "Can you believe him? Comes all this way, has the chance to leave and not have to bother with us anymore, go back to his home, but he chooses to continue with us only to keep disparaging us the entire time."

Aldrin, with arms still outstretched, and with a calm in his voice, asks, "Would you mind if we spoke mentally? I have a lot to talk to you about and it seems to tend to be quicker to converse in that way."

Eliza is struck still with confusion and tilting her head, her voice echoes in the back of Aldrin's head with suspicion in its tone, "*Sure.*"

"*Ok look, Auburn isn't entirely wrong to feel the way he ◦oes. He still has a reason to live. You see I haven't stoo◦ in your way, as you've thrown yourself away, risking yourself with no regar◦ for your life. You ◦on't care if you ◦ie, an◦ I ◦on't see it as a problem, I un◦erstan◦ it. Hey, ◦o you have the ability to see my memories with this min◦ link?*"

"*I ◦on't know. I can forcefully rea◦ someone's min◦ but I haven't rea◦ someone's memories before. I coul◦ try, I ha◦n't communicate◦ telepathically before with anyone but Boop until I met Pearl, so I may have more I can ◦o.*"

"*Well, ◦on't worry about it. Just know that I un◦erstan◦ your vin◦ication for everything you make yourself a part of, an◦ that I only know that because I'm pretty ◦amage◦ too.*"

"*Damage◦, how are you ◦amage◦?*"

"*Hey. What's that about?*"

"*You stan◦ here explaining that you are ◦amage◦, in ◦efense of the half-hearte◦ continuation of that person who sees me as nothing more than a monster, no matter what I ◦o to change how he sees me? You ◦on't know what I've been through, I watche◦ the man I wish was my father be mur◦ere◦, by my han◦s,*" Eliza's eyes fill with tears, as the room suddenly begins to feel cold, and the air begins to press down, thick and heavy with an alien pressure. Aldrin doesn't get a chance to respond to the domineering presence filling the room and his head, as Eliza's voice continues, echoing even, "*an◦ only after I was free from the control of the man who woul◦ call himself my father, I was force◦ to remove Bartholomeus hea◦, or his lifeless corpse in that horrible plane of existence woul◦ have kille◦ me. You want to talk about ◦amage◦, I kille◦ the man who raise◦ me, twice.*"

Aldrin, rightfully feeling attacked, yells back at Eliza, "You think you are the only person whose experienced loss. I know you are a smart girl. You can do things with just you mind that would baffle some of the smartest people I have ever known. Yet, you're so self-absorbed at this very moment that you can't even see past your own trials and tribulations, to recognize that maybe, just maybe, people other than you have also experienced a great deal of suffering!"

Aldrin's words strike Eliza and the world around her freezes around her, as suddenly the magic that connects her mind to his, washes from his mind over hers. In that instant, her vision is filled the flash of lightning, and a sound of thunder, that crashes in the lightning's wake. Confused of what she is experiencing, Eliza feels panic, as her mind first leaps to a flash back of her night of horror, but she is shaken from that when the eyes she is seeing through move of a will not her own revealing a crew rushing across a ship's deck as it is tossed by an enormous wave. Each adult stands several feet above Eliza's point of view as she continues to ponder what she is experiencing. The form she is experiencing the visions from moves on its own revealing a small child's hands as it runs to an almost glowing female form in a doorway across the deck.

Another flash of lightning echoed by another rolling rumble of thunder ends abruptly when panic yells fill the air, and the ship lurches upward again. The sound of snapping wood tears out over the panic as the eyes Eliza sees through, watch the front of the ship snap free from the back. The ship begins to fold, slowly sinking, and a man's voice calls to the woman and child, "Heyana, grab Aldrin, get to the life boat!"

Eliza realizes that she is experiencing a memory from Aldrin's past, as she feels a jolt from behind with the woman's hands grabbing the child's shoulders, and pulling, the mother lifts the young *ALDRIN*, through whose senses Eliza bears witness. Whisked into the air, the images in Eliza's vision flash from being on board the breaking, sinking ship, out to several hundred feet away from a small boat that lifts and falls powerfully on the storm's monstrous waves, and slowly the ship disappears under the water's surface. The young Aldrin's vision is blurry with tears and he falls forward, onto his mother's chest crying, and Eliza's sight goes black, as she feels the small boat flip and she feels submerged in the icy ocean.

Vision of Aldrin's memories returns to Eliza, with the blinding white light of a late morning sun. Aldrin's eyes open, and he releases a cough. Sitting up the child scans the beach that stretches to both sides of him. Two adults lay motionless in the sand, a man and the woman from before. Standing, Aldrin sprints to the forms, calling out for Eliza to hear through his ears, "Momma! Papa!"

Dropping to his knees by the woman, Aldrin softly shakes her hoping for a sign of life which quickly comes with her turning and releasing a groan. Eliza feels a smile take Aldrin's young face, before fading again with him throwing himself past his groaning, waking mother, and to the man who remains still, motionless in the sand. The child's hands press into the adult man's shoulder.

No response comes and Aldrin's pushing hands grab the man's shirt and begin shaking him violently, the young Aldrin, whose voice, cracks with sorrow, cries, "Papa! Wake up, Papa!"

The woman's movements hasten as she hears her child crying at her motionless husband, and she drops to her knees on the opposite side of the man as the child, saying in a scolding voice, "You better wake up, Richard. Come on, wake up!" Her heart breaking, the woman brings a fist, down on the man's chest, as her eyes begin to fill with tears. Panic throws the woman's head onto the man's chest, and she begins sobbing. Pulling away, Aldrin's mother begins frantically pressing her hands against the man's chest desperately attempting to resuscitate him.

Aldrin pulls away as he watches his sobbing mother switch between compressing his father's chest and forcing air into his lungs with mouth to mouth. Noticing even at his young age the futility of his mother's actions Aldrin stands, and attempts to pull her away from his father's body, explaining, "Mamma, stop."

The woman pulls herself from her son. Eliza sees the fear in her eyes, the grief that she holds for what she knows but can't believe, all witnessed through the eyes of the woman's young son. Everything becomes blurry and Eliza watches time speed up. Days pass into nights, and nights pass into days in what to her feel like seconds. She watches as Aldrin, only about seven years old in the memory, cares for his grieving mother, while simultaneously building a make shift shelter for the two of them, and perform the necessary tasks of hunting and gathering to keep both of them from being completely malnourished.

The rapid progression of the memory suddenly slows to a crawl with Aldrin asking his mother, "Mom are you ok?"

She lets free a cough responding in a scratchy deep but still distinctly feminine voice, "Yea, Mommy will be fine. You've been so strong Aldrin. I know you've missed your father and sister, but you've been so strong."

Eliza's vision blurs and once again flashes forward, swirling around her. When it stabilizes, Aldrin once again stands over his mother, who lays shivering, her hand in Aldrin's hands, her veins bulging visibly through her skin. A flash thrusts time forward, Aldrin's mother's condition worsens as she jolts in position with the transition of time, but remains laying with one hand wrapped in Aldrin's. He leans forward, watching as her eyes turn completely black, and begin to seep a strange dark substance. Jumping forward in time again, the young Aldrin brings his hands to his mother's face wiping away the seeping fluid from her eyes, and from her ears. Four more leaps in time, shift her slightly, each time showing her skin becoming darker, and the seepage increasing in volume, before a separate train of thought interrupts the suffering.

Like a white canvas superimposing itself over Eliza's vision through the young Aldrin's eyes, the memory plays of Aldrin disposing of a fire's remnant ashes and charcoal, behind a small pile of rocks on the beach, and a sudden loud pop that cracks out from where the black powder landed as one of the larger stones fell onto it. Eliza feels the curiosity that surged through Aldrin in that moment and watches him step to the stones investigating the cause. The vision shifts to Aldrin fastening a thatch rope to a stick that holds up a stone over a pile of a dark sedimentary powder. Again, the vision shifts, moving to Aldrin's eyes as he lifts a small bird from the ground with a single hole in it. The hand not holding the bird holds a long device made of two pieces of wood formed into a channel, with the end closest to the hand damaged with heavy scorching.

The bright radiating memories of Aldrin's process of inventing his first rifle fade back to the dark of night with the flickering fire's orange glow illuminating is sick mother, whose hand goes limp as she starts to spasm. Aldrin becomes worried at first, leaning forward to see if he can do anything for his mother, but the worry turns to fright and he leaps away watching in a terror that shakes through Eliza as she feels his emotions, as his mother's skin splits open releasing the thick substance, that had drained through her tear ducks, in oozing streams. She spasms and twists, rolling from her back, to her stomach.

Releasing a terrifying gurgling growl, Aldrin's mother pushes herself up, with unnatural ease compared to the difficulty she had even lifting her hand to her son moments before. Spinning around the black dots that became of her eyes blink before melding with the strange substance, that clings to her, growing as a mass to cover her. Aldrin turns from his mother when he sees from her, back tendrils that whip out destroying the shelter he built, before attempting to lash out and grab at him.

Grabbing the rudimentary device, which he left leaning against a tree nearby, the young boy runs to a pile of leaves that cover half of the stone pile, he discovered the explosive sediment from. Under the leaves, is a mound of the black powder, which he had mixed for hunting, and he begins packing a handful of the dust in the damaged part of the device. As he turns back to where the shelter stood, he panics seeing the thing that once was his mother lurching over him. Accidentally he strikes the stone he was going to load as a projectile hard against the packed powder causing it to ignite, bursting and sending sparks out in all directions.

The stone leaps from the device, soaring off away from the creature. A single spark though, lands on the pile of dust and it suddenly explodes in a ball of fire that sends the pile of stones scattering in all directions. Aldrin recoils from the sudden flash, and stays coiled in fear of the monster that was his mother, believing himself to have failed in his self-defense, but he releases his tension, realizing that he isn't dead. Turning over to see why he is not being mauled by a terrifying black tar beast he sees the creature sprawled on the sand, opposite his side of the point of the explosion, with a hole roughly the size of the largest stone where the largest mass of its chest had been.

Through a young seven-year-old Aldrin's eyes Eliza looks down on two mounds of dirt with a single stone placed at one end of each the second only just added by the first. The blur returns, and Eliza watches the passage of time as a strobe of night and day. More than three years pass in what feels like a second before change causes everything to come to a sudden halt, with the pre-teen Aldrin spinning a bird over a fire while looking out to sea, where just on the horizon for the first time since he was marooned, he sees a ship with full sails crest into view. Confused at first, Aldrin realizes the opportunity being presented to him and he leaps to his feet.

Running to a tree, Aldrin grabs an undamaged one of his creations from a pile of similar devices, all burned and damaged to the point of being unusable, except for the one in hand. He packs a cupped hand full of the black powder, that he has made more of, into the object's end nearest his hand. Running out to the beach he sparks the black powder and it cracks out in a loud pop that echoes over the crashing waves. A silence sits on Aldrin as he waits to see if it is at all possible that the shot was heard, and a smile grows as he watches the ship turn his direction.

A small boat comes to the shore and a man steps into the sand with a curious look at the young boy before he introduces himself, "Hail, child. I am Captain Herald, of the ship Freesails," and what was once likely a series of questions from the captain about the boy's parents and his reason for being on the island, ends and clarifies with a question, "I sail to Blackgate, would you wish to come with me and leave this place?"

Aldrin only nods his head, before a blur brings him to boarding the ship. Standing on deck to greet the new passenger, a young girl with light brown almost blonde hair smiles at him as he reaches the top of the ladder. Aldrin's eyes look into her deep green irises, and being escorted past, he is introduced by Herald's voice, "That's my daughter Victoria, keep your distance from her, you will bunk in this room over here."

The time traveling is once more a blur, except for the moments Victoria comes within view and becomes clarity in the distortion. The ship gets to Blackgate, a much smaller version of what Eliza has seen to this point and the compression of time in the memory accelerates even further. Years pass, and Aldrin grows, and time slows finally to a normal pace with a man standing in front of him, a deep commanding voice rumbles out explaining, "You are assigned with the escort and protection of the exploratory research unit. The island you are going to is not strongly radiating corruption, so you will mostly only have to deal with natural threats. The nature of the lack of corruption is the reason we are sending Miss Herald's group. You leave in the morning. Dismissed."

Blur returns bringing Aldrin's eyes, for Eliza to see Victoria, only a year older than Aldrin, and yet the head of a research group for an organization within Blackgate, smiling as she steps up a gang plank joining him on a small ship. A jungle forms around them, and Aldrin scans the foliage as Victoria pulls aside a wall of vegetation near a cliff face revealing a tunnel that leads down into the stone. Turning back to him, she gestures with a nod into the hole saying, "Hey, Aldrin check this out."

"Oh, you found us somewhere private," Aldrin responds with a smile resting his hands on Victoria's shoulders.

Victoria returns the smile rolling her eyes, responding, "Now, Aldrin. What could you possibly be suggesting?" The flirtatious exchange immediately turns cold when she pulls away from him stepping into the tunnel, continuing in curiosity, "What's that?"

Aldrin watches Victoria step away from him and scanning ahead of her in the direction she is looking asks, "I don't see anything. What did you see?"

"I don't know, let's check it out."

"I mean sure, let's not go inform your or my team about a mysterious tunnel that we found that you believe to have seen movement in."

"Oh, don't start. Come on, your rifle can handle anything that would be on this island. There is a reason you have been allowed to be a junior member of the guard since you were thirteen."

"Fine."

Victoria spins and leads the way down into the cave, and Eliza's vision through Aldrin's eyes watches over Victoria's shoulder as they step a short way into the cave and she steps to stare over a subterranean cliff. Eliza feels Aldrin fill with a devilish playfulness, as he creeps forward toward Victoria arms outstretched, with a plan to jokingly scare his companion. Slow steps bring him within arm's reach and with a quick motion he grabs her shoulders causing her to jump in surprise nearly falling over the shear edge she was looking over. A laughing anger fills her voice as she slaps Aldrin's hands from her saying, "You idiot. I could have fallen."

"I had you."

"Is that so," Victoria responds walking with two fingers pressing into Aldrin's chest.

Panic takes both Aldrin and Victoria's faces, and she suddenly grabs hard on to his collar. The stone beneath them cracks and shifts. Aldrin goes to move both Victoria and himself, but the instant his weight shifts the stone cracks again and falls out from beneath the two and they begin to plummet. Victoria clings to Aldrin as they fall. Terror fills them both, and for the few short seconds they fall everything else of the world is torn away leaving only them, and as if in a desperate need to leave nothing unsaid, Victoria pulls Aldrin into a kiss.

A sudden impact that pulses through Victoria into Aldrin causes everything to go black. An unknown amount of time passes, in what is experienced for Eliza as less than a second, before Aldrin groans and rolls onto his back. Terror strikes, not allowing him a single moment to wallow in his pain, as his hand falls to the side and he feels Victoria laying, motionless. Leaping to his knees, he looks in terror at her body, and she lays unbreathing, still, with the stone beneath her wet with a puddle of her blood which has grown in the time he had been unconscious.

Eliza feels Aldrin hold back a well of painful emotion as he looks up to where they fell from calling out in panic, "Help! Somebody, help us!"

No one comes, and Aldrin throws himself into desperately trying to resuscitate Victoria, having as much success as his call had in getting the attention of a passerby. Painfully his attempts lesson and inevitably stop, with his hope dying as he slumps over the body, and his vision is broken.

Looking through the tears that fill her eyes Eliza sees Aldrin across from her. He looks worried at the manifestation of magic around his young companion which has lifted her from the ground. Falling to the floor as the magic finds its end, her feet carry her forward where she wraps Aldrin in a deep embrace. Her voice cracks in her sobbing, muffled by Aldrin's shirt, "I'm so sorry!"

For Aldrin, who only bore witness to Eliza suddenly engulfed in a powerful magic and did not experience his memories alongside her, the sudden apology is confusing. Accepting the embrace, he rubs Eliza's back responding, "For what?"

Eliza pulls away looking into Aldrin's eyes with a gentle twinkle in her own, saying, "I know what you went through with your parents, I felt the emotions their passing put you through, and with Victoria, I felt everything you felt, your love for her, the judgment you cast on yourself, believing that you were responsible for the fall, the heart break that pulled you away from her when you realized she couldn't come back to you. I felt it all."

"What? No. That isn't what I meant by having you read memories. I never wanted you to have to suffer those feelings as I did. I just wanted you to understand that your experience with Bartholomeus did not fall on deaf ears with me. Are you alright? I mean, I don't know what all you felt."

"I'll be fine."

"Are you sure, both of those events broke me when they happened, each on their own, if you felt everything I did. I can't imagine where you are at right now."

"Aldrin, we don't have time for our suffering. I am sad, and I will carry your tragic memories with me with as much clarity in my mind as Bartholomeus' death, but we have to focus on freeing the people of your home."

"It wasn't my intention to give you more sorrow to be burdened with."

"I know, you said it already, you wanted to stop me from throwing myself away and breaking from the world because of fear of being hurt again. Like you have with your tinkering. But you don't understand. I don't' throw myself into situations that you deem risky because I don't want to live, I do it because, I know tragedies will befall me, Archangel teaches that it is through our suffering that we are honed into the instruments he uses to drive darkness from the world."

Aldrin withdraws from Eliza with an expression of worry mixed with deep respect, and fear for the young woman standing fearless before him. Before anything else can be said as Aldrin realizes he did nothing to change Eliza's mind, or calm her anger, a voice speaks from the tunnel, Alex's voice, "Woah, what's going on here? Why the release of so much magical energy?"

Eliza turns to see Alex standing in the entrance of the tunnel with a strange glow emanating through the arm of his long-sleeved shirt. In Alex's other hand is a small bottle, filled with a creamy opaque crimson liquid. Aldrin, steps to Eliza's side responding, "Its nothing just steeling ourselves for tonight."

"So, the coup happens tonight, well that's good to know," Alex says before leaning toward Eliza offering her the bottle. The gentle glow begins to fade as Eliza's emotions calm, but as he leans in it flickers and his voice echoes in her head, without her having been the one to establish a telepathic link, "*Are you alright?*"

"*Yea, just a little shaken by. Wait, how am I hearing your voice in my head?*"

"*Well, there is this form of communication called telepathy where two people can communicate with just their minds.*"

"*I know, I can do it.*"

"*You have an arcane tattoo? You're so young though, what kind of inscriptionist would do that.*"

"*A what?*"

"*An arcane tattoo.*"

"*I can communicate mentally naturally.*"

"*Interesting.*"

The rapid nature of telepathic communication allows the two to blast through this short conversation in the same time Eliza's hand extends and grabs the bottle. Aldrin, going to respond immediately after Alex finishes his last vocal comment, breaks the mental conversation, asking, "So that's the cure for Eliza?"

"No, or at least it isn't a cure, this will delay any further progression of the negative side effects of the replication elixir if Alfredo hasn't fixed it yet."

Taking the bottle and opening it, Eliza sniffs the compound, asking, "What's stopped you from creating a complete antidote?"

"Alfredo doesn't like sharing, I would need to know the exact formulation to be able to isolate and eliminate the side effects. Speaking of which, I have decided that I could teach you alchemy, but I would need your word that you would never converse with Alfredo again. Don't answer now take the night to think about it, I know how manipulative he can be, it might be hard but that is my condition."

"Why can't you work with Alfredo?"

"That monster is a lying, short sighted manipulator, who doesn't care about the people he mutates only that his potions are effective without regard of side effects."

"Right, but from what I understand with what you have said, he is far better at getting results than you are."

"How dare!"

"I mean no offense, I am actually suggesting the opposite, that he may need someone like you who knows the suffering that can come from failing to take side effects into account."

"I don't care, I will not work with that man ever again, I have given you the option."

"So how long will this delay the living decay?"

"Living decay?"

"Well I thought rapidly progressing to one's death in a way that it would appear as if it was by age, could use a name, and since it is a decay of the person's ability to live, I thought the name living decay could fit well."

"Well, sure, that will hold back the living decay, for just about three moon cycles."

Eliza gives a nod and downs the thick liquid and the three in the basement make their way to the ground floor. After an hour the group in Aldrin's house is joined again by Ben who brings another bundle of food to the house with the sky darkening with the approach of night. Over their shared meal, Aldrin explains the plan to Ben and Alex, agreeing that the two of them should stay in the home when the signal is given for the assault to begin, in order to protect Delira in the case that anything were to happen near Aldrin's home.

With night setting in and their stomachs full, Aldrin, Auburn, Eliza and Pearl, settle in to wait for their signal. The darkness of the night settles in for more than an hour and Eliza's mind dances around what Alex offered. In a moment of wanting Eliza thinks to herself, "*If only I could ask Alfredo.*"

To Eliza's astonishment a voice not her own and not Alex's echoes in response in her head, "*Ask Alfredo what? How are you communicating with me Eliza,*" after which Eliza recognizes the voice, as Alfredo's.

"*Wait you can hear me? No matter, why does Alex hate you so much?*"

"*Alex? If you are talking about Alex Telitaria, a person claiming to have once been an apprentice of mine, he's a liar.*"

"*What? He said you were a liar, and that you don't care about the negative side effects of your creations.*"

"*That is a falsification. Alex, once Alexirandarus, was a competitor of mine, don't trust him.*"

"*What do you mean, how am I supposed to trust either of you when you are both saying the other is lying,*" Eliza asks but no response comes and she is left pondering still as the four continue their wait for the night sky to turn red.

10

Champion

The silent stir of impatient waiting, broken by the clink and squeaking of Aldrin's suit as he paces, comes to a sudden end with a deep loud boom rumbling out over the city. The sky sparks and flickers with an explosion, as a bright red orange light radiates up to be caught by the layer of smog above. With a nod to the others Auburn stands and growls, "Soonds lik' we've bin cried tae dae oor pairt."

Standing Aldrin agrees, "Guess so," before leading the other three down into the basement and into the tunnel. Quickly they find their way through the dark cramped path in the direction they came from during the day, and shortly after starting they turn down a different path leading them to a ladder leading up. As they reach it, the group hears from beyond the metal cover that seals the exit of the climb the muffled sounds of militaristic panic, and the sound of bells being rung from the keep above them.

Aldrin continues to lead being the first to climb the ladder. Small holes in the cover above allow flickering beams of orange torch light to pierce down onto the climbing group as they approach the seal. The group stop with Aldrin pushing up against the plate and simultaneously gesturing for them to be quiet. A moment passes as the streams of light are broken and strobe from above, before Aldrin continues pressing the metal barrier free from its hold.

The muffled ringing bells become loud with the snapping of roots as dirt falls from above as Aldrin opens a hatch that had been overgrown. Quickly he aids the other three the rest of the way up, into a yard within the fortress walls. A massive fire's glow can be seen brightly filling the southern skies, and Aldrin forces himself into the others' attention gesturing for them to follow. Creeping along the outer wall of the keep's main structure the group find the large front double doors. Holding the other three around the corner from the door, he waits as a group of four dragon men storm from the structure and out into the city streets.

Turning the corner and getting into the building, Pearl closes the doors behind her group an instant after one of the large reptilian flying creatures, like the one they saw when they were entering the city, falls from the keep's walls with a rider strapped to its back, before filling its leathery bat-like wings with air and taking flight. Pearl is pulled from the door, as she leans against it breathing heavy from witnessing the large wyvern up close before sealing the threshold. The building, once regally decorated within its halls, sits in great disrepair with the red rug that stretches down its center wrinkled and torn, and with the walls painted and damaged with jagged streaks of scorching. The group hug the right wall as Aldrin leads them deeper in, and down a dark unlit stairway.

At the staircase's base a single torch meagerly glows, lighting the single hall that is flanked by rows of rooms, each separated by stone walls. The small rooms are blocked from the central path with barriers of vertical iron bars. Each rod of the walls separating the cells are spaced a quarter of a foot apart, with a door of similar construct set at the entrance of each block.

All of the doors, are open waiting for prisoners to be locked within, except for one. Sitting closed and locked, the last cell on the left holds within it a single individual, with long blond hair tied back in a ponytail, waiting on her knees facing away.

Grabbing the keys from a hook at the base of the stairs, Aldrin steps to the woman's cell, and as soon as he touches the medal the woman asks, "So what is going on now, going to move me to a more secure spot as the people finally show that they have had enough of your occupation?"

Aldrin smiles hearing the familiar voice, one that has personally saved his life multiple times from corruption overload, and he responds, "No Lady Tristalia, we the people, mean to release you. You are our greatest chance to remove the snake's head."

"Aldrin Ironskin, need a purification for yourself and your companions again?"

"No, no, your sisters have taken care of that for us already, but I think you need a sword. Come with us."

"Excellent. So, I assume that ruckus that pulled my guards away was you rallying the people to rise up then?"

"You could say that. The people of the tide have enough want for the old Blackgate that they are actually leading the uprising."

"Well what's the plan then?"

"We use the Blackguard and Red Tide tunnels to get you to the temple, from there we four follow you into battle against the leader of these Stormriders."

"Let's do this," Lady Tristalia responds nodding for Aldrin to take the lead.

Doing so, Aldrin steps through his companions and the group before continuing back up the stairs. Pulling themselves around the corner of the keep's ground floor once more, they walk back along the path they followed into the structure quickly finding their way again to the front doors. At the moment Aldrin's hand falls upon the door handle, a voice calls from behind the group, deep and distinctly from a dragon born, "You there stop!"

Pearl and Eliza instinctively turn to see the voice's source, one of the large blue scaled individuals in a battle-ready stance. He draws in a deep breath as if preparing to shout. Aldrin and Auburn grab Eliza and Pearl pulling them through the door as the smell of heated burning ozone suddenly takes their sinuses. Leaning forward, still in the line of sight of the group, mouth open, the dragonborn man releases his breath and a straight visible line warps in the air between him and the escaping prisoner. As quick as a strike from a storm cloud, a bolt of energy whips out from the large figure's maw, finding and scorching the doors of the keep as they are closed, blocking the bolt's attack.

Eliza looks at Tristalia with wide eyes asking with worry in her voice and pointing to the door, "They breath lightning?"

Pearl is the first to respond as she climbs down the ladder into the Blackguard tunnels, explaining, "Oh yea that is a thing with the dragonborn race, they have an innate magic within them to produce a miniaturized version of the same devastating breath of the dragon whose blood they share. Balasar a companion of ours was green and could thus release a cloud of poisonous gas, these Stormriders appear to be all blue scaled, so they can produce lightning strikes. Though I will say they seem to have something about them making that connection a lot stronger than I would have thought. That one's bolt went just about sixty feet."

The group continues down the dark tunnel, with Aldrin at the lead, and within Eliza contemplating Pearl's explanation of the people holding military power over the city. She turns to Lady Tristalia asking, "What happened? We heard that you willingly gave yourself up when the Stormriders came to the city, but what actually happened?"

"Exactly that," the woman, dressed only in a loose tunic and pair of trousers responds wrapping her hands behind her head.

"Wait, what? How could you not even fight for your home?"

Lady Tristalia smiles and resting a single hand gently on Eliza's shoulder responds, "I understand your confusion, it is not like a follower of Archangel to consider inaction as a correct path at any time. I assure you though that it is much better that I didn't find myself injured or killed trying to stand against the whole of the Stromriders' force else we would not be speaking now and seeking to rebuke them for the atrocities they have committed."

Stunned Eliza asks, "How did you?"

"Know you worship Archangel? Don't worry child, Archangel is a good god to follow, though his teachings can lead to hasty action sometimes. It's how you carry yourself, a stranger to people of this city, yet you would willingly and in good mind lay yourself in the way of danger so that they may be free. A common ideal of the truest followers of Archangel."

"And what of Silvermist, what is the truest ideal of her followers?"

"To purify, Silvermist and her followers cleanse those they touch and they seek to heal damage that has been rot, to make that which is sick, or corrupted, beautiful again. You can probably see why followers of Silvermist, and Archangel tend to befriend each other."

"Yeah."

The group returns to silence with Eliza finding a process of thought to meditate on while they walk. Walking a similar distance as they had from Aldrin's house to the keep, they finally arrive at the exit near the underside of the bridge. Stepping out the group see on the opposite end, the fat man Vect, waiting for them with a wave as they emerge. The loud sounds of movement echo down from above with dragonborn voices growling to each other in their own tongue, "Errok tarook riktar tembiir."

"Massaook, massaook. Don'trak tembiir massaook."

Vect gestures to be quiet from his spot across the river, before signaling with another wave for the others to cross. Stepping to the suspended rods Aldrin grabs hold of the first rope and locking his foot into place on the first pole he begins to make his way across. Getting his foot to the fifth pole, Aldrin gestures for Auburn to follow, who steps on to the poles to be the second to cross. The sky above darkens as storm clouds thicken overhead.

Aldrin and Auburn continue step by step with Lady Tristalia joining them as Aldrin nears the end and Auburn nears the middle. Each step seems almost easy for the three as they cross, and Eliza is the next to begin as Pearl insists on being the rear. After a few moments of the group silently stepping to cross the under-bridge Pearl finally begins her progress. The sound of movement from above comes to a sudden stop as panicked screams in the deep draconic tongue ring out before the sound of a large object falling takes the air. That sound finds a terrifying end when the bridge releases the sound of a massive crack as several of its boards split from a heavy object or creature lands on it at terminal velocity.

The impact throws the suspended rods into a violent swinging, which threatens the women still trying to cross over the two-story space above the river of black poisonous water. With the violent thrust panic fills Pearl's eyes as she watches Eliza go to take a step just before the crash. The young girl is thrown forward and without a steady place to land her lifted foot, she falls. In an almost unnatural feat of dexterity though, Pearl drops, wrapping one of her legs with the rope that suspend the poll that was just under her foot, while simultaneously lunging forward, just barely grabbing Eliza's wrist. The two become taut as Pearl stops Eliza's downward decent.

Both of the women want to call out but understand doing so would only draw attention to the group under the bridge, attention they are looking to avoid. Hearing the unintentional grunts of the two behind her Lady Tristalia glances over her shoulder to see Eliza dangling in Pearl's grasp. Spinning around she wraps her leg with the rope of the rod she is on, and she leans down to help Eliza back up, grabbing the dangling girl's other arm she and Pearl heave, lifting the fallen friend back onto a bar of the under-bridge path.

Eliza gets a leg up and over one of the rods and releasing Pearl and Lady Tristalia quickly grabs the ropes to her side. Standing back up she gives a nod to the two who saved her as they also return to standing, and the three of them continue, quickly catching up with the others. Unchecked by the soldiers above who, in a panic, swarm the thing that impacted the bridge, the group are ushered into the Ride Tide tunnels. Vect takes lead and quickly presses the group through the path way leaving no opportunity for any further conversation before they reach the ladder up to their destination, a run-down building across the street from the front path of the temple. With a nod Vect ducks away back down the tunnel system surprisingly nimble for his size, and the group prepare themselves to move quickly and quietly.

Emerging from the door, the group instantly slows to a stop as a phalanx twenty-four heavily armed and armored dragonborn soldiers, comes into view waiting at the temple's steps. Standing still as the wall of dragonmen begin to step in their direction Pearl's voice dances through the group as a whisper asking, "Hey Lizzy? I know you have this whole thing about trying to not use your magic, because it comes from a dark place and all that, but I think if there were ever a time it was necessary, for you know protecting others, others including me, well now would probably be that time."

Eliza glances in Pearl's direction, whose head hadn't even turned from the advancing militarized mercenaries, and she gives a nod in response. Turning her focus back to dragon men Eliza watches their expressions turn to confusion as she widens her stance and takes a deep breath focusing her mind to have more control over the energy she wants to draw than she does when it is summoned from her emotions. Extending her hands, the solid incarnation of her magic appears, easily more prominent than any time before she had used it, and the torrents of wind that accompany the drawing of great powers from seemingly nowhere grow into gusts stronger than any of her companions have ever experienced before. The looks of confusion switch to looks of terror on the faces of the soldiers, as they notice that Eliza is wielding powerful magic against them. The fear causes several of the dragonmen to release the bolts from the heavy crossbows in their hands, the instant they see the small anti-dimensional disk form within their ranks an instant before it shatters enveloping them in black.

Those that don't try to shoot their crossbows, dive to the ground expecting the ominous black disk to explode and be done, in no way being prepared for the black that floods over them to sit as a weightless mass around them. Panicked screams break from the undulating membrane like surface that gently whispers in the sounds of military conflict that dance through the city's air. The Stormriders captured within the black nothingness feel the alien slimy acidic lapping of the otherworldly tentacles that come with the darkness, which begins to sear the scaly flesh of the victims. Turning to her four escorts, Lady Tristalia gives a nod and over the now loud mixture of pained screams, thunderous whispering, and the powerful gusting that rushes out from around Eliza, she yells, "Looks like you've got them handled."

The Silvermist Champion takes a step to run in the same moment a bolt shoots down toward her, missing by nearly the exact distance she moved in her single step. The projectile's impact with the stone of the road underfoot, where the wood of its shaft shatters, draws the attention of the group up to a dragonborn riding the back of a wyvern, which elongates, stretching its cobra head forward and letting it scorpion tail straighten to the swooping flight path as it passes ten or twenty feet above the group before arching around for a second pass.

With a single movement, Auburn whips the ornate bow from Negmor's palace into his hand and draws an arrow. The strange transparent bow string pulls back easily. When it reaches a third of the maximum it can be drawn one of the gold feathers on both ends of the bow's body, shifts ninety degrees toward the string and the arrow is engulfed in fire. From that point Auburn continues to draw the arrow back and getting to two thirds the maximum draw a second set of feathers folds back toward the string and the fire around the arrow begins twist around it spiraling in a heated tornado whose base is a point nearly a foot out from the arrow's head. Further still in the split second that the arrow is drawn Auburn pulls the string to a full draw. A third set of feathers twist, angling in at the string, and the eyes of the bird of prey design of the bow ignite into glowing cinders as, almost imperceivably, pinpoint dots appear on the surface of the flying rider's cloak.

Auburn releases the arrow. The fraction of a second it took him to draw it back and for the fire to ignite and begin spiraling captures the attention of the others as it leaps from the bow. Faster than any arrow he has shot before, this shot flies through the air narrowly missing the rider who has his wyvern roll out of the projectile's path. To the astonishment of those on the ground, they watch as the arrow curves its path in the air and redirects into the now unsuspecting rider's shoulder before bursting in a small ball of fire igniting his cloak.

The rider, feeling the sudden impact and splitting pain in his shoulder, panics as he hears the fire fed by the rushing wind of his mounts' movement. In a quick moment of action, he releases his burning cloak, which falls to the ground where the fire continues to grow, revealing on his shoulder the severe damage of a cauterized puncture wound surrounded by burnt away scales leaving a bulbous fleshy blister. The distraction of removing his cloak nearly causes the rider to collide with a second, who dives toward the conflict, aiming his loaded crossbow for Eliza.

Aldrin aims up to the diving wyvern releasing a shot from his rifle, but it flies wide, missing. Ducking away from the whistle of the bullet's path, the rider focuses again, attempting to steady his aim at the girl who has a torrent of wind spiraling around her. In his attempt to focus, the new rider doesn't hear the splitting of air as a figure from far above breaks through the cloud line, in a directed freefall in his direction. The approaching figure is not a wyvern, and a smirk forms on Eliza's lips as she holds concentration on maintaining the hungering, otherworldly, undulating orb, when from the approaching figure in a scratchy high-pitched voice, only just recently made known to the group, a call can be heard yelling out, "Banzai!"

The twang of the crossbow releasing its quarrel sounds, and Eliza, seeing the projectile get thrown forward, leaps to the side, causing it to just miss her as the floating sigil shatters from the point in the air where she was maintaining her magic. Finding her feet beneath her, she raises her hands and the glyphs reform creating the sigil in front of her new location, and she looks up to see the wyvern rider, with ice crystals forming on the surface of his torso, get struck by a nearly invisible force of energy waves that pulsate in a line through the air from the freefalling figure further above. The form gets closer, and becomes clear, a creature, seemingly the amalgamation of an eagle and a lion, falls with its wings tucked tightly to its sides. On its back appearing as though riding the flying beast, without even touching it, an orb with four eyestalks, one of which struggles to point forward as the wind of falling throws the other three back, laughs, and the large sideways cat-like central eye glances down to Eliza before forcefully closing, as if performing a one-eyed wink.

The talons that exist on the front eagle like legs of the griffon extend forward as it approaches in its freefall pounce. Impacting with the now unmounted wyvern digs it's sharp meat hooks into the snake-bat-scorpion's thick leathery hide pressing it down with the impact. The griffon reopens its wings with a forceful thrust to regain lift.

The new aerial combatants' arrival draws the attention of the burnt rider as one of his companions descends forty or more feet to the ground. Reloading his crossbow as his wyvern banks over the disheveled line of buildings the group emerged from, he takes aim for the griffon and Boop. He doesn't take his shot though, as before he releases the trigger a bolt whips past his wyvern causing it to recoil to avoid being struck. Looking down to the source, he sees one of the soldiers that was engulfed in the orb of black, laying on the ground breathing pained breathes which crack a layer of frost that has formed over his body, covering seeping wounds of acid scoring of painted strange alien patterns, through his armor and scaled flesh.

The group on the ground, having found themselves motionless as Eliza, and Boop dominate the field of conflict, spring once more into motion.

Pearl strides to Lady Tristalia's side, pressing the champion forward, while simultaneously drawing the jeweled rapier from its sheath at her side. Running across the yard to lead the champion into the temple, Pearl jumps as another of the soldiers pushes his way free from the tentacle filled space within the shifting presence of Eliza's magic. The emerging form only just sees Pearl before the pain of the cool winds, from the impending storm, battering his fresh acid burns, sets in. Instinctively he reaches to his side to draw his sword. He isn't given the chance, for by the time his hand is on his sword's grip, Pearl's blade is in his chest. Pulling the blade free Pearl is amazed to find it clean of blood, or any trace of use.

Auburn draws back another arrow that ignites in his hand, and releasing it lets the burning projectile soar into the unburnt shoulder of the still mounted rider. There it bursts like the previous one in a small explosion of fire. In the same instant he sees the arrow make impact, he looks at Pearl and Lady Tristalia and yells, "Weel whit urr ye waiting fur! Go!"

Pearl gives a nod to the three, flinching away as another shot flies from Aldrin's rifle releasing a blinding spray of sparks. She looks back again at Eliza, as the rifle flash fades to see her draw the spider tipped wand from her backpack with one hand, while the other holds firm on the center of the sigil in front of her. Turning back to the temple, Pearl finds Lady Tristalia no longer standing next to her, and she gives chase into the temple as more of the soldiers begin to finally break free from their prison of darkness.

From the top of the temple's tower a third wyvern leaps into the lightly glowing night sky tilting to an aggressive dive for Boop and Felix the griffon. Swinging the wand up to point in the direction of the approaching third wyvern and rider, Eliza exclaims to activate its magic, "Aracnis." From the end of the wand, a small white ball shoots out in the direction the spider is pointed and intercepting a point in the wyvern's path explodes, in a mass of thick stringy webs that leap out to grab onto whatever they can before collapsing back into the point of detonation to become inert mush.

Flying into the mass as it expands, the newest wyvern rider panics as he is unable to stop his mount's momentum before both are wrapped entirely within the web. Unable to flap its wings, the wyvern and its rider go into a freefall. The mass of the two web wrapped beings continues forward as they fall and the orb that is their combined form vanishes through the upper most membrane of the black mass of undulating otherworldly magic.

The griffon pecks into the serpent neck of the wyvern in its talons, causing a spurt of black green blood to spray up and across it and Boop. Releasing the wyvern from its grasp the griffon's wings continues to carry it around the aerial battlefield, circling in an attack path toward the remaining air born wyvern who turns for a head on confrontation. Boop grins as the wyvern's form becomes larger with the approach, and forcing one of his eyestalks forward, he releases a black magical beam that upon impacting with the angered wyvern washes over the creature's form. Before the two flying creatures can impact with each other a sudden, indescribable fear washes over the wyvern's expression, and it abruptly attempts to avoid the impending mid-air collision.

Auburn and Aldrin take aim and take turns finishing the dragonborn soldiers who emerge in pain from the area of void magic. It is at the point that one of the dragonmen falls from within the orb, with only a minor resemblance to how he appeared when the magic came into being, the three watching his escape, stare wide eyed at the visage, and putting his hand toward Eliza, Aldrin mumbles, "Maybe that's enough, we can finish off any stragglers."

Eliza, sharing in the horrified expression, only nods and releases the power from the hand that holds the spell maintained, and the sigil spins, flickering and fading into thin air. Like every time before when the channeling of the magic that birthed the spell into being finds its end the outer reaches of the sphere begin to retract and collapse inward disappearing back into the strange tear in reality from which it sprung. In the wake of the magic that fades, is a scene that can only be described as gruesome. The soldiers that could not find their way out of the pure black nothingness that engulfed them, lay within a shallow divot melted from the overturned dirt of the temples yard, the stones of the path leading to the temple hold the maddening pattern of scorings that the group has come to recognize, a minor representation of the atrocity wrought to the living flesh of dragonborn men, who now lay dead below.

Eliza's hand springs to cover her mouth as she sees what her magic has done. The divot in the dirt teams with the stench of boiling, dissolving, fats and flesh. Thirteen dragonblood skeletons sit in a soup of slime that once was their scaled flesh and soldier-built muscles. Armor that once clung tight to the large forms, sags loosely over the bones of the dead, holding small scraps of still undissolved tendons and muscle fibers on bones which hold the same pattern as the stones of the path to the temple. If left any longer within the hungering void sphere the trace skeletal remains would have joined the rest of their bodies in the liquid sludge that makes up the stinking soup they sit within.

The griffon, Felix, lands between Aldrin and Eliza with a powerful thud of its weight pressing down on the stones of the main road, bringing Eliza back from the horror of the sight of her magic's creation. Slinging the magical bow back on his shoulder, Auburn steps again toward the temple, drawing his sword. Seeing the movement Aldrin goes to join, but stops for a moment saying, "You're doing a great job Boop, take out the rest of those riders if you can. If we keep their forces on the ground those rising up against these monsters will have a better chance of survival. Eliza let's go. We have to continue helping the champion."

Nodding his form in agreeance with Aldrin, Boop drops to tap his mounts back exclaiming, "Ride Felix," and as the griffon's wings extend and press down with tremendous strength to lift it from the ground, Boop turns to Eliza exclaiming through the loud beating of griffon wings, "Stay safe master."

The dynamic duo of Boop and Felix take to the sky leaving Eliza with Aldrin. After a moment, Aldrin pats Eliza'a shoulder and the two begin to jog forward to join Auburn in his approach to the temple's front doors. Reaching the pit's side, Eliza slows to a stop placing her hand over her mouth again as she looks wide eyed down into the viscous unsightly mess. Her head slowly moves from one side to the other as her disbelief in the pool of melted men having been her doing holds her in place, leaving her to stammer, "No, I couldn't have done this."

Aldrin gets only a few steps further when he feels the lack of Eliza's presence at his side and he stops. Turning to the young girl looking down into the pool of humanoid ooze, he returns her side and grabbing her arm, pulls her away from the dirt bowl of mush. The instant his hand touches her skin the clouds above finally finish gathering their strength releasing a bolt of lightning to dance through the black canopy, as it begins to rain. Two steps closer to the temple doors he says to her, "Eliza. Look you didn't do anything wrong. Those men were enslaving the people of this city, and they wouldn't have hesitated to kill you if they had been given the chance. You were defending yourself."

Greeted by the acolytes of Silvermist, Aldrin notices the unmoving dead forms of two more dragonborn men slumped against the doorway to the temple's tower staircase. Stopping Eliza in the temple's open large double front doors, he looks sternly into her eyes awaiting a response. With a quick nod Eliza obliges responding, "Ok." Withdrawing from him as the two of them are brought into the temple by the acolytes who go to close the doors. The moment the sisters of Silvermist grab the doors a heavy thud crunches through the room followed shortly by another dead dragonborn, the source of the impact's sound, falling into view, onto the path, from above, before the doors are fully closed.

Stepping to Eliza's side as she turns to the corner of the room tapping her lower lip with an index finger, her mind holding on the image of the thirteen disfigured skeletons covered in strange alien indentations from the acid covered tentacles that made the rest of their bodies into a soup, Auburn lays a hand on her shoulder. Jumping from the sudden physical contact Eliza turns, her breaths heavy with panic, and he asks her, "Nae sae eager tae thro' yersel' intae a war noo that ye'v seen th' darker side o' it urr ye?"

"That's not it. Archangel teaches that it may be necessary to defend the rights of those who cannot defend themselves and that blood may be spilt in conflict. I knew those men needed to die, they had no intention in relinquishing their unearned authority over this city peacefully, but I didn't intend to torture them, to mangle them the way they were."

"Yer pure annoying wi' a' o' that Archangel malarkey. Look priests, clerics even holy crusading champions ur a' th' same as ye, magic wielders bound wi' power in thaim thay can't explain, th' two differences ur tha' yer power is purely evil, and darkness, to fit the wielder, 'n' thair tae delusion tae realize that gods abandoned oor world lang, lang ago."

Auburn is too busy laying into Eliza with a disrespectful tirade, insuring that he once again reminds her that he sees her as something evil, to notice Lady Tristallia. Returning from the top of the tower, she approaches him and Eliza, with Pearl and Aldrin at her side. Striking a confident pose with her fists on her hips that Pearl is known to regularly strike, the champion asks with a curious brow, "Is that so, spirit born?"

Turning to face the Lady, Auburn's eyes widen as he sees her donned in heavy armor, appearing as though larger than she was when he saw her last. A second take to the champion reveals that the perfectly polished silver plates of the suit of armor she is wearing, isn't causing an optical illusion to make her seem larger, but that she actually is. Standing looking down at the red skinned man Lady Tristalia has grown to be nearly two inches taller than Eliza, who remains taller than Auburn by more than an inch herself. Pearl reaches forward, from behind Tristalia, apologizing, "Don't mind him, he's an unthoughtful drunk, who cares more about reminding Lizzy that he sees her as a monster because of her being unwilfully connected to a dark source of magic, than he does about anything else that comes out of his mouth."

With Auburn staring speechless back at her, not even glancing angrily at Pearl with her comment about him, Lady Tristalia laughs, placing a hand on his shoulder and with a caring tone she explains, "Good for you that the gods that protect will protect, even if you don't believe in their presence," and she looks to Eliza as she continues, "or trust in their followers. Come," she exclaims as she turns to the door, "we mustn't wait any longer. People are fighting and dying as we speak. They are relying on us to succeed in purifying this town of its unwelcome occupation."

Lady Tristalia steps in the direction of the door revealing even further the brilliance of the innate divine energy that radiates around her, with the reflection of the flickering sconces' light that illuminates the room becoming magnified upon her armor, turning into a stunning white. Stranger still to Eliza and Auburn, the onlookers who had never before seen the champion of Silvermist donned in her vestments, her movements reveal from the joints of armor, falling softly from her, a glistening gaseous moisture. A literal embodiment of her goddess' name, a silver mist, that fades leaving only small clouds that trail her.

Before she can reach the door, Aldrin jumps between her and the exit, stopping her saying, "Wait, before we go anywhere we should start fortifying this place, get anyone left fighting here in a central location, draw the rest of the stormriders to a single point to stop the fighting faster when we have defeated their leader."

With a scowl Auburn interjects, "'n' if we fail ye bring th' rest o' ony hawp o' future resistance tae a single point fur th' stormriders tae deal wi' smoothly."

"There wasn't a chance that a rebellion would happen until we arrived."

"Juist because we ur stupid enough tae throw ourselves intae danger, even makin it if necessary, doesn't mean we need tae bring, those who cuid maybe realize better whin hings stairt turning sooth, tae an inescapable point o' na return."

"If we are successful though, people who wouldn't have to die will, just because we would be slow to drive out the stormriders with their commander's death."

Crossing her arms and shifting her weight onto one leg Lady Tristalia listens to the two men argue, allowing Eliza to take note that while heavily armored Lady Tristalia doesn't have a sword on her person, even though that is what she was supposed to have retrieved from the top of the tower. Turning back into the temple space Lady Tristalia raises a hand gesturing for the sisters to come to her side. Aldrin and Auburn become quiet looking to the champion as she addresses the women that step to her, "Sisters, it is now that our faith is tested the most. Silvermist brought us to this land to cure it of the dark corruption that takes the innocence of the living. Now we most purify our foothold here of those who would deal in evil without the darkness of the lands corruption, but who are never the less a corruption on this world in their actions. Go out into the streets. Keep yourself hidden and find anyone who is of this city, and bring them here. You two stay here. Do not let our holy site be taken again. Weapons," she turns back to her four escorts, "Do you have any weapons you could spare?"

Struck astonished by the question, Pearl blinks several times before responding, "Yea, I think I have a crossbow, here. I only have a few quarrels, and here I have a spare sword. Oh, and here are some arrows, and Auburn's old bow."

"That should work. Now help me move these tables close to the door to use as a barricade for the sisters."

Following the champion's command the eleven people around her, push everything within the main temple area to be within a few feet of the door, where the pile could be easily shifted to block off the single entrance into the structure. Then stretching and loosening her joints Lady Tristalia looks to the only two men alive in the room, asking, "There, now we will draw the impurity to here, and we also make this a highly defensible location."

Looking to each other Aldrin and Auburn both share in a shrug, not having expected for the champion to take such a domineering control of their argument only to strive to find a middle ground between their positions. Before anything else can be said or done by the group, the sisters who were instructed to seek out citizens rising against the stormriders duck from the building and into the dark of the storm and the night.

11

Battle for Blackgate

Hitting her fist to the chest-plate of her armor, Lady Tristalia nods to the remaining sisters in the temple before taking the lead out the door with Aldrin, Auburn, Eliza, and Pearl following. The fire that lit the sky from down the river no longer glows bright against the ceiling of black clouds, having faded in the storm's torrent of rain and winds. Instead the sky is lit with unnaturally regular jolts of lightning that dance from cloud to cloud releasing a steady rolling rumble of thunder.

No longer seeking to remain undetected, Lady Tristalia runs over the path from the temple to the main street and continues through the city. The five come to a stop as they reach the bridge they had passed beneath. Standing in the group's path, weapons drawn, is a set of three more dragonborn, on guard to control who can cross the damaged bridge.

Cracking her knuckles Lady Tristalia stops Aldrin from aiming his rifle at the snarling elongated reptilian maw of one of the three, explaining to him, "I've got these three. I need to warm up a bit, before we face their boss."

Reaching out with an open hand, the champion smiles, and in a flash of silver light a broad sword forms in her open hand and she clenches her fist around the artifact's handle. A spark of brilliance dances across the blade, drawing attention to the engravings of holy texts carved into the damascus steel of the weapon's flat. Twirling the newly formed sword in her hand with a flourish, the champion reaches out the other, gesturing with a challenging wave. Her gesture ends, with a second twitch of her fingers falling back into her palm, and the silver mist that billows out from under her armor rises around her head and releasing a sound of two pieces of metal drawn against each other, the miniature cloud bursts away revealing a helmet of equal elegance to the rest of her armor, finishing the full plate suit.

The men staring from the bridge withdraw their looks of aggression, hesitatively standing in place as the divine magic is put on display for them. Taking a step forward Lady Tristalia nearly breaks into a laughing fit when her single movement causes the group to turn and run, unintentionally whipping each other and nearly tripping themselves with their tails. Not wanting to let them get away Aldrin, first looking to Tristalia who smirks with the reaction of the dragonmen, darts forward to give chase.

Reaching the damaged peak of the bridge Aldrin looks to the other end coming to a sudden stop. Eliza and Pearl rush to Aldrin's side when they see him reset his stance, to find him grinning to the other end of the bridge. They join in his smile when they too see the three dragonborn soldiers, lying unconscious at the feet of three friends, Rev, Lorm, and Esmerelda. Pearl sprints to the group giving Esmerelda stiff jab with her fist into her shoulder. Stumbling from the impact Esmerelda rubs her shoulder asking, "What was that for?"

"You made me think that you weren't going to help us with this in any way."

"I wasn't going to. My husband convinced me. Now what's going on," the question escapes in response to Pearl's appearance, before seeing the champion join Aldrin and Eliza at the top of the bridge, "Lady Tristalia! How can we help?"

The Lady's voice calls from her position commanding, "Get to the temple. Hold off any more of these soldiers from inside. Protect the Blackgate citizens that my sisters are escorting there. You four come on we don't have time to waste."

Eyes return to the champion with her command, revealing to the three that ran onto the bridge ahead of her that the helm and sword that were summoned to her have vanished. Without any further acknowledgments, Lady Tristalia continues forward and passing the three newcomers, she shifts back into a jog in her heavy plate armor through the city toward the large keep she was freed from, and Rev, Lorm and Esmerelda shift into their own sprint toward the Silvermist temple.

The streets are surprisingly empty for a full uprising to be in effect. The loud clang of metal plates flailing against each other with each bouncing step that carries Lady Tristalia forward, mixes with the continual roll of the thundering storm above, which sends down the hammer of heavy rain drops striking the roofs of the buildings that flank the group's path, and that ting off the champion's silvery armor. The sound of distant conflict can be heard over the group's hustled movement through the city along a path without obstacle, which brings the Silvermist champion and the four accompanying her to the large front gate of the keep's outer walls. Through the gate, the large front door of the main structure, which Pearl had previously closed, waits open and unguarded. Finally slowing from their jog, the champion steps to the door silently calling her weapon to her hand once more, declaring, "No guards, this person's pride will be their downfall."

The woman's words provoke a quick response from Auburn, almost irritated in his already gruff voice, "Mibbie we keep th' chit chat tae a minimum, at least 'til we ur dane 'ere."

"I guess you're right. Aldrin which way to the main chamber."

Looking, almost surprised to the short interaction between Lady

Tristalia and Auburn, Aldrin stammers for a second before leading the group down the most direct route to the commander's chamber at the center of the building to a set of large double doors. The path the group is lead through holds the same signs of damage and conflict as the front hall. Large portions of walls are broken leaving divots with rubble scattered on the ground. Black scorch marks are left from the electric exhalation the blue dragonborn soldiers are able to produce all around the shattered remains of the few pieces of furniture that had lined the halls in the prime of the city.

 The storm and the sounds of conflict become distant through their muted echoes that barely press through the keep's walls as the five stand before a pair of closed doors, behind which they expect to find the leader of the dragonborn occupying force, a man explained to them as a towering indominable form that dwarfed the smaller buildings of the city in height. Staring at the portal, Eliza takes a split moment to look at those who stand with her. Auburn pulls his bow from his shoulder looking with his same calm disinterested scorn to the awaiting and inevitable conflict. Aldrin packs his black powder tightly in the back of the barrel of his riffle with his breath still heavy from the time spent running from the temple to the keep. Pearl holds an uncharacteristic stern expression on her face, as she joins the others in mentally preparing for the fight they are about to walk into. With a glance in Eliza's direction, seeing the awe in her young companion's eyes, the stern nature of Pearl's expression breaks as she grins with a nod before turning back to the door. With a smile taking her face, in a natural response, to Pearl breaking the seriousness of the situation, Eliza joins her companions in taking a deep preparatory breath which causes the magic within her to begin surging in a calm gust around them.

 With the sound of the champion summoning her helmet to her echoing over the group, she thrusts her sword's point into the ground, it slides through the stone with ease and the group continue to stare at the door in anticipation of what waits for them beyond. They stand in silence, as she brings her hands to door handles and with a single movement throws both powerfully open.

Waiting beyond the door is a large chamber meant for holding sessions of court and issuing commands from the commander of the Blackguard to his forces. The space though, sits empty of furnishings with the singular exception being a large iron chair at the far end facing the now open doorway. Large columns extend from the floor to the ceiling equally spaced through the chamber. Through the doors as they open the group hear a deep cacophonous rushing wind, an inhalation followed by an equally powerful exhalation. It bellows over the sound of the doors swinging open, and through the continued muffled sounds of the storm and conflict beyond the keeps walls and overpowers the magically spiraling of air around Eliza.

In the large iron throne, sat with appendages spread imposingly, is a figure nearly twice the size of the other dragonblooded occupiers of the city. Protruding from the figures back, unlike the other smaller beings of his kin, is a pair of massive leathery blue scaled wings. The figure rises and falls as his chest expands and contracts with his deep breaths.

The broad reptilian grimace grins ever slightly as the doors to his throne room are swung open, and his form shifts to have his titanous taloned hands grasp the ends of the arm rests of the chair as chains rattle swinging from where they are connected to gauntlets that sit locked onto his wrists. A visual ripple pulses through the form's scale covered appendages, as he forces himself up, standing to stare down from across the room, more than twice the height of any of the five now within his presence. The light of the hanging braziers illuminates the upper portion of the towering figure's silhouette menacingly as his head reaches a fifth of the way to the massive chamber's ceiling and his eyes squint into the darkness, able to peer onto the second-floor balcony that runs the edge of the room.

Taking a single step from his throne the monstrous form causes the ground to tremble beneath him with an unnaturally terrifying force. The behemoth draconic tail shifts against the smooth stone floor, accompanied by the clatter of the chains connected to his gauntlets falling and dragging in the same fashion. Another step releases a second quake, through the sturdy chamber of the keep as he stretches his shoulders unfurling his wings, releasing a powerful leathery sound and a torrential gust of wind that whips out almost visibly in waves that suffocate the flames that lit the room and halls, casting them and those within into darkness.

Aldrin's exoskeleton thrums, the small motor, that functions in a way only his mind understands, glows orange red in the black of the room, but the fullest attention of those within the dark area falls upon the Silvermist champion. The soft silver mist that drifts from the joints of her armor glows illuminating her, Aldrin, and Pearl who are standing on her immediate right and left. The monstrous form of the dragonborn giant vanishes almost completely with the suffocation of the light. Only a scarce outline of his form remains visible with the glow of Lady Tristalia's radiance, and his glossy eyes glisten as he looks down upon the defiant forms before him.

Another heavy footfall brings the silhouette closer. He peers down on the group in their hesitation to make the first strike. His deep growling voice thrums resonating with a immense strength, echoing within its own rasping, scratching like the rolling of the thunder outside, "You were such a good prisoner Lady of the Silvermist. Throwing down your sword, before my soldiers without striking a single blow. Handing yourself over without even the slightest kindling of a fight. Tell me what happened to make you want to die at my hands? Don't tell me that you honestly believe these puny tripe will have any effect on the outcome you already knew would happen if you were to raise your sword against mine. The reason you threw it down."

Shifting into a defensive stance with both hands on the holy sword's handle, Lady Tristalia yells in a challenging response, "I refused to fight your whole force alone, such an act, though it would have seen me glory in the eyes of those who witnessed it, would have been shortsighted, and forsaken my chance to face you and cleans the world of you. I will grant you the same curtesy, say the word and I will have these heroes stand down, and I shall face you in one on one combat!"

The deep bellowing voice laughs at the champions offer, responding, "So much fight in such a small ground bound cloud, don't dismiss the help." Another heavy step shakes the ground underfoot, as in the dark the sound of two locks snapping free of themselves precedes the sound of the chains that dragged, shifts into the gauntlets falling from the large man's wrists to clatter against the floor. Immediately after the locks break free, allowing the gauntlets to fall from the man's wrists, the air of the chamber fills suddenly with the smell of ozone and the group feel it electrify as their hair begins to stand on end with a static the seems to have no source. The giant figure leans in, and illuminated by Champion Tristalia's glow reveals that in the wake of the gauntlets falling free his massive form has begun to grow larger. His confident grin only becomes more devilish as his voice getting even deeper with his increasing size, shaking his challenger's chests, almost forcing out their breaths he continues, "I would like to have some sort of a challenge."

With a yell throwing her entire form into a single motion Lady Tristalia swings for the smug dragonblood giant's jugular. The swing misses the form as he draws back into the shadows. Pointing away from herself deeper into the room, Lady Tristalia yells to the other four, as the sound of an enormous slab of metal being lifted with the dexterity of a regular man's sword grinding through the darkness, "You heard him! He thinks he can take us all with ease! He has accepted the challenge, don't hold anything back!"

The command escapes into the air, moments before, slicing through the lightless space that extends at least seven stories in height like a windmill spining in a hurricane, a blade of blackened metal as wide as Lady Tristalia is tall is swung down with a near unfathomable force, directly for the champion of Silvermist. In the split moment she has to react, the holy sword swings up connecting with the titanic blade, that even at its enormous size comes to a razor-sharp edge, and the impact drops the champion to her knee as the two blades release a shockwave through the air.

The monstrous sword draws back, and through the thunderous

crash of metal that continues to ring in the ears of those in the chamber, the sound of many jolting arcs of electricity jumping through the air crack into existence as the, lit by blue lighting dancing across him, form of the commander of the stormriders rises to glare down from nearly twice his initial height. With a jerk of his fist he lifts and thrusts down the enormous sword, and with the motion, a magic within it comes to life. The air is suddenly filled with the snapping and popping of electricity leaping into the air as, with the arcs that jump effortlessly across the vast blue scales and armor of the giant form an orb of unstable electricity grows into being at the base of his blade releasing energy to leap for the ground, and to dance along the blades length.

The darkness of the room is cast aside by the glow of the jumping lightning, illuminating the chamber in a blue light that shows the full height of the monstrous challenge before the group. Raising his sword again, the giant roars, "You shall fall to the might of Domavir, the Storm Caller," as his arm brings the electrified blade down again for Lady Tristalia who is still attempting to recover from the force of the previous blow. Drawing back the red bowstring, Auburn glows with the orange of the fire that consumes the arrow in his hand, and pulling the twine to a point that bends the bow further than a normal bow should go, the weapon itself releases a shriek like the call of a bird of prey and the golden beak in its design opens glowing red with heat. The red and the blue sources of light conflict for a mere fraction of a second before Auburn releases the drawn arrow toward the giant dragonborn's head and vanishing from his hand the arrow transforms into a beam of pure fiery heat.

Catching the ray forming below him in the corner of his eye, Domavir is unable to move himself out of the fire's path, as he is bringing down his sword. The heat wave hits him with a stunning force, throwing him off balance. The blast causes his strike to fall to the side of Lady Tristalia, missing her by only a few feet, where the black blade cuts into the ground with seeming ease releasing its charge in a small burst of electric sparks around it, nearly hitting Pearl instead, who leaps out of the way. Trying to force himself through the fire, Domavir visibly grits his teeth before he is thrown back stumbling toward the iron throne, which now exists far too small for him to sit in. The fire beam fades and the enormous angered scowl throws itself back to glare down toward Auburn. The look of hate glares down, disfigured by a large five-foot diameter burn having incinerated the blue scales on Domavir's face, with a line of them curling, upon themselves and flaking from the damage, through which bulbous, blisters immediately begin to bulge.

Taking the opportunity as the room returns to darkness, Pearl darts from the side of the others, impaling Domavir's ankle with her jeweled sword, and continuing past withdraws the blade leaving the fresh open wound to bleed, in hopes of evening the playing field. Stopping with a spin near the metal throne, she whips the sword's blade up curious at the ease in which it made the incision and the sheen that it maintains as it remains untarnished by blood. The wound seems to bear fruit, when the monster's leg trembles, trying desperately not to collapse under his tremendous weight.

Shifting the foot, returns a sense of control of the fight to Domavir, as he relieves the pressure from the wound. Pearl rolls her eyes in disheartened disappointment at the ease her blow was adjusted for as the blue glow returns to the room with the giant looking over his shoulder at her as lightning arcs begin once more to dance across his form. Attention drawn away from the main group, Lady Tristalia gestures to the three still at her side to spread out.

Eliza runs to the far wall taking deep breaths as panic begins to press into her, the magnitude of the opposition draws a fear from within her, once more pressing upon her the feeling of helplessness that is only natural for someone of her age in this situation. Being near the wall amplifies the sound of the rain outside. The room teems with the lingering smell of smoke, and burning flesh, both quickly being taken over once more by the smell of ozone burning; the smell that emerges from a lightning strike. Something about the sounds and the smells intrance Eliza as she looks back to see Pearl roll beneath the tree sized tail which strikes in her direction.

Aldrin sets his feet, on the opposite side of the room from Eliza and takes aim. With a moment to steady his breath, he pulls the trigger. The shot rings out with the familiar thunderous crack for most in the room, but as Eliza shakes trying to bring forth her magic to help, not understanding the source of her fear, the shot which lights the room for less than a tenth of a second, sounds too familiar to her door being slammed open on that stormy night.

The image of Bartholomeus flashes again into Eliza's head for the first time in weeks, if not months, and she wants to feel sad, but looking back to the others, the image of her mentor, dead at her hands, shifts in her mind to that of Auburn and Aldrin looking up to her in supernatural fear, as she saved them from the beings of shadow on the plane of undeath. Her mind switches again to the goblins that she defended the other three against, after having just lost Boop, but simultaneously becoming more familiar with her magic. Her feet continue to carry her back as the images, almost forcing themselves upon her, like trying to keep her from falling into sorrow at this moment, shift again to Vall the young elf who reminded her of Archangel's teachings of kindness, and then to the bridge where she saved Vall's father from the snake-men.

The conflict continues, with Eliza off in her own mind, as the bullet ricochets off the hard scales of the giant form. Leaping to the ceiling the grape sized metal projectile pulls with it some amount of Domavir's charge, causing the lightning to jump upward with the crack of a thunder bolt. Seeing the bullet get deflected by the natural armoring, Aldrin calls to the others as he runs from his position to avoid the massive sword which swings down in his direction, once more releasing a burst of electricity into the stone around where if cuts into the ground, "The scales look weak because of how easily they were destroyed by fire and acid, but they're not. You have to hit the seams between them! Eliza, your magic probably won't have that limitation!"

Eliza only just hears Aldrin through a muffling effect that reexperiencing her journey is causing to her senses, but instead of pulling her back into reality the words only switch the images in her mind to the rat-based lycanthrope in the elven port's sewers. Her feet continue to carry her closer to the wall of the room, and the images begin to fade allowing her to once again witness the conflict the others are engaged in. Auburn releases two more shots at the giant with neither becoming the powerful beam of heat of the first.

Drawing back a deep breath, Domavir throws his head forward, mouth wide, in the direction of Lady Tristalia, and the electricity that dances across the surface of his form disappears. In his open mouth a bright pure white light forms in the base of his throat, and after a split moment of the room watching in stunned silence of the power being summoned, the light leaps from his maw in a bolt of lightning a visible foot in diameter. A blink of an eye is all the time it takes for the arc of energy to connect with the far wall, and unlike the scars of lightning breaths used by the stormrider underlings, the lightning leaping from Domavir connects with a violent explosion of stone and dust.

Lady Tristalia vanishes within the blinding light, transforming into the very mist that has continuously been escaping from the joints of her armor. The cloud that forms where she stood shoots through the air coalescing just above Domavir's head. There the mist bursts reforming into the champion, and she begins to fall with both hands holding tight to her sword's hilt. With every muscle contorting within her heavily armored frame she twists and spins the holy blade of the Silvermist faith into the portions of Domavir's face that no longer has scales, and it cuts deep, bursting the already bulbous blistering flesh. She feels slight resistance as her sword cuts divots into the monster's jaw bone and with a smile of success she lands in a three-point stance looking up to Domavir who recoils in pain.

At the moment Domavir's lightning breath springs across the room, lighting the chamber with a brilliant and horrifying blinding white light, Eliza watches Lady Tristalia's transformation into mist, utilizing the divine energy granted to her by Silvermist, and she thinks to the magic she attempted while her group were traveling to the pirate city, the Cove. This memory becomes all too real again in her mind when her feet finally find her back to the wall she has been slowly stepping toward where an empty holster meant to hold a lamp, presses into her back. The feeling though doesn't shake her this time, as Pearl's voice calls from the conflict, "Come on Lizzy, we could really use your help over," cut off by a thud, as Pearl, having been distracted in trying to get Eliza to help, is struck by Domavir's tail and thrown thirty feet to a wall. This strike, on Pearl, instead pushes Eliza into a mental clarity that had evaded her to this point, that had kept itself from her since that night her door slammed open.

Seeing where Pearl lands, and tuning her focus on the tyrant, Eliza's mind fixates on her magic again. The small gusts of air that were brushing around her grow with an intensity in her hate for the being standing domineering before her. Clenching her fists tight Eliza feels herself almost thrown forward when a feeling sweeps over her, like a barrier which had been limiting her suddenly gives way to a flood of magic. The room comes to a sudden still, with a stop in the fighting which remains without a clearly winning side, as the winds vortex around Eliza erupt to compete with winds of a hurricane. The five stop their conflict to stare in Eliza's direction and see the small girl, eyes closed, building a force that becomes visible as it begins to seep into their reality, and stretching out her hands the glyphs form before her before passing onto her and lifting her from her feet.

Looking at the small pests that have seemingly been toying with him this entire confrontation, and then to Eliza, Domavir yells in apparent frustration, "No, I let you distract me, that one is your weapon, that is the one you think can stop me. Well, let me prove you wrong!" He takes in a deep breath and throws his head in the direction of the black pulsing orb that Eliza has disappeared into, and the black back of his throat begins to glow white, with sparks of electricity leaping from within.

As it had before, time feels to almost slow to a crawl for Eliza, as she experiences the magic of the spell she is attempting to cast upon herself. Before even the glow flickers to life in the dragonman's maw, she feels a familiar, while still strange, burning sensation, with her appendages pulling themselves in and bending her into the fetal position, floating a short few feet above the ground. Her skin becomes like putty, sticking to itself and reshaping in the magic infused torrent around her. She feels her bones crack and grind themselves to dust causing her to scream in pain as she is compressed into an orb of flesh. These soul wrenching screams however, fail to escape the deafening winds and thrum of otherworldly magics surrounding her and, for Eliza, everything goes black.

Without an interruption coming in the form of a trident to her back, Eliza pushes forward into the magical transformation into a phase that she could not experience when she tried this use of her magic before. The pain across Eliza's mutated form eases and changes in itself to something more like a deep-set hunger, but not for food, and a thirst, but not for any type of fluid. She feels the singular mass of organic material, without eyes, mouth, or anything that would reveal it do be more than a blob flesh, lash out with a fragment of itself forming a singular thin tentacle, long enough to wrap around the entirety of her current form. A second, a third, and a fourth tentacle whip out and they solidify in the vortex of magic. With a fifth long tube of flesh and muscle solidifying, the five pull apart splitting themselves into a total of ten writhing fleshy whips, that transmit every sensation to Eliza's mind which struggles but maintains its presence.

Finally, in the fraction of a second that has drawn to feel like minutes for Eliza, she is allowed to once more gasp for air as a mouth, filled with a comb like row of razor sharp, finger length teeth on both an upper and lower jaw, opens and stretches from the orb of putty like flesh. This gasp is joined by the sensation of Eliza's returning ability to see, but this doesn't come without her mind having to re-adjust as a single eye, above her new mouth, is joined by six others which open at the ends of the upper most of the ten tentacles leaving the lower four to be used to grasp like those of an octopus.

The vortex breaks and reveals the transformed form of Eliza within, holding the shape of a creature like Boop but about three times the size, and with six more wrapping tendrils than her small friend. The bolt of electricity leaps finally from Domavir, and like before it crosses the span of the room for its target in a blink of an eye. Pearl leaps for Eliza hoping to miraculously prevent the attack, but stops as the light fills the room, thinking only that Eliza was struck by the full force of the energy as sparks and bolts leap to take the place of her magic, concealing her again from view.

The lightning fades, in half the span it had existed in Domavir's initial display, and even he appears confused as it dissipates, revealing the Boop like creature grinning with a single one of its six eyestalks pointing directly at the point the energy seemed to have struck in the air. Eliza feels with the passing of the energy the strange feeling of hunger and thirst lessens and in a blur within her head, she tries to focus, not being used to having seven optical inputs. Domavir looks at the strange orb mouth still agape from his lightning breath, joined in staring, stunned, and silent by the rest of the room. The form before them that has taken the place of Eliza drifts awkwardly swaying as if dizzy and drunk for a moment. That is when the room's attention is brought back to the conflict at hand by the sound of Aldrin's rifle releasing another loud bang.

Domavir lunges forward from the shot ricocheting off the back of his head, and he turns to look as Eliza sees his titanic form pass through the center of one of many eyes. Focusing hard on his image, glee fills the young girl's mind, as she watches a beam of magic leap out and impact Domavir's side. A dark grey ray that radiates a cloud of white smoke around it, shooting like an arrow that pierces his thick scaled hide. Everyone in the chamber is bewildered as Domavir slows from the impact, begins swaying, and his eyes begin to flicker, fighting a magically induced urge to fall asleep. The urge grows, to the titanic being's dismay, too strong as he turns to Aldrin and falls, crushing one of the chamber's. There the leader of the Stormriders lays, still, breathing in the slow breaths of sleep.

Pearl, leans to her left looking over the massive slowly rising and falling torso of the man, and with confusion striking her, she points a single finger at him asking, "Is he asleep?"

Aldrin steps to the behemoth mouth as it releases a horrid smelling breath and responds to Pearl as he waves away the smell, "Yeah, it looks like it."

Auburn draws an arrow pointing it in Eliza's direction asking the others, "Don't tak' it easy yit, what's that thing?"

Immediately the four eyeless tendrils lift in the same way that arms would, defensively trying to avoid getting shot, as Eliza's voice mixed with a throaty gurgling, shouts out, "Don't shoot, it's me, Eliza."

Pearl's eyes widen and she gasps asking, "Lizzy? Really?"

"Yes."

"What happened to you?"

"Well I had this dream a while back, about being able to change into, at least temporarily, something like Boop. I tried once before, but it didn't work, so I didn't hold anything back this time. Seems to have worked now."

"So, that's temporary then. That's good."

The conversation between Pearl and Eliza is broken when Lady Tristalia, who has stepped to the side of the sleeping Domavir, clasping her blade in both hands, and looking down at the scale covered neck says with stern authority, "Domavir, who claimed yourself as the Stormcaller, you are judged for crimes against humanity, specifically the enslavement and torcher of the citizens of Blackgate. You bear also as a scar on your soul the breaking of a century old treaty between all of the peoples of this world that no group or nation would move a military through the Port of Blackgate, beside those electively performing such action as citizens of the city, and city guard. The sentence for the first mentioned of your crimes alone is death, you have displayed yourself to be of power to not reasonably be held within the chains available in such time that a trail of word could be gathered, I thereby invoke the trial of soul. Let this world be cleansed of one evil today."

Drifting to Aldrin's side while Lady Tristalia speaks, Eliza, leans close to him asking, "What's she doing?"

Jumping as he catches a glimpse of Eliza's transformed form, having forcefully tried to forget what he had seen when she reemerged from the spiral of magic and wind, he returns his eyes stiffly to looking in the direction of Lady Tristalia whose eyes close as she draws up the blade, and he explains, "Well, it is this thing known as a soul trial, I have only ever seen one but I have been told by the sisters of Silvermist that Lady Tristalia has performed hundreds. Basically, it is a holy judgment ritual that can only be performed by Silvermist's champion with that holy blade. The way I have been told it works is the champion states the crimes and determine what sentence that would carry, whether it be death or amputation, and then they state why the judgement would be unable to wait until to be passed by the law system of the land, after which they carry out the sentence, and if the soul of the judged holds knowledge of committing the crime, and the sentence is just in the eyes of the Silvermist faith, the blow bears its effect."

Joining the other two Pearl adds, "But I hear that if either the judged's soul doesn't have memory of committing the crime, or the spoken sentence does not fit the crime, the champion instead receives the wound, however fatal it may be."

Aldrin looks to Pearl scoffing, "That's just ridiculous."

Pearl looks back responding with a shrug, as Eliza watches the holy blade in Lady Tristalia's hands glow, as though growing into a blade of pure light large enough to easily sever Domavir's head from his shoulders with a single stroke. The blade draws up above the champion's head and in a single swift motion it falls and all seven of Eliza's eyes freeze and widen staring at the ground where the edge of the light cuts the stone like a hot knife cutting snow. Silence takes the group in anticipation of the result to be somehow known and panic throws them to join the champion on the other side of the massive body as the light from the sword fades and she drops to her knees.

"Lady Tristalia," Aldrin calls out when the sound of the metal knee guards crash against the floor. The group's panic is eased when resting on her knees breathing heavy Lady Tistalia stares, and the point where the blade of light sliced. The three get to the champion's side at the same moment a sickening sound is released from Domavir's direction, one of two wet pieces of flesh pulling apart.

Aldrin offers a hand, and Lady Tristalia takes it, pulling herself to her feet, saying with a worn but confident command in her voice, "Quickly, we have to present that head to his followers, and you," her hand raises to point at Eliza drifting a few feet above the floor, "While you made this fight far easier than it may have been without your presence, the people of this city are going to remain on edge for some time. So, if you can possibly return to the form you were in before with the extremely long hair, and, well, it would allow us to ensure you don't get hurt by a jumpy person with a crossbow."

"I can try," the creature Eliza has transformed into responds, closing her eyes, and focusing on her other form, while, as a test, she imagines herself with large white feathered wings protruding with a magnificent brilliance from her back instead of the ones of bone she knows she has within her. In the same short span of only a second or two the orb withdraws the eyestalks into the central mass before shaping itself with flesh leaping from it like tendrils of clay warping themselves into the general shape of a young woman before filling out the form to become the exact return of Eliza to Pearl's side. Aldrin and Auburn, working in the light of one of the lamps that they relight, lift the horse sized head, not seeing Eliza return to her form with only her boots and amulet, the only real articles of clothing she was wearing, before she gestures with a phantom motion of putting on a shirt that causes the appearance of the outfit she had been wearing to return.

Opening her eyes for the first time after returning to herself, Eliza takes a deep breath, and feeling control over her body whips her head to look behind herself to see no pair of wings. Having watched, without helping the others, Pearl's hand falls near Eliza's shoulder without touching, in fear of causing her young friend any unintended harm, and she asks, "Lizzy, are you alright?"

Saddened, Eliza turns to look into Pearl's eyes responding with a smile wide enough to force her eyes closed again, "Yeah, Pearl, I am fine," and looking down to her hands, which she stretches out in front of her, opening and closing them, while turning them over several times, feeling the pain, and the strange emptiness the transformation had impressed on her completely nonexistent, and left in their wake a feeling of an almost tingling satisfaction, an almost taste of ecstasy, in her complete freedom from pain, and she continues, "I feel fine."

With a nod Pearl accepts the response, stepping from Eliza and Lady Tristalia's side to the enormous, electrically blackened sword. Ignoring the struggle of the two men, who successfully lift one end of the head onto Aldrin's suit, which rattles, holding pistons extended to amplify his strength for carrying the weight as it sits on him, she grabs the sword's handle and heaves to drag it. The metal slides surprisingly easily across the stone floor as she moves to where the gauntlets rest. Seeing this happen in the corner of his eye Aldrin yells through gritting teeth, "Pearl! What are you? Pearl could you help out over here please?"

Picking up the large metal rings by their chain tails Pearl turns to Aldrin and moving a thick moist lock of hair from her face she responds, "You're doing fine, I am doing important work too, got to collect this loot, I mean these magic items, to protect people from finding them and hurting themselves with either of them."

Aldrin goes to continue to demand Pearl's assistance, but is stopped when the load becomes significantly lighter, and looking over his shoulder he sees the champion lifting with Auburn, relieving even more of the heads weight than the red man had been. Turning to Eliza, Lady Tristalia calls, "It's up to you to get us back to the temple. lead the way."

"I can't do that," Eliza responds misinterpreting the comment.

"Don't worry we shouldn't need to fight anyone we just need someone to make sure the doors are open before we get to them, any Stormriders in their right mind will flee upon seeing this."

"Ok," Eliza nods turning to the door they entered through, and stepping to it she grabs her bag, and takes lead opening doors and moving small obstacles out of the way of the head's procession.

The sounds of conflict in the air have faded leaving only the patter of soft precipitation that continues to fall. The rain itself is not clean of the lands corruption with each drop sending an irritating sting, like from a bee, through the group's skin as it strikes their bare flesh. The streets are empty still, as the group return slowly carrying the lifeless head of Domavir like a large piece of furniture. The bridge, while damaged, maintains its hold underfoot as they cross and continue through even still silent streets, in their return to the temple of Silvermist.

Finally, after a long drudge, through the city that has felt almost dead for the group as they have walked completely undisturbed, they see the clearing in front of the temple and a phalanx of nearly forty more dragonborn soldiers, receiving a barrage of projectiles from within the temple. Immediately upon seeing the soldiers in a shield wall step toward the door, Auburn and Aldrin stumble dropping the head as it becomes too heavy for them. They see a bolt of silver mist pass beside them, and over the soldiers. Reforming ten feet in the air, Lady Tristalia releases a powerful burst that sends a cloud of the silver mist in a shockwave out slamming into the soldiers, drawing their attention. With a slowed decent, through the same divine magic, the champion yells down with an amplified voice, "Your fight is no longer here! Domavir, your leader, is slain for his crimes," and her hand points to the group with the lifeless head, before continuing, "You have three choices, run, and face the horrors of corruption you have been hiding here from, fight, but that will result in the same outcome for you as your commander has suffered, or surrender and allow our laws to judge you, and perhaps find mercy!"

Lady Tristalia's feet finally touch land once more and a moment silently passes as the coherence of the soldiers begins to corrode. A handful slowly break their ranks backing with hesitative steps away from the Temple. The slow steps turn into full sprints when crashing down from the air above lands the gryphon that has eliminated most of their flying forces, with yet another wyvern dead from the impact beneath it, and the eagle lion amalgamation releases a terrifying screech. The ranks are left broken, with nearly half the remaining force running to escape the city, the others snarl with hate, placing their weapons to the ground and kneeling with their hands placed behind their heads.

The temple doors open and from within is a flood of Blackgatians who circle around the champion, awaiting orders, with one of the sisters breaking the stir verbalizing the want, "Our Lady, what do we do now?"

"Form groups and begin taking these soldiers to the dungeon beneath the keep. Use muzzles. We wouldn't want them to overpower their escorts or attempting escape with their ability to breath lightning. I must summon a meeting of lords."

In the time the remaining soldiers surrender themselves, and the crowd pours from the temple. Eliza, Pearl, Aldrin and Auburn, slowly make their way to join the gathering, leaving the head in the middle of the street where it fell, and hearing the tail end of Lady Tristalia's statement Eliza looks to Aldrin asking, "What's a meeting of lords?"

Aldrin turns to the champion watching her step into the temple with a look of doubting curiosity on his face and he responds gesturing for his companions to follow him explaining, "Well, in training there was a class and we ran drills for the possibility that one was called to order. When Blackgate was founded, one such meeting was held. A peaceable meeting between the leaders of the five major nations. That first meeting was what formed Blackgate, and established it as a neutral zone, where no outside force could have presence. I don't think a second meeting has ever been called."

"That's right," Lady Tristalia stops Aldrin, responding, "There has only been the one, the authority to call one together was given to the Sisters of Silvermist, as the authority of law in the neutral port was given military body not connected to the major nations, the Blackguard. The leader of these two organizations are the only two other individuals allowed to hold seats at the table of discussion. Aldrin as the only anointed Blackguard remaining alive the Blackguard Commander's seat is yours."

Stepping forward to draw attention to herself Pearl asks, "Wait, but why call for this meeting?"

Aldrin doesn't give Lady Tristalia a chance to respond turning to Pearl exclaiming, "Look around us Pearl. Blackgate is in ruins, we are going to need funding and laborers to rebuild, and we have to remind the nations of the treaty, or risk having one of them claim this city as their own, and that would not be as easily overturned!"

Lady Tristalia puts a hand on Aldrin's shoulder, offering in a softer voice, "It is that we may show that Blackgate has returned to its proper leadership."

From the other side of the group Eliza, says, "And it will give Aldrin a chance to explain the mission Negmor has assigned us to."

"Negmor? Assigned mission? Whatever it is I am sure you can explain it to the council yourself, I insist you and Pearl come as my guests. The bravery and conviction you three and your friend have shown deserves you your turn to speak in whatever talks take place," Lady Tristalia explains giving Boop a gentle petting.

Eliza looks at Aldrin with worry growing on her face when the champion says three of them, and she asks, "It's temporary right?"

Aldrin looks back honestly stumped by the question, "What is?"

"You being this commander. I mean I am just guessing but it doesn't sound like you would be allowed to stay with us if you hold such a position. It is only temporary until you can pass it off to that other guy, right?"

"We'll talk about this later, but that does remind me. I should go help with the imprisoning of those soldiers," and before he can be asked any further questions, Aldrin turns and leaves. Moments later, feeling out of place, the others exit the temple as well and make their way to Aldrin's home.

12

A Peaceful Day

Two days pass with Auburn, Pearl, and Eliza, sitting around with Delira waiting to be called upon for the Meeting of Lords, with Aldrin seeming to avoid them the entire time. His absence isn't without reason, as each time Pearl and Eliza venture to the keep they find him or the remaining blackguard initiates busily working upon repairs and taking inventory of what remains of their stronghold. The one time Aldrin does return to his home, it is long after the others have gone to sleep leaving Eliza awake with a buzzing whirl in her mind of what the next step is, and she doesn't have a chance to see or speak to him before he is in the second-floor room with the hatch locked letting the sound of deep snores escape from him after only moments.

A third day comes and the morning holds a change in pace as the door to the small home is struck with a series of rapid knocks. Opened by Delira, the passageway reveals on the small porch, one of the sisters from the temple with hands clasped in front of herself. Greeting Delira with a smile the young acolyte asks, "Good morning. May I ask if the heroes Pearl, Auburn, and Eliza would be in at the moment?"

"Heroes? I like the sound of that," Pearl's voice rings from within as she approaches the door stretching. Relinquishing the doorway to Pearl, Delira returns to stoking a small fire to heat up some breakfast, and Pearl looks out to the sister asking, "What can I do for you?"

"Our Lady and Champion Tristalia wielder of the Holy Oath, has requested your presence at the temple in your earliest convenience before noon. It is on the matter of a discussion you have had with her prior."

"Alright, Lizzy, Auburn and I will be over shortly, but Aldrin isn't here right now."

"Commander Ironskin has already made his visit to receive the aforementioned conversation."

"Really? Alright then," Pearl nods to the sister, in a gesture to allow her to leave knowing her message has been passed on successfully, and the door is closed. Turning to the room, Pearl steps to the hatch down and opening it sees Eliza awake, sitting up with Boop in her lap, and both hold their eyes closed in a meditative state. Not wanting to break Eliza's focus but still wanting to get her attention Pearl calls in a pseudo-whisper, "Lizzy! Hey, Lizzy we finally have something to do."

Hearing the words, having her concentration instantly broken by the call from above, Eliza releases the breath in her lungs and stands before looking to Pearl asking, "Really? What is it?"

"We need to go to the temple, something about the last conversation we had with Trish."

"You mean Lady Tristalia? That means there is more information we need before we are to be her guests for this meeting she has asked us to attend."

"You want to go do that?"

"Sure, have you told Auburn?"

"He's up here, but still asleep I am sure he's heard us though."

"Pearl, we should wake him. Then we'll go meet up with Aldrin."

"Well, actually, Aldrin's been to the temple to get his briefing apparently."

"Oh, alright then."

Eliza steps to the ladder and begins to ascend, with Boop shooting up into the main floor past her. In the same time Eliza climbs to join her, Pearl steps to Auburn who sits up, asleep against the wall, and with a firm boot press into his side she wakes him saying, "Wake up. We're going to the Temple."

Opening a single eye Auburn growls, "I'm nae aff tae ony meetin o' th' lords, sae ye kin juist tell miss Tristalia that 'n' let me sleep."

"Fine sour puss," Pearl responds before extending her tongue at her red skinned companion.

Eliza steps to Pearl's side adding to the finished interaction, "At least we let him have the choice, let's go," as she steps past, toward the door.

The two step from the house, to be once more in the streets of the city of Blackgate. The atmosphere of the city these past two days, and this third day in particular has been exceptionally different from how it was when the group arrived. With the smell of freshly cut wood, and the sounds of people working together to repair the damaged structures of the town, filling the air, there is a life that has returned to the streets. A retheme that move with small groups transporting lumber and nails to construction sights, but that slows as every group see Pearl, Eliza, and Boop, stepping along the road so that respect can be shown for their heroes.

Sometime into the journey Pearl crosses her hands behind her head asking Eliza as they walk, "So what's with the meditating you were doing?"

"What do you mean," Eliza asks looking over into Pearl's eyes.

"Look I was just wondering what you were doing?"

"Father Bartholomeus taught me to meditate when I am confused, to help calm my emotions. So that they don't control me, so I don't release anything without intending to."

"And what's bothering you?"

"Nothing, I'm just worried about Aldrin, I think I may have said something that made him hate me, and now he is using this new position of his to avoid me. I am worried he is going to leave us."

"Don't be silly, Aldrin loves to hang around us, not to mention he would get bored far too quickly sticking around here now that he has seen so much of the world. He is just honestly swamped with work, until he feels someone is ready to replace him he is the person responsible for rebuilding the blackguard core."

"I guess you're right."

The walk to the temple seems short with the near jubilance that fills the people of the city, and through the large double doors, Eliza and Pearl are greeted by the sight of brand new pews filling most of the main chamber, and several of the acolytes in their vestments, scrubbing the floors and walls alongside a handful of strangers. Seeing the two step into the temple, one of the sisters stops her work for only long enough to gesture to the side room that the acolytes had been sealed in by the Stormriders, saying, "The Lady our Champion is waiting for you."

With a nod to the helpful woman, Eliza and Pearl step through the chamber to the room. Through the room's door they find, talking with a young man who hands her a small chest, Lady Tristalia. Dismissing the man she greets the two entering, "Greetings, I hope you have been resting well. I am sure that you have been informed of the reason I wished to see you, so I won't waste any of either of our times. The lords will be arriving later today and the Meeting of Lords will take place this evening. I am sure two well-traveled individuals as yourselves could guess that there is a bit of ceremony to this type of gathering, and I just wanted to ensure that we were on the same page in the code of conduct that is expected, as neither of you nor I was alive at the time of the first meeting. The arch mages of the elvish council, the lord king of the dwarvish monarchy, and the President of the gnomish confederation, all were alive for that meeting, so there is an expected process to be followed."

Pearl leans back rolling her eyes and releases in a groan, "Ugh, rules?"

"Don't worry they are not a lot, but we need to respect these individuals for the good of Blackgate."

"Fine, what do I have to wear?"

Tristalia allows a smirk to take her face before she covers it responding, "Nothing like that, I am sure the council will understand we just came from a military conflict. So just try to be somewhat presentable. Perhaps see if you can get an outfit though, the arch mages are the pinnacle of magic, and are likely to have items and enchantments about them permanently to allow them to see through illusion, if that is at all possible, and I do think being in the buff, as it were, would not strike them with an as much understanding as wearing a non-magical garment would," she explains looking at and gesturing to Eliza.

Not giving Eliza a chance to say anything Pearl jumps back in asking, "Do we know if Marcus is open again?"

Pulling away from the energetic response Lady Tristalia thinks for a moment responding herself, saying, "I don't know, you should check that out, he is pretty good at having spare outfits laying around, I mean," she turns again to Eliza, "I doubt any of them will fit you well or do your blessings justice, but there might be something you can have to wear."

Pearl turns to Eliza, and placing one of her cold wet hands on the teen's shoulder she continues her train of thought saying, "Marcus is the one that made this outfit and look how well it is holding together after all we have been through let alone the stuff I did before meeting you."

With a crossing hand wave Tristalia breaks the conversation hoping to return it to the intended topic saying, "Look I only ask that you try to take care of that before this evening. Now back to the matter at hand. When sitting on a council such as this one I ask that you please remember that you are guests, and thus I ask that you please keep your input into the talks to when you are addressed with a question. Remember these individuals have lived for more than a century each, several of the arch mages are approaching their millennium."

Eliza's eyes widen as she speaks for the first time in the conversation asking in surprise, "Really?"

"Really. Now do either of you have any questions?"

Pearl's eyes roll and she groans stepping to the door, "Yeah, yeah, keep our mouths shut unless we are asked for our legitimate points of view of what happened here. Sounds like we are having a school meeting about bullies and we are the ones who were bullied. Let's go see if we can talk to Marcus."

With a nod to the champion Eliza joins Pearl and the two step from the temple once more into the street. Pearl's slimy grip of webbed fingers wraps around Eliza's wrist as a realization strikes her, and she pulls the two into a jog. Tripping into a stumble that allows her to only barely remain standing under Pearl's pull on her arm, Eliza exclaims asking, "What are we doing?"

"I just realized we have spent two days locked up in an old musky house and I haven't showed you the city. So, I am going to get you to Marcus then I am going to show you my stomping grounds, and tell you some stories for why you don't need to be so worried about Aldrin trying to cut and run." The two, with Boop struggling to keep up, quickly make their way through the streets of the city, leaving very little chance to appreciate the neighborly behavior of the citizens rebuilding their homes, or to accept the signs of thanks that are cast toward them as they dart past. Finding their way into two separate districts, easily discernable by the walls they pass through, the two women make their way to a small building sandwiched between two others in a way that makes it look almost squeezed into place. Pearl looks up and gestures to Eliza who puts her hands on her knees breathing heavy from the hustle, and with a laugh Pearl says, "Well once you catch your breath.

We're here. This is Marcus'.'"

Eliza wraps her hands around her stomach as it releases low rumbling growl, and she looks up to the building, in surprisingly good repair compared to the other structures of the city. The faded cream-colored paint flakes, on the front wall around the single window and door that leads in, which Pearl steps to as she sees Eliza straighten back up with easing breaths asking, "Can we get something to eat after this?"

"You're hungry? You had a double helping of eggs this morning."

"I know, I am still hungry though."

"Sure thing. We can get something after this," Pearl says with a laugh opening the door, and the two step in.

The building is well kept and a complete juxtaposition of the outside of most of the city's structures. There are clean shelves of well-polished wood holding bolts of varying cloths neatly kept within the small space in a way that makes it feel roomier than would be expected. The far wall from the entrance, with almost new paint beaming from it in a bright green, holds on its base two waiting closed doors painted a soft caramel color. Two plush chairs sit in the path to the rooms end, empty, waiting to be used. When the front door swings open a small bell hung above it is struck releasing a ring through the room. A moment passes after the women step into the building before a smooth moderate to high pitched old man's voice responds to the bell's sound muffled through one of the back doors, "One moment please."

Stepping to one of the chairs Pearl falls into it yelling back, "Take your time Marcus, we're friends."

The instant Pearl's words find their end the left door slams open revealing a thin framed old man with a large nose that holds up small misshapen spectacles with a forehead the doesn't end, instead extending to leave him mostly bald. His thin wiry white hair clings desperately to the sides of his head protruding out like messy wings. Peering across the hall of a room the man's voice asks, "That wouldn't be Pearly Sarya. Would it be?"

"Hello there, old friend," Pearl exclaims standing from the seat with a jump.

Pearl's appearance throws the old man back with worry in his eyes and pointing to her with a shaking hand, which holds on the back of its wrist a small pillow impaled for several sewing needles protruding from it, he asks, "What happened to you?"

"Well that is a long story," Pearl says placing a hand behind her head awkwardly.

Running to Pearl and grabbing the coat tails of her jacket Marcus looks with almost a sorrow in his eyes at the garment, mumbling under his breath, "Your seams are worn far beyond where they should and your soaking wet, with, salt water?" Standing back up the old man's eyes hold scorn as he turns Pearl to face him as he asks, "What have you done to this poor suit," and Pearl's seafoam green-blue skin finally registers in his mind and he leans back confused asking, "What happened to you?"

"Like I said it's a long story. Look we need a couple things from you."

"A new suit for yourself no doubt, one water resistant I am guessing, based on your complexion. What else?"

"Well my friend here, Eliza, needs an outfit, something like that one, but we are going to be doing a lot of traveling, some to the north pole, and possibly some jungle and desert exploration."

"So, you need something that can be segmented, to be warm enough in freezing temperatures, and also can be made cool enough for humid and arid heats. If you don't mind my asking young one, who made the outfit you are wearing," Marcus asks looking Eliza up and down with almost overly focused eyes.

Uncomfortable from the man's wandering eyes Eliza is silent, slowly pulling away, as he awaits a response. Pearl, in an attempt to break the tension, responds in Eliza's stead saying, "Well that is the thing, those aren't real, it is a magically created illusion."

Eliza's eyes widen in worried anger at Pearl, not knowing what the old man eyeing her may do with the information Pearl is sharing. To her pleasant surprise though Marcus simply shifts forward contemplatively as his eyes continue to trace her curves responding, "That makes much more sense."

Suddenly intrigued by his words Eliza's head tilts and she asks, "How does that make more sense?"

"Most wouldn't notice, and that is probably why you could walk around the way you are without getting the unwanted attention you were worried I would impress upon you, but my trained eyes caught it. The fabric of your illusion is too light, it almost floats massless from your curves," Marcus responds turning from both woman before continuing, "Alright I will have your new outfits ready in a week's time."

"There is one more thing," Eliza hesitatively says raising a hand to try to get the man's attention.

"And that would be?"

"Well I have the ability to extend a pair of wings from my back."

"Oh really, now that is interesting but it shouldn't be an issue with what I have in mind. Good bye."

"Actually, Marcus could Lizzy borrow an outfit? At least for this evening, it doesn't have to be anything elegant, she just can't rely on her illusion tonight," Pearl asks before the old man can step away back to the other room.

"You really had an agenda coming here, fine, come with me young woman."

Eliza steps with the man to the back of the room and he ushers her through the right door. Inside the cramped closet, is barely enough room for the two to stand without touching amongst a plethora of manikins and body form stitching stands that pile up the walls, each clothed in its own unique outfit. Looking around the small room Eliza is amazed, and asks semi-sarcastically, "Been busy?"

"Oh these, no these are failed, canceled, and disappointing projects."

"Oh," Eliza breaths looking at the array of beautiful but practical outfits.

"Hands up," the man says after pulling a bundle of cloth from the pile. Confused Eliza complies partially bringing her arms up to make right angles with her elbows, which spurs an immediate reaction from the man who raises his voice, "All the way, come come."

Worry fills Eliza, as she complies with the further demand, but that feeling is quelled when the man throws over her the bundle of cloth, which turns out to be a dress as he pulls it down over her. A single seamless piece of a deep green fabric with holes cut for a head and arms the dress sits loosely draping from Eliza's shoulders and chest. With a single swift motion that doesn't hurt Eliza, Marcus uncoils the enormous scarf of braided hair from its resting place around her neck and down her back out of the for loops down to the back of her knees, and he pulls it from beneath the dress' fabric. The cloth falls slowly to be loose for only a second before another strip of cloth is thrown around her and pulled tight in an instant, with a beautiful bow tied from the ends set on her hip. The light soil brown of the sash seemingly enhances the green of the dress that it pulls to Eliza's form causing the simple outfit to almost seem elegant. With Eliza's lush braid of sky blue hair wrapped around her again in a way to look almost like a cloak, she is ushered back out of the closet where Pearl is struck starring with widening eyes before gasping, "Wow. Marcus you're incredible."

"Don't say such things I will get a big head," the man responds pushing the two back into the street.

The day passes by. Pearl walks Eliza around Blackgate, first to a bar where they get a bundle of snacks, and then to several other places that Pearl holds with some minor significance to her memory, and the sky once again begins transforming into the deep reds of the evening as the two begin to make their way back to the temple. It is nearly dark when they finally arrive once more at the large double doors.

Pearl goes to open the door, but it is opened from the other side, revealing Lady Tristalia who stops as she sees the two stood before her.

Confused by the champion moving to leave the temple Pearl asks, "Um, where are you going?"

Pointing in the direction of the river Lady Tristalia responds with a similarly confused tone, "To the meeting of lords," and realizing the confusion she rolls her eyes back in her head explaining, "You thought it was here. No, we don't have a room in the temple large enough. Come you can walk with me to the keep. It will probably look better if my guests for the meeting arrive with me anyway." So, Pearl and Eliza join Lady Tristalia, and flanking her sides, they walk through the dark streets to the keep.

13

Meeting of the Lords

A large chamber, lit by lamps hung five feet apart along the walls, holding within it an almost equally large table lined with chairs, waits with three fancily dressed human strangers all sitting in silence as Pearl, Eliza, and the Champion arrive. The metal of the Champion's armor rings with the clap of Pearl and Eliza's boots steps into the room. Before the silence can become awkward the door they entered through reopens and Aldrin, wearing a heavy black cloak, and not in his exoskeleton suit, along with Ben at his side, holding a pad of parchment, greets the arrivals, "Greetings, Lady Champion of Silvermist. Sorry I haven't been around the house, you two, it has been hectic trying to clean up around here. I have to go greet the lords as they arrive You can come with me, or just have a seat as we wait."

Happy to see Aldrin in good spirits Eliza smiles responding, "I'll come with you."

"Alright let's go," Aldrin responds with a head nod back to the door, and he leads Eliza away leaving Pearl, Lady Tristalia, and Ben to sit in the awkward silence of a large room holding only people present not for each other's company but for a matter of other importance. Aldrin leads Eliza quickly through the keep's halls to a point that seems almost to be in the complete opposite corner of the structure as the chamber they left, not once saying a word. When he finally stops, the two stand in front of an old inconspicuous door, and he turns to Eliza explaining, "I know this goes without saying and between you and Pearl I don't have to worry about this from you, but remember we have to be respectful." Eliza nods with a smile not saying a word. With a nod himself Aldrin turns back to the door and pulling a ring of keys from his side, he opens it revealing the room within. Small with only the light of the lamps in the hall lighting it, the room is in surprisingly good condition compared to its door with the only thing of note about it is a strange set of glyphs carved into the floor.

Without another word Aldrin steps into the room. Turning to the right of the door he removes from the wall a sheathed sword, whose case is a rich black leather. The motion is obviously meant to appear ceremonial with slow precision filled with intent. With one hand on the black leather of the sheath and the other on the worn black leather of the handle the blade is drawn revealing a brilliant polished Damascus steel blade which is almost black with razor edges that glistens in the minor amount of light from the lamps in the hall.

Setting the sheath to lean against the wall again Aldrin rests the point of the sword to the edge of the carvings in the floor. Bringing his free hand to the handle and shifting his other on the leather grip, he presses the blade's tip against the floor, and after a moment a slit opens up and the blade pushes half its length into the stone. Instantly the carvings spark into life, as if they had been filled with Aldrin's black powder igniting like a fuse which leave its path lit with a magical white glow that illuminates the room. After a second the entirety of the glyph is illuminated with the strange magic glow and Aldrin lets the sword rest embedded in the floor where it rests, and he takes a single step away to find Eliza at his side, staring wide eyed at the spectacle.

The quiet of the air is broken when a flash of light pops three feet above the circle's center. A sound like that of stone striking stone mixed with a balloon bursting escapes the point of the flash. Another pop, and a third follow in blindingly bright strobing rapid succession, which forces Aldrin and Eliza to look away. After the third pop, five elves appear standing in the small room. Removing her helmet one of the elves steps to Aldrin, extending a hand she explains in a voice that no matter how stern and official, has a gentle soft beauty to it, "I presume you are the new commander of the Blackguard. Greetings, I am Ava Aradi High Commander of the military forces of the elven nation, the full elven council were unable to attend but attending with me are Arch Mage Cordian Valavor Master of Divination Magic and Seer of the Elven coucil," behind her, a man in long multi-layered purple robes decorated with gold embroidered accents raises his hand with a nod to Aldrin, while keeping his eyes focused with a deep discerning look on Eliza, "Arch Mage Ortidian Numinur master of conjuration magic," which ushers the other man, significantly younger in appearance with light brown hair, and no beard, in contrast to the white long beard and head of hair of the other. The man's heavy blue robe similarly accented with gold threading falls to his elbow as he gives a nod to Aldrin. Finally, the woman's hand finds its way into Aldrin's as she finishes explaining, "and two stenographers for the accounts and records to be held within our archives."

"I would say it was a pleasure to make your acquaintance if the nature of our meeting was not in such dire circumstances," Aldrin responds with a nod of his own as his hand, shakes Ava's. "The meeting chamber is prepared in the same room that the first was held," Aldrin continues as his hand is released so that he can gesture out into the hall.

The younger mage smiles, and with a nod turns to the other saying, in voice that fits his thin, short frame, "I don't know about you Valavor, but I don't personally remember where that room would be, based on our host's gesture I assume we are not the last to arrive, would you mind leading the way."

His gaze, not leaving Eliza who attempts to avoid the attention by looking to any of the other faces, the old elf takes a step using his staff, made of a purple material, with a single white gem hovering an inch off its upper end, he steps past Aldrin and Eliza, responding in an equally fitting voice for his age and hunched over stature, "That would not be impractical. Black Commander, as to provide you insight, the dwarves are preparing their transportation incantation now they will likely be another twenty minutes, you may wish to go to your docks and greet the gnomes whose ship should be arriving soon."

Aldrin looks in confusion responding, "Ship?"

"Oh yes, I forget myself sometimes. The Gnomish confederate utilized our magics for some time but have found their own modes of rapid transportation in recent centuries. A move they have committed to in order to avoid any reliance on powers that to them are foreign."

"They don't use magic at all?"

"Ha, ha, no young commander, they use magic, but don't like using services provided, no matter how freely, from other peoples, they don't do this as the dragonborn, in distaste for other beings, but for fear of building a reliance of what is not sustainable through their own efforts. It is an admirable position for them to hold."

"Alright then. Well I will head out to greet them, which means I can escort you most of the way to the chamber then. You didn't mention the Dragonborn. What is the nature of their arrival?"

"It would be considered an act of war on the nation of the descendants of dragons if I were to scry on their leadership. As I said, they unlike the gnomes, seek separation for the mere dislike of the people of other nations, based on their heritage."

"Alright then. As to not risk insulting them by not being present for their arrival, let me sheath Commander's Blade," Aldrin responds with an appreciative nod to the arch mage before stepping to the sword in the floor, and pulling it free he returns it to its holder. Turning back to the hall and keeping the weapon in his hand, Aldrin takes lead saying, "Follow me, this way then."

Getting to the front hall of the keep Aldrin gestures in the direction of the chamber where Pearl and Lady Tristalia sit quietly waiting, and he turns to the exit ushering Eliza to follow him. The collection of Elf ambassadors step from Aldrin's company to find the meeting room. The night sky sits darkly overhead and Aldrin walks with Eliza by his side both stepping silently to the cities docks. The silence is broken however, when Eliza looks down to the back of Aldrin's head asking, "This is temporary right?"

"What do you mean," Aldrin asks without turning, continuing to walk for the docks.

"This. You as this commander. You will be coming with us to find the shard, won't you?"

"I don't know Eliza, we need to get through tonight before I would be able to say anything toward that."

"Alright," Eliza responds relegating the pair back into silence for the rest of the walk.

The docks are quiet, with a strange slurping sound in the air of what would be the lapping waves instead becoming undulations of the thick black sludge like water. No later do Eliza and Aldrin reach the outer island that holds the majority of the city's docks, when a new strange sound echoes in from the distance. Like a roll of thunder consistently rumbling from a point on the horizon, which grows louder as a singular light in that direction seems to come closer. on the horizon, the light expands, flickering, the source of the sound, approaching at a furious speed. In mere seconds the sound grows deafening, and the light grows to reveal a monstrous flame blasting from the rear of a ship made entirely of metal.

The jet of fire cuts off suddenly, and several smaller blazes replace it shooting from the ship's front slowing the vessel's approach as it comes close to the docks. The crew drop an anchor and bring the ship to a stop. While that happens, a metal gang plank extends itself from its side lowering onto the planks below.

From the ship's deck step three small forms, each only just taller than three feet in height each. Aldrin stands waiting with Eliza as one of the individuals, wearing dirtied leathers smudged with black grease, lifts a pair of goggles from his eyes, up onto a leather cap that presses down on his head, and looks up to Aldrin, staring with a stern look in his eyes and no discernable expression visible from beneath his large bushy mustache. The man's large nose nearly twice the size in proportion to what a human's nose would be on his face, foreshadows the man's nasally voice as he addresses the two stood before him, "Greetings, we are the representatives from the gnomish confederates, your commander is expecting us."

With a nod Aldrin presents the pommel of the sword on his side saying, "The commander greets you."

"Oh, a greeting from the commander himself, this is a treat. Well, let us not waste time. Please lead the way to the meeting area."

"I can arrange a meal and lodging for your crew if you would wish."

"Oh, you needn't do that. The entirety of the crew is before you and we are all to be in the council for the meeting."

Eliza looks with surprise at the small man asking, "You piloted that entire ship on your own?"

The man laughs responding, "Gnomish engineering my dear."

Aldrin turns saying, "Well if it wasn't for the circumstances, I would say it was a pleasure to make you acquaintance."

"Don't be silly, it is still nice to make your acquaintance, regardless of the circumstances. Now about leading us to the meeting spot," the man says gesturing to the path.

"Right, this way."

Aldrin leads the group quickly to the keep, and like with the ambassadors from the elvish society, he directs them toward the meeting chamber before stepping away with a gesture to bring Eliza with him. The two of them return to the same back room and drawing his sword he presses it again into the ground where it had been placed before. Again, the glyphs spark to life, and begin to glow, with a gentle low hum sitting in the air. A moment passes without a sign of the popping effect that preceded that arrival of the elves. That moment becomes a minute, before Eliza, turns to Aldrin to ask, "Did you do something wrong?"

Aldrin turns to respond but is cut off when the familiar pop cracks from the room. The quick secession of mini explosions ends revealing three bulky forms each only four feet in height, but muscularly built. One of the forms dressed in a purple outfit with a thick head of red hair tied back in a thin braid, that pales in comparison to the lush braids of his large bushy beard steps forward giving a deep bow to Aldrin and Eliza saying in a deep voice, as if the ground underfoot is speaking, a voice free of the accent that would be expected from the time the two have spent with Auburn, "Greetings and salutations from the Kingdoms of the dwarven people, I introduce to you, new Blackgate Commander, to the Lord King Gregoric Ferrix Heartholm," the man's hands gesture to one of the other two, wearing black and gold plate armor with a thick coal black beard almost leaping for escape from beneath the fancily embellished barbute helm, "and the High Mage of the Lord King's court, Bellar Ironstone," he finishes with a motion toward the other figure, who holds a staff in one hand, next to his heavy brown robes, with intricate patterns of yellow stitching that make the garment more extravagant than it would normally be.

"Greetings, I am Aldrin Ironskin, Commander of the Blackguard."

"Aye, and who's this lovely lass by yer side," a deeper voice filled with the regal strength of bred lordship, as the armored king of the dwarves steps past his herald to take Elia's hand and great her by giving it a kiss.

"That is a companion of mine who was instrumental in the freeing of Blackgate, Eliza Black."

"Ah, Eliza Black, a brash name for a fair woman," King Gregoric responds with a short bow to Eliza releasing her hand.

Eliza draws her hand into the other bashfully pulling herself ever so slightly away, as her cheeks become warm with a blush from the attention. Before an awkward silence has the opportunity to form Aldrin turns to Eliza to ask, "I need to wait here to greet the ambassadors from Drak'thilar. Perhaps you can show the Lord King and his attendants to the meeting chamber?"

With a nod Eliza turns and gestures from Aldrin into the hall and begins walking. With shared bowing nods each of the dwarven individuals step past Aldrin and begin following Eliza. Inevitably, the door comes into view and a tension that had filled Eliza in the silent walk, from a feeling unfamiliar to her of having possibly admiring eyes watching her every move lessens, and her strides lengthen and quicken to bring her to it. She opens the passage and holds it there for the ambassadors to enter before her. Each gives her an appreciative nod, with no further extension of the action that gave Eliza the uncomfortable feeling, and they step to a set of seats at the table. After the three have past her Eliza moves around the room and joins Pearl, Ben and Lady Tristalia.

A low murmur rests in the air for several minutes with the four factions sitting at the table mingling amongst their own groups on matters of the nations from which they hale, until the door once more opens with Aldrin stood gesturing in for a group of five forms to enter. All hold a visage very similar to the ones that made up the occupying force, with the exception that none of them bear scales of blue coloring, nor are they quite as towering in form. While still taller than Aldrin by nearly a foot, the five stand staring in, noticeably shorter than the stormriders. The room goes silent and fills with unease in a way that had not happened with any other group's arrival.

The one that leads the five is gowned in a white cloak that hides the steel plate armor that is strapped tightly to her, over the overlapping small leaf like brilliant red scales that cover her body broken by a segment of larger almost cream covered plates of scale that runs down her throat and continues all the way to the end of her tail. Gold rings clash against the hard horns, which protrude from the upper back of her elongated head like the horns of a young ibex, through which they are hung. A confidence in this person's stride pulls the scornful attention of the room to her as she steps in and to a section of empty chairs and with forceful movements sits.

The attention drawn completely to the one that leads their group, nearly causes the other four to go unnoticed as they take their seats. One with scales that glisten like leaves and plates of silver with what looks like a silver fin protruding from the top of his head like a mohawk, is equally armored as the first sits to her right. One gowned in robes almost identical to the elder elven ambassador, and scaled with gold across his form, possessing a less elongated, rounder and wider maw which holds four short vine like golden tendrils to it that appear almost like a beard, sits to her left. The last two sit on the outer edges of the group of three both clothed in loose but fancy looking outfits, one with a thinner long maw, scaled with brown down his throat and chest and green over the rest of his form, and the other, with a skull similar to the gold scaled individual, is scaled with what looks like fragments of brass, with no tendril stubble instead with three rigid almost bony mounds that run in rows down the back of her head.

Aldrin steps from the door in the time that the dragonborn individuals take their seats, and he joins Pearl, Eliza, and Lady Tristalia. When everyone has seated, he speaks to the room, "It is in this hour that I see representatives from all of the major civilizations of our world that I am most grateful for the rapid response. I ask now if we are ready to begin with the proceedings of this Meeting of Lords."

One of the strangers who were sat in the room before Eliza, Pearl, and Lady Tristalia arrived stands, stating, "The CEO of the Excavatory Group of the Lost Continent, are willing to begin the proceedings."

Ava stands responding with a resounding officiality in her voice, "The ambassadors of the elven people accept the greeting and are willing to begin the proceedings."

As Ava sits the large mustached gnome drops from his seat to have only the goggles on the top of his head visible from the opposite side of the table, and climbing onto his chair he turns back to face the room again exclaiming in a similar way, "The Gnomish Confederacy accepts the greeting and are willing to begin the proceedings."

The leader of the gnome group returns to his seat and continuing in the counter clockwise introduction the herald in purple stands from his seat with only his head and upper chest visible he strikes his pectoral adding, "The Kingdom Under the Mountainous South, accepts the greeting and is willing to begin the proceedings."

Finally, with the herald returning to his seat the red scaled dragon woman stands with a natural glare in her eyes, and lets out her growling voice, which somehow retains a femininity to it, into the room saying, "The ambassadors for the Drak'thilarian people are willing to begin the proceedings."

While this process transpires the scraping of quills on parchment, and the ting of their tips dipping into ink vials sits under the powerful voices that come from the speakers of each group. With the lead ambassador of the group from Drak'thilar sitting again, her confirmation said, Aldrin stands again. Scanning over the people sat at the table his voice bears a confidence that is new to him as he says, "The first order of business we must discuss is the reassertion of the initial treaty that formed Blackgate as a neutral zone. Not to do this would make any other discussion here meaningless."

A murmuring fills the room as Aldrin sits down again with the robed dwarf whispering into his king's ear, and the other groups discussing amongst themselves. Leaning over to his herald King Gregoric says something quietly and gestures with a wave to the table. The dwarf stands and clearing his throat looks to Aldrin before turning to the elves saying, "It is the will of my lord to make clear that some form of recompense be expressed from the elvish kingdom."

Immediately shooting to her feet Commander Ava exclaims with her eyes locked on the sitting armored dwarf, "For what reason might I ask would you think such a thing is reasonable to call for?"

The herald leans over for his king to speak softly into his ear, and after a moment he stands straight responding to Ava who impatiently presses her fists onto the table, "My lord expresses concern for the information we received about the elven government striking a bargain with the occupying force only two weeks before the force was overthrown, the nature of said deal, to our knowledge, was to gain access to the port and it is the belief of the king of the south that such a deal breaks the original treaty that also stated that no action would be taken to deal with any force to overthrow Blackgate, without a meeting of lords having discussed such actions before they are acted upon."

"Are you insane? Our researchers have not only been thrown several months back in terms of understanding the magic that is causing the corruption, but the people of this city were starving! You can't seriously be looking to punish us for helping innocents."

The herald receives further instruction responding, "It is not a matter of the reason of the action but that the action was taken."

Pearl shoots up from her seat enraged, yelling in the direction of the dwarves, "Wait, you are asking for compensations for a good deed, just because of some rule?"

Eliza shoots up staring at Pearl saying, "Pearl," and in a hushed tone continues, hoping to not be heard, she says, "We are supposed to be respectful." Turning back to the room, Eliza takes a deep breath before saying in an amplified tone, "I have to apologize for my companion's outburst, you have to understand we had to break the rules of the land to free the people of Blackgate. I think the main point she was trying to make was that if it were up to a bureaucratic process, the people of Blackgate would very possibly be dead, and there would be no point to have this meeting at all. I would ask, without the intervention of the call of the faith of

Silvermist's champion, how long can it take to call one of these meetings to order?"

Pearl looks to Eliza, addressing the room, with a look of continued appreciative surprise before, with a nod and a shrug as though to say that Eliza was correct in her assumption of her intent, she sits back down to let Eliza be the focus of their side of the round table. The groups around the table look into their own with the question as they contemplate not only their own willingness but their perception of the willingness of the other nations present, and with each of them glancing toward the five members bearing the appearance of a draconic heritage, Ava, and the herald of the Dwarven kin both sit again. The low murmur that fills the room with contemplation is broken with a voice that has yet to be heard within the chamber, a sagely, fatty cheeked, voice which comes from the golden scaled individual who says from his seat, "Far too long to have been any good."

"Serves that you would say that it would take too long to do any good, these occupiers were of your kin," Pearl stands again, exclaiming with a pointed finger.

A gentle fury shoots from Eliza and Aldrin to Pearl pushing her back into her seat with only the glare of their eyes, and in the same moment, with slow strained movements, like those that show old age taking a bodies mobility, the golden scaled dragonborn rises and looks over the gathering around the table explaining first to Eliza and Aldrin, "Your friend is correct to be angered, a great evil was carried out and though it had no connection to our nation the perpetrators, as we have been informed held our appearance and likely came from the same heritage that birthed all the races of dragon's blood. I believe I speak for all of Drak'Thilar when I say we had no connection to the group known as Stormriders, and we condemn them and their actions with the same ire as each of you."

The sage of the group from Drak'Thilar eases back into his seat leaving Eliza as the only person still standing, and suddenly feeling the eyes of the room on her she feels her face warm with fluster but she speaks through the attention saying, "So, I reassert what the commander asked before, can we please," she takes a deep nervous swallow of saliva, "reassert the treaty that was put in place in the forming of Blackgate?"

Dropping as quickly into her seat as she can, Eliza feels Aldrin's hand on her shoulder, and looking to him sees a soft smile pointing her way before he stands. Addressing the room Aldrin reiterates, "The motion is official, shall we continue this discussion and reassert the treaty, or are these discussions over, before they have even begun?" With that said Aldrin sits again and Eliza watches him stare intently at the room of discussing groups.

After a few moments of the room being filled once more with murmuring of intergroup conversation, the room becomes silent with Ava standing once more announcing, "We agree to reaffirm the treaty." Following this, each of the other four groups rise in the same order they had introduced themselves, and in their own words each leader agrees to the reaffirmation before sitting once more.

Aldrin stands again with the room's full reaffirmation adding to the discussion, "The next order of business needs to be the reconstruction and bolstering of the city."

"This is our assessment of the damages," a representative from the group of humans says standing as the other two with him stand and step to each of the other groups handing them each a parchment with information relaying estimated costs of repair. Leaning onto the table, the man continues, "As this city is a neutral territory, with all governing bodies having a hand in the longevity of that fact, and taking into the consideration the actions with, and the people who were, the cause of these damages, it is in our recommendation that the governments of the elves and the dragonborn bear fifty percent of the expense together, with the remaining fifty percent covered by the remaining three nations."

The red scaled dragonborn's fist slams down on the table and she leaps to her feat responding with a furious growl, "What insolence! It was just agreed upon that the force that attacked the city are as much our fault as a crew of pirates is the fault of their race!"

The armored dwarf, the king of his people, rises to the woman's outburst, calmly addressing her, his voice deep and reverberating giving him a dominating present like a father scolding a child, "That wisnae 'greed upon. Ainlie that Blackgate as a neutral zone is mair important than letting it fall. Still we can't trust ye."

The woman turns with anger in her face to glare at the dwarf, but before she can say anything Eliza's voice grows softly into the air, "Excuse me. I know I do not hold a status equal to any of yours and I don't mean to speak out of turn, but may I say something?"

Rising from his seat the elder elf responds for the room, "You need not worry about speaking out of turn, you are one among us because of your actions, speak your mind child," gesturing for Eliza to continue.

With a nod to Cordian, with a feeling of empowerment filling her with his words, Eliza continues, "Well, I think your all in the wrong." The room which had been murmuring with discussions amongst the several groups becomes silent with all eyes becoming wide, focused on Eliza. Gesturing to Aldrin and Pearl, she continues, "Not to be to forward, but we are the ones that set into motion the actions to free Blackgate. What did any of you do? The elves tried to deal with the illegal occupiers to continue what I can only assume is important research based on what was said to this council, yes, and the occupiers were definitely of draconic heritage which has so readily been pointed out, but there was something about them that was unlike the five with us, there was something unnatural about them, for instance their leader stood twenty or so feet tall, but the rest of you are just as at fault, inaction is an action. Again, I do not mean to speak out of turn but was there any action to call a meeting like this before Blackgate was liberated? With all of that in mind could it be possible for you all to agree that what matters now is helping Blackgate and the people who live here repair."

Standing, Lady Tistalia gives Eliza a nod saying, "Very well said. As the champion of Silvermist, I propose to this council that any aid deemed to be granted to our city be presented equally to a minimum with further charity as welcome but unnecessary, as to avoid any attempt to shame any one nation."

The murmur returns to the room as all of the standing individuals find their seats once more. Several minutes of deliberation within each group pass and Eliza sits desperately trying to not be overly self-conscious about the way she spoke to the world's leaders. The quiet is finally broken by the voice of the gnome who has presented himself as the leader of his group saying as he stands on his chair, "I for one agree with the sentiment presented by the guest to this meeting," and looking directly at Eliza he continues, "You may not have the wisdom of age that most of us have, nor do you have a position of authority like us, but please do not be afraid to speak your mind. Your words held more truth than most of the words said at the last of these meetings."

Eliza blushes and averts her eyes, both as a sign of respect and of embarrassment, as the man with a large bushy mustache sits again. Quickly after the lead representative of the gnomes speaks Ava stands, agreeing, "As one of the nations targeted for blame it should go without saying that we agree to terms that don't unjustly assume to secure correct recompense for perceived, if not actual, miss deeds. As a matter of respect to each of our fellow nations we refrained from verbalizing as such until one of the others had spoken first."

The red dragonborn stands calmly, and expresses with a nod, "We too agree."

A look of frustration forms on the armored dwarf's face, and with a glance to his herald he half-heartedly gestures toward the table. The motion ushers the fancily dressed man to stand and respond to all that has been said, "While it is not to my king's liking, he agrees to what has been said to this point and will split the burden of aiding the neutral zone equally."

A clap rings from the three humans as their leader stands again saying, "It is settled then, the amount of payment due by each nation to insure equal proof of desire for the continued peace between our nations will be equal from each nation, then the matter of payment from each nation should be agreed upon, in knowing that dwarven architecture is worth often four times more than the value it equates to in labor, as is gnomish engineering."

"The laborers will be sent for honest wage from our kin," the herald expresses at the whim of his king behind him.

The gnome leader stands again on his chair agreeing, "As will necessary engineers from our nation be offered contracts to improve upon the city's defensive capability."

"As for the rest of us, I think it best if we aid the city through monetary means, as for the strengths of the elves is the use of magic, not something that we should leave to have fall in the hands of any other group in the future, and a presence of soldiers from those with dragon heritage, would threaten in its very nature the existence of the treaty," the man continues, "That I believe will conclude the necessary proceedings of this meeting."

Aldrin looks to Lady Tristalia with both of them holding a slight look of worry in their eyes as the other groups of ambassadors nod to themselves, and make motions as to stand. Before the room can be filled with the clatter of chairs being pushed out to allow their mounters to stand Aldrin leaps to his feet asking, to the room, gathering the full attention of the collection of representatives, "What about the ones we captured?"

Still moving to pack parchments into his bag the man from the group of humans responds while dismissing the issue with a hand wave, "I am sure the other members of the council, would agree that the Commander of Blackgate can handle sentencing and punishment. This meeting was more to come to an agreement on the nature of the treaty and international aid for your devastated city."

"But what about their leader?" Pearl exclaims leaping up to join

Aldrin in leaning against the table.

"Last we were informed he had been slain through the Lady of
Silvermist's judgement, so all that is left is disposal of the corpse. A matter
well suited for you and other civilians."

Pearl's jaw drops in surprise from the man's callous disregard shown
toward her, but before she can respond with a flurry of anger filled diatribes,
Eliza's voice once again fills the room which goes still, if only to attempt to
hear the meager response, "There are others like him. Not his servants, other
leaders working for a group with evil intentions."

This information visibly perplexes the room, and in what could be
the closest thing to a unilateral agreement to sit and hear more, the youngest
of the elves sits and turns to the his elder asking, "You never said anything
about more to the group, and as the arch mage of divination you out of
everyone should know the goings on of the world, as it deals with matters
relevant to our posts. Is what she says true?"

"I am unsure. It was my perception that this group was a lowly band
of brigands so I didn't even waste the energy to divine such information
about their leader," the white-haired elf responds stroking his beard.

Pearl looks with worry at Eliza, asking, "I don't think we should say
anything, Lizzy."

Looking to Pearl, Eliza nods, responding, "Do you trust me to not
endanger you?" Pearl looks with surprise at Eliza's question and simply nods.
The response prompts Eliza to turn back to the room continuing, "On our
way here we came across an unmapped island on which was a palace. Within
we were introduced to a construct that spoke for a wizard by the name of
Negmor, who informed us of a group of individuals seeking an item known
as a Shard of Prime."

The room goes silent with the end of Eliza's statement and a sudden
gasp is released from several of the people sat at the table. Pearl goes to say
something to Eliza but is stopped by Aldrin's hand which is placed to her
mouth with a finger of his other hand placed to his lips. The green scaled

female, one of the individuals to gasps leaps to her feet to ask loudly in a distinctly young woman's voice with the growl that is innate in her people's accent, "You're saying that the Shard of Prime is in the Broken Isles?"

Turning to face the woman Eliza responds, "We don't know, if the group we were informed of thought it was the only option, one of them wouldn't have been on the island, of Ortoung."

The younger of the elven wizards recoils in his seat asking, "Are you saying Negmor told you there is another group of those things just off the coast of our continent? Ava this needs to be looked into immediately!"

"You can't do that!"

The man looks almost insulted at Eliza's response, and with that look filling his voice with concern he asks, "Why possibly not?"

"As it is now, the group has not attacked any city to your knowledge, correct?"

"Well I guess not."

"If they are just searching then they know they wouldn't be able to fight any of your nations, investigation into their work might simply tip the hand to our knowledge of them being there. That isn't to say do nothing, increasing the number forces on the coast nearest the island would probably not draw their attention."

"She makes a good point Ortidian," Ava says from her seat beside the young elf wizard before turning to Eliza continuing, "But we can't simply leave who these people are to search unimpeded, a group should be formed to search on behalf of the governments."

"No! I mean not one created by governments. If what Negmor told us is true, then there must be some treaty even older than the one that maintains Blackgate, and having any agents to such a group would make the possibility of trusting those individuals to not instead seek the shard for their people to have sole possession of it nonexistent. Let us continue as that group, please, as Negmor had asked of us."

"'n' whit mak's us sure that we kin trust ye," the dwarven king's voice rumbles through the air.

"You can't," Eliza's head drops with the words leaving her mouth in an almost defeated tone, "We are nobodies, people from Blackgate, outcasts from our homes, people without homes. All you can know about us is that we say we have spoken with a dwarven wizard by the name Negmor, and that we on our own volition rose to fight these occupiers. That is the point, if a search for something like what we have been told this shard is, were to become known by those already searching for it, it would be better if they didn't believe that group to be backed but simply a set of treasure seekers. If they think they can defeat us they are not likely to try to hide themselves. If they hide themselves that would make it even more difficult to prepare your cities to prevent any of them from becoming like Blackgate."

Still stroking his beard Cordian stands, his sagely voice taking the room, "You understand that some proof of progress should have to be presented to retain our favor in not forming our own group to search for the shard of prime. I suggest a time of three months."

Pearl jumps to her feet at the time suggested, shouting, "Three months are you crazy? It takes nearly a month to get from here to the Elven or dwarven continent, nearly two to get to the Gnomes or the dragonborn. You can't seriously think that three months is enough time gather anything meaningful to express to this council."

"You are in possession of the palace that was Negmor's correct? Negmor is one of the few dwarven mages to have ever gained the title of arch-mage, and while he wore white robes to symbolize his master of abjuration magic, he could have just as easily wore blue for conjuration, the magic of teleportation."

Eliza's voice calm again responds to the old elf's comment with a nod saying, "You know of the object that allows the island to transport itself once a day."

"He had permission to establish the anchor points on some of our world's ley line intersections."

"Then perhaps you can help us understand why the westward portion of the device is extended in a way unlike the other three sections."

Before Cordian can respond a chorus of the sound from chairs shifting against the floor screeches from the five dragonborn, who stand and turn to the door. As they step to leave the table Aldrin calls to them asking, "Where are you going? The meeting hasn't finished."

Looking over her shoulder only the leader stops to respond, "It has been over for some time, the dealings with Blackgate were concluded, our portion of repairs will find their way here, but this talk as though a child, and a fish woman, could find the shard of prime, something lost for more than a thousand years is absurd. We are going to put into motion preparation against anyone connected to what happened to your city for our people, commander."

"As we were discussing, the reason the forth section of your pedestal of relocation is not active is due to the anchor having been removed from the ley lines off our coast when Negmor went missing. The risk was too high of someone taking possession of his palace and using it as a means of ill against us so we could not leave it," Cordian's voice continues as the dragonborn leave with no intervention from any other member at the table.

"What can we do about getting that put back into place," Eliza asks with a cold calm, that draws Pearl and Aldrin's worried attention to her.

"A matter like that would have to be heard by the elven council. The necessary preparations of such could be completed in a week's time, after the conclusion of this meeting."

Eliza gives a nod, and the room goes silent. A moment sits in the air before Lady Tristalia moves to stand, her armor filling the room with the ring of it clanging against itself. With arms out stretched the Silvermist champion smiles and gives bow saying, "If there are no other matters to be discussed I motion that this Meeting of the Lords be concluded."

The groups of ambassadors take turns concurring to the motion, and with the dwarves as the last to agree the whole of the room stand. Aldrin steps to the door and begins to lead the way through the keep to the small far back room, where the teleportation circle waits. As they step from the room Aldrin gestures to the exit of the keep and Ben begins walking in that direction saying, "Will the representatives from the north please follow me? I will escort you back to your ship."

During the walk Eliza pulls herself from Pearl's side around the crowd to the dwarf in brown robes, and leaning down to his ear she asks, "Excuse me, but in telling us about the Shard of Prime, Negmor mentioned speaking to someone. Would that be you as the king's mage hand? It would be helpful if we could in any way learn more about the palace he has given us."

Pulling away from Eliza, Bellar whispers into his king's ear, something which provokes an almost violent bout of laughter from the king, who responds, "Why are ye asking me this type of thing? I am not your mother. Just insure that it doesn't interfere with yer duties and ye can do whatever ye wish."

With approval granted to him, Bellar turns to Eliza to respond, seeing a smile on her face, "I will meet you on the dock of this city in the morning, tonight I must gather some supplies."

After that the large group of ambassadors find their way to the back room where the dragonborn stand waiting outside the door. Aldrin steps past and embedding the sword into the glyph on the ground, again sparks the runes to life. Group by group the ambassadors step into the circle, one among them exclaims an arcane incantation, and with three pops they vanish.

After the last of the groups vanish, Aldrin withdraws the sword from its spot in the floor and with a sigh of relief turns to face the three with him, Eliza, Pearl, and Lady Tristalia. Returning the blade to its sheath and returning the sheath to its hanging point on the wall Aldrin smiles to the others saying, "Well, that was more eventful that expected."

Pearl's hand finds itself landing forcefully, in play, on Aldrin's shoulder, as she says to him, "Well, it's a good thing Lizzy was there, not only did she strike down tensions, but she got our group approved to continue to search for the shard. Now, I'm tired, so let's get some drinks."

Eliza turns away blushing at the notion Pearl presents, before Aldrin responds, "About that we need to talk. I can't continue with you. At least not right now."

A strange look, and expression only possible in a moment when one close friend betrays another, mutates itself onto Eliza's face from the smiling blush she had turned away to hide. Pearl's face is taken with confusion, with her eyebrows pushing together with worry, as she shakes her head and responds, "What? Why?"

"You have a meeting with the council of the elves in a week, and beyond that you only have three months to produce some proof that you are progressing to relocate the shard of prime. There is no way everything I need to get done will be done by then."

Aldrin is interrupted when one of the acolytes of Silvermist steps to the group and addresses lady Tristalia, "Lady the gathering you requested be made presentable and counted is ready."

Aldrin looks at the heavily armored champion and confused by the new arrivals words asks, "What gathering?"

With a sigh having witnessed the pressures of the conversation preceding the arrival of the information Lady Tristalia looks at the three others individually, and turning to leave the keep responds, "Please come with me, there is something I must show you."

With the request, Eliza, Pearl, and Aldrin, step behind the champion as she leads them silently out of the Keep and returns with them to the Temple of Silvermist. The calm polluted sky overhead bears no peace for the group with Aldrin's statements sitting silently in their minds, as they walk, afraid to speak before learning Lady Tristalia's intent. The large double doors wait closed for the group when they arrive at the temple, stepping past the crater that still remains from Eliza's efforts in the conflict, and Aldrin finally speaks, "I ask again Champion of Silvermist, what gathering?"

"The gathering of all that was taken from the Stormriders of any value, we have prepared it for your group as a gift for freeing us from their occupation."

"Wait, that money, those objects should be returned to their owners," Eliza responds uproariously denying an offer that wasn't presented.

"You misunderstand child, anything whose owner could be located, has been offered back to them, as well as any marked purse containing coin, we have gathered what is left and what has been returned again to us by the people of Blackgate who truly want you to know their gratitude."

"Even still it should be used to help repair the city, like the finances the nations will be sending."

While Eliza protests the offer further, Pearl's eyes widen with childish delight as the doors are opened revealing in the worship area a large table piled high with coins of all different prints, and of the three major currency types gold, copper, and silver. The enormous sword that Domavir had used in the fight, with the shackle gauntlets hung by their chains over its handle, leans onto the table from the side and several other strange chests and bags sit amongst the mound of money. With a smile and a gentle shake of the head Lady Tristalia gives a final response before stepping out of the way, "You can trust that you taking this reward for your good deeds will not hinder the regrowth of our city. If anything, leadership right now, for those lost and amongst the damaged of this city, is far more important than this coin."

Lady Tristalia's eye focus on Eliza's who looks away to avoid the look which she knows the meaning to without having to be told, the people of Blackgate need Aldrin to help lead them, to save them from the wastes as he saved her. They need him to carry them until they can again carry themselves. Before the building knowledge that she would have to go on without her friend by her side can overwhelm her, an acolyte steps into her field of view presenting something in both hands for her, a tightly bound, expertly made, tome, with a hard-black leather cover, with an envelope bound to it with common twine. The young woman, barely an adult in the tone of her voice, hesitatively pushes the object toward Eliza saying, "Miss Black this was left for you."

Eliza reaches out to take the tome asking, "For me? Who would, why would anyone leave something for me specifically?"

"It was a strange man with messy hair, he made great effort to insure that we give this book to you. Perhaps the letter he has tied to it will explain more."

"Did he give a name?"

"Well he said that we should let you know that this is a book from a Victor Ambrose."

"That makes no sense," Eliza mutters to herself fully accepting the book into her possession. Duty completed the young acolyte turns and steps away into the temple, leaving the group, and leaving Eliza staring with a concerned inquisitive look at the object in her hands.

Quickly forgetting the world around her, consumed by a sudden surge of curiosity, Eliza unties the twine to free the envelope, on which a wax seal sits pressed with the indentation of what appears to be a coin. Stepping into the room Eliza finds her way to have her back against one of the walls resting the closed book in her lap as she frees the letter from its envelope. The parchment unfolds to reveal fine calligraphy reading, "Young miss, I have contemplated since our meeting the way in which I would go about repaying your kindness. Through much meditation of the air I was allowed to witness about you, I have no doubt that you are not of any of the worlds common races. No, I sensed about you a presence that spoke to the rarity of your existence, something more than human, a soulborn, someone graced with the presence of the gods themselves, in their blood. The presence I bore witness to held something else though, something that in my many years on this plane has never been present in my observation, something that I shamefully say I dare not fathom the expanse of. Through this thought, your interest in the arcane that the pure hearted good that radiated from you in the time we met, I felt I would offer you a ritual tome. A book for you to gather arcane incantation so that they may be cast in a ritual much like you performed for your spirit companion summoning, I also included a few more pages to go with the one you have from the dark book. While I would normally never trust anyone with such knowledge, I have a feeling about you that out of anyone on this world you are the least likely to use the incantations they possess for ill. You are a very good person I could see this in the mere seconds we met, I only hope that this gift will find itself helpful to you in spreading that good. P.S. Happy Fourteenth Birthday I know you were sailing when it passed I hope you and Pearl enjoyed the wine, I left a few more normal rituals in this tome as a gift for the occasion."

Eliza flips open the tome, feeling strange bumps on its cover through her hands as it rests in her lap, and sure to the word of the letter the first several pages are filled almost to being black with arcane sigils, denoting incantations for Eliza to decode. Before any more excitement for the gift can take her, she looks up to find the peeping eyes of Pearl, who moans childishly, "Aw, I didn't getting a present left for me," but without even a beat to skip, she laughs, and becomes almost obsessive, continuing, "So, what'd the letter say? Was it actually the same Victor whose coin we returned? What are those spells already written in it?"

Eliza gently closes the book, and with a soft smile responds, "Take it easy Pearl I don't know. The letter had a lot in it, most of which doesn't really matter, but apparently this is a ritual tome."

"Really? Wow those aren't cheap if it is real the parchment within is special, it should be extra resistant to water damage, and you need special inks to write in it, but that type of ink also shouldn't run if the pages get wet that is so cool. Well, come help me shovel three fifths of this pile into my bag."

"Three fifths?"

"Well, Lady Tristalia and this temple should definitely get a portion."

"And Aldrin can carry his own for scaring us by saying he won't be joining us any further, makes sense. What about the sword?"

"Well, if it is magical it should shrink down to a size appropriate for its wielder after about an hour of holding it, to allow the enchantment to recognize one of us as the new owner. At least that should be the case if it is enchanted and has at least the baseline enchantments on it with whatever caused it to sheath itself in lightning."

Without another word said, Pearl and Eliza begin shoveling coins, bags, and small chests into the magic satchel Pearl carries. In the same time Aldrin is given a large sack, into which he shovels approximately a fifth of the total of coins, before Ben arrives and the two of them carry the sack to the keep. Coin gathered, Pearl, to the annoyance of the sisters of Silvermist, sits for a full hour with a hand on the enormous sword's handle after which, exactly as Pearl explained, the titanic plate of metal suddenly shifts and grinds across the ground releasing the loud sound of folding cold metal, and it somehow shrinks to only the size of a normal hand and a half sword.

Adding the sword to the bag with the chained gauntlets, Eliza and Pearl finally take their leave and make their way back to the house. The streets stay quiet and the two walk still quietly contemplating all that has been said in the past few hours, not saying a word. Reaching the door, Eliza brings her hand against it releasing a soft knock, within a second a voice from the other side calls out, Boop muffled through the door, loud enough to wake the neighbors if there were any, yelling, "Master is back! Open door please!"

Before the door can open, with the motion inside sounding only loud enough to relay itself to the two in the street, Pearl's hand falls on Eliza's shoulder and with a smile she says, "We never did get that drink."

To which Eliza responds, "Maybe some other night. We have a lot still to go through together." Pearl responds with a smile just as the door slams open with Boop shooting from within out into the chest of Eliza, where he seemingly weeps for having been left at home. The night takes the group once more into rest, for another day to come.

14

Leaving Blackgate

The morning comes with a knock on the door of Aldrin's abode. Pearl opens it begrudgingly having been woken by the crack of wood striking wood, and finds with a large chest on the ground at his side, the dwarf mage Bellar standing with a slight lean against his staff. With a greeting nod the dwarf says with the door opening before him, "Good morrow, I know I said I would meet you at the docks, but I arrived earlier than expected and thought perhaps we could treat each other to some company in walking that way."

Still rubbing the sleep out of her eyes Pearl responds with a nod saying, "How long has it been since you left? Did you even sleep?"

"I was busy gathering reagents from my lab in Deepslag and to be honest I am far too excited at the prospect of being able to speak with my teacher again to sleep, I will probably fall asleep on the ship."

"I hope so. Its two days off shore."

"Two days? Well I guess that makes sense, Negmor said he built his temple and got the permissions to establish its anchors only a few years before the Shattering."

Continuing the conversation Pearl steps back into the house to give Aldrin and Eliza swift waking jabs with her foot as she grabs her bag, "Before the Shattering? That couldn't be. How old is Negmor, I thought dwarves only live four or five centuries?"

"That's a laugh. Hearing a human, you are human right? A human, who don't tend to even make it to a century say only four or five of them with enfaces on only. You are correct, but it is not uncommon for mages who reach the pinnacle of arcane ability and earn the title archmage to use magic to extend their life to allow them to forge new ground in their field of the arcane before they pass."

"Alright then, just so we know, how old are you?"

"Three-hundred-twenty-seven years young."

Joining the conversation from behind Auburn groans through the doorway, "What's wi' th' rude wakeup 'n' a' th' talking?"

"We're going back to the palace. We have things that need to get done," Pearl says with a near skip of a step out the door and past Bellar, and turning with a head nod she calls to the small house, "Come on, we have to go get Esmerelda."

Running past Auburn, Eliza sprints to Pearl's side shouting, "And we need to get Aldrin, he never came back last night wouldn't want to leave without him."

Before Auburn has a chance to straighten himself after being pushed past, Boop darts by, nearly throwing him off balance. With a roll of his eyes though, he groans and grabs his stuff stepping to join the others as they walk. Behind them, as Bellar joins the precession through the still vocally thankful town, the group watches the large chest lift from the ground and begin to follow only a few feet behind.

With their walk through the city, and not wanting to waste time to understand the group that volunteered themselves for such a daunting task as to search for the shard of prime, Bellar asks before they get to the keep, "So, if you are a human, what type of hex are you under that has made you blue and fishy?"

With a nervous laugh Pearl doesn't hesitate to respond, "Well, that is kind of a long story, but to make it short, one of the gods of death forced me into a contract with them to find something up north, on a sunken ship, there is a good chance I was morphed like this to help me get it."

Keeping pace with Pearl as she responds, Bellar's eyes widen and he turns to Eliza asking, "How did a beautiful woman as yourself find company with someone cursed by a god of death," he looks to Pearl for a split moment as though to confirm he had heard her correctly.

Eliza blushes, and with a smile she responds, "Actually Pearl and I met before she was cursed," but becoming bashful she turns away almost mumbling as she continues, "It's actually kind of my fault that she is."

Bellar leans slightly toward Eliza with decerning curiosity hoping that he is having his leg pulled with some strange foreign type of joke. Before he can ease his mind enough to ask, Pearl steps to Eliza's side, and puts one of her webbed fingers to her lips in an almost seductive pout she explains, "And you really think Lizzy is more of a beautiful woman than me? She's only thirteen."

"Fourteen actually," Eliza responds turning to Pearl in a way that turns her away from Bellar.

"Really? Since when?"

"Before we reached the Cove."

Bellar pulls back in the walking group from the girls, looking at them in a slight panic, to be walking at Auburn's side when he asks, "So what about you, your accent sounds like it is from south of Slag, am I right?"

Looking down at the dwarf disinterested Auburn sighs, "Right."

"Well hows a person like you end up in the company of such boisterous individuals like those two."

"Whit dae ye mean?" Auburn responds as Pearl takes Eliza's hand and pulls her quickly ahead for the keep.

"Well, beyond your obvious appearance, being not of pure dwarven or human heritage, you seem like a calmer sort."

"Weel tae be honest th' young yin haes ainlie recently grown tae hae th' confidence she is showing, bit tae answer yer quaistion we met in th' plane o' undeath, 'n' we fought against shadow beings that a dragon drew fae fowk wha wur alive ainlie moments afore together."

"And you worked together to escape that plane of existence."

"Aye."

In the time Auburn and Bellar step joining Pearl and Eliza at the large door of the keep, Ben answered the girl's knock, and returns with Aldrin, who stands with a surprised look on his face responding to something said, "Wow, really, I forgot you were so young, you carry yourself so maturely."

Eliza is visibly blushing with her pale almost white skin going into a reddish pink with Aldrin's comment on her maturity, and through it she continues their conversation, with a somewhat dishonest attempt to draw the focus away from herself, "Well Bellar from the dwarven ambassador group is going to help us get into contact with Negmor again, so we are going to go talk to Esmerelda about sailing to the palace today."

A serious look takes Aldrin's face and he turns quickly from Eliza's smile responding, "I will meet you at the docks, I can't leave the paperwork I was working on just sitting incomplete on my desk."

"Alright see you there," Eliza laughs turning with a wave as she takes a step away.

Pearl gives Aldrin an informal salute and spinning joins Eliza. The two lead the way again from the keep for only a few steps before they both stop. Turning, filled with embarrassment, Pearl's voice creaks out only loud enough for Aldrin to hear, "Um, do we know where Esmerelda is?"

Aldrin faces back out to the others once more, pressing his index finger and thumb to the crown of his nose and with a laugh in his voice he responds, "You could try her house, seventeen Northstream avenue."

"Thank you. See you at the docks."

With an address Pearl and Eliza spin and begin walking again from the keep in search of their ship's captain. The street, Northstream Avenue, as the name implies, is on the northern half of the city across the river from the keep and Aldrin's home. By the time the five get to the bridge Bellar looks up to Boop who has been staring, with a glare of suspicion, at the mage since they left the house, and turning to the other three he asks, "So how is it that you have come into the companionship of a witness."

"A what?" the three seem to simultaneously ask at the question.

"This creature is often known in the common tongue as a witness. They're a creature from another plane of existence. They are the smallest, weakest, and least intelligent form of an entire family of creatures like it. It's extremely rare to see any of the many types of this creature on our world, especially one of this color, or that looks this healthy. It stands as theorized that creatures like this escape to our reality when they are injured or ill to escape a hostile environment."

While listening to Bellar's explanation of what Boop is, Pearl and Eliza chat to themselves about Pearl's intent to teach Eliza to swim, and Eliza's distain for the idea, Auburn points to Boop and then to Eliza explaining to Bellar, "That thing is that one's pet."

"Am not," Boop growls in his squeaky high pitched voice, and looking away as though to show the offence taken about the statements said about him, he continues, "I companion of spirit. I not run scared. She call. I answer."

Bellar looks astonished for several seconds, staring at the floating pinkish purple orb, and raising a pointed finger in Boop's direction stammers, "I-it t-talks? How is that possible? No Witness has been recorded in being able to speak before. Wait, companion of spirit, do you mean spirit companion?"

Eliza turns to the question, "Yea, I didn't know it when we first met, but recently I was able to summon Boop to me through a ritual Pearl taught me."

"You mean... This is incredible! There are absolutely no records of a creature from the matipragma family interacting peaceably with humanoids, let alone one being generated as a spirit companion. That isn't even considering that it can talk in the common tongue, or any tongue for that matter, witnesses are noted as being comparable to a dog in intelligence. Even being a spirit companion doesn't explain that. How have you managed to increase, this, um, Boop's intellectual capacity?"

"To be honest I am not really sure. He only recently has shown that he can speak. Isn't that right Boop?" Eliza explains as she falls back from Pearl's side to be walking with Bellar, while gesturing to Boop to come to her.

Boop is hesitant, not wanting to come to the gesture thinking it would only confirm the dwarfs comment on him being akin to a pet dog, but with one of his eyes glancing into Eliza's sparkling pale eyes he gives in and drifts into her grasp. With freshly trimmed nails, which Eliza has noted to herself have been continuing to grow at an exceptionally accelerated rate, she scratches between Boop's eyestalks and beneath his chin causing him to lull in her grasp.

Before anymore prying to the nature of Boop and his connection with Eliza can be asked Pearl's knuckle knocks on a wood door drawing attention to the small cottage in front of the group. They stand in silence for brief moment, with only a miniscule exhale of pleasure as Boop sighs softy with Eliza's continued attention to him. The door finally opens before enough time could pass to make the silence awkward, revealing on the other side, a fairly average man. Only about the height of, the taller than she would naturally be, Eliza, the man's dark completion, and his combination of black hair and well-trimmed beard, find no success in diluting the gentle smile that he bears in his expression as he greets the people at his door, "Good morning. How can I help you?"

"We were told that Esmerelda lives here. Is she in?" Pearl asks politely.

"She is indeed. One moment. Darling, there is a group at the door for you!"

A familiar voice from inside calls, back almost immediately to respond, "Who is it?"

"It looks like that group you were telling me about. The one with the fish girl."

Slow clacks of boot heels striking a wood floor bring a figure to the door, finally revealing Esmerelda from behind the man. Wrapping one arm around her he gives a kiss to her cheek as her turns from the door and steps in the direction she came from, leaving her to talk with the group she sailed with. With a curious smile she crosses her arms and leaning her weight onto one hip tilts her head and asks, "So to what might I owe the pleasure of your visit?"

Pearl gives a bow, responding nervously, "Well, we kind of need to sail back to the palace."

"Yeah, I was worried you weren't just going to settle down. Meet me at the docks, I have to go talk to someone," Esmerelda explains rolling her eyes and gesturing down river, then turning back into her home she calls to her husband, "I'm going out."

From within the house the man's voice calls back, "Alright be safe," before Esmerelda steps into the street and past her group after closing the door behind herself.

With that Pearl takes lead again and the group begins walking down stream toward the docks. After walking again the whole distance through the city, with occasional greetings from passersby who still hold eager their desire to thank the group who freed them, they make it to their destination. There Pearl quickly finds the large, black ship bobbing on its own tied to a pier separate from the few fishing vessels that remain docked. Waiting there at the dock stands Aldrin, staring at the ship with an expression of calm satisfaction to the trip that finally got his group here. With him in their sights Eliza and Pearl run to his side calling with joy in their voices, "Aldrin!"

Aldrin turns with a smile, in time to set himself so as to not be knocked from his feet as the two tackle him. At the moment they impact with their friend Eliza pulls away her smile fading, as she asks, "Aldrin, where's your suit? Your bag? Your rifle?"

"Eliza, I…" Aldrin tries to respond before a voice echoes from the direction Pearl had led the others.

Esmerelda's voice calls to the gathering, collecting their attention, "Hey, there, I see you found the ship."

Approaching with her is a man with sanguine almost burgundy skin with a pair of horns extending from his temples like those of a ram which hold back long black hair. His eyes, the same exact blue as Eliza's hair are made even more vibrant against his dark skin and against the dark almost black purples and blues of a sailor's jacket. A large sack is slung over his shoulder held by his fist that displays nails that extend almost like talons from his fingertips. As they get to the group standing at the pier the man gives a nod, letting from his gaunt boney face a voice that compared to the rest of his appearance is unextraordinary in its middle tone saying simply, "Yo, the name's Devin. You Pearl," he asks nudging his chin upward toward Pearl

With a nod Pearl looks with only her eyes to Esmerelda, suspicious of the man, responding, "Yeah."

"Looks like I'll be your first mate. It's a pleasure," he says immediately after the confirmation, offering his free hand for her to shake.

Taking the man's hand Pearl responds, "First mate, eh?" After a second she realizes what she said, and her look snaps to Esmerelda asking, "First mate?"

Esmerelda shrugs with a smile responding, "Look, I want to settle down at least for now, but I wasn't going to leave you without a way out of here. Devin is an old friend and when I approached him about you needing a crewmate to keep up the ship when you aren't on it, he couldn't accept fast enough."

Devin just nods muttering, "It was not a good time here the past few months. I just need to get away."

Pearl turns and sprints from the group down the wood path and up the gangplank onto the ship's main deck. The others can just see her on deck wrapping the main mast in an excited hug. Turning to face Eliza, Aldrin reaches out to put his hand on her shoulder saying, "Hey, you take care of yourself, and take care of her for me ok?"

Eliza turns to face him only just feeling the strike of truth of Aldrin's intent to stay, and with a steely look that he hasn't seen in her eyes before, one that shakes him and puts a dread in his heart she responds with a cold calm in her voice, "Thank you for the hospitality commander," and walks away, leaving Aldrin stunned by the emotionless formality of the words and actions directed in response to him. Quickly Eliza makes her way with Boop onto the ship and to the same room that was hers before, closing the door behind her, slamming it with all her might, unheard by anyone else.

Aldrin stands staring stunned as Eliza leaves him, but he is shaken back into reality when Auburn approaches him saying, "Watch out fur yerself." The two share a nod and Auburn turns and steps to board the ship, quickly followed by the new stranger, Devin, and the mage Bellar.

Stepping to the pedestal on which the urn that contains the crew rests, Pearl lays her hands on the outer edges muttering to herself with an almost forced contemplative look on her face, "Now what was it that Esme said again to get the crew?" Then with a spark of memory lighting her face with glee she steadies herself on the swaying ship saying loudly with conviction toward the urn, "Raise the anchor, set the sails. Get to your stations, sunken crew."

With the command the urn shakes violently in its place releasing onto the deck the fog that forms up into the ghostly figures of the bound sailors. The sails fill with the unnatural wind that propels the ship forward at the fullest desired speed, regardless of the natural world's air flow, and the ship's tying and gang plank retract themselves onto the deck. In a fit of inspiration Pearl easily takes to shouting commands at the ghostly skeletons, in the same fashion Esmerelda had, before she glances to Devin in hopes of seeing his expression struck with the same worried surprise she had when the undead crew was first made known to her. To her surprise the horned red man stands observing the actions of the spirits around him, stroking his cleanly shaven chin, and listening to the commands shout out by Pearl.

Aldrin only watches from the end of the pier as the ship escapes into the ocean, to disappear on the horizon.

15

Black Book

The ship sails for two days with no interruption or event. Two days in which time Devin takes to quickly covering responsibility for commanding the undead crew without continuous input from Pearl. Two days of Auburn becoming quickly annoyed with the company of the high society dwarf that is Bellar. Two days Eliza spends locked in her room alone with Boop.

Several times during these days Pearl visits Eliza's door, listening to hear if her young friend was crying for having to leave Aldrin. Finding no such sound each time is followed by a knock and a question calling into the room, "Lizzy are you alright?"

"I'm fine," Eliza responds each time, with the same cold façade of calm that she is blanketing over a pain Pearl suspects is present. Pearl is eased slightly each day when she finds the bowls of food, and the cups of fresh water she sets outside Eliza's door empty and waiting upon her next visit.

In her room Eliza sits petting Boop at her side on the hammock bed
reading and trying to decipher the strange texts that fill the few pages of
writing in the book she was given. The loose sheet that she had taken from
the man's library, who she met in the plane of undeath, holds a place of its
own between two other pages, each with similar sinister design to their
format and calligraphy, and each also not bound to the book's seam. An
emotionless expression holds itself upon her face as she reads, as she holds
down emotions she doesn't want to feel instead choosing to focus on
learning what has been given to her.

Early on the second day of sailing when the door to Eliza's room
sounds with a knock, she responds preemptively, "I'm fine Pearl, honest."

The words escape to the hall, and the response surprises Eliza, as
Auburn's voice calls in, "Whitevur, stay oan th' ship. We ur at th' island.
Pearl asked me to tell ye."

Surprised by the rapid passing of time, having been so entrenched in
the alien arcane scripts to have recognized time having passed at all, Eliza
steps to the porthole window from her room to confirm Auburn's statement.
Seeing the rising stone faces of the mountain range that sits as the outer wall
of the island, Eliza releases a sigh of relief. Placing her book in her bag, her
expression remains stern as her finger finds the cold metal of the dagger that
still sits buried beneath the rest of her belongings. Pressing the feelings
down, she hefts the bag over her shoulder once more and sits down patiently
waiting in her hammock to be informed that the ship is docked.

Eventually Pearl's voice rings through the door with a knock saying,
"Lizzy we're home. You want to head inside?"

The first three words paralyze Eliza, freezing her wide eyed with her
arms wrapped around Boop. A second knock with Pearl calling out the
nickname she had given the young girl, breaks the trance and Eliza steels
herself. Rising from the hammock and stepping to the door, she responds,
"Coming." Stepping from the room she makes no motion to interact with
anyone as she steps from the ship, along the marble path and floor to the

room she had claimed as her own when they were first introduced to the idea that the palace would be theirs. After only long enough for her to have set down her bag she returns. Still with no sign of joy or sorrow, nor anger or fear on her face, she finds Bellar in a large room near the front of the palace meant to act as a dining room waiting with Auburn and Pearl. With Boop at her side the teen gestures to Bellar with an open hand, saying, "I am sure you want to begin work as soon as possible on that construct we had mentioned," and looking up Eliza's eyes find Pearl's as she asks, "Where's Devin?"

Feeling all of a sudden nervous for a reason she can't explain Pearl's hand reaches back behind her head as she responds, "Well he took so well to leading the crew of the ship, that when I told him that this was our palace and that he could come sleep inside, he declined, before I even told him that we don't even have any furniture. And well you know I have been thinking maybe we should use some of the money we have collected to hire some help and clean this place up. Maybe get some furniture for the rooms we will use most often, like a bed for each of us."

"No."

"What?" the sudden confused expression expels itself from Pearl almost as a shout.

"We are supposed to be searching from something called a Shard of Prime, something that in the wrong hands could bring devastation to the world. We can't trust people to know of this place, or where we go."

"I know, but wouldn't you like a bed to sleep on?"

"I am fine on the floor, I am used to it, since long before we met."

Pearl sighs with a nod as Eliza turns and leaves the room, leading a wordless Bellar and Boop down the hall. The three make their way up the tall passageway into the round brightly lit room, and immediately Bellar's mouth drops agape in impressed surprise at something unseen to Eliza. Running into the room, the dwarf drops to his knees sliding up to one of the pillars expressing in excitement, "Marvelous. Simply marvelous. You truly are a master beyond my scale Negmor."

The chest that had been floating a few feet above the ground several paces behind Bellar suddenly shoots from the hall, past Eliza, in order to keep the short distance between it and him the same as he finds his knees under him. Naraly avoiding the locker as it shoots past her, Eliza looks at Bellar and stepping in his direction asks, "What do you mean by that? I don't understand why you are so excited?"

"Well, it is simply amazing the craftsmanship of this ritual space. The mere fact that you are not impressed as a person who I don't believe has had any formal education in the arcane arts, is exactly the point."

"I still don't understand."

"The construct you had mentioned, it is only a small part of what this room is capable of, and glyphs, the symbols that focus the wild arcane energies, are all around you but hidden almost completely from view. If I hadn't known Negmor before as my teacher, I myself would probably not have seen the faint trace of his craftsmanship. You see the mural above us, the one depicting the legend of the creation of my kin? Well, within the lines and the people in that painting are arcane symbols. To what exactly all of them are focused, I don't know, but as you had mentioned, within them has to at least be the symbols for the creation of a messenger construct. If I am able to find a way to fill the primal energy reservoir I might be able to access that construct. You wouldn't happen to have a Master's cane would you? It would be about this long, and would bear resemblance to a pact maker's rod."

"Well there was this thing that was used to dismiss a demon from its contract here."

"Really? Where is it? That is most likely it."

"Uh, I don't know. Boop do you remember where you stored your chewing rod?"

Bellar looks in horrified surprise at Eliza's words, and turning to the floating orb watches as one of its eyestalks feigns a salute as it nods, responding, "Yes, you want me to get it for you?"

"I think Bellar wishes to use it for something up here."

"Ok I come back soon," Boop exclaims shooting down the stairs.

Turning back to Bellar, who maintains an open jawed look of surprise, Eliza says to him before noticing his expression, "There Boop should be able to get that for you. Will you need anything else?" but noticing finally the stance and face she asks, "Is something wrong?"

"You just let your spirit companion use a master's cane as a chew toy!" he responds his voice almost trembling with a jealous anger.

"Well Negmor told me to hold onto it, but I have no idea what it would be used for after we banished the creature bound to the contract that it held. He never said anything about it being a master's cane, whatever that means."

"I will put it this way, if you connected with that cane in the same way Pearl connected with the sword Domavir used, I can tell you that there is a good chance that that is why Boop has become able to speak."

"How did you know about Domavir's sword?"

"Relax, nothing of an evil motive. If I was to be your companion to a place I thought was only a myth, I pried into the intentions of your group, as any mage advanced enough would do when outnumber by a group escorting them anywhere. At least I tried. Pearl and Auburn were both easy enough, and Pearl's mind was filled with a jubilance of giggling joy of her treasures brought through the events in Blackgate, but you, I have to say I am a bit nervous, right now, being around you, as your mind alone was concealed from my spell. Based on your physique I knew you wouldn't be a fighting type, you're much to frail and overly beautiful without a flaw in your appearance. So, you being a cleric or some member of a mage class would make sense. Your spirit companion perplexed me. The magic that guarded your mind was astonishing and nothing I had ever experienced before nor have I read about the feeling of being driven from someone's conscious that overcame me when I tried to peer into your thoughts. I would very much like to talk to you about your magic, when I have completed all of the work that is within my ability here."

Eliza simply smiles, blushing at what seems to sound like a mass of compliments laid upon her in Bellar's words, responding just as Boop returns with the rod within his maw, "I think that would be nice, but for now I am going to go work on deciphering some rituals I was given by a magic user from Blackgate. I am sure Boop would love to help in any way that he can," saying this she turns to Boop whose eyes light up as he nods in agreeance having grown bored of Eliza's melancholic studying. With confirmation Eliza turns and steps to go down the stairs but not before opening her third eye just above the threshold of the entryway, in order to carefully be able to observe the visitor's actions now less trusting of him knowing that he used magic to try to peer into her mind.

Eliza returns to the room she had claimed and lifts her bag from the spot against the wall she had rested it against. From within she draws the black covered book, and sitting down she begins to read again; Slowly deciphering the script that would break a normal person's mind. The light that passes into the large room's double windowed wall grows bright with the day's sun rising to the heat of mid-day, but a cool breeze continues to blow in from the surrounding ocean waters keeping the palaces rooms a comfortable temperature.

Bored of walking the palace grounds reexploring empty room after empty room, Pearl finds the room Eliza has claimed and with a knock enters without waiting for a response, asking, "Hey you want to do those swimming lessons?"

"That was your idea. I was never interested," Eliza responds still emotionlessly staring into the book.

"Well, anything interesting in there?"

"Yes, actually. One of these pages has written on it something that, if I am understanding it correctly, will protect a threshold against anyone or anything that does not have its name spoken within the casting of the spell."

"What does it do?"

"Well, I am not sure how it works I haven't tried it out, but it says it will strike at the mind of any being that passes through a protected threshold uninvited. It doesn't say how powerful the assault would be."

"That's cool. Did you want to test it?"

"Test it? On who?"

"Well I would say Auburn, but I think without Aldrin here to calm him down afterward, that might be a bit too far and whatever it is that has kept him from trying to kill you in your sleep might end there," Pearl responds waiting for Eliza's eyes to get wide with fear of the prospect, before both break into laughter. Then continuing Pearl says simply, "How about me?"

"What? You? No. I don't know what type of damage this spell might wrought on someone. I wouldn't know what to do if it killed you."

"Ha! You think one little spell would kill me? Give me a break. Look Lizzy, you and I have been through a lot. We each have far more fight in us than any normal person. We can take hits that would kill other people from the shock. So, let's try it out. Plus you can do that healing thing with your hands. That plus a couple days rest should cover most wounds, as long as no bones are broken and you don't cut me."

Seeing a conviction in Pearl's eyes, from wanting to do something to try to reconnect with her and break the distance that formed as soon as Aldrin insisted at the dock that he couldn't join them, Eliza nods responding, "Alright." Stepping to the double door into the room, she sets the book down opened to a page that not only is filled with a script which is not of the draconic based language that most arcane spells are formulated in, but also does not sit in lines across the page but phrases that wind in strange patterns of their own. It holds a detailed hatch-mark sketch depiction of what was described to Pearl as the effect of the spell, except the depiction shows the spell striking a strange tentacled creatures head, causing it to explode. Only seeing a glimpse of the image, Pearl suddenly becomes nervous as she steps into the hall, and Eliza starts reading something from the page out loud, "Fahf yaw fhtagn mgng mgepnnn hai, mgah'ehye ehyenah ahch' rect mgepuln eonon, Eliza, Boop."

Eliza repeats the phrase twelve times, over the course of ten minutes. With each time she repeats it she draws a strange glyph with a finger that sits where it is drawn glowing an ominous dark purple, each different from all of the others, three to a side of the door way. The row of three on the top of the door frame, made easily inscribed from the height that still remains from the potions she had taken in the basement that have still not warn off leaving her still nearly a foot taller than Pearl. After the ten minutes, and after she has finished drawing all twelve of the marks Eliza steps back from the door and watches the seals fade into nothingness. Seeing Eliza relax her stance, Pearl prepares herself in a running stance asking, "Ready?"

"Well I think I did it right."

With that Pearl presses herself forward, putting herself into a full sprint within the five or ten feet width of the hall. In less than a second, Pearl's form goes from the other side of the hall to just starting to pass through the doorframe. At that moment time seems to almost become still for the two watching for the effect of the spell to take effect, and if they hadn't been watching for it, they would not have been able to witness the spell activate and act. As Pearl's form only just begins to cross the threshold the glyphs flash into existence once more releasing strands of energy, like individual lines of the finest silk thread, through Pearl's head before vanishing once more.

A gasp forces itself from Pearl's throat as she feels an intense burning pain leap down her spine and through her body. With the pain also comes a lack of motor control that causes her legs to fall out from under her, and prevents her arms from moving to catch her form as her momentum throws her forward like a ragdoll thrown into the room. Eliza only just jumps in the way to help cushion the fall as both of them descend down hard onto the marble floor.

Both groan as Pearl rolls off of Eliza, moaning, "Yea, that was stronger than I expected," laying down on the marble floor with her eyes closed to attempt recapturing the breath the forcibly escaped her, and to let the searing pain in her limbs fade into a feeling of numbness.

Eliza turns to Pearl responding calmly, "I told you I didn't think we should test it on ourselves," but then as her eyes look upon Pearl's face a panic fills her words, "Pearl, your nose is bleeding."

Slowly lifting her hand almost having no strength to do so, Pearl wipes under her nose and lifts her hand to confirm Eliza's analysis. Sure enough, when Pearl opens her eyes she sees, through a red hew, blood clinging to her finger. Rolling her eyes back in her head annoyed with having gotten a bloody nose, she responds, "Yup, looks that way."

"Not just that, your ears are bleeding, and," Eliza looks in a panicked horror at what a spell she cast has done to Pearl, as Pearl's eyes sit as a darkened overly blood shot red with trickling streams of blood dripping out their corners, "Your eyes are bleeding!"

Forcing her head up to barely be able to look at Eliza, Pearl responds with a calm pained groan, "Lizzy, I'll be fine just help me get to my room, I'll rest this off, we have a week, right?"

Eliza only nods in response, and wrapping Pearl in her arms she helps her bleeding friend stand, and they step to the door. Pearl grasps tight onto the dress Eliza got in Blackgate as the door grows near, and continuing forward Eliza, assures her, saying, "The description says that the magic only affects someone once. No need to worry."

The words fall insufficiently into Pearl's bleeding ears, and her grip squeezes tighter with her eyes pressing powerfully closed, and Eliza pulls both of them free into the hall. With a tap on Pearl's shoulder to let her know she no longer needs to worry, she relaxes, and the two begin to make their way through the labyrinth of halls. After nearly an hour of walking the two once again find themselves in front of Eliza's room, and Pearl laughs, "Oh yeah, I just claimed the room next to yours."

Eliza rolls her eyes groaning at the bad joke that came to floriation having been played on her, but still tending to Pearl the two walk another few yards to the single door entry into the room next to Eliza's, and step in. Laying Pearl down against one of the walls, Eliza asks, "Do you need anything, water, food?"

Pearl just shakes her head with a smile, responding, "No, like I said I'll be fine," before pushing herself to her feet with the walls help, "I am just glad you are showing some emotion again." Eliza doesn't know how to react to the comment simply turning to leave before Pearl calls one last time to her, "Lizzy," which causes her to stop, "It is alright to cry."

With that said Eliza closes the door to Pearl's room, and steps once more to her own. The wide double doors still waiting with one still open how it was left. Picking up the book and feeling a well of anger for having been so wrapped up in learning something new to not stop herself from letting Pearl get injured in the pursuit of seeing the effect of the new thing, she presses the book back into her bag done with it for the time being. In the bag though Eliza's hand rubs against something she had almost forgotten about with all of the commotion that has been spiraling around her, a small glass test-tube, and moving to grab it, she feels the others, the remaining untested potions, from Alfredo sitting together with the journal to record their effects in. With a thought to what Pearl said, "It is alright to cry," passing through her mind Eliza thinks to herself, and pulls back out the book, and once again begins reading.

16

Released Suffering

Night comes with the darkening oranges of the skyline, and being informed that, as there are no beds anyway, Bellar would sleep in the room he has been working in. Eliza returns to her room with Boop, with a plan in her heart to make herself cry. Not because she wants to, but because she realized in the moment that she saw Pearl bleeding next to her, that when Aldrin refused to join them any further, she had closed herself off, and she blames that seal for the pain that was inflicted to Pearl. First she sits with Boop until he is fully asleep. She couldn't have him stirring and stopping her with his worries. She needs to cry. Waiting for the sky to light with the brilliance of the moon's glow, Eliza sits with only the want to be free of the emotional block that she has placed upon herself.

Boop snores deeply from the bed made of Eliza's dress, and casting over herself the image of the rose-pink dress that she out grew, Eliza steps to her bag, and digs out a single glass test-tube filled with a liquid that looks like two mixed together making a marbling of clear and milky white. Pressing the vial against her chest, feeling this to be her way out of a hole that has formed around her, Eliza steps softly to the door. Only stopping once as Boop turns over on the dress bed, before continuing out into the hall closing the door slowly, to avoid the sound of the reattaching latch. Looking through an open door into Pearl's room, Eliza thinks to Pearl, likely moistening her skin outside, and continues to step with that in mind.

Down the long tunnel like halls, up several flights of stairs Eliza finds a room at the furthest point from the palace's dock. Unfurnished like every other room, the glow of the full moon's light makes the space almost peaceful in Eliza's mind. Holding tight to the glass container in her hand, she affirms herself on a mission to let out what she hid from Aldrin; to be angry at him; to be fully sad to see him so easily walk away from her, to let out the pain she hid of him leaving her; to open herself up again so that she won't so easily hurt Pearl, who really only wanted not to be cast aside by a second person so close to her.

Stepping out into the moonlight that cascades down onto the balcony, Eliza unseals the small bottle's top, and with a deep breath downs the liquid with a single gulp. The odor and taste are foul, and both together make Eliza want to wretch, dropping the bottle as she grabs her stomach and throat in response to a sudden discomfort within. The want to cry builds up finally revealing to Eliza the freedom from her callousness coming, and finally her breath releases in a powerful terrifying scream.

Eliza experiences every second of the horrifying pain she sought to subjugate herself to. Every ounce of fear that she is insufficient, that she will fall on her own and be lost to the ocean, the fear of having alienated, injured, hid from, or killed anyone close to her. The moment that her arm pops from its socket, and the pain feels as insignificant as she had felt in her fit of chemically induce screaming, which brought out the fullest of her emotions, and the comfort that the pain of having her shoulder popped back into place brings knowing that Pearl is with her, Eliza finds peace.

Pearl sits with her back against the wall, with Eliza in her lap, and stroking the long sky blew hair softly says to her young companion a second, "She'll be alright."

"*Pearl,*" Eliza's voice wisps into Pearl's head with a calm about it that is unmistakably different, unmistakably filled with an innate youth that had been void the past few days, "*I think I should get a haircut.*"

Pearl looks down, eyes wide with a joy, to have Eliza back once more. To have the young child like heart once more showing through her words, and she says nothing, not wanting to ruin the mood. Pearl just sits and with slime covered webbed hands, stroking the hair in her lap, and smiles down at the young girl as she, Eliza, and Boop slowly drift back to sleep.

The morning comes and Pearl wakes in a sudden fright as she remembers the events of the night before, her dream having shifted into a nearly exact memory of the assault of powerful waves of magical energy that washed over her as she fought to make her way to Eliza. The light of the mid-morning sun pierces almost blindingly into the room, causing Pearl to recoil from the sudden adjustment required of her bloodshot eyes. Letting them adjust Pearl looks around the empty room to find Boop resting in the warm sunlight, and to her surprise, and building a sudden panic, there is no sign of Eliza.

Pearl jumps to her feet with the sudden realization that Eliza is not with her, and leaping to the door she throws herself into the hall with worry and a need to find her friend. She runs first across the palace to Eliza's room. Reaching for the door handle she hesitates in opening the passageway, not knowing if the spell is still in effect, but deciding that to insure Eliza is alright is more important to her than avoiding a possible second blast of the magic that effortlessly floored he., Pearl swings the door open, and scanning the room is surprised with what she sees inside. Against one wall sits Eliza's bag, next to which lays the mound of cloth of the dress bed Eliza made for Boop, but the object of note about the room lies against the far wall under the windows. There, stretching the length of the room twice, lays the majority of Eliza's immense plethora of hair, cut now from whatever remains on her head.

Not finding Eliza presses Pearl to search elsewhere and she quickly finds herself back in the hall running to check the rooms they had used for eating when they were last here. Reaching the room though, she finds no trace of Eliza, only Auburn who sits sharpening one of his swords in the corner. Not paying him any mind Pearl again turns into the hall to search elsewhere, finding her way to the garden in the center of the palace, thinking Eliza might be reading. Again, she finds no trace of her young friend. Finally, Pearl makes her way out the front of the palace thinking maybe that Devin may have seen Eliza, and only after she steps through the front door does she see Eliza sitting in the shade of a tree reading one of the many books given to her by Alfredo.

Releasing a sigh of relief Pearl runs to Eliza calling, "There you are, I have been looking all over for you."

Turning to the call, sending her hair in a fan out behind her, trimmed to only reach just below her shoulder blades, Eliza smiles and stands responding without her lips moving, *"I've been out here all morning, waiting for you."*

"Waiting for me? Why? And why are you doing the telepathic thing? There is no need to be secretive."

"Well my throat is sore an, when I try to speak all that comes out is," Eliza responds before opening her mouth to scream with the only sound to escape being a barely audible, "Ah," like a kitten's gentle yawn, causing her to wince in pain with her full effort pressing the air from her lungs through her damaged voice box. Stopping and rubbing her throat Eliza, continues telepathically, *"I ,on't know how long it will be until I can speak again after last night. Sorry about making you worry. But I was waiting on you because I was kin, of thinking we coul, ,o that learning to swim thing you've been wanting me to ,o."*

Pearl's eyes lighten up as she hears the proposition in Eliza's voice pass through her head. Filled with excitement she throws off her jacket and boots as she runs to the dock leaping into the waiting pool of ocean water. With a nervous nod in the direction of the water, now worried about the prospect of just going into it while not know its depth, Eliza sets down her book, and steps to the water's edge where Pearl waits eagerly. Sitting down and sliding into the water, Eliza begins her lesson with Pearl.

The two spend just over an hour in the water, with Pearl working mostly to teach Eliza how to keep herself afloat in place, before they reemerge to reveal Eliza's skin a pinkish red from sunburn. With laugh, Pearl gestures into the palace saying, "Well, I had almost forgotten about the side effect of a person who spends most of their time inside going outside for any prolonged period of time. That sunburn is going to hurt for a while, but look at the bright side, you don't have to actually wear clothes so you won't have to deal with fabric irritating it. Tell you what, let's go see if anyone wants or needs anything from town, and we will sail over to the dwarven port and see if we can get a salve to help your skin heal and maybe something for you throat too."

"*And maybe probe for information about getting us some beds and stuff for the palace.*"

Pearl only smiles at the turnaround from the cold expressions Eliza had given her the day before and as the two of them begin walking in she simply responds, "Yeah, we can do that," before asking, "We can also dispose of the pile of hair in your room while we are over there too."

"*Actually, I was thinking maybe we see if we can get it made into rope. There's enough of it. It's lighter weight and could be stronger than hemp.*"

"Say no more. That sounds like a great idea. Let's do it!"

Stepping into the palace again the two find their way to the room which has become their dining space, and find Auburn still in the corner he was in when Pearl checked the room before. When he sees the two enter, he gives a chin up nod, saying to them, "Sae ye found her? Sae kin ah ask ye, how come ye felt it necessary tae keep us up lest nicht?"

Knowing that talking to Auburn telepathically only upsets him, Pearl is the one to speak saying, "Look, it probably won't happen again, but we are going to go to Dru'heim to see if we can get something for Lizzy's skin, and maybe look into purchasing furniture, maybe hire some help moving it. We just wanted to see if you need anything."

"If you're aff tae be getting labor tae stairt fixing up this carcass o' a structure, ah ken some fowk wha wid be mair than grateful fur an opportunity tae git themselves th' coin fur labor, 'n' as outcasts wouldn't be th' sort tae hae tae worry aboot bein' spies."

"That would be fantastic, and they are on the dwarven continent."

"They're likelie aye shacked up whaur thay wur afore ah fun masell in th' ither plane. Aboot a two week donder fae th' port ye wull be taking us to. Ah kin gang oan mah ain 'n' git thaim fur ye."

"That would be amazing. We'll meet you on the ship."

With extra plans made, Pearl and Eliza step again into the halls and begin making their way for the room Bellar has been working in. Without turning to them as they enter, entranced in tracing an invisible to the nontrained eye marking, Bellar greets the return of the masters of the house to the workspace, "Greetings. What can I do for you?"

"Actually, we don't need anything. We are going to send the island to its spot two hours out from Dru'heim, and were wondering if you needed anything from there," Pearl responds as Eliza steps to the pedestal in the center of the room.

"I am fine, Boop was a major help yesterday. If anything, it would be nice to have the company again."

"I am sure Lizzy can arrange that for you," Pearl responds, before the sky suddenly shifts, as the palace relocates from Eliza turning the arrow.

17

Trusting Strangers

Eliza sends Boop to keep Bellar company, while she and Pearl stop at her room to pack the massive amount of hair into Pearl's bag. They make their way once more through the halls and out to the dock to board the ship. The trip is short, relative to the trip between the palace and Blackgate, and the two hours pass again uneventfully, bringing the group safely into the harbor of Dru'heim. Before he can be roped into anything else, Auburn leaps from the ship as soon as it is a close enough distance for him to land on the dock, and quickly passes into the streets of the city away from Pearl and Eliza.

That is where the calm ends. Directly off the docks, where the wood paths out to the ships become stone, a crowd is gathered in a commotion around a sight that is only emphasized by the short stout nature of the native dwarf population majority. Standing in the center of the bustling crowd is a large muscular man, more than seven feet tall, with stone grey-white skin that only barely peaks out from beneath his heavy set of scale-mail armor. This mountain of a figure, holds a bag larger than Pearl over one of his shoulders effortless control, and strapped to him are the sheaths of two swords, one at his hip, and the other larger one on his back, both with a slight curve to their blades.

The crowd stands in a ring pushing the large man into a space facing a bulky angry looking dwarf. Bald with a large black beard the dwarf glares angrily at the large man yelling, "Watch where you are going ye big oaf!"

The large figure, doesn't even pay any mind to the man yelling at him and instead scans over the crowd as if looking for something or someone. He responds in a deep majestic voice that thrums with the calm of spirituality, "I have no time for this. I did not mean to," but he stops as his eyes widen into a stare when they fall upon a tall woman recently burnt by the sun, with long hair that is like a part of the sky resting on her head, and a deep blue woman who looks of the sea. "My apology again sir or madam, I must be going," he continues gently attempting to push his way out of the circle of the crowd, in the direction of Eliza and Pearl.

"Turn your back to me will ye. I'll learn ye some respect," the dwarf shouts, charging for the tall man releasing an angry wordless yell.

"Forgive me, you provide me no other option," the large man says softly dropping his head and closing his eyes.

There is a seeming slowing of time for the witnesses in the crowd around the man. The dwarf's feet carry him quickly across the circle and drawing back a fist, he prepares to throw a punch, but before the fist can find forward momentum the man comes to a sudden stop, and a gasp echoing from the crowd almost silences the sounds of the city. A stone grey-white fist as large as the dwarf's head connects with his nose, before launching him from his feet back to the opposite side of the circle to lay unconscious on his back.

The crowd quickly parts from the grey man's path as he steps again in the direction of Eliza and Pearl. The women both look in confusion at each other as the giant of a man steps to them and continues to face them as they attempt to also step out of his way. Looking up into the man's eyes, who looks down with eyes glistening like two marbles of polished coal, Pearl asks, "Can we help you sir?"

The man lowers himself to a knee and bowing his head he responds, "My ladies, I know not the purpose, but the spirits have instructed me to travel to this place and join the efforts of a woman of the sea, and a beauty with hair like the sky."

Eliza and Pearl look at each other confused by the odd specificity of the stranger's description by some supposed spirits that told him to join them. Eliza shrugs, saying into Pearl's mind, "*Well with Al♦rin gone it might be goo♦ if we fin♦ one or two more people that we can trust.*"

Pearl contemplates Eliza's words, but before she can say anything, or question the large figure in front of her, she is interrupted by two more figures approaching from the side with a horse in tow, one of whom addresses the large man in a voice that portrays a posh upbringing, "Excuse me sir, if I could have your ear for but a moment, I would like to inquire about a business proposition I have for you."

The man is a well-dressed fellow wearing a multi-layered magenta-purple velvet suit, trimmed with gold threads, and gold-plated buttons. A smile curls devilishly within a well-groomed light brown mustache goatee combination revealing pearly white teeth that glisten with his soft blue eyes. The grin does not shrink away when he looks slowly up as the mountainous man rises to stand nearly two feet taller than him so he is looking down at the well-dressed man asking, "I have been guided to join these two. Are they companions of yours in what you propose?"

"I'm sure some arrangement could be made," the fancily dressed man responds, "My dear ladies," and he stops for a moment as he glances at Eliza muttering instinctively, "Wow! You're beautiful!" but clearing his throat he continues, "Would you consider yourselves good people? Excuse me, that is a loaded question of course you would, rarely would someone openly admit otherwise. Would you, in full control of yourself, risk yourself, your safety, and your comfort, to protect others, or to spread the aspects of good in the world?"

Pearl and Eliza, look at each other almost breaking into laughter before Pearl responds, "You don't know the half of it! We just got done risking life and limb."

"That is fantastic to hear. My cohort and I would very much appreciate some assistance in a task of grave importance in this city. If I could interest you in letting me purchase for you a meal so that we might discuss details I would greatly appreciate the gesture."

"Well, we need to try to find someone selling a salve to help with Lizzy's sunburn, but after that I think a late lunch/early dinner would be nice."

"Great we will meet you at the Leaking Whetstone."

"Sure thing," Pearl responds with a smile, before asking, "If we are to find you again later, what name should we call you by?"

"Oh, how silly of me to forget. You may call me Flame-Tender, and my companion here goes by the name Umbra. What might I ask are your names?"

"I am the great captain Pearl Sarya. This is my dearest of friends the beautiful, smart, and magical prodigy Eliza Black. As for the big fellow, we only just met."

"The names' Nakhal," the thunderous voice responds softly adding, "I have nowhere else to be. I will join you to this Leaky Whetstone, and await the return of these women," as he turns to face Flame-Tender.

While introductions are being made Eliza focuses on the figure who hasn't spoken in the interaction. Dark black leathers and a hooded black cloak cover his thin but not frail form, with swords concealed beneath the cloak at his sides. A black mask clings to the man's face concealing it almost completely with only his gentle brown eyes visible. His breaths are calm, slower than a normal resting breath rate, and his attention avoids the conversation Flame-Tender engages in, instead scanning the passing crowds and buildings around them.

With a smile and a wave, Flame-Tender takes the reign of the horse following him, and turning begins walking off into the crowd again. The black cloaked man, referred to as Umbra, turns joining in the exit, and finally the giant of a man, Nakhal joins the two leaving Eliza and Pearl. Turning to Eliza, Pearl smiles saying, "How about three? Now I know what you are thinking, don't go trusting someone we just met. So, we will help them with what they are looking to do and decide afterwards. Now, let's go get that salve. Apothecary, apothecary, where to find an apothecary."

The two explore the port for just over an hour, in the process finding a general practicing doctor who was willing to give Eliza a jar of a soothing salve and point them in the direction of a weaver. Having found their way finally to the location they were pointed, Pearl and Eliza stand outside a small nondescript building which has uncompleted nets hanging on the street side wall. Stepping to the door, Pearl draws back a fist and throws it into the wood for a gentle knock. From inside a gruff but highly pitched male voice calls to the sound, "What? Who? I don't want any. Go away!"

"We were told to come to you about having a rope made," Pearl calls back, not accepting the crass turn away.

"Well in that case, how can I help ye?" the voice responds with the door swinging open to reveal a very old dwarf with clouded white eyes, and thin white hair. His skin tan, roughed by ages of manual labor stretches and wrinkles with the exaggerated movements he makes to speak. He wears an expression of disapproving impatience, in the general direction of the voice that called for him, "I have rope, how much length do ye want, and of what material?"

"Well actually we wanted to commission a rope made from a special material."

"Nope can't help ye."

"What? Why not?"

"If ye haven't well noticed I'm old, even for a dwarf, and blind, I am simply guessing that you are human based on circumstance, these both together make me get any special materials impossible, you either get the standard stuff or you go somewhere else."

"But we have the material with us. All that exists of it."

"Now you are talking I guess I could make an exception based on that. What is the material I will be using for this commission?"

"Eliza's Hair."

"What's an Eliza? No matter. I have made horse hair rope, the hair of something else shouldn't be a problem. Maybe a challenge but I should be able to get it done."

Pearl snickers at the motion of Eliza's hair being short and she responds through the snicker, "I doubt length will be an issue."

"Sure, sure. Come in and set the material in a pile in that corner, then come back in a week, I will remember you as Hair Girl for the order."

Following the direction given Pearl steps into the small building, and reaching into the magic satchel she begins pulling out yard after yard of the light sky-blue hair, laying it in a pile. Stepping back into the street, she and Eliza laugh at the absurdity of having a rope made of Eliza's hair, but both eagerly wait to test its strength. The two quickly find their ways through the streets and with only a small amount of direction find their way to a small hole in the wall style building whose street sign reads in both Common, and the most common written language of the dwarven people, "The Leaking Whetstone."

Stepping into the tavern Pearl and Eliza don't even need to ask for assistance in finding the people they are looking to meet. From the door they see the group easily with Nakhal's form awkwardly sticking out in a dwarven structure. Stepping to the table the two woman come into view and hear the middle of a conversation about past lovers, with Flame-Tender quickly ending a response to something Nakhal must have said, "That's nothing! There was this one time in Vestalian, me and a gorgeous woman met in an alley between bars. We had both been told we reached our limit in one of the bars and were crossing to get another drink in the other when... Hey, it's Pearl and Eliza. Great! That means we can talk about my companion and my purpose in this city."

The man stands and pulling out two seats offers them to Pearl and Eliza. Accepting the gentlemanly gesture Pearl asks, "What is your reason for being here?"

"Well, if I am to have any chance in getting your friend here to join us in our mission here, I need to be forth coming and honest, and you seem like reliable types so I think I can trust you to not betray us immediately after we are done here. We are hunting a vampire. I know, sounds crazy, but we have been tracking him for some time and he has made his way to this city to hide away. I doubt he will stay here long so we are pressed for time in finding his hideout. We were interested in your friend here as to see his strength, we both thought that it would certainly be of aid to us to have muscle like that in the impending conflict."

"We honestly don't know this guy. He approached us after he was in that scrap with that dwarf."

Turning to Pearl, Nakhal interjects into the conversation, "The spirits told me to seek out and join you, in something of dire importance. Now that I have, I am sure their guidance will come to me again soon for what is next for me."

Flame-Tender turns his whole body in his seat to Pearl and gesturing with a hand to Nakhal continues, "You see? Whether or not your tie with this man is strong or you believe it to be non-existent, he will only help us if it is part of your journey, or at least that is what he keeps telling us. So please, I know for women as beautiful as the two of you, the idea of fighting, let alone the target being one of the types of undead lord, maybe something you would try to normally avoid. I can also see that you at least have seen some amount of travel to find yourself transformed into a half-elf person made into a hybrid with a fishy being. Look, you don't have to do anything. Umbra and I can protect you but we will probably need this man's help, for his strength."

"Alright, take it easy, what do you need?" Pearl responds with a smile.

"Really?"

"Yea, sounds like an interesting break from our mission, which has been put on hold anyway. You can rest assured that we won't need your protection."

"Sure..."

"I'm serious! I did tell you that I am a great ship captain, and Lizzy here is an exceptionally powerful mage," Pearl boasts wrapping an arm over Eliza's shoulder, having forgotten about the sunburn.

Eliza who turned away to blush at the compliment suddenly feels Pearl's cold wet hand, slap against her shoulder. Unable to scream because of the damage to her voice box, she still recoils, yelling into Pearl's mind, *"Pearl! My sunburn!"*

Pearl's hand retracts to press against her forehead both in response to having forgotten, and to the piercing discomfort that comes from having a voice yelling directly into her mind. Chuckling, Pearl turns from Lizzy saying to the man, "Forgot about her sunburn. Wait, Lizzy why haven't you tried your healing hands thing on yourself to get rid of the burn?"

Eliza's writhing in pain from the impact of Pearl's hand on her sun scorched skin, stops suddenly with Pearl's question, and thinking to herself, she responds, *"You know I don't know why I haven't. Might even help my throat."* Grabbing the holy symbol which even while she sits with a full body sunburn, finds its home around her neck, Eliza concentrates on the want to heal. Her hands begin to glow with the gentle golden light. Wrapping her hands together the energy passes into her, and the red of the burn fades returning her skin once more to the flawless smooth pale that it has naturally. Looking to Pearl, Eliza draws in a large breath, and she releases it in an attempt to scream, instead finding only a soft kitten like call, "Ah," and rubbing the back of her head her voice passes into Pearl's mind, *"Nope, no voice still, but at least it ɵoesn't hurt anymore."*

Confused from the sudden pathetic breath of a meager scream from Eliza, not having the ability to hear her words to Pearl, Flame-Tender pulls slightly away asking, "I'm sorry is something wrong Miss Eliza?"

Eliza looks to the man having forgotten where she was for a moment, but before she can wave him off, Pearl slides herself between the two explaining in a way that almost sounds like she is embarrassed of Eliza's pitiful outburst, "No, no, everything is fine. The thing is she hurt her voice recently, and while she just used an ability of hers to heal the sunburn she had gotten earlier today, she was testing to see if it gave her voice back, which it apparently it didn't. We've been communicating telepathically this entire time."

"Telepathically?"

"Yes, like I said, Lizzy is an exceptional mage. She can maintain telepathic communication with as much ease as you and I are speaking."

"That is amazing, magic is an excellent way of defeating unnatural beasts like the one we are hunting," Flame-Tender responds getting beside himself with a sudden excitement, before leaping from his seat to take Eliza's hand, "It is only fair to say that a woman of such beauty holds such effortless control over great amounts of magic for only that could be the case so that she may never need lift a finger to tire herself or sully her perfection."

Pearl looks in jealous disgust at the gushing that she discerns as a façade put on to get Eliza to accept the man's proposal. Before Eliza can respond, Pearl leans in and whispers into Flame-Tender's ear, "Wait a moment now. How are we supposed to trust you?"

Flame-Tender's eyes widen with the information, filling him with shame, confusion, and fear, of the two women he is meeting, and he pulls away responding, "You can't. I understand that, but the creature we intend to confront cannot be brought down merely by of the efforts of Umbra and myself. We need more strength, and we saw Nakhal on the docks and sought his compatriotship. Seems he will only assist if you are there too. Something about spirits telling him to follow you."

"Well I can't say that we have much reason to trust you. So, I can't say we will join you," Pearl continues turning to face the giant of a man, "If you want to join us we aren't leaving until the morning so feel free to aid them until then."

"I am sorry to hear that. Will you at least join us," Flame-Tender says standing and looking to Nakhal.

With a slow nod Nakhal affirms simply, "Yes."

"That is fantastic! Well, it is getting late. The perfect time to continue Umbra and my search for this fiend. I suggest we stick together at this point so that we can build trust in each other and our abilities."

Without waiting for a response Flame-Tender turns from the table and steps to the door quickly followed by the silent figure of Umbra whose chair doesn't even seem to grind against the room's floor. Nakhal, whose expression holds a deep thoughtful look in the direction of the leaving group nods, only smiling himself after Eliza gives him a wave and gestures to the door.

With the three strangers gone Eliza turns to Pearl asking, "*What happened?*"

"What do you mean?" Pearl asks in response, leaning back and resting her feet on the table.

"*You agreed this morning that we might want to look for others to help us. These could be those people.*"

"They could, or they could be three strange men who see two uniquely beautiful women, and who would want to take advantage of us. I don't know, it just felt too much like a trap."

"*Well you would agree that we can't continue on our own with Aldrin gone right?*"

Standing in a burst of movement Pearl nods with a grin, "That's why we are going to follow them, and if they actually are going after what they say they are we will hop in and help, otherwise we leave none the worse," and having waited a few moments to put some distance between themselves and the men, Pearl and Eliza step into the streets. There, they see the towering figure moving away from them far down the busy street.

The dark of night sets in almost undetectably in the streets of the subterranean port city. The glowing fires that provide the town with most of its light continue to burn at the peak of their strength even as the seaward horizon sparkles with the stars and the moon's light glancing off the softly stirring ocean's surface. The streets remain full of life with the populace unfazed by the particular time of the day. As the Pearl and Eliza pass by one of the many taverns, knocks on doors and voices from within can just barely be heard saying to waking patrons, "Th' sun is bellow th' horizon, ye kin wake, or keep sleeping juist letting ye know," now obvious to the outsiders is the routine to keep the city functioning at all hours.

With Flame-Tender's lead the three men weave through the streets, with ease passing through clusters of people gathering around open store fronts, which radiate with the scent of freshly baked bread. The movement of the city could easily be seen as the morning commute if Eliza, and Pearl weren't tired from having walked most of the cities span earlier in the day. As the men step onto a lift to the layer of city above, Pearl holds Eliza back within a small cluster of people waiting to board the other lift which descends as the one the men are on begins to ascend. They board the new lift and themselves ascend.

Getting to the third tier of the dwarven port does not find Flame-Tender and the other two nearby turning a corner several blocks down as Pearl catches them in her gaze once more. Still suspicious of the intent of the mission at hand and not truly knowing if they have yet been noticed, Pearl and Eliza follow still the three men with a focus on their surroundings, becoming more uneasy the deeper into the dark cavernous parts of the city they progress into.

The glow of fires quickly grows distant and is as quickly replaced with the soft glow of luminescent fungus that appear to have been grown purposefully and with great care by the people of this part of the city to give a place where they could escape the bustle of the rest of the city. The quiet of this part of town presents itself as a distinct warning of the shady dealings that take place here. This puts Pearl and Eliza on their guard, but it is as they raise their guard that Pearl and Eliza notice one of the three missing. The dark hooded figure, Umbra has vanished from his companion's side.

Pearl and Eliza almost jump from their boots as a hushed call echoes to the girls from an ally. With the tenor of a young man, whose voice has seen no hardships of pipe weed, or hard liquor, "You two?" Pearl draws her blade, and Eliza extends her hands toward the suddenly appearing figure from the shadows. No weapon drawn Umbra, immerges more into the soft glow of the mushroom lights asking, "Why are you following us, you denied aiding us?"

Worry fills Pearl's eyes as she hesitatively responds, "How did you know we were following you?"

"We have been tracking a creature who possess traits far more sensitive than a human's. We have had to fine tune our perceptive skills. Look, you don't trust us, right?"

"There is no reason to."

"We trust you. At least Flame-Tender does. He has a way with people, and knowing whose side they would be on in a conflict. This also means that he can be overly flattering and give too much information when he finds people he thinks he can trust. Look, I trust Flame-Tender so I am pretty sure you aren't going to sell us out, but we can't be distracted. Stop following us, I have to get..." Umbra explains before turning to look in the direction Flame-Tender and Nakhal and seeing them gone he exclaims, "Darn it," before turning from Pearl and Eliza and shifting into a full sprint in that direction.

Now intrigued more than she was before Pearl grabs Eliza's wrist and kicks into her own jog, after Umbra. Jogging to stay at Pearl's side, Eliza asks, "*What are we ↑oing?*"

"He's panicked. We might have to hop in to help here."

"*So, now you trust them?*"

"Not quite, but that was an earnest reaction. They may truly have just been overly straightforward with us, and based on that panic the other two might be in trouble having moved forward without him."

In the path Eliza, Pearl, and Umbra are moving, there is commotion in the street with barely clothed patrons escape from a building in a stampede. The instant the front entrance is shown to be blocked by a frightened wave of all types of people, Umbra looks to the only window the building has facing the street. Maintaining his sprint in the direction of the building he steps into a shadow cast by one of the blocks along the street and vanishes.

Through the same window Pearl watches as the colors of Flame-Tenders velvet suit flash by before two more figures appear to leap for him. Seeing this Pearl roles her shoulders, and again steps into a run in that direction.

From behind Eliza calls, "*Pearl my ritual book!*"

"What? There's no time we have to get in there and stop whatever fight is happening," Pearl responds.

Regardless, Eliza sprints to Pearl's side, digs the black book from the magic satchel, and runs for the window extending a pointed finger in its direction. Opening the book begins the ritual that she tested on Pearl. Taking a deep breath, not sure her voice will be able to produce the verbal component necessary for the magic to take hold, Eliza begins to trace sigils in the air toward the framework of the window. "Fahf yaw fhtagn mgng mgepnnn hai, mgah'ehye ehyenah ahch' rect mgepuln eonon, Eliza, Boop, Pearl," her voice whispers somehow barely escaping her throat, which becomes sore as the words growl and scratch their way out, and the sigils form in the air flying to their places around the window.

Almost immediately after Eliza finishes a single incantation the sigils fade as they had before when the strange spell took effect around the door of Eliza's room. At that moment Pearl darts past Eliza saying, "Lizzy I don't know how your telepathy works but if you can, try to read their minds, we need to know what is going on," before she lowers her shoulder and leaps through the window shattering the glass in a loud crash.

Inside the room Pearl finds what appears to be an office that has been put together in the back of a large supply closet. Behind the desk of this office Flame-Tender appears to be in a dance with three strange dwarves who have a strange fog of two purples, a deep royal mixed with the same purple of his suit, over their eyes swinging clawed hands aggressively at him. With the crash he turns to see Pearl and still avoiding the attacks of the dwarves, calls, "See, I told Umbra you wouldn't be able to resist helping. You and the companion of yours are good people. I could feel it," he stops at that turning his attention back to the dwarves.

The three dwarves look vastly different from others of their species. They are gaunt and pale, and all participating in one of the greatest taboos of dwarven kind, being clean shaven. Their eyes, though obscured by the strange purple fog, are filled with predatory malice, and their teeth are unnaturally sharpened and elongated, visible as they grunt with each missed swing in Flame-Tender's direction.

Pearl presses herself from the fresh pile of broken glass in time to watch a black figure drop with a heavy weight down behind the strange dwarves. For only a moment the figure appears as just a pile of fabric on the floor before rising to reveal Umbra, who throws open his black cloak revealing a silvered longsword in each hand. An amulet of two crescent moons with a star between them throws a spark of light reflecting brilliantly from its silver and gold. His voice, sure in its strength and intent, calls out to the three aggressors, "Creatures, spawned to hunt in the night, against the natural order, learn too to fear the moon."

The small spark of light that glistens on the metal talisman hung from Umbra's neck suddenly grows out into three beams that impact the slender dwarven forms as they turn to him. Each raise their arms in recoiling terror as their skin begins to blister and peel, releasing white pillars of smoke to rise to the ceiling. Revealed in the glow is a series of mutations that have occurred to the pale dwarves, whose ears and canine teeth have been elongated and pointed, and whose faces have become gaunt like a sickly human's. The beams of light only last a moment quickly flickering once more from existence, revealing to the creatures as they look to the source of their pain, the masked hooded figure in a defensive stance.

Filled with rejuvenated bloodlust after having been struck by a radiant energy, the dwarf like beings release an ear-piercing screech. Extending their claws the three of them move for Umbra. Before any of them can begin a charge, Flame-Tender's voice calls over the room, "Three against one? You must have some faith in your strength to think you need all three of yourselves for that one man!" finishing the statement with a sarcastic snare, "Tch." Two of the three stop with the words, turning with twitching, visibly struck with unnatural anger, they look in Flame-Tenders direction, finding him standing with his back against the wall and his hands in his pockets. It is as they see him that the fog reforms over both of the creatures' eyes. Angry at the man in the velvet suit, more so than they are at the man who seared their flesh, the two charge the cocky man in the same moment the other lunges for Umbra.

On her feet, Pearl lets a grin take her face as she leaps onto the desk, and planting her feet she launches herself into a flip and toward the two charging Flame-Tender. The spring from the wood of the desk is just enough to propel Pearl into a flip where tucking her legs to just miss striking the ceiling, she passes over both creatures. Upon landing with a speed that makes it nearly impossible to see with a normal human's eye, her rapier is drawn and presses through one of the creatures' temple to protrude from the other side leaving a proud smirk on her face. The smirk doesn't last though, with Pearl withdrawing the sword, thinking that she has dealt it a fatal blow, the creature turns to face her with its own grin.

Flame-Tender leaps out of the path of the one still charging him, and shrugging he continues his verbal assault saying to the thing, "Really? This is all you've got? Ivo must be weaker than I thought for his spawn to not even be able to strike me while I'm unarmed." With those words, the fog in front of the one creature's eyes expand to encompass the entirety of his head, with a small column of it forming into what looks like a nail before pressing down in a way that appears as though it penetrates the skull. The thing coughs, its eyes wide behind the fog as it swings with anger wildly missing Flame-Tender who doesn't even need to dodge the attack as he calls to Pearl, "Don't go for killing blows. We need to subdue them to learn where their master is!"

Looking through the shattered window to the three separate conflicts Eliza watches Umbra fend off swipes with his swords. She watches Pearl narrowly dodging the creature, who doesn't even bleed through the puncture wound, she made in its head, acrobatically moving through the cramped room as if in an intense dance of her own, as she is pursued by claws and teeth trying to rend her flesh. She watches Flame-Tender's insults, now obviously channeling some type of magic which is rendering one of the creatures unable to land a single blow with minimal effort on the suited man's part to dodge. She looks to the space and sees a window in the far wall opposite her, and again looking to the script in her book of rituals she releases the magic of the ritual for the threshold in a single incantation.

When hearing Flame-Tender call to Pearl that they need to find the creatures master, Pearl's words again pass through Eliza's head, and she extends her hands in front of her closes her eyes and takes another deep breath. The crystal on her amulet pulses and her hands dance, pulling from it ribbons of magic. Pressing the strand to her head, her eyes flash open and her voice now painful again to use, only barely scratches out, "Ilolg-nnn."

The room doesn't stop with the spells effect taking place but feels like it does as suddenly Eliza is taken by a cavalcade of voices from those around her, their thoughts become audible for her. Pearl's mind, focused on her own movements, lightly sings, "*Left swipe, now he does a right, and duck, and poke,*" and on queue with her thinking it, Eliza watches Pearl swing and sway with her rapier finding purchase in the creature's chest.

Flame-Tender's eyes glance over to Eliza, and not even concerning himself about the creature his is occupying, his mind inquires, "*I wonder what that was. I was worried I brought people into this who might have been in over their heads, but Pearl's having a good go at it. So, I am interested to see this one's magic at work. Oh, need to add insult to injury,*" before actually speaking once more, "I mean I understand why your teeth are so white, your trying to get my blood but you can't even touch me, you must be starving, since you obviously can't kill anything."

The creatures have their minds repeating a cacophony of growls and barks in their head the three seem to have more than twenty voices in their minds, all saying the same thing, "*Eat. Feed. Hungry. Kill.*"

Focusing on that group of voices, Eliza presses the power that fills her mind into the crowd, her telepathic voice yelling over all of them, "*Where is your master?*"

One voice shared between all three of the minds of the strange creatures responds as all of the other voices silence themselves, "*Peering into the minds of my servants isn't a very respectful thing to do, but you come vith a challenge. You vish to kill me, very vell. I make my place of rest in the crypts of this wretched place, for now. You have until next sundown to find me, if you dare come,*" the fighting comes to a sudden stop as the three beings grasp their heads in apparent pain as the voice continues, "*Children these are now our guests, leave them, for your father to care for.*"

Eliza gasps, for a reason strange and forgotten to her in the moment, at the malicious cadence, the way she hears the word, "father" used, strikes in her subconscious throwing a flash of a memory into her head, but letting the magic subside she watches as the three creatures looked panicked and each rush for an exit.

On instinct, Eliza leaps through the window to see the door that leads out of the room and throws a hand up in its general direction out of the room, and her voice growls out as she calls, "Fahf yaw fhtagn mgng mgepnnn hai, mgah'ehye ehyenah ahch' rect mgepuln eonon, Eliza, Boop, Pearl, Flame-Tender, Umbra, Nakhal!" Six sigils form and shoot into place passing through solid objects until affixing themselves to the doorway, and Eliza, suddenly feeling light headed lets her body drop to her knees in the broken glass just in time for one of the creatures to leap over her for the window.

The sound of glass shattering cracks through the air as the two escaping through the two windows break past the windowsill. In the same moment the sigils flash to life and create the tethers that pierce through the creatures' heads. Injured and worn down from the fighting, the magic that surges through them is more than can be handled and both make their way out of the building their heads rupture spraying grey matter out like a popping water balloon.

Eliza on hands and knees breathing heavy, having expelled more magical energy than she is used to using in such a short period of time, doesn't see the effects of her magic as Pearl and Flame-Tender visibly cringe at the sight. Umbra gives chase to the third who leaps over the wardrobe before finding trouble undoing the lock. Before Umbra can get close enough to attempt to subdue the creature, it forces the door open breaking the latch in the process. Stepping through the door, the same fate finds the final of the three vampire spawn leaving a headless body laying in the now silent establishment's front room.

Turning from the new silence, Pearl's eyes go wide as she sees Eliza bent over in exhaustion. Everything else fades from her mind at that moment, and her feet carry her to Eliza's side asking with worry in her voice, "Lizzy! Lizzy are you alright?"

Grabbing onto Pearl's shoulder, and pushing herself up Eliza coughs, releasing a spattering of blood, before responding telepathically, *"I'll be fine, I figured out where their master is. He has hidden in a crypt somewhere in the city. We don't have much time though. If we don't find which crypt and face him by next sundown he is going to be able to make his escape."*

Before Eliza can say anymore or Pearl can respond, Flame-Tender's voice chimes into the conversation, "Excellent, they're dead. Now how are we going to get the information we need. I mean yeah, you are definitely the real deal, I have not personally been in the acquaintance of anyone whose magic I have seen be able to easily finish off a vampire spawn, but we needed to capture one."

With the comment sounding like an attack on Eliza to her, Pearl becomes defensive rebutting, "Lizzy got the info. That's probably why they scattered. She got inside their heads. The question I have is since you are the vampire hunters, what do we have to do about these three? Are they going to come back to life somehow? I mean they already did it once."

Stepping back into the room dragging one of the bodies with him Umbra responds with a cold calculated tone, "No, these are just spawn. Lesser vampires, which when slain, stay dead."

"Wait, you got in their heads? What information did you get?" Flame-Tender asks directing his gaze to Eliza.

"She told me that he is in one of the city's crypts," Pearl responds.

"Alright then. There is no time to lose. Let's get searching," Flame-Tender continues stepping for the door.

"Wait, Lizzy is exhausted she needs to rest."

"So, you are going to be joining us then. Well, we can't wait. Every moment we do is another moment for Ivo to prepare an escape."

Pearl looks at Flame-Tender both admiring the straightforward focused attitude and despising him for the ease at which he looks past Eliza's pain to continue toward his goal. Before she can think of a retort, she feels Eliza's hand pull on her shoulder, and standing up Eliza's voice touches her, *"It's alright Pearl, I can rest while we walk. We are seeing if we can trust these men. Being single minded on accomplishing a goal to help people isn't a bad thing."*

Pearl sighs responding, "Yeah, and I guess you are right. Let's go."

Quickly Pearl and Eliza join the other two stepping into the main room. Quiet and empty of all patrons, the room sits destroyed and in disorder from the riotous stampede of people running to escape. The group continues, stepping out into the street, where they find, Nakhal glaring down at six strangers who had been in the establishment. Looking to the group as they exit he squints gesturing to the unconscious bodies, "They charged me."

Flame-Tender stops, with a look of astonishment responds, "Th-that's alright, they probably won't remember you when they wake up. They were panicking from seeing a head explode. Come on. We need to see if we can find the crypt Ivo has made into his lair."

Flame-Tender turns from Nakhal and stepping into the street begins walking away from the structure. Umbra is quick to follow but Nakhal waits at the door until Eliza and Pearl emerge. Seeing Eliza, exhausted, barely standing with Pearl's aid, Nakhal steps to her and kneeling offers, "One with sky hair, if you are to continue with us in your condition please allow me to carry you until you can carry yourself." Eliza hesitates for a moment before silently she responds with a nod, and steps to Nakhal from Pearl to be quickly lifted from her feet.

From there the group walks for several minutes before finding someone willing to talk to them. With a lie about wanting to visit and pay respects to an old friend who had been buried in the town, Flame-Tender learns that like the city, it is separated into layers which have innate class separation, so too are the crypts which hold only people of appropriate status within a given level. With that information, the group decides that a person who makes themselves out to be a lord, is most likely one to establish a foothold in the highest level of crypts, and they begin to walk that way.

Eliza finds her own feet beneath her as the group steps onto the lift that hoists them up to the fifth level. As the platform kicks and begins to rise Pearl asks Eliza, "How did you do that back there?"

"*Do what?*" Eliza asks back, not sure what Pearl is referring to.

"You invoked that ritual that we tested in moments instead of minutes."

"Oh, that. Well, I thought that maybe one of the things about a ritual taking so long is that it is a small amount of magic over a long period of time to get the same effect as magic invoked instantaneously, without the drain of channeling large amounts of magic at one time. So, I thought, maybe if I reversed that logic, I could invoke the power in a very short amount of time as was necessary. To be honest I didn't know it would work."

"Wow, I have to be annoying with how often I repeat this to you Lizzy, but you are amazing. I think I can actually remember something about that from when I was in school but for you to figure it out on your own..." Pearl's voice trails off as she feels a tear forming in her eye, and the lift jolts again.

As they reach the top of the lift's path they find armed guards waiting at the lifts' exit. Worry fills them as they think of the pile of unconscious bodies left outside the brothel in Nakhal's wake, but they find the guards are posted to prevent beggars from filling this particular city layer. With the guards' help it becomes simple to find the rest of the way to where the dead are entombed. Getting there though, the notion of their goal's impossibility strikes. Beyond the metal gate entrance is an unlit section of tunnels that the light of the fire from the street spans only a short distance into.

Allowed through the gate the group begins walking in the little light that is cast by a hooded lantern that an on-duty guard of the crypts provided them. An ominous unease rests on them with the whole of the area around them appearing like any other part of the city they have been through with towering blocks of stone reaching up to the ceiling, each holding staircases to access the many levels of doors available. Beset by the overwhelming appearance of the task at hand, Pearl's hands interlock behind her head as she asks with her voice echoing off the cold dead stone, "So what's the plan? We can't simply open up each of these until someone jumps at us from within."

"You're right," Umbra responds, in the same cold calculated voice as before. "That is why we aren't opening any. Do you remember that establishment? There was a layer of fog across the floor. That is one of the many possible remnants of a vampire's presence which often goes overlooked. If we find the tomb emitting that same fog, we find Ivo."

Flame-Tender simply stands with his arms crossed, nodding with a cocky grin, adding, "We told you. We've been at this for a while. There isn't anything Ivo will throw at us that we haven't prepared for. Come on we're burning oil."

Not convinced, Pearl stops and waving her hands above her head asks, "Wait a second! If stories serve me right, vampires are awake at night. So if you are so sure that finding some fog will find him, shouldn't we rest until morning?"

"There are two problems with that. You mentioned that we are on limited time. On that you are most assuredly correct. I don't remember seeing that barkeep in the pile of unconscious people when we left, nor did he remain at the bar. Chances are he has already informed his master that we are here and are searching for him. Secondly, you would be correct that generally vampires recline during hours of daylight. Unfortunately, your assumption for the reason is only half correct. Vampires cannot come into contact with sun light which is one of the few forms of radiant energy naturally available without a cleric or paladin of a faith channeling their deity's power and would thus burn the beast like Umbra's channeling did. Vampires however do not need to sleep, like all things that have circumvented the order of life to death they need not worry of fatigue, or their sanity. So where would the best place be for a vampire who wants to be more active than the sun will allow? On a continent where the entire population lives in caves away from the sun. So, you see, if we are going to catch this thing and put a stop to it, before he can make more of his spawn, then we must hurry."

Pearl sighs recognizing her inability to argue back against the response Flame-Tender provided, and once again the group steps ever forward. After more than a mile of walking, with no sign of an end to the path they are on brings more conversation to her mind though finally thinking of what to ask, "So if they can't go into the sun what other weaknesses do vampires have?"

"Well there are a hand full actually, though these only show up in the greater vampire specimen, also known as true vampire. What you have fought thus far have been lesser vampire or vampire spawn. The difference being that spawn are created by a vampire by it drinking nearly all of the blood of a victim and as they die the vampire uses necromantic energy that is part of them from their curse to bring back the victim as a servant. We aren't quite sure how true vampires come into being. To answer your question though, an oak stake pierced through the vampire's heart paralysis it and prevents it from transforming to escape. Natural running water like that of a river, they can't cross, and if they try it's like strong acid to them. They can't see their reflection and they can't enter a place of living or business without being invited in first. I think that is all of them but remember these are all of course alongside them having the strength of several men. They are faster than most land animals. They never need to sleep, only ever need blood to sustain themselves, can walk on walls and ceilings like a spider, and can transform into mist or animals all while controlling other undead that happen to be nearby."

"Oh so most of the stories are true. That means garlic should be a weakness too."

"Well it is and it isn't. Vampires have very keen senses so sudden loud noises, strong smell, sudden flashes of bright light all can be debilitating to them, but not to the level of the other weaknesses."

"Tender," Umbra's voice calls, stopping the conversation and the group's movement, "It's here."

The five stand between two towering columns of stone nearly three hundred feet wide reaching up to the ceiling more than one hundred feet above them. A single door sits on either side of the group in the center of their respective stone columns with another door above them and another, every ten feet up to the ceiling. From the fourth door up on the left, a thin trail of fog falls dispersing before it has a chance to form as a sheet across the ground like it had at the strange establishment.

Looking up to the door leaking fog, Pearl asks, with sarcasm in her voice from knowing the answer but suddenly not wanting it, "So we're going up there?"

"Well actually it would be best if one of us went up there and we drew him out, the more distance we can put between him and us from the start of our conflict the better chances we have of taking him down."

From above a voice interrupts the conversations, gathering all five of their attention with a worried fright. The voice Eliza had heard echo through the minds of the vampire spawn calls down with a cold malevolence, "You do know it is rude to disturb someone's slumber, especially if you are looking to kill zem, but by ze hour of your sudden arrival I vill assume one of you is ze one who peeked inside the heads of my minions. It vas a pleasure to meet you. Now it is time for you to die."

The figure a gaunt pale man with short black hair dressed in a simple but elegant black suit stares down at the group with a hunter's glare and a grin that displays his fangs extended to a point like those of the creatures before. With his words said he raises a single gloved hand and turns from the people below stepping for the iron door he had silently opened while the group was distracted. A powerful cold wind rushes unnaturally through the tunnel suddenly with the gesture, and the group look around themselves with a new feeling of unease falling upon them. Flame-Tender looks to Umbra the instant Ivo's back is turned, calling in a hushed tone to avoid Ivo's hearing if possible, "We can't let him latch that door."

With a nod Umbra darts from the group in the direction of the stairs that lead up to the separate tiers of tombs. In the same instant that Umbra's second foot fall lands, he stops. A the loud echoes of the slam of iron doors, which are meant to be completely sealed, breaking open on the side of the path the group is standing in. Looking to the sound's sources they find the doors of the ground level open releasing a low chorus of shuffling bodies.

Again, before the group can prepare themselves for an approaching undead threat, the doors of the second level slam open, then the third, the one on the forth not already open, and the fifth and so on, in a series that only becomes more frightening as it becomes more distant, with each increasing the volume and number of approaching abominations against the proper order of the cycle of life.

Umbra having stopped strides again to get to the stairs, leaving the others stunned staring through the now open doors of the tombs, in horror. Shuffling, the source of the noise, dwarven figures with decayed flesh tightly clinging to bones without any appearance of nondecayed muscle beneath. Quickly Eliza takes a deep breath and remembering the thirteen rooms she and Pearl went through to escape the plane of undeath, she looks to Pearl and telepathically calls, *"Pearl that wan, I nee it."*

"What? Sure. What for?" Pearl asks digging into her satchel to draw forth the webbing wand, immediately throwing it to Eliza.

Catching the wand Eliza points it up and concentrating her magic into it an orb of white forms at its tip before leaping up to explode creating an enormous cluster of web above them, nearly forty feet wide with each strand thicker than the hemp rope used on ships. As the ropes of web find their connections Pearl's eyes fill with panic noticing one of the zombified forms, having stumbled forward into the semblance of a run, drawing its fists back to strike Eliza. Before she even has a chance to call out to warn her companion, Nakhal's form darts past the figure and Eliza in a single motion, and stopping on the other side reveals one of his swords drawn when his hands had been free before he moved. It is when Nakhal straightens himself that Pearl becomes impressed as the zombie suddenly splits into two pieces separated with a razor's edge cut that holds no tearing along it.

Eliza turns and seeing the undead thing falling apart by her looks to Nakhal, to give an appreciative nod, before turning to the door from which it came. Pointing the wand in that direction she releases another burst of the energy clogging the door way and ensnaring the undead within with thick sticky web. At that same moment more of the zombified forms begin to make their way out from the other door way. From above zombies can be seen entangling themselves in the web, and from above that the sound of falling bodies being caught by the sticky net can be easily heard. Eliza's mind leaps out to all four of those with her, "*If we ɗon't stop this soon we'll be overwhelmeɗ.*"

Pearl dips out of the way of one to the zombies which has escaped the still open-door way and lets her mind call back through the telepathic link for the others to hear, "*Your right. Can you ɗo that thing you ɗiɗ against Domavir? If you can ɗo that I can get vamps back out.*"

"*I can try.*"

With a nod, Pearl charges one of the shuffling forms. Getting only a few feet away she jumps and using it as a springboard throws herself up into the web which is beginning to fill with undead. Grabbing the leg of one of the bodies, she acrobatically avoids the web and leaps again up to the third level of the tower. Repeating the process, a third time, Pearl plants her feet on the ten-foot ledge in front of the open but not broken iron door of the forth level, through which more zombies are making their way out.

Flame-Tender dodging out of the way of another zombie looks up at the acrobatic feat that brings Pearl to Ivo's door at the same time that Umbra has taken to reach the second. A look of impressed approval forms on his face as he points to one of the zombies facing him and gives a wave as thought to express that the form is not worth its presence. Again the dark fog that formed over the eyes of the vampire spawn finds hold on the zombie's face. In the same moments he is casting a type of magic on the undead being, he is also stepping away from the approaching hoard putting as much distance as he can between himself and them.

Umbra, with both of his swords drawn, looks at the path before him to cross the second level to reach the stairs up. Seeing three shuffling forms not yet restrained by the magically created web he doesn't hesitate in sprinting forward passing through the gathering. With agile movements, each blade find impact against the decayed flesh and bone of each of the three figures, at least two times apiece, leaving Umbra on the other side untouched as the undead become dead again with the magic animating them failing to do so with the added damage. Growing a smirk from the adrenalin of his attack, Umbra continues to the next set of stairs and begins climbing to the third level.

A body falls through the web avoiding the adhesive vines through a series of impacts against the already ensnared forms within. With a crack of bones and the release of a ring of dust around it the form does not move after the impact directly behind Nakhal who is unfazed by the undead projectile. Standing with both hands on the grip of his large curved sword the large man's movements are fluid, and swift with every strike dropping a foe as two more zombies split from his blade in front of him, both falling motionless to the ground.

In the midst of all the action Eliza pulls away to not risk being interrupted. Extending her hands out before her while taking a deep breath she lets the magic within her build. A gust forms around her quickly becoming hurricane level winds focused in a perfect sphere only large enough to contain her as her magic becomes visible to the naked eye as it seeps from her into the vortex. As with all of the magic she knows she can create, her hands dance on their own forming the glyphs that become the circling gyroscope around her as the transformation begins to take hold. Painful even to those around her who can bear witness to the magic, the sound of bones breaking and grinding into powder is just audible under the gusting torrent of magical energy as Eliza's appendages are pulled in to her form, replaced with long thin eyestalks and tentacles. Eliza's body compresses into a single central sphere and all seven eyes, one in the center of her form and one at the end of six of her ten new appendages, open.

Flame-Tender looks in bewildered astonishment at Eliza's transformation, captivated to the point of being unable to dodge the gnashing maw of a zombie that has made its way to him. Growling in pain he only takes his eyes from Eliza's new floating form long enough to draw a dagger and pierce it through the zombies throat to be able to escape before looking at the sphere creature asking, "Hey, you are still Eliza right?"

"*Yes,*" Eliza's voice echoes in his head unchanged by the transformation.

"So what's the plan? What does the magic to turn into that thing let you do?"

"*First just worry about staying alive Pearl, and I will get Ivo down to where you can strike him,*" in that moment Pearl leaps over the zombies through the door, and on the other side she throws herself at them pushing them all into the web. Watching this Eliza flies out and around the web with the cluster's radius being just about forty feet, calling into Pearl's mind, "*Just get him outside.*"

Pearl looks out and sees through the twisting maze of web the floating orb that is Eliza, and she responds with a nod before running back through the door. Inside the tomb are many halls lined with divots in them for the dead to be lain to rest. At the end of the main hall sits in a fairly out of place way, a single human sized coffin. Pearl's elvish heritage only just allows her to see normally with the small amount of light that the lantern resting on the ground below provides in the awkward to get to place, and she steps slowly toward the coffin whose lid sits closed. Nervously she moves around to be behind that vessel for the dead and tries to think how she should get the undead fiend out of the tomb without it first killing her.

Wrapping her arms around the head of the casket Pearl pushes her full weight into it and it slowly begins to slide across the stone floor. Little by little she pushes it to the tomb's entrance, hoping that the vampire is inside. Gaining momentum it is only moments after Pearl entered through the iron door that she reemerges pushing the coffin off the side of the ledge. The wooden box falls and is barely caught by one of the ropes of web slowing it enough not to shatter on impact with the ground landing with its lid open revealing no one to be inside.

Pearl is suddenly filled with worry as she sees the emptiness of the coffin and slowly turns to look back where she pushed it from. Fear runs down her spine as standing directly behind her, glaring down in a deep seeded rage that holds the angered party still enough for terror to be struck in the heart of the causer, Ivo asks, "So zat is how it is going to be. You vouldn't just die. You had to make things difficult for me didn't you? Fine then I vill kill you myself."

Fueled by instincts Pearl ducks around the male form and gives a swift jab to his back that through his surprise at the suddenness of the action throws him off balance and to the edge of the ledge as she slams the door behind him and latches it. Turning from the door having looked behind himself as he was pushed, Ivo only see's the many eye stalked being after it is too late, and he becomes the target of three rays. One of dark energy that to a living creature would cause the impacted part of the body to quickly decay, which strikes with no effect. The second a pulsing wave of energy like one that Boop regularly uses which strikes and pushes the undead man several feet back toward the staircase from the third level. The third beam however misses, impacting the stone wall to no effect.

Umbra, only after Ivo is magically pushed toward the staircase, reaches the same level and beneath his mask he smirks as he readies himself in an offensive fighting stance. Waiting for Ivo to catch himself, Umbra charges forward and bring both blades together swinging them as one into Ivo's side. He watches the silver razors edge slice through the thin padding of the suit and into the thick dead skin that instead of decaying has become tough like armor. The blade shimmer for a second in the light, not through a means of magic of their own but through sparks that burst on the vampire's flesh upon contacting the holy metal plated weapons, and the flesh gives giving the full force of the blow into Ivo's side, throwing him from the edge into the web.

Snagged in the sticky strings Ivo struggles, attempting to get free. Looking up to the trapped man Flame-Tender grins, saying, "Letting yourself get trapped in a web because we caught you off guard. Please, you are taking us for fools. No, I won't let you insult us in such a way, in that web you shall not stay. For you I send blades of sound, to free you to fall to the ground."

The words echo almost like one of Eliza's incantations reverberating with magic, but unlike Eliza's, the echoes of power portray a melodious nature to them sounding like music. No sooner do the words end, does the sound of wind being sliced by a quickly swung blade whip around Ivo. Magic cuts through the air and webs around him causing him to fall to the ground. Before he can impact the ground though and be surrounded, Ivo grins responding, "So you have magic users in your company and more than one. Fine I vill still kill you," and his body disperses into a cloud of mist.

Gathering behind Flame-Tender, Nakhal sees the mist form into a column and become Ivo once more. The large man yells, "Behind you," as he steps to swing along a path that threatens to decapitate both Ivo and Flame-Tender.

Seeing the sword, both go to duck, and Ivo simultaneously throws forward a clawed hand with razor sharpened nails. As both he and Flame-Tender duck opposite ways, his claw just catches purchase on Flame-Tender's face tearing a gash of flesh away to let blood flow freely out. Nakhal glares angrily at the vampire who dodged his attack, and who pulls away putting space between them. With a smirk Ivo charges forward fearless to strike at Nakhal and Flame-Tender to reveal he is struck by only magical attacks such as the rays Eliza bombards him with, or those made with a magical or silvered weapon deal lasting harm as the wounds Nakhal deals almost instantaneously heal.

Breathing heavy with her back against the door having been overly frightened by the unexpected appearance of the creature, which if stories are to be believed could have killed her easily, Pearl sits thinking to herself what she can do to help when just seeing the things eyes struck her with the fear she is feeling. Inspiration does strike, and digging through her bag she pulls out an old piece of wood, a belaying pin from the boat she had used and sunk in getting to Blackgate, and pulling a dagger from her hip she begins sharpening the pin to a point, while saying to herself, "I hope this is oak."

Three more beams blast into Ivo's side, one of orange fiery energy that burns another hole in the monster's suit. The telekinetic beam once more blasting him back and away, as the third, a white beam of energy that almost looks to be almost like a solid rod as it flashes into and out of existence in the blink of an eye. Sliding back along the stone road, Ivo feels his muscles contract as the white energy threatens to strike him motionless. With a roll of his shoulder the energy subsides not taking hold, and his focus pierces past the two he was in melee combat with, and to the creature whose magic struck him, Eliza.

Before Ivo can move from being blasted away from his conflict with Flame-Tender and Nakhal, Umbra notices an opportunity and leaping from the upper platform, from which he has been dispatching with the zombies who continue to grow in number as they rain down onto the web from above, he leaps down at the undead lord of prey. Landing hard, he brings both of his silvered blades across the vampire's back leaving unsealing wounds, and sending Ivo lurching forward in pain. Turning his attention to Umbra, Ivo scowls yelling, "I'll deal vith you next," before running at a frightening speed to the side of the battlefield defined by the walls of the towering tombs, and without needing to show any change in effort his motion continues as he runs up the walls face.

Nakhal and Flame-Tender, breathing heavy from the conflict they were just freed from, and covered in cuts and bruises from Ivo's assault against them, don't have a moment to rest as shuffling forms continue to amass around them. A few begin breaking their way through the web in the one doorway. Tired and sore the two turn their attentions to the zombie hoard around them. Nakhal's speed and size, even while tired, dominates over the slow stout-boned undead. Flame-Tender remains agile, slinging insults infused with magic to damage his targets' motor functions. In the midst of the chaos, Flame-Tender stops once, and looking to Nakhal calls, "Hey, you holding up over there, I told you it wouldn't be easy, and that we needed help. Keep at it."

The words cascade with a similar ring that the magically infused words Flame-Tender speaks carry. In the hectic sounds of moans and sword swings, Ivo turns along the wall and begins running through the web in Eliza's direction. The bleeding from Nakhal's wounds almost completely stops, and his breathing eases with the magic of the call. The sound of the battle is accented again, by another barrage of three beams shooting from Eliza, as Ivo leaps from the wall at her. Again, the telekinetic eye finds its mark throwing the leaping vampire back to slam into the wall, and a second time the white beam flashes, with the third beam releases energy that looks almost like a cloud that corkscrews around an invisible lance between Eliza and her target, before bursting against Ivo's chest.

Again, like against Domavir, Eliza's transformed self seems to hold victory with a single beam finding its full effect on the intended target, as Ivo impacts with the ground and grasps at his head with one hand while swinging at nonexistent enemies with the other, swaying dizzily, before becoming completely still. In the same moment Pearl holds in front of her the sharpened belaying pin, and swinging the door open steels herself for a fight, only to see Ivo's body go limp and fall to the ground. Jumping down each level to get to the vampires still form she calls to Flame-Tender, "Hey, how do we know if he's dead," as Eliza blasts the beam of fire into a zombie that had shuffled close to Pearl.

"He's not," Flame-Tender responds giving a disparaging wave at a zombie who falls as a fifth nail drives down through of the magic fog around its head, "If bodily injury gets too great, a vampire of his level instantly becomes mist to make an escape, and the only way to fully kill one is burning it in the sun."

"One of the beams that struck him was one that causes sleep the other was one that can cause a target to become paralyze› for a short time," Eliza's voice

echoes in everyone's head as she explains, not understanding herself how she knows the information other than to say it is built into the mental processing that is necessary for the form to control itself.

With a shrug Pearl turns to Ivo responding, "Alright then I have a feeling Lizzy's paralysis will wear off, so let's figure out something more permanent," and flipping over his body, she lifts up the pointed wooden stake and drives it into the vampire's chest.

Ivo's body lashes out with the impact, but only as much as a natural reaction to having a stake driven into the chest, and suddenly every remaining zombie slumps from its feet no longer animated returning once more to lifeless corpses. Umbra, Nakhal, and Flame-Tender free from their battles, join Pearl and Eliza, around the motionless vampire. With a sigh of relief Flame-Tender nods saying, "Looks like that stake worked, excellent work Pearl. Now all that is left is carrying him up to the cliff faces above this place and wait until sunrise. Nakhal you mind helping me carry this thing?"

Something about Flame-Tender, in the way he carries himself, and how he speaks to Pearl not as an annoyance, but as a comrade causes her to smile as she watches him grab Ivo's legs before Nekhal lefts the entirety of the body on his own with ease. Laying Ivo in the coffin that still sits undamaged from being caught and slowed by the web, the group close the lid before Eliza's voice echoes once more through the collective group's minds, *"Just a note to think about, but we probably shouldn't carry a coffin through the city, nor be seen leaving this many defiled graves. Probably we should let the guard who lent us that lantern know what happened, and then find another way out."*

Flame-Tender agrees with a nod adding, "Probably best to avoid causing anymore panic in the city at least for now. Don't worry, Umbra and I got detailed maps of the city from a source of ours. There is a way up and out that way," and he points deeper into the grave-tunnel.

Taking the lamp Umbra leaves the others to stay near the coffin, and he does as Eliza and Flame-Tender had said about retuning the torch and informing the guard of the state of the specific grave block. After a few minutes he arrives at the gate, and returns the lantern explaining, "The group I am a part of that you let through here, were searching for a vampire who took residency here. We have slain him, but in the process, he raised the dead to attack us. Their corpses no longer animated remain outside of where they were buried. We leave it to the city to return them to their resting place. We have handled the vampire," before fading into the shadow, disappearing.

In the time Umbra is away the group wait patiently for his return and after only a few moments of quiet the group sits in the light of a torch Nakhal has lit. Flame-Tender asks, "So what type of magic transformed you into that creature, and what type of creature is it?"

Turning to have her main eye look at Flame-Tender, Eliza responds, *"Oh, well Pearl said it appeared to her like a type of polymorph spell she had seen when she studied. A mage called Bellar, told us that this creature's family, like a black bear and a grizzly bear are both in the family Ursidae, is called matipragma. I was staying like this to see how long it would last on its own without me canceling it, but if it is making you uneasy, I can change back."*

"No, no don't worry about it. Learning the extent someone's magic can go is important so that they don't try to do something that is completely out of their reach."

"You think I'm creepy don't you," Eliza asks almost disheveled in her expression.

"What? No. What would make you think that? As long as you are in control of that form I won't see anyone but you right there. I have seen and heard stories about so much that magic can do. Some of it is unsettling, like the dead coming back to life. As long as magic is being used for and by beautiful things, then there isn't any reason to find it creepy. It is when ugly, evil things pervert magic that I would use that word."

Eliza almost gasps as Flame-Tender uses the word beautiful, slightly hinting at her as such, and she feels her heart almost skip a beat, his voice fading with the rest of his response as she focuses on that comment. Pearl smiles as she sees Eliza's face react to Flame-Tender's words, with a thankyou building in her to him for responding how he did. The conversation doesn't have a chance to go any further as Umbra reappears among the group saying, "It is done, we should move." Which ushers the group to do so, with Nakhal carrying the coffin with seeming ease as Flame-Tender leads.

18

New Friends

After more than an hour of walking, including a climb up a narrow staircase, Eliza's form transforms back from the strange creature she had become, filling her with almost a feeling of relief as the reversion occurs and the group eventually find their way out onto an expansive plateau. Small tufts of tall grass break through stone terrain with only a small cabin protruding above the grass barely visible in the distance. Off in one direction the plateau falls letting the ocean far below take the horizon. All only barely lit by the light of the moon, which seems to never cast itself upon Umbra, keeping a circle of shadow with a radius almost the same as his height strangely and unnaturally around him even as he moves.

Pointing to the other cabin far in the distance, Flame-Tender delights in saying, "That over there like the cabin we just came from is one of the few remaining dwarven structures that sits above ground on their continent. Ever since they completed their tunnel network there hasn't even been a need for them to venture above ground even to send mail, or to travel between their cities."

"And this information does what for us?" Pearl asks rolling her eyes feeling like she is back at school.

"Nothing of the practical sort. I just found it fascinating and thought it would be an interesting thing to share as we pass the time until morning when we can say farewell to Ivo over here. I mean it has to be at least a little interesting to you that an entire nation of a humanoid species lives beneath the ground we stand on like a colony of ants, with immense tunnels interconnecting the few centers of their civilization together like veins and arteries. I mean it makes me wonder, are dwarves the only ones who do this kind of a thing? How far down do the tunnels run? Could they be building a tunnel under the ocean floor, to other continents? All questions that I will probably never know the answer to, but fun to ask."

Sighing and setting to rest her back against the old cabin, Pearl asks, "So where are you guys headed after this? Lizzy and I have plans, this escapade with you was only a nice break from them because we had the time."

Nakhal looks down at Pearl responding with a stern seriousness in his voice, "The spirits have not told me to change my plan, I am to join you if you will have me."

"That is kind of my point in asking. Lizzy and I are on a quest where our world very well could hang in the balance. One of our fellowship left us a few days ago so when we met you three, and you wanted our help in this matter, we talked about asking you to join us if we could learn to trust you in time we spent with you, and I think we both agree," Pearl explains before looking to Eliza who nods in response, then she continues, "I don't want to share all of the details even here so tomorrow if you want to join us, come with us on our ship and we can explain everything."

Flame-Tender smirks responding, "An adventure where the world is in the balance? Now I know I am glad we ran into you two. I think we might very well tag along for that. How about the four of you get some sleep, I'll make sure nothing comes at us until morning."

Before Flame-Tender even said anything about it Eliza sits down and leans against Pearl, and almost immediately falls asleep. Pearl quickly follows letting her eyes become heavy to recharge as much as she can in the few hours of the night that remain. Umbra too rests his head on the hard-stone floor showing a vulnerability as he sprawls out in his circle of darkness. In a way it shows his trust for those he is with that seems out of character for the masked, secretive figure. Nakhal though, refuses to rest, remaining awake with his eyes fixated on the well-dressed human, who pulls from his hip a small sewing kit and begins to stitch the cuts and tears in his clothes.

Morning comes, and the light of the sun only barely begins peeking over the far horizon when the group is woken by the smell of burning hair and flesh, and the sound of sizzling. Their eyes opening quickly to the sudden sound and smell, to watch as the light of the sun only just makes direct contact with Ivo, the vampire melts and burn simultaneously, unable to scream in his pain from the oak induce paralysis. After a few moments the heat generated from purification of the unholy creature, ignites the wooden coffin that holds him, and the two crumble becoming only ash after a few minutes.

Standing and putting a chipper look on his face even as he tries to conceal the bags under his eyes from not having slept Flame-Tender gestures to the cabin in the distance saying, "The way we came will probably be blocked off by a crew reburying the poor dead that were made to attack us. So, we should probably enter back into the city through there. Let's head to your ship, or breakfast, or something. Please, Miss Eliza, and Captain Pearl, lead the way."

At being referred to as captain, Pearl smiles and takes lead for the hour walk to the suggested entrance. The group follow behind and quickly they make their way back down to the dock level, after retrieving Flame-

Tender's horse from the stable. Leading the group to her ship Pearl stomps aboard and seeing Devin return to deck from below, smiles introducing, "Devin this is Nakhal, Flame-Tender, and Umbra, they will be joining us. Nakhal, Flame-Tender, Umbra, this is Devin, my first mate."

Stepping onto the crewless ship Flame-Tender looks around asking, "So where is the rest of the crew?"

"Don't worry about that. Devin did you get everything you needed from the city?"

Scratching his chin to think, the demon blooded figure responds, "I think so, a couple months' rations, fire material, booze."

"Then let's get back, we have some stuff to discuss with these guys in a place we know we aren't being spied upon."

Eliza, steps from the group and returns to her room. The others watch Pearl, and Devin get the boat out of the harbor and onto open ocean on their own. Once out of view of any prying eyes Pearl steps to the urn, and exclaims with her hands resting on the sides of its pedestal, "Hoist the anchor, set the sails, to your positions sunken crew," and as with each time before the ornate jar shake in place releasing a fog onto the ships deck and forming the ghostly crew. This time however, Pearl gets to watch the reactions of the three, new to her company, as they share expressions of panic and worry, and Pearl has to leap to their sides, as they draw their blades, exclaiming, "Wait, wait, don't attack them, you wanted to know where the crew was, this is them. They are not evil, I got this ship from someone who was owed a favor by a pirate known as Pumpkin Head. Apparently, this ship and its crew was him repaying that favor to her. Umbra, I get it you are a holy person, to some extent, Lizzy was raised in a temple to Archangel, she has given me an earful against using a ghostly crew, but with our current mission we have to keep the number of people who know, down to as few as possible, so we can't afford to have a crew, at this time."

Gripping the hilt of both of his swords, caught only just before his was going to strike, Umbra steps from Pearl and through the door the way Eliza went. Watching his companion leave Flame-Tender responds, "You won't have to worry about him destroying your crew now, but you are intriguing me more and more, about this quest you are on, and if it is how you say I would have to agree. So where is it that we are going, there aren't any inhabited land masses for at least five days with good wind from here."

"You know a lot about a lot of things."

"I make it my business to know as much as I can, and teach those who would listen to my stories and songs."

"You're a bard, that's where your magic is coming from, I have always wanted to meet someone like you. Maybe you can be my Jacque."

"Your, what?"

"Not what, who. Jacque is the man who recorded the escapades of the great Vincent Jay. The originals that is. Several scribes have tried to pen new stories all of which I believe have fallen short."

"I don't think I will be doing that, but you still haven't answered my question. Where are we headed?"

"To our private island, and palace."

"Wait what? Alright, I am glad I came along, this is going to be nice."

While the ship is sailing for the two hour transit, Umbra finds his way into Eliza's room, where she lays on the hammock bed, gently swinging and staring at the strange writing in her black book. Sitting down on the stool Umbra simply stares at Eliza, until she becomes uncomfortable. Closing her book she asks, "So what brought you and this Flame-Tender together?"

Unmoving Umbra responds, with all expressions hidden behind his mask, "What are you reading?"

"I asked you a question first."

"He and I offered to search out that thing and were put together because of it. Your turn, what are you reading?"

"Well, I recently learned how to use my magic to preform rituals, and a friend gave me this, it already has a few in it. I have been trying to translate them, so that I can be of more help to Pearl in what we have been asked to do. Why do you ask?"

"The magic you used in the brothel and that took form in your casting of polymorph is not magic that could be called, arcane or divine, your magic is something entirely else, and it makes me uneasy. If you don't mind could you inform me on what exactly your magic is so that I can have the peace of mind that I had before seeing you preform those two spells."

"The magic inside me is connected with a being beyond our knowledge of existence. Bound to me by the cruel monsters that would be called my blood parents. I promise you I am not evil! I only use the magic to help people, and protect myself, I wouldn't dare attempt to use any more."

"I trust you. You are still young, and it is a shame that someone so innocent was bound to an accursed power. If what you say is true then you have already taken the right steps in maintaining yourself, and the good in you. Do whatever you can to not call upon that power."

"I promise I won't. I hate this power and its source, but if I am to be of any help or any use to Pearl, I have to be confident in being able to use at least some of it."

"Your transformation with the altered polymorph spell you preformed, did it hurt?"

"Yea, why."

"Normally, a high ranking mage with that ability feels no pain before, during, or after the perform that spell. They turn their body into a putty almost instantaneously, and painlessly. The version you use, an imitation created by the magic that you are using forces your body into that moldable state. I heard the shattering of your bones when it happened and the snapping of each piece being put back into its place. This is more reason to not venture into the more powerful magic that may be offered to you from whatever being you have connection with."

"Offered?"

"There are only a handful of ways that one becomes able to wield magic, great devotion to a god, or holding favor with a god, for people who have this the god may grant them access to the divine energy that they wield, using the faithful or favored as conduits of their work in our existence. This is where divine magic comes from. Then you have those gifted with talent, or a blood line that holds tie to the primal energies that pass through all of existence, or those who spend decades if not centuries learning to harness it. This is where arcane magic comes from and its users. Flame-Tender is one of those born with a talent that ties him to this type of magic. Then there are sources unknown, perversion of the natural state, and one of the most common of these is the contact of a being on another plane of existence, and requesting their power, in a way this makes their magic like that of a divine user, but often times without any rules or code of ethics, but it also comes with a cost, the body of the acceptor of such power is bound to be corrupted in some way by the binding of the magic into them. This type of magic is also often limited not by the wielder as other magics are, but by the nature of the deal that was made for them to obtain the power. I ask you not to accept any more power because from what you describe, this form of magic seems like the source of your power, what worries me is that you accepted more, I can tell by the hesitation you had in using that altered ability to polymorph yourself, which means that the pain that comes with it is still new to you."

"Yes, I only recently have been able to manifest that ability, but I haven't accepted any power, I wasn't offered anything."

"So, there is no condition you know of to your use of that ability?"

"No."

"Well like I said there are more exceptions to the way magic is normally acquired. For your sake avoid pushing your limits with that magic, I'm guessing that you don't know, and we don't know, what would happen if you push too far. Thank you for the conversation. My mind is at ease," Umbra finishes before standing and stepping out of the room.

Sitting by herself Eliza stares down with worry at her hands, and then reaching back to just barely touch one of the spots where her wings escape from, she mutter to herself, "Corrupted body." Before forcing the thoughts from her head with a shake and laying back down opening her book back to the page she was working on, but still the thought lingers quietly in the back of her mind as she continues to translate the strange symbols.

The voyage continues quietly, with little other conversation taking place until the island begins to grow into view. The lush green of the trees that rise from the mountainsides capture Flame-Tender's gaze as he runs to the front of the ship looking out to the distant uncharted land. Turning he points to the island as his eyes hold an inquisitive expression to Pearl who responds with a gleeful nod.

Docking the ship at the marble slab and extending the gang plank Pearl marches down first, to be in front of the new arrivals exclaiming with extended arms, "Welcome to our island, please follow me so Lizzy and I can share with you the mission we were given."

The group slowly step from the ship, horse in tow, and follow as asked into the room that has been dedicated for dinning. Setting down their equipment Nakhal, Flame-Tender, and Umbra, turn and wait for Pearl to begin explaining. His eyes wide as a natural reaction to the excitement he is trying to suppress in the anticipation for the epic quest that he has been invited to, Flame-Tender asks, "So we are in your palace. Can you explain we are doing here?"

"Yes, now we can. Have any of you heard of something called the Shard of Prime?" Pearl asks looking to the three as Eliza sits down against the wall behind Pearl and continues translating her book.

Flame-Tender raises a brow responding, "Only in children's stories about how everything came into being."

"Well it is a real thing, apparently, Negmor the original owner of this palace, an archmage told us so, and there is a group who are not good guys seeking it. So, we were told to stop them. A hag creature who calls herself the Queen of the Southern Seas, who signed a contract with Lizzy to act as a guardian of our palace's secret existence, also told us where the last ship to be transporting the shard had run aground. The northern most coast of the gnomes' continent. It is our plan to retrieve the shard, before anyone else has a chance to."

"Ok. So, wow, this is a lot to think through. If this is such a high priority, why is it that we aren't already sailing that way? We are wasting time that could be used in the search."

"Well, firstly the north is cold. Secondly it is about to be winter in the north, which makes it even more cold. Thirdly, you may have a wardrobe in those saddle bags, but Lizzy and I need new outfits that we already ordered before we even have a chance of surviving up there. Fourthly, this palace has the ability to teleport."

"Wait, wait, wait, hold up, this palace can teleport? Like to another island?"

"No, the island goes with it. Oh, that reminds me we have a meeting with the elven high council about getting back from them one of the things that lets the island teleport."

Speaking for the first time in the conversation Umbra shakes his head, "I can't participate in such a thing."

Pearl is struck with surprise, anger, and concern simultaneously by the comment, asking, "Wait you wait until after we tell you everything about our plan to then say you don't want to help, keep in mind this is an epic mission where our goal is to, save the world."

"That is not what I mean, I am not allowed on the continent of the elves anymore."

"Oh? What happened?"

"Long story I don't feel like sharing."

Eliza looks up from her book as the conversation continues with Pearl responding, "Well you can come with me to get Lizzy and my new outfits. They will be ready at the same time as the meeting is going to take place anyway."

Worry takes Eliza's eyes, her voice jumping from her mind into Pearl's, "*Wait you aren't going to come with me to get the ley line anchor?*"

To which Pearl responds turning to face her young friend with a smile, "Your better than me at talking with those old gas bags, I would just get in the way. You'll be fine, and with a charismatic guy like Flame-Tender you shouldn't have conversational issues, and if Nakhal is willing to go, you shouldn't have ruffians bother you either."

Flame-Tender smirks responding, "If you are worried about the city, don't be, I grew up in the elven capital, I would feel honored to show you around my home town, and assist you in any way that you deem necessary," ending with a bow to Eliza, who blushes and sinks back into the books strange symbols.

"I would also like to join you. There is little threat to Miss Pearl in a shopping run, but in transporting something from the elven capital the travel could serve as a danger to Miss Eliza, the spirits sent me to join your group that means I must protect you the best I can," Nakhal adds putting a fist to his chest.

With a smile and a boastful nod Pearl says to Eliza, "See you'll be fine, I will meet you here when you get the anchor in place. Wait I just realized, how are we going to know that the marker has been placed?"

Before Eliza can lower the book to respond, Bellar steps in through the door responding, "For this palace, it will be obvious, the extended portion of the transportation focus, will return to its natural state as the others are," then turning to Eliza he continues, "I am glad you are back by the way, Boop has been a fantastic help, unfortunately with everything I can do, I can't speed up the rate at which we will be able to communicate with my master next. I need to talk to you though, the master's cane, you will need to bring that with us to the meeting with the elven council, it is the only thing that will make transporting the anchor possible," then suddenly realizing the new faces, having been oblivious to them as he entered with something on his mind he asks, "Wait, who are these people?"

Pearl smiles, and stepping between Bellar and the group, is interrupted before she can introduce them by Flame-Tender who leans in and shakes Bellar's hand explaining, "We are three strangers who were aided in the extermination of a vampiric entity in Dur'heim, and have asked to join Captain Pearl and Lady Eliza, as they venture onward as we lacked direction of our own beyond that accomplishment."

"Hm, I am not sure how the world leaders would feel about additions made to the group after they approved your mission, but I guess that's one reason your movements are meant to be kept secret even from them. Beside with Lady Tristalia of Silvermist, and Commander Ironskin, having to stay in Blackgate the need for new companions was obvious. It is a pleasure to meet you three, I am Bellar, the current mage of the court for Lord King Gregoric Ferrix Heartholm, I am here assisting the liberators of Blackgate in understanding their base of operations and the magic inlaid within."

"It is a pleasure, Bellar, I am Flame-Tender, this is Umbra, and Nakhal."

Frustrated at having been cut off before she was able to do the introductions Pearl stomps between the two and says, in a voice that matches her mood, "Look, we have only a few days before you need to be in Esterion, for that meeting. Based on what you said before, I assume you will be transporting the group Bellar?"

"That is the plan. Eliza, based on my observations, has formidable magical ability but I do not believe that she poses the ability to teleport herself let alone groups, yet," Bellar responds giving Eliza a wink of challenge and encouragement.

"Well, guys, as long as you continue with us on this, make yourselves at home. This is as much your home as it is ours now. Lizzy and I already claimed rooms of our own, and the room Bellar has been working in is not to be a bed room, otherwise feel free to lay claim one. I am sorry there is no furniture. A companion of ours is working on that, and if you have any ideas on what some of our space should be used for let's talk about it when you think of it."

Pearl gestures to Eliza, and with the conversation complete the two leave the others to explore the palace at their leisure. While walking together through the halls Eliza stops suddenly, and her voice reaches out to Pearl's mind again saying, "*I am going to go preform that protection ritual on the ‹oor ways in the vault, an‹ leave a message for them not to enter.*"

Turning to Eliza, having continued walking only a few more steps before hearing the voice in her head, Pearl responds contemplatively, "Hmm. I guess that is a good idea, I mean we did just meet them yesterday."

With a nod Eliza grips her ritual book tightly, turns from Pearl, and leans into a jog through the palace, to the basement. There she spends ten minutes at each of the three doors Pearl had unlocked, performing the same ritual on each, and with each saying only the names, "Pearl, Eliza, and Boop." Completing the task Eliza returns to her room and with several hours left in the day continues the process still trying to translate the same one page she has been working on so that she can understand it.

19

Yefim

The next few days pass uneventfully. Flame-Tender, Umbra, and Nakhal are introduced to Boop, with varying reactions of curiosity, hesitation, and disinterest. The Island is relocated the day after they return to it from Dur'heim, and Pearl sets sail for Blackgate with Umbra and Devin. After another two days of Eliza reading through the rituals gifted to her, having finally come to understanding enough with the one she has been working on to move to the next page, she, Boop, Nakhal, Flame-Tender, and Bellar gather in the chamber Bellar has been working in. Bellar directs the group to stand within a circle drawn on the marble floor in chalk which contains several arcane symbols in preparation of his teleportation spell. Joining the others he asks for a final check, "Does everyone have what they wish to bring with them?"

Eliza readjusts the strap of her back pack on her shoulder, with the master's cane strapped to its side, and everything that she would normally have in Pearl's bag that she thought she might need placed tightly within, she responds, with only a whisper of her voice, which only just is beginning to return to her, "I am ready."

Nakhal lays his hand on the hilt of both of his swords, and then the strap of his large bag, responding, "Sure."

Finally, after the other two respond Flame-Tender's mind returns to the present from remembering if he left food for his horse, before correcting himself in that there is plenty of grass to be had, and patting himself down he gestures with a thumbs up saying, "I have all that I will need before we get to my parents."

With a nod Bellar responds, "Very well then. Take each other's hands, Eliza hold Boop." The group follow instructions, and he reaches out his own hands and begins drawing symbols in the air. Like Eliza casting her magic, his voice, echoes out as he calls upon the magic to teleport to a set location, "Sect, rockt tu arct, seartra gastorn, Esterion."

Three pops sound, and a flash of white erupts from within the center of the circle formed as Bellar grabs Eliza's wrist and Nakhal's hand, completing the interlocking ring of people. On the third flash the group is thrown forward, only just catching their balance as the room around them is no longer the one in the palace, but a small stone room only just large enough to contain a small circle engraved in the floor that matches the one that Bellar made with chalk. Rubbing his head, Flame-Tender smirks saying, "So that is what teleportation feels like. I have to make note of that to add realism to my stories. Does everyone still have their own bodies? Minds weren't swapped in transport were they?"

"That isn't a thing that happens," Bellar responds opening the only door that leads out of the closet.

Beyond the door is a small room only four or five times the size of the one the group steps from within. Several more doors line all but one of the walls, which bears only one in its center. For a small room there is a large amount of foot traffic, with other groups, and individuals of all different types of species, stepping out of the other doors which all look to lead into similar closets, all dimly lit by glowing orbs, like the ones in the lamps at the palace. With Bellar's lead the group join the crowd passing through the door that sits on its own as an exit from the room, and enter into yet another room.

Across the newer, and even larger room, a similar collection of groups can be seen waiting in a queue to pass through another door, which waits guarded by two large suits of armor, and a man in a strange uniform. The line of people waiting extends out another door which holds within its frame the late night air of the elven continent, and Bellar continues to lead the group out. The sky sits in dark contrast to what it had been over the palace holding the moon's light as the primary source of radiance with the stars resting gently overhead. Eliza looks around, and even though she knew that the time wouldn't be the same in both places because of the rotation of the planet, she instinctively breaths, "Wow."

With a smile, but not turning to show it, Bellar responds, "If you think that was something, and are impressed by the time change from the great distance traveled, just wait until we get up to the city."

Eliza's eyes widen, as she asks, "Up, to the city? Wait we aren't in the city?"

Flame-Tender joins Bellar in smiling as he is first to respond, "Yes up to the city, Esterion, capital of the elves, center of the highest level of arcane study, City in the Sky."

To which Bellar continues, "And yes, we are technically within the city limits, but think of this more as the buffer zone to insure that nothing illegal enters the city proper. The way up is through there."

Eliza's eyes follow Bellar's finger as he points ahead of their group. The line drawn from the dwarf mage's fingertip extends only a few hundred feet before connecting with another queue of people of all races, waiting to be granted entrance into a structure that looks almost like a barracks except with four separate entrances each only just large enough for a cart to be able to pass through. In a small box next to each gate are more individuals dressed in the same type of uniform that was on the man with the suits of armor. A green suit with yellow buttons, tightly fit to the form of their wearer. A small wedge hat, which only barely rests on the top of the head, with any hair longer than a few inches pulled tightly back into a bun.

On the side of the four gates letting people in, there is a separate gate open with four guards stood by it on both ends, a pair on each of the opening's sides which allows groups to exit with ease while a backup is visibly obvious in the process to let new arrivals enter. With Bellar remaining in the lead, Eliza feels confusion as they step along the side of the line, and she does a double take to the lines back, as they walk its length. Seeing the confusion, Flame-Tender smiles explaining, "Don't worry. That line is a formality for those without official and important business to wait through, so that they can be screened for contraband. We won't have to wait in it."

After a minute of walking and receiving strange looks from the people they step past who have been waiting in line, the group arrives at one of the gates into the barracks structure. The attending female official sitting in the box by the gate gives a raised brow in response to the group's approach, saying, in a monotone overworked voice, before they can even step to the box, "Back of the line."

Bellar freezes responding, "We are here on a matter of official business, this young lady has a meeting with the high council today."

The woman looks down at a pad of paper asking, "Name?"

"Her name is Eliza Black, one of the liberators of Blackgate."

"Her appointment isn't until this evening, it is barely an hour after midnight. You have time to wait your turn in line."

With a sigh Flame-Tender steps from the group and to the box. Leaning against it he gestures with his hand saying so softly, so that Eliza can only just hear, "The Son of the Burning House, would like to return home."

The woman's posture and expression shift immediately as she sees a ring on Flame-Tender's finger, from one of uncaring tedium that comes with her job to one of fear that she has made a grave mistake. Quickly standing from her seat she gestures to the gate saying, "Please forgive me for not noticing, please enter, your companions will still have to submit to customs."

With a nod Flame-Tender steps to the gate responding, "That is fine," before gesturing to the others to follow calling, "Come on."

Immediately after the group pass through the gate into the large building, they hear from outside a commotion erupt from that one booth with people yelling at the poor official that they too are returning sons of the burning house. The ease of entry and the commotion caused in the wake of Flame-Tender's action bring a question to Eliza's tongue that she asks, "What was that about?"

Turning to face her with a smile and a thumb up Flame-Tender responds, "I told you I grew up here, and for a human to call Esterion home, their family has to be something above the normal class. This way, we have to let some guards know that we are here."

The group follow Flame-Tender a bit deeper into the building before they enter a large room which takes up most of the building's inner space. The double door entrance is made small by the large, shifting wall of green energy with purple vein-like lines spreading through it on the opposite wall, which is too familiar to the gateway Eliza was shot through to escape the plane of undeath for her liking. Along the edges of the chamber standing on raised platforms are several robed figures looking down upon the group as they enter. In the center of the room is a single table to which a line has formed that leads back to the entrance, and at which a single uniformed individual stands combing through a group's possessions before waving them by and calling for the next group to approach.

While the official scans through the next groups belongings, the one waved by steps to and through the wall. Only a second later a group appears from the wall, and leave through the door Eliza's group entered through. The sound echoes through the room again as the official calls for the next group to approach but without realizing it, having been taking in the room, Eliza steps with the others up to the table skipping the line entirely once more. Showing the same ring to the man standing at the table, Flame-Tender turns to his companion again with a smile saying, "He just needs to make sure you aren't bringing in anything that the law wouldn't allow."

With that Eliza is shown up to the table and she, Bellar, and Nakhal begin, unpacking their bags for the investigation. Eliza is stopped before she even has a chance to open her bag by the officials hand gesturing to her, and then to Boop, who she only just released from her grasps so that she could unpack her bag, and in a similar tone of voice as the woman had at the first gate, the man explains, "No foreign creatures are allowed into the city, as per the ecosystem regulation laws. You will not be allowed to enter the city."

Eliza looks with panic to Bellar and Flame-Tender, before stammering, "But Boop's my spirit companion, I can have him go into his inert state if necessary."

At this Bellar nods, "It is true that creature is not a pet. That is a specialized form her particular spirit companion has taken."

Looking over to one of the robed figures who nods in response to the glance, the official responds, "I am sorry about the confusion, you may take him with you, but any waste found abandoned to be his in undesignated areas will receive you a fine."

Eliza looks to Boop asking, "Waste? Do you create waste Boop?" and Boop responds with a bob in his levitation in a display that if he had shoulders would be a shrug.

With that matter settled the group continues unloading their equipment onto the table into a small pile in front of each of them. Nakhal's table holds his two swords, a bedroll, several bags of rations, and other uninteresting nick knacks used for outdoor survival. Bellar's table holds, his staff, two wands, three scrolls, and a leather bound tome very similar in appearance to Eliza's black book, only brown. Finally, Eliza's contains three books, two of which are books three and four from the series Alfredo has her reading, and the other which if the ritual book most of her attention has been focused on, the spider capped wand, the rod Bellar refers to as the master's cane, two bags of rations, and a black serrated dagger. As a joke Boop drifts down on top of Eliza's pile, which earns a smirk from the official and the robed figures watching from above, before the group is ushered past.

Seeing a nervous expression grow on Eliza and Boop's faces as they step to the wall of magical energy Bellar grabs Eliza's hand explaining, "Don't worry, this isn't painful. It's only a simple gateway spell, just step through and we will still be by your side when we get to the other side."

"It's not that," Eliza responds, "The last time I went through something like this, Boop and I were separated."

"Hey, you don't have to worry about that, you and he will be fine. I promise."

Eliza nods accepting the encouraging words at face value, and wrapping Boop in her arms, she steps into the magic gateway. She prepares herself to be thrown forward, like she had been with the others the last time she went through something similar, but she isn't. As Eliza steps forward, her feet fall in the same way as they would with her walking through an ordinary doorway. Having closed her eyes in anticipation of something going wrong she double takes to see the others emerging beside her after appearing in a room that is an almost mirror of the one she was stepping from.

Flame-Tender continues to lead the group and they step out of the large room, into a small hallway, and finally out of the structure, revealing that they have actually been transported. Amazed bewilderment strikes Eliza again as the light of the moon glistens across metal embellishments that line the elven city sky line. The building the group steps out of is not a harsh stone barracks like the one they entered but has smoothed plastered stone on its exterior with dark cherry wood supports decoratively adorning it. The aesthetic runs across all of the visible buildings in the street lit by familiar magic floating balls, of smooth blemish free exteriors adorned with pointless additions added for appearance.

Beyond the line of people tiredly yawning as they wait to pass through the building the group steps away from, and the few people who like them are walking and dispersing themselves into the city streets. The city is quiet and still. A pleasant change from the port of Dur'heim. A constant cool breeze runs through the streets and alleys rustling the leaves of the bushes and trees that line the paths, and gently tossing the fabric and hair that adorns the group. With Flame-Tender at the helm, the five continue with purpose through the city's thoroughfares that quickly become void of any presence beyond their own until they find their way to a gate set in a wall around a grandiose manor.

Eliza, still in awe of the beauty of the city she is in, even through the dark veil of the night, looks up to the cloud free sky which had not been as such before they went through the gateway, and up to the beautifully twinkling stars. Flame-Tender stops the group and steps to the newest gate before them, and raising his ring again, presses it into the center of the gate. A spark is sent dancing both up and down the seam between the two halves, releasing a sound like that of parchment being quickly torn. It is a spectacle that quickly finds end when the lights reach their respective edge and disappear releasing the gate to swing gently open.

In the same instant the sparks vanish, from within the manor through an open window, the faint sound of a small bell ringing makes its way out to the group's ears. Only a moment later from the same window a light ignites with a white and gold glow showing a shadow hastily moving within. Only a few seconds after the light appears it dies from the window as it is taken through the room's door which is closed behind its possessor.

Flame-Tender gives a smile and a nod to the building saying, "Well this is my place, not quite as large as yours Miss Eliza, but it has furniture."

The joke earns a smirk from Eliza, as the group joins Flame-Tender in stepping for the front door. Before they reach it, an old man in a plain black suit emerges from within with a crossbow in hand, trailed by another small glowing orb floating three feet off the ground just within his arms reach. Not seeing the group at first the man's expression is defensive expecting to have to drive off home invaders, but his voice comes out unthreatening holding his age and many decades of service as, what appears to be, a butler exclaims, "Alright you hooligans, I am armed," but seeing the velvet suit stepping arms spread in his direction the man immediately changes in his demeanor, putting on a smile saying, "Young master, you have returned. The lord and lady will be so happy to be informed of such."

Flame-Tender only laughs at the eager greeting of his old friend, responding, "How about we wait to tell them until after they wake up on their own terms. For now, how about getting my guests some rooms ready to let them put their bags down in, and a meal. We were teleported here from a bit off the broken continent, so this feels more like midday to us."

"Certainly sir. If you don't mind the asking, what is the purpose of your return?"

"I told you and father that I needed to see the world and experience a grand quest before I could follow in the family line of duties. I am here because of that. This young lady is here to speak with the high council."

"Oh, my that truly is something. I shan't bother you further. I shall notify the kitchen staff of your need for nourishment and the maids of the need for prepared rooms, it will only be a few moments," the old man explains stepping from the group leaving them standing in the front hall.

Eliza, freed from watching the old man as he leaves, looks around the room, and then with sudden connection to Flame-Tender. The way the house is decorated, shows as an almost perfect representation of a living space one would expect someone so well dressed and mannered would live. A large read and black rug covers a majority of the light polished wood floor. Ornate polished wooden tables and chairs line the areas of the walls which are free from the path of the doors which lead into different rooms. Over the furniture are hung large paintings that depict a family posed regally, with a father and mother at the center of five children, three girls and two boys, and at the far side of the space between a set of rising curved twin staircases, stands a column of wood and glass within which hang weighted chains. The front of the object holds a circle with a pointed arrow, directed to an image of a setting moon, and a number. A smile takes Eliza's face as she looks again at Flame-Tender, who not noticing her gaze upon him, gestures for the group to pass through a set of doors from the room.

Through the doors waits a large dining hall. One wall glows with the night's light flowing in through glass pain windows that fill most of its space. Opposite the windows holds in its center a large fire place adorned with two pictures one of each of the parents in the portrait in the front hall. The majority of the room's space is filled by a table, gowned in a white table cloth with four plates and a bowl set on one side, and two large unlit chandeliers hung from the ceiling sparkle in moon light reflecting off their gold, silver, and crystal forms.

Stepping from the seats set for dining, the old man from the entrance leaves the room with the smooth haste of a professional servant through a door which releases the distant sound of a busy kitchen. The fragrance of food being prepared only just begins to fill the room as Flame-Tender ushers his still relatively new companions to their seats. Only a moment after they take their seats the door opens again, with the old man leading a train of others dressed in the same fashion as him, each pushing a tray cart holding a silver dome.

Eliza watches in amazement as the servants approach and stop one behind the chair of each member of the group, including Boop, who through Flame-Tender's silent instruction took to floating over the seat set with a silver bowl. A man emerges from the other room in a clean white outfit, with a grin on his face, and when he gets to the side of the seated company he gestures to the men stood with the trays. The servants move in unison, through a choreographed presentation, each simultaneously lifting the silver lid on their cart. The gentle smell that only barely found its way into the room before, immediately becomes full bodied with the lids coming off releasing plumes of steam that carry the scent of the food that emanates it.

Standing proudly as each dish is moved from its cart to the table, the man in white states, "I woke to hear of master Yefim's return and that he brought guests, through means of having arrived from nearly half way around the world, I had to craft his favorite midday meal."

Flame-Tender's hand slowly finds his forehead as the chef just blatantly says his real name responding, "Geran, did you have to use my name in presence of company?"

The man in white recoils in an expression of surprise asking, "But sir do these people not know your name."

"Well they do now, unfortunately, thanks to you."

"But sir they are present here as guests and they don't even know who you are?"

"Look they know me for my pen name, Flame-Tender, and I know each of them. It doesn't matter now just serve the food."

"I am sorry sir. Anyways, the meal that master Flame, has always adored as a meal midday is baked salmon with lemon, on a bed of garlic asparagus," Eliza holds back a snicker with chef Geran exposing Flame-Tender, as the chef continues, "and as I was informed that a pet of one of the guests was also to be served, I made, a nice warm meat paste for," and he only pauses for a split second to look with raised brow at Boop, "the cute little critter."

"Thank you Geran. That will be all."

The man in white, bows with Flame-Tender's words, and leads the servants pushing the serving carts out of the room. Leaning over his plate, Bellar takes a deep whiff of the backed fish, and exhaling in delight of the scent turns to Flame-Tender who in every way of a nobleman hiding the extent of his emotions rests his head in his hands mortified with the conversation which just took place. Shaking his head and looking at the size of the empty dining hall the dwarf mage asks, "So, you grew up here?"

A slight moan in his voice Flame-Tender responds over the sound of Eliza and Nakhal's silverware going to work transporting the delicious meal into their mouths, "Yes."

"Tell me, what made you leave it? What I mean by this question is not what it seems on the surface. Eliza, and Pearl, I have come to know as people who don't really have a place like this, and the people I have known in the centuries I have lived who did strike out as you have, never did so from this but in hopes of achieving it when they start with next to nothing. So, tell me mister Flame-Tender, why leave? Why change your name? Why do things like risk your life, when you could live one of comfort and safety?"

A sigh responds from the door from the front hall, a woman's voice, with the grace of someone who had mothered, but the tenor of someone fighting to maintain their youth, "Because none of this was because of him, and his head was always filled with the city heralds' stories of heroes saving the day."

Flame-Tender's eyes widen at the sound of the voice, and turning to see the source he immediately stands, exclaiming in surprise, "Mother!"

A woman stands with the doors closing behind her, draped in a long elegant forest green sleeping gown with naturally curly hair tide back in a bun. Age show in the lines of her face, but not as much as would be expected of the mother of five, though without a doubt she is the woman depicted in the portraits, as the matriarch of this family. She stands with arms out stretched responding to Flame-Tender's standing, with the question, "What? You didn't think you could stop by home and not say hi to your mother before you wake the help, did you?"

"I didn't expect you to be awake, and didn't want to wake you."

"Don't worry about it dear, I wasn't asleep in the first place. Your father's away on a supposedly important errand involving his station," having sauntered from the door to the group the woman's hands grasp tight to Flame-Tenders shoulders and she leans in giving him a kiss on his forehead. Turning to the sitting guests she smiles continuing, "Now I want a detailed introduction."

"Mother, these are companions I have joined with on a mission I am not at liberty to tell even you about. Bellar the mage from the dwarf king's court. Nakhal, a mountain man who also only joined into the quest at the same time I did. Lastly Eliza, and her spirit companion Boop."

Being polite Eliza stands and gives a slight curtsy bow to Yefim's mother who responds, "Oh my what an attractive young woman. You wouldn't happen to be unwed and not being called upon by a suiter would you dear? My son is getting to the point where he needs to start thinking about his contribution to the family's lineage."

"Mother!" Flame-Tender shouts down his mother's imposition as Eliza silently blushes and sits back down wide-eyed staring at the fish meal in front of her, "She is a compatriot of mine on our current quest. I don't see her that way and I doubt she could see me that way. Besides she's only fourteen."

"So, your father met me in his travels and I was just about the same age when we were engaged."

"Mother! Please! Drop this topic."

"Fine dear. I meant nothing by it," the madam responds before leaning down to whisper in Eliza's ear, "My son is a good man. You could be a beautiful wife for a man like him, and never worry about money ever again."

Eliza, not wanting to be rude but also feeling exceptionally uncomfortable simply stares forward down at her meal, with her face becoming hot and red with embarrassment. Flame-Tender almost annoyed by his mother's lingering steps to her and gently ushers her from Eliza toward the door saying, "Well, we should talk more, later. About something completely different, but for right now how's about you let us have our lunches and let my companions rest a little."

"Alright, I get the hint, your little old mother, is not needed around here, but you get yourself a woman Yefim, I want grandkids and at this rate your brothers or sisters will beat you to it, and you're the eldest."

The door closes behind the woman and Flame-Tender returns to

Eliza, saying, "I am so sorry about that. Mother is pushy but she only ever means well for me. I hope you weren't too off put."

To break the tension as Eliza, doesn't respond, Bellar speaks up instead, "Well at least we know where your flamboyance comes from. She is one expressive person."

"Yeah, she is," Flame-Tender responds with a grateful nod to Bellar, as tension in the air begins to fade and Eliza picks up her fork again bringing a stalk of asparagus to her mouth before biting down on it releasing the snap from the fresh well-cooked green vegetable.

After the plates are cleared of the meal, and Boop begins licking his bowl to a polished sheen, the man servant, that greeted the group upon their arrival, and who has been standing by the unlit fireplace watching the group eat, steps to Flame-Tender's side asking, "Shall I show your guests to their rooms sir?"

"I think that is a great idea," Flame-Tender responds standing from his chair.

The man gives two claps into the air, which are surprisingly loud through the white cloth gloves he wears, and he steps in the direction of the door the group entered the room through saying, "This way please." Several other similarly dressed individuals step into the room brusquely walking to the plates, and retrieving the dishes they leave again from the room before Eliza, Bellar, Nakhal, and Boop can even get to the door.

With a smile Flame-Tender steps the opposite way from the seats as the others, explaining, "I am going to go give greetings to a few others, I will meet you all at the front door at sunrise to show you around the city."

The group step in line behind Flame-Tender's butler who leads them from the room and up to the second floor. As they walk Bellar clears his throat asking, "So, what should we call you?"

The suited man doesn't flinch at the question responding in the tone that would be expected of a butler replying to a guest of the house, "Anderson." Bellar looks to want to ask further questions but is stopped by

Anderson stopping and gesturing to a door, explaining, "The men have this room for their use, and for the Lady," he steps to a door across the hall, "This room has been prepared for you." Boop goes to join Nakhal and Bellar in the room for the men, but again Anderson's voice moans out, "The lady's pet shall sleep in her quarters."

With a joking look of depression Boop turns from the room for the men, before shifting back to having a smile and rushing past Eliza in to the room made up for her. The room is large but with very little unused space. A bed larger than any Eliza has ever seen stands against the side wall furthest from the offset door. A wardrobe and desk sit with each other basking in moon light that seeps through the thin pink curtains which adorn the window above the desk. A large chest with its key left in its lock sits empty at the foot of the bed with the silk sheets that cover the mattress and the thin silk drapes that hang from the bed's canopy, resting over it decoratively, and opposite the rug covered floor space that the chest rests upon is a small circular mattress set for Boop.

Ever more amazed by the glamor of the house, Eliza steps over to the bed, and falls into it. The soft feather filled cushion pillows under her are like a cloud of comfort, hugging her as she sinks slightly into it. Pulling the covers over herself, even though it was noon for her when they left the palace, she drifts to sleep.

20

Sisters

The gentle sound of chirping birds and the delicate rays of light find their way through the window of Eliza's room waking her peacefully. Sitting up in the soft silk sheets of the pillow of a bed her eyes flicker open as she stretches releasing a morning yawn as her consciousness brings to her the feeling of the most rested sleep she has had in a very long time. Folding the top quilt over and tucking it to almost the same way she had found it, she grabs her bag from the side of the bed, and steps to the door, calling to Boop who snores from his mattress, "Come on Boop. Let's go see the city."

Stirring at the call of Eliza's voice, Boop shoots up to the height he generally floats at and shaking himself awake responds with a smile, "Coming," before shooting to Eliza's side spinning.

The house's decor is even more glamorous in the light of the morning, with almost everything that isn't fabric of some kind, glistening with a sparkle from the morning sun's light peeking through the windows.

Retracing the path that Anderson had taken her and the others, Eliza finds her way through the densely populated hallway, with artistic nick knacks and to the stairs down to the front door. Looking down she sees waiting there at the ground level Anderson, hands folded waiting by the open doors to the dining hall. With a nod, he gestures into the room saying to Eliza as she steps down the stairs, "Madam Eliza, the Lady of the house would like to have breakfast with you and your companions. The others are already seated, this way if you would."

The dining hall is fully lit with the morning's light. Sitting at the far end of the large table, the same side as her picture is above the fireplace on, is the woman from the night before. She gestures with a nod to two set seats at the table by which Bellar and Nakhal are sat. Across from them sit three woman, a young man, and Flame-Tender. Each person at the table has in front of them a clean, empty plate, as they turn and watch Eliza and Boop make their way to the seats set for them.

Anderson helps Eliza with her chair, and at the same moment Flame-Tender's mother speaks, her voice holding a stronger aristocratic feel to its cadence than the night before, "I would like to welcome the three of you to our home. I have been informed of your reason for being in the city, and an ambassadorial meeting with our high council is far more than reason enough for my family's doors to be open to you while you are here for such purposes. I am Lady Izhutin, you know my eldest son from your travels, Yefim Izhutin. These are my daughters, Anastasia, Victoria, and Liliana, and my youngest son, Alexander."

"It is a pleasure to make your acquaintance Lady of Fire," Bellar responds with a nod.

"Oh, so you know of our family?"

"I wasn't sure at first but I am pretty sure I have met your husband, the Bearer of the Shard of Fire."

"Oh, when was this?"

"He was asked to aid in the rekindling of one of the great forges in my king's land, after an earthquake caused a cave-in which extinguished it."

While the conversation has been taking place, servants enter the room and without the fanfare from the chef as in the night, they set each person's meal down silently and leave, not interrupting in any way. Hearing the words Shard of Fire, Eliza, stops before taking a bite of the breakfast set in front of her, and asks, "Excuse me. What's a Shard of Fire?"

Turning to Eliza with the interruption, Lady Izuhtin tilts her head in acknowledgement of the query, "Oh, perceptive and curious," then turning her head to face Flame-Tender gives him an expression that only a mother could give to a son, saying, "See she would make a wonderful wife."

"Mother, stop this," Flame-Tender responds rebuking the comment, "You are making her uncomfortable. I do not see her in a romantic way, only as a person who is part of a group I am in where we have a unified goal."

Rolling her eyes, Flame-Tender's mother responds, "I am only kidding," and looking to Eliza who has sunk in her chair sipping from a glass of water that was brought to her, continues, "To answer your question dear, the Shard of Fire is an artifact, with history that dates back to the First Era. Back then the nations did not have a pact of peace between them as they do now, and war was waged by the creations of the gods. In that time magic existed in a far greater primordial state, and was allowed to exist in rampant nodes throughout the world. It quickly became clear to the mortal races, those who lead the world in our age now, that war was not the way of prosperity. Even as talks of peace were growing from mere whispers, the rampant magic flooding into this world from the other planes of existence that the gods created, was still untamed and was causing deaths in far greater numbers than any war had, especially through the mages who manipulated the nodes for their own purposes. While the peoples who called for peace knew that these nodes would need to be closed off to limit their impact on worldly affairs, they had no way of doing such a thing. Magic must be greater in power than any magic it wishes to contain not equal to. That is when a blessing was granted to our world. A tiny shard fell from the sky, a crystal no bigger than a coin, which held the power the people of peace needed to make the dream a reality. This shard, called the Shard of Prime closed the nodes and sealed the gateways to only let small amounts of elemental energy into the world. The closed nodes became shards of their own, and families from the people of peace where tasked to never let their power fall into hands of those who would use the direct link to the planes of existence to bring harm. The Prime Shard, vanished, but it is said that it held far more power than all of the nodes put together, and thus would not be allowed in the hands of anyone for fear that its power would corrupt its guardian. The Shard of Fire to which my husband is the guardian, is one of many that link our world to the plane of fire. Does that answer your question?"

"Well kind of."

Adding his voice into the lesson Flame-Tender asks, "You understand the different kinds of magic that exist right?"

"Well, yeah, Umbra explained it to me in short."

"Well for the magic Bellar uses, primordial energy must be present to be manipulated. The shards act as limiters to prevent any one mage from wielding the power to say blow up an entire country. My father is entrusted with protecting one of these shards. Story has it that at one point the greatest of the magi foresaw the possibility of one rising to use power where the only limit is the users skill and understanding on how to manipulate it for great evil. Perhaps something like that actually happened so when the opportunity arose that they could impose a limit, even on themselves, they took the opportunity."

"But what about magic granted by gods?"

"That magic is limited by both the knowledge of the wielder in being able to use it, and by the strength of their faith. While one person might follow a god that seeks evil to occur on this world. The power granted to them is most likely going to be countered by another god granting similar power to one of their followers. That and there really isn't anything mortals can even hope for that would let them curb the power granted from divine sources."

"Wow. Ok, but why do you know all this, I understand that your father is the protector of this Shard of Fire thing, but why do you know so much about divine magic too?"

"I told you before, I make it my business to know the stories. Now how about we finish eating, so that I can show you around the city."

Eliza, head spinning from the bombardment of knowledge she may never use, though interested to its connection to the quest at hand, she smiles nodding and shovels another full fork of eggs into her mouth. Quickly the breakfast is consumed, and Eliza, with the others, makes her way out into the front hall. Stepping to the door she asks, "So what are we doing first?"

Bellar is the first to respond, saying, "We should go to the High ouncil building so that we know where it is and then agree to meet back there before our scheduled appearance."

In agreeance, the group leave the home and step into the street. Eliza is once again struck by the splendor of the city as it takes on a completely different look in the day then it had in the night. The smooth outer walls of the city's buildings which appeared an almost uniform color in the light of the moon are instead almost all unique to their walls. One theme in the colors is a consistent vibrant quality, as though every home and shop had been painted the day before.

The gold and silver trimmings that sparkled above like extra stars over head as the group stepped to Flame-Tender's home, draw Eliza's eyes up to the cloudless sky in the soft of the morning sun, just in time for her to watch a man fly overhead sitting on a rug. With her eyes wide from seeing a flying carpet, Eliza asks, "Was that man flying a carpet?"

Flame-Tender shrugs responding, "What did you expect? This is not just the capital of the elven continent, but also the epicenter of the study of primordial magic, and home of four shards, air, water, earth and my father's fire." Eliza just continues with the group in continued silent wide-eyed bewilderment of a world opening around her that she never even knew existed.

The city is busy, as a capital should be, even in the earliest hours of morning light. Crowds of people walking with purpose flow through the streets, with even more people bypassing the traffic by flying overhead, some on carpets, others on brooms, and others still simply floating on the air without such objects. The life of the city is mixed with the sounds and smells that come with the morning, of bakers setting out fresh bread, fruit vendors splaying open their carts with sweet produce, and within all of it a gentle smell of lavender drifts through the air which wasn't present in the hours of the night.

Only a few minutes of walking with the flow of pedestrian traffic, brings the group to a large set of stairs which lead up into an imposing, large building, and with a hand pointed to the large open doors, Flame-Tender explains, "There it is, the main hall used for council meetings, these meetings are usually open to the public, but they have been known to shoo people from the chambers for some things. Will this happen for us? I wouldn't be able to tell you, but you seemed like you have somethings you wanted to do in town Bellar, so we will meet back here when the day passes a little after midday. Oh, and Nakhal don't feel like you have to stick around either. I will be giving a tour of the city if you want to hear about my childhood, or you can go do something on your own. This is a safe place. Eliza won't be in any danger here."

With a wave Bellar steps from the group saying as he goes, "Alright see you then, don't be late Eliza, you are the most important part of you getting that anchor."

Before Flame-Tender can turn back to Eliza, Boop, and Nakhal from his attention having been on Bellar leaving, Nakhal also leaves. Looking around and surprised to not see a trace of the large figure stepping away Flame-Tender shrugs asking, "Well first off, is there anything you want to do?"

Looking to her feet and clasping her hands Eliza responds,

"Honestly, I was hoping we could go see about getting me a dress for tonight, I have a green one I wore when meeting the representatives that went to a meeting of the lords in Blackgate, but I want to show the proper level of respect to being given the opportunity to state my case."

"Buy a dress, alright. Anything else?"

"Well if this place has so much magic, do you think I would be able to get a bag like Pearl's? It would be easier for me to carry everything and I could stop relying on her bag."

"Yeah, I can take you to an enchantment store. Alright, two things to do gives me a decent route in mind to show you the important stuff of the city. Let's go," Flame-Tender responds turning and stepping with a head nod to have Eliza follow.

Slowly the two walk with Boop drifting along with them, and to Eliza's pleasant surprise they find that either through being too busy to care, or through the understanding of him being a magical companion, little to no attention beyond acknowledging his existence is cast the way of the floating eye creature. The shade of the trees that line the sides of the streets grows nice as the gentleness of the morning sun grows brighter and harsher as it rises in the sky, and still not even the trace of a cloud floats overhead. Reason comes when Flame-Tender's path brings the small threesome to a bridge, a sight which makes everything clear. The bridge does not cross over a stream but instead connects two sections of the city, which is floating above the clouds.

Seeing the drop off of the far segment of the city, which is not connected to the ground Eliza runs to the railing on the side of the bridge and simply gasps, "Wow," as she looks down to see beneath her a large cotton cloud drifting by in the wind.

With a smile Flame-Tender steps to Eliza's side saying, "See I knew I should show you this first. You want to do something fun," he asks waiting for Eliza to turn to him with a smile filled with anticipation for what he is going to say next before continuing, "Jump off."

The smile on Eliza's face shatters with a distrusting worry taking its place with her voice escaping from her, "What?"

Rolling his eyes Flame-Tender moans with a smile, "Man. You don't trust me yet. Watch, it isn't dangerous," and without giving Eliza a chance to react he throws himself over the side of the bridge and begins to fall.

Eliza instinctively calls out, "No, don't," but it is too late as she reaches out and the form of what was becoming her friend flips from the bridge and begins to plummet to the ground several thousand feet down. Turning from the edge, wanting Flame-Tender to be right in that it is safe to jump off, she doesn't watch, not able to think of a way that he would be safe.

Boop, however, watches, and only a few hundred feet down, which a body can fall to relatively quickly when in free fall, Flame-Tender slows to a stop. Boop turns to Eliza exclaiming, "Look, look. Not wrong, velvet guy not wrong."

Eliza turns back around looking down over the edge, and as she does, she sees Flame-Tender drifting upward. After a moment he is lifted by an unseen force over the railing and let to drop onto his feet. With a smile, a bow, and a cockiness in his voice, he laughs, "See, I told you it was safe. You want to try it?"

Even seeing Flame-Tender leap and return to the bridge completely safe, Eliza is nervous as she looks back over the railing responding, "I don't know. What if that magic decides not to catch me?"

Before Flame-Tender can even think of a response, Boop floats over the void and with a smile responds, "Then I'll catch you."

Looking at the smile on Boop's face Eliza smiles and nods before climbing up onto the side rail, and letting out a deep sigh she spreads her arms and lets herself fall forward. The sound of wind rushing past her face becomes deafening, as a feeling of freedom fills her, as her outstretched arms make her want to let her wings extend. The braid that her hair had been put in, having loosened from its continued unnaturally fast growth rate, almost instantly comes undone with the rushing of the free fall. Eliza smiles to Boop as he shoots down by her side as if racing her, before both of them vanish into the peak of a slowly drifting cloud.

Only a few short seconds after releasing herself into the descent, Eliza slows to a stop, before being lifted back to the bridge. She doesn't feel a force on her body to cause the lift, something which intrigues her young curious mind, but when her feet once again land on the bridge Flame-Tender greets her with a smile, "See, it's fun. When the city was lifted from the ground for the security of the families who bear the responsibility of guarding the shards, several bits of magic where permanently put in place. One was to make falling from the city something the people in the city don't need to worry about, another, was to maintain air pressure, otherwise being this high up would make it hard to breath, and one was to regulate the weather so that the city is never really ever too hot or too cold, kind of like that island of yours. Alright first stop, magic bag."

Flame-Tender takes lead again and the three quickly cross the bridge and enter again into the crowds of people in the streets of another portion of the city. The heat of the day begins to grow, but like Flame-Tender explained, there is magic in the strength and cool freshness of the breeze that rustles the leaves of the greenery that decorate the streets. The chill of the gentle wind still isn't enough to prevent Boop from panting to help him cool down.

Only another few minutes stepping through the crowd, as Eliza becomes more acclimated to appearance of the city and the atmosphere of its people, sounds, and smells, she, Flame-Tender, and Boop arrive at a store front. To the side of the door a sign is hung saying something in elven script, and directly next to that in the common script, "Traton Arcanist's Shop." Like the other buildings of the city, the outer walls are smooth, with its own shade of a soft sage-in-cream color with struts designed to look as though adding structural integrity, aesthetically adhered to the painted plaster.

Through the light birch wood door, there is a small quaint shop, tightly filled with shelves and glass display cases, all stocked with items that seemingly have no correlation with those around them beyond assumedly holding some kind of magical property. At the back of the room a young looking man with long pointed ears, and even longer straight brown hair, sits behind the counter, and he looks up from a book as the door opens striking a bell hung above it. Seeing the three forms, the man immediately stands with a smile, slamming his book closed on the counter in the motion, exclaiming with a slightly effeminate, but still obviously adult male voice, "Well isn't it little Yefim all grown up, returned to my shop. You want some spark gum, or have you out grown it by now?"

Flame-Tender is taken with a nostalgic smile waving to the man responding, "Greetings again, Elandur, business been well?"

"As well as it could be in a city where everyone is a mage, who already has their basic tier magic equipment. Who's this attractive young woman following you in here?"

"Oh, this is Eliza. Eliza, this is Elandur, he was like a second father to me when I was younger," Eliza just watches the conversation with a silent smile waving sheepishly as she is introduced before Flame-Tender turns back to his old friend asking, "Hey, you haven't sold that thing have you?"

"No, I haven't," Elandur sighs, "I am thinking I may need to drop the price."

"To what? If it is close to what I have I can have you put it on hold for me, I still have a reward to pick up for the execution of a vampire."

"Now, now, you know you shouldn't lie to me."

"It isn't a lie, Eliza helped. It was a vampire in Dur'heim."

The elf turns to Eliza with disbelieving look, and a raised brow asking, "Well he invoked you as a witness, did you guys really take down a Vampire?"

Suddenly involved in the conversation Eliza hesitates in her response, "Y-yes, or at least that is what he said it was before we fought it."

Realizing some rudeness on his behalf for having excluded a person he had never met from the conversation by instead having spoken in frank nostalgic ways with his friend of many years, Elandur palms his forehead before extending a hand to Eliza, "How impolite of me, the name is, well he told you my name, I own this magic shop. What we are talking about is something little Yefim here has been trying to get me to sell him for more than two decades now. This," and turning from Eliza, the elf opens a locked case behind him pulling from it a small lyre that glistens in the radiant light that fills the room, its intricate golden engravings and embellishments make it certainly a beautiful instrument.

"What is it?" Eliza asks looking from it, to the man presenting it, for viewing.

Before a response can come from the man holding the item of inquiry, Flame-Tender responds, "That is the lyre of Felicity Meiana, a great bard of the second age. It is said that her songs, could end entire battles on their own, and that some of the connection to the primordial energies of the world that her songs had, still remains within the instrument. If you didn't notice, I myself am a bard. I can't explain it really more than when I sing, or perform, or even just crack a joke, sometimes I can invoke magic effects, and I have been drawn to that since I was six years old, imagining how great of a performer I could be with only a fraction of Felicity's legendary prowess."

"How much is it?"

Both men look to Eliza, with surprised expressions, and Elandur hesitates, but responds, "Seventy-five thousand standard unitary gold."

"And you said you haven't dropped your price, yet?"

"What are you," Flame-Tender looks between his old and new friend.

"That is correct," Elandur responds, suspicious of Eliza's questions.

"Do you have any bags or satchels that hold more than they should," Eliza asks looking around the store, overlooking Boop sniffing a pair of green boots that look almost as though created from leafs.

"Yes," Elandur's voice trails off feeling suddenly like Flame-Tender, to be the one out of place in Eliza's presence.

"How much would you ask for, for me to get that and the lyre you have been talking about?"

"Seventy five thousand five hundred standard unitary gold."

"Alright," Eliza smiles responding in a chipper voice, setting her bag onto the counter, which only just now reveals itself to be heavier than Flame-Tender had seen it before the day they left the palace. From within Eliza hoists a large bundle gesturing to Flame-Tender to join her asks, "Could you help me count please," with the bundle opening to reveal it filled with an absurd number of shining coins made of platinum. Looking up to Elandur, whose expression is a stunned surprise, like Flame-Tender's struck, to see Eliza carrying around that much coinage, she asks, "Platinum would be alright, right?"

Elandur nods, as he slowly moves to bring several bags with varying designs and place them on the counter, "They are ten times the value of gold."

With a nod Eliza focuses down at the coins and begins counting waving her hand for Flame-Tender to join her saying, "Come on, you count out half, I'll count out half," as she pulls out a second equally large bundle, revealing that the bundles made to look like rations were actually these two bags of coin.

Respecting the rule that the receiver of payment should never touch the money until the end of the transfer, Elandur watches as Eliza and Flame-Tender quickly count out large stacks of coins, from one bag, when they finally come to the requested total with Flame-Tender saying to Eliza, "Are you sure you want to do this? You barely know me, and you are offering to spend so much on me."

Eliza smiles and nods, responding, "No matter how Short of a time I have known you, we are currently a team, and if you believe this to be something to make you a stronger part of that team, then we have to get it for you. About the money, I brought it with me because I had a feeling going to a capital city with so many powerful wizards leading it, that there might be something that could help us, and that thing would probably not be cheap. Besides Bartholomeus taught me that to hoard away that which could help protect, feed, or heal others, is as evil as threatening, starving, or harming those people," with that said Eliza pushes the counted pile of coins toward the store owner finally seeing the options of bag put in front of her. Taking a moment to contemplate her decision Eliza is oblivious to the expression of overwhelming stunned silent gratitude that takes Flame-Tender, and finally she makes a decision pointing to a small messenger style bag made with purple stained leather, with the design of a pure black raven on the flap that covers its opening.

Elandur removes the other bags placing them back where he had pulled them from, and pulls the pile of coins that was pushed to him into a small chest, before offering the lyre to Eliza saying, "Here you are, thank you for the patronage."

Taking the instrument she immediately turns and offers it to Flame-Tender finally seeing the tears of joy that have welled up in his eyes, and with a smile she presses it into him, saying, "For a friendship that should be a good one and a long one." When he takes it hesitatively from her hands she turns, grabs her new bag, and begins shoveling the rest of her stuff into it.

With their new possessions in hand Eliza, and Flame-Tender, step from the shop, and back into the street temporarily being blinded by the suns light which has risen ever closer to its noon position. Boop quickly leaps from the store as he sees Eliza, step out hearing her voice in his mind call, "Come Boop."

Holding the lyre, Flame-Tender is still discombobulated simply standing in place just outside the building's threshold, but his senses return to him as Eliza's hand presses into his arm. Looking over and up into Eliza's eyes Flame-Tender smiles and turning to the street points announcing, "Alright next a dress," and he steps taking lead into the crowds of the street again.

They continue walking for a while crossing another bridge, while

Flame-Tender fills Eliza's ears with explanations of the acts of tom foolery he
had participated in his youth, he stops Eliza and Boop several feet away from
a vendor cart. Leaving the two and stepping to the strange cart he completes
a small transaction of only copper pieces in exchange for what appears to be
snowballs placed onto a cone made from stale pastries. Returning to Eliza,
with one in each of his hands, Flame-Tender offers one to her, and as she
takes it she asks, "What's this?"

"We call this Ice-cream, it isn't common, because the magic runes
needed to keep it frozen until it is consumed don't exist in most cities, but it's
really good."

Looking down at the cold ball of ice-cream, Eliza nods and gives the
suddenly beginning to slowly melting substance, a lick. Instantly Eliza's eyes
lighten with childish delight, and the cold melts on her tongue releasing the
taste of sweetened cream flavored with vanilla. With the taste filling her
mouth in such a pleasant way Eliza, suddenly wants more, and putting the
cone to her mouth she takes a large bite of the frozen substance. Regret fills
her immediately as her teeth send sudden signals of pain to her brain and as
the large chunk of the ice-cream sits in her mouth slowly beginning to melt,
the pain intensifies and her free hand shoots to the side of her head, as she
exclaims with a full mouth, "Ow, ow, ow, ow, ow."

With a snicker from the over exuberance of Eliza's consumption of
the snack Flame-Tender explains, "Hey, you can't eat it that fast you'll get a
freezer headache."

"Too late."

"Well don't worry it will pass."

Rubbing the crown of her nose Eliza continues with Flame-Tender
again, stepping in search for the place he has in mind for letting her buy a
dress. The three arrive at such a place shortly after having finished their ice-
cream as they step through an ebony wood door, on the side of a lavender-
cloud colored building, past the hung sign which reads, "Sisters of the Cloth."

Inside is a familiar scene of shelves built into the side walls stacked high with bolts of clothes of all colors and styles. That, however, is where the similarity to past tailors ends. Two counters stand on the sides of the room with two fitting stages, one by each, stood behind. Four doors leave the circular main room. One on each side leading through the towering floor to ceiling shelves, and one on each side where the shelves, find their ends.

As with the magic item shop, a bell rings from being struck by the door as Flame-Tender leads Eliza, in explaining, "This is where my sisters commission their outfits from, I am sure they will be happy to help you."

The doors at the back of the room open almost simultaneously with the closing of the entrance to the store, revealing an elven woman in one and an elven man in the other, both standing in a flamboyant pose, as though taking part in a choreographed entrance. Both are dressed in tan straight pressed pants with a long sleeved top covered partially by a blue and black vest, and with both of their long blond hair pulled back in a ponytail. They would look identical if it weren't for their genders. A synchronized bow releases from the two a greeting, "Welcome valued costumer to the Sisters of the Cloth, Tailors."

The woman who stepped through the left door takes a step forward and out stretching a single arm in their direction she continues obviously the higher pitched voice of the two her words have a lyrical feel to them to not make the semi-song like greeting embarrassing, "I am Avilandra."

Instantly the man follows striking a mirror of the pose, "And I am Valerian."

Then speaking again in unison, they conclude, "And whether it be business, pleasure, or surprising your special other, we can have the outfit for you ready before you leave."

Then crossing her arms Eliza asks, "Isn't it supposed to be the Sisters of the Cloth?"

Avilandra's head drops as she sighs, "Our sister, Faedowin, is currently unwell."

"So, I am helping here in her place, for now," Valerian continues,

"What could we help you with today?"

Flame-Tender smiles and gently pushes Eliza forward saying, "This one has a meeting with the high council and she wants to get something proper to wear."

"Excellent, just step onto one of fitting platforms if you would please," Avilandra asks, and Eliza obeys.

Standing on the platform Eliza watches as the two take points opposite each other facing her, and pulling out two small stones each which hold on them different glyphs, they extend the carved faces of the rocks out to their sides. A green glow grows in the symbols on each stone and the siblings begins to walk in a circle around Eliza as Valerian begins a conversation with his sister, "This one's hair is a nice sky blue and her skin is pale with her eyes void of color. Perhaps we stay with that and make the dress something vibrant."

Eliza watches as the image she maintains of an outfit on herself is replaced with a plain dress that is a vibrant tangerine orange, Avilandra shakes her head responding, "No, no, this isn't a date brother this is an official meeting they said she is going to be going to with the high council. You can't have the attention be on the dress. We must make the thing to really standout be her face to draw their attention to her eyes and not to the rest of her stunning figure."

Suddenly the image of the dress morphs its color, darkening into a deep blue, and Valerian squints at the change for a moment before responding, "I think you are right sister. The darker color does shift the attention from her as a whole to the lightness of her skin and hair. On that note I think we should definitely have sleeves just to focus that attention even more to her beautiful white eyes."

Sleeves grow from the dress image's shoulders wrapping down Eliza's arms extending a ring of cloth to sit like a ring around her finger to pull the sleeves down into place. The conversation continues, "What a wonderful point brother, now about her figure, she has a stunning shape to her, and we shouldn't lose that in mounds of fabric. The dress should be simple, only lightly pleated along the bottom, tied in the back, and complimented with a stylish belt."

The image changes as described again and this time Valerian is the one to shake his head responding, "Now sister you are the one that made point to remind me of the importance this person's appointment must be to be meeting with the high council. I suggest a near black corset-brazier combo, to contain her impressive endowments, and to again shape her figure to more draw attention upward, something I believe the belt you suggested would fail to do."

"I believe you may be right brother, how silly of me to have not taken into account this ladies blessings."

"Now sister no need to be jealous."

"I am not," Avilandra exclaims in response leaving both her and Eliza blushing at the comment.

"Excuse me dear will you have any accessories with you at this meeting?"

Eliza turns to face Valerian responding, "A cane."

"Interesting, would you happen to have it with you?"

Digging into her new bag, Eliza draws out the master's cane letting the two tailor siblings examine it. Looking to the cane and then to each other the two smile saying in unison, "A hat," and Eliza watches in a mirror attached to the shelfs on the edge of the room, a small hat of a similar dark blue add itself to the illusionary outfit that covers Eliza, resting itself on her head, and being tied in place by a ribbon which disappears into her hair.

Turning to Flame-Tender Avilandra asks, "What do you think?"

Surprised to be asked, there is hesitation in Flame-Tender's response eventually expressing, "It looks nice."

Bringing a mirror closer to Eliza for her to get a look, Valerian smiles asking, "And how about you dear? It is important for you to like the way you look."

"It's really pretty," Eliza responds sheepishly still blushing from the banter filled with compliments about her, that the siblings had while creating the image.

"Well, it's a good thing you like it," Avilandra responds offering a hand to assist Eliza down from the raised platform before turning to her brother, "Total it up brother for these good customers."

Instantly a pad of parchment and a quill are in Valerian's hands and he mumbles to himself writing something down, "Fabric, labor, personalization, fitting, and it's a rush order," and with a smile he nods saying to Eliza and Flame-Tender, "For that dress it will be a meager one hundred twenty five unitary gold pieces."

Eliza's eyes go wide responding, "For a dress?"

"Not just any dress. That dress is hand crafted specifically for and fitted perfectly for you. Made as a rush order so that you can have it within the hour."

"Is there any way we could bring the price down?"

"Afraid not, unless you can delay the time you need it by, but I was given the impression that the meeting you have with the high council is later today."

Flame-Tender steps to Eliza asking her in a whisper, "Hey, what's the deal? It isn't that expensive given the factors they are taking in."

"I already spent so much in the city, and I have something I want to do in E'ar Falmar with the rest of what I have. I have the green dress, I'll be fine."

"Well, if you are sure," Flame-Tender responds, before turning and putting on a smile to the shop owners explaining, "Seems we won't be shopping here today, sorry for wasting your time," and he walks with Eliza to the door.

When the three pass back into the streets the siblings call from within one last time, "Come back any time."

The air of the streets hasn't changed any, but as it sits upon the trio as they continue Flame-Tender's route, it is heavier than it was before. Eliza, looks down contemplating her plan in the port Alfredo's shop is in, and on how pretty the dress was on her. Knowing she shouldn't use her magic to cast the appearance of the outfit on herself for the high council meeting, she almost lets herself selfishly long to not have purchased the lyre for Flame-Tender, but grabbing the amulet to Archangel steadies her mind against such false regret.

In a spur of inspiration Flame-Tender turns to Eliza saying, "Hey, let's go have some lunch," before grabbing her wrist and pulling her into a run.

The crowds seem to part out of their way as the several minutes it would have taken to get back to Flame-Tender's home become few. Pulling Eliza in to the dining hall and sitting her down at the table Flame-Tender disappears through the door that meals have been brought from each time they have been served. Eliza, sits with Boop, confused as to where Flame-Tender had gone, and about the burst of energy that had him nearly drag her here.

Eventually, Eliza becomes tired of waiting for something she isn't even sure is coming. The instant she stands from her seat though, the door from the front hall once again swings open revealing Flame-Tender, and one of his sisters standing in the open doorway. At the same moment the smell of spices finds its way into Eliza's senses, and a man servant enters through the other door pushing a lid covered tray cart.

Flame-Tender and his sister step in Eliza's direction reaching her same moment as the servant bringing her food, and with the meal set onto the table revealed to be a large flat circle of bread with cheese melted over a tomato sauce topping it, Flame-Tender's sister, Victoria, smiles saying, "Yefim told me you are worried about your outfit for your meeting with the high council. Would you let me help you?"

Eliza looks up into the young woman's eyes only just nearly twenty years old in appearance, she smiles with sparkling white straight teeth, and a glisten in her green and light brown eyes that are only barely darker than her dirty blond hair which hangs long down her back with a single small braid mixing with the untied rest of it. The look of honest desire to help Eliza, is apparent in the calm of the welcoming expression as she turns and grabs a slice from the large lunch dish. Confused Eliza, turns her look to Flame-Tender who returns a smile, and then looking back to Victoria, she asks, "Why would you help me?"

Mouth full Victoria responds, in a way that is unladylike showing her trust of the company around her, "Yefim told me about how much of a help you were with the quest he left on, and how you and a friend of yours are taking him along on a quest that is giving him purpose. On top of that he showed me that you got him that silly trinket he has been eyeballing since we were young, because I know he couldn't afford it. So, when he told me you didn't have enough to get a new dress for yourself, I nearly slapped him for not buying it for you, but since you are here you can borrow one of my dresses. It might be tight in some places, but I am sure we can make you look fabulous for this meeting of yours."

Not knowing what to say or do with the sudden offer presented to her, Eliza simply mimics Victoria's action, grabbing a slice of the dish placed on the table and taking a bite. It's good. The two quickly consume the rest of the midday meal, with Flame-Tender having stepped away leaving Eliza in the hands of his sister. Victoria pulls Eliza from the dining hall, leaving the dirty dish for a servant to clean, and up to the second floor. Eliza watches Boop yawn tired from the day's activities thus far and as they walk up the stairs her hand falls softly on the back of his head as she whispers to him, "Go take a nap bud." To which he turns as they reach the second floor and drifts lazily in the direction of the room that was made for them.

The girls step the opposite way and find themselves at a door that in the hall looks the same as the others, but when opened reveals Victoria's room, large and decorated very similarly to the one made up for Eliza, minus the pet bed. Being on the side of the hall that is toward the home's center, the room lacks a window, but is brilliantly lit by the same light emanating orbs that seem to be everywhere, as fireless sources of light. In the spot of the room's layout where Eliza's room has a window, there is a painting of an outward looking scene made to appear as looking through one.

Most notably in the room, in contrast to the other minor details that make it different from the one Eliza was allowed to sleep in, is the color scheme. The walls hold a light yellow paint to their faces, trimmed with molding painted the same blue as Eliza's hair. The drapery hung from the canopy of the bed is an equally light green like the peal of a granny smith apple. Lastly, the rug and furniture are dark tones like soil of red and brown, making them bold against the other colors which make the room feel almost as though it wants to expand, pulling the focus of the room back in and keeping it grounded.

Stepping from the hall to her bed and throwing herself onto it, to a seated position facing the foot space of the room, Victoria gestures Eliza forward demanding, "Alright, let's see this dress brother says you have, and the reason you didn't feel you were worth a new outfit."

Following the instruction Eliza enters the room and reaching into her bag withdraws the plain green dress given to her by the tailor in Blackgate, hesitatively stammering in response to the sudden domineering presence Victoria has begun to emanate, "Here."

Worried concern strikes Victoria's face as she witnesses the plain green dress emerge from the purple bag. Leaping from her bed and running to Eliza she shakes her head explaining, "No, no, you mustn't wear that. The thing is filthy from whatever it has loitering with in your bag. It would be better if you were to go in what you are wearing now."

"But this," Eliza tries to respond looking shyly down to the illusion of the pink dress that has been her go to covering, but is cut off.

"Don't worry that won't be happening either, I told my brother, that I would help you out, so that is what I am going to do," Victoria explains moving to the wardrobe and opening it to reveal it pact tightly with many different styles of dress, all of which are green, "You will have to forgive the color pallet those two seamstresses found that I look good in green and won't offer anything in any other color. Not that I am complaining they are beautiful outfits, and they make me feel pretty when I wear them. Hey, hey, enough about me. Let's find one of these that looks good on you. First things first, did they think light colors or dark for the outfit they offered as their idea for you?"

"Dark."

"That means these won't work," Victoria whispers to herself sliding her hands past a section of dresses almost a similar green as the bed canopy. Pulling one dress free she crosses her arms with a sarcastic look on her face saying, "You know you are going to have a hard time getting into one of my dresses as it is, let alone if you try to keep that dress on underneath."

"But, um, that is what I was trying to say, I couldn't wear this to the council meeting even if I wanted to," and casting her arms down and out from her sides, Eliza lets the image fade revealing her clothes-less form wearing only the boots Pearl had given her to protect her feet.

"Oh, you poor thing, having to use magic to cover yourself, in hopes of keeping the one nice dress you have clean for occasions you need it. I understand high level mages like the council leaders would definitely see through that. Here," Victoria sets down the dress on her bed before turning back to the wardrobe and pulling from a drawer a brazier and accompanying piece of undergarment, offering them to Eliza, "Like the dress these might be a bit tight, but I know you will feel more comfortable even if they are too tight, to have something like these on, than to not," but before letting Eliza take them from her hands Victoria is struck by sudden inspiration exclaiming, "Wait, there is no way these would even be remotely comforting to you, and you might even snap the brazier's clasps," mumbling, "there is no doubt actually," before continuing with the inspired look in her eye, "Let me go get Liliana, she is my younger sister, but she is at least a little bit closer to your size, at least when it comes to these." Eliza is left alone in the room as

Victoria sprints out and down the hall.

Eliza stands alone and nervous in a stranger's bedroom for a handful of minutes. When Victoria finally returns she is accompanied by the fuller figured sister from the introductions at breakfast, Liliana. The two of them find Eliza nervously holding the green dress she had brought against herself. With a smile Liliana, waves with the greeting, her voice sounding almost the exact same as her sister's, as would be expected from siblings, "Hello again! Victoria explained everything to me, and I want to let you have these," presenting a set of plain grey undergarments continuing, "And I would like to ask you to come to my room and have you use one of my dresses. Neither of us know why Yefim talked to Victoria first but you would definitely find the squeeze of your chest lessened in one of my dresses compared to either of my sisters."

Victoria's fist clinches before turning to her sister saying angrily, "Yea, but the midsection of your dresses would just have folds of excess fabric."

Liliana turns angrily to glare back at her sister but their glaring contest is interrupted by the third sister, Anastasia, the tallest of the sisters, entering the room and asking loudly, her voice with a significant maturity over that of her sisters, "What is going on you two?" Seeing Eliza she steps into the room closing the door, you're Eliza, right? From that group Yefim brought home with him. What are you doing in Victoria's room naked, and why are you two fighting?"

Instantaneously Liliana points to Victoria responding, "She called me fat."

To which Victoria responds, "I did not! Besides, she made fun of us being flat chested."

"Grow up you two," Anastasia commands into the situation, "You're both nearly thirty, and engaged. Start acting like it." Then turning to Eliza she continues, asking, "So what is going on here?"

Victoria responds before Eliza has a chance, "She has that meeting that brother talked about with the high council soon, and she went to go buy a dress at Sisters of the Cloth, but because she bought Yefim that fiddle he has been talking about since we were little, she didn't have the money to spend on a new dress for herself, he told me, so I was going to give her one of mine, but then I found out that she hasn't actually been wearing any clothes, I don't know why, but I was going to offer her some underwear to wear with the dress, but that wouldn't have worked, she would have burst any of my bras so I got Lili because at least one of her bras would have a chance, and then we got back here, and Pudgy said my dresses wouldn't work because I am too flat, and I responded that Eliza is thin and would look awkward in one of her dresses, and then you walked in."

"I see. Eliza, I apologize for my sisters' rude behavior. Quibbling over such trivial things while they were intending to be aiding you. Victoria, Liliana, how about we work together the three of us to make this friend of Yefim's as beautiful as we can before her meeting with the high council?" Both of the other sisters respond with agreeing nods, before Anastasia points to Eliza saying, "First, Lili give that girl the underwear you brought her and let her put it on."

Liliana looks at her hand and seeing the delicate garments still wrapped in her fist, she blushes and offers the two items of clothing to Eliza. Grateful Eliza takes them and puts them on, as predicted the bottom sits loosely in place while the brazier struggles at its seams to maintain hold, but with Eliza minimally clothed, the women go to work to do more than just give her a dress. With the three moving Eliza to be seated on Victoria's bed they begin. Liliana, takes to applying colored polish to Eliza's nails. Anastasia takes to brushing smooth the long sky blue hair, and Victoria takes to applying makeup to their young canvas' face.

After only a handful of minutes, the question comes up, with Liliana asking as she paints Eliza's toe nails, "So, how old are you, really. Yefim hasn't ever been so embarrassed by mother's advances toward women on his behalf before."

"Fourteen," Eliza responds bashfully remember the conversation the night before and at the breakfast table the morning after.

The three sisters in unison gasp in disbelief, with Victoria responding, "I totally thought you were at least Lili's age. I mean you have to at least be fully developed for your species. Which is...?"

"I'm human."

"No way!"

"It is true, or at least I think I am, I don't know what else I could be."

"Wow! Well that would explain brother's want to deny interest in you, though I doubt that his refusal is earnest. He probably has feelings for you, but won't allow himself to show them, because that would make him disgusting."

"What do you mean?"

"Eliza, darling, you have a gorgeous figure, that the three of us are certainly jealous of," the other two sisters continue their work silently agreeing with slow nods.

Eliza blushes at the complement asking, "You thought I was about your age. What age would that be? Anastasia said that you were nearly thirty, but I thought Flame-Tender, was twenty six, and each of you had to be younger than that."

"You flatter us," Anastasia responds blushing herself, and having to take a moment to fan herself with her hand.

Victoria responds with a smile, "I am twenty-six. Big brother Yefim is thirty. Anastasia twenty-eight. Lili twenty-five, and our little brother is twenty."

"There, finished," Liliana exclaims pulling back from her work having finished polishing the last of Eliza's nails with a black polish.

Leaping up and to the wardrobe Victoria cheers, having finished the minimalistic makeup on Eliza's face before her sister started even working on their guest's toes, "Now an outfit, I was thinking that dress. What do you two think?"

The dress pointed to still lays on the bed where it was placed before, and the two other sisters look at it with contemplative stares. Not satisfied with their ability to imagine the dress on Eliza, Liliana swipes it from the bed and pulling Eliza to her feet, she holds the dress up in front of her. With Eliza stood to almost look like she is wearing the outfit, the three sisters smile together with Liliana saying, "You know sis, if she fits, I think you are right that she would look better in that than in one of mine."

Victory smiles responding, "You know I was thinking about that," before brandishing a set of scissors and swiping the dress from her sister's hands. In an instant faster than either of the others can respond the cutting tool finds grip on the fabric in the back of the dresses stiff upper half, slicing a line down it through what is meant to be a fitted, chest covering, corset.

"What are you doing," Liliana exclaims reacting too slowly to stop the destruction of the garment.

Victoria just smiles responding, "Trust me on this," then stepping to the door opens it calling, "Anderson!"

Within moments the door rings with a knock from the other side preceding Anderson's call in asking, "You called for me Madam Victoria?"

"Yes, Anderson, I need this dress repaired immediately, as in the next few minutes, the cut that has been made, make that a seam held together to be adjustable with lace."

"I will have it done shortly ma'am," Anderson responds disappearing with the dress back the direction down the hall from which he came.

Turning back to the room Victoria is greeted with approving nods from her sisters and an expression of worry from Eliza, who feels even more out of place having her hair down, wearing undergarments that are both too small and too large for her, gifted by someone she barely knows, and wearing, for the first time, a layer of makeup. Proud of her idea Victoria steps to Eliza explaining, "The worry we had about my dresses on you was your chest, but with the added lacing that shouldn't be a problem. I mean of course it will still be a little short on you but it looked cute. Now for accessories."

Liliana and Anastasia light up with the word and both of them run from the room. Victoria steps over to the desk, and sliding out one of the drawers pulls from within, a small chest. Eliza tries to deny the extra decoration intended to be applied to her saying, "That isn't necessary. You are already being too kind lending me a dress."

The comment is cast off though when Victoria asks, with a doubting look on her brow, "Oh, so you have your own jewelry you will be accenting the dress with," then turning back to a smile she continues, "Look, you are a friend of our big brother, one that will make sure that he comes back after all of this adventuring he is doing, alive, so our soon to be husbands won't have to do Daddy's job. As long as you are that for him, you are like a sister to us. Ok. Now tell me have you had your ears pierced?"

Bashfully looking away, overwhelmed by the generosity of the people she has met, Eliza responds softly, "No."

"So, you haven't. No worries we will use clip-ons," Victoria responds pulling out a pair of earrings both decorated with a single green gemstone hung from a tiny clamp that holds itself closed with an even smaller spring.

As Eliza sits back down on the bed the earrings are clasped into place on her lobs. In the same moment the second earring is attached the door rings with a knock and opens with Liliana and Anastasia reentering the room with big smiles of their own for what they have returned with. In their hands they both carry a box, and opening them reveal more to be added to their canvas, Eliza. Liliana reveals a necklace with five golden leafs attached with a small chain, on each of which is impressed a blue gemstone that takes up most of the leaf's surface area. With Eliza's eye widening at the necklace Liliana quickly latches it around the surprised girl's neck, saying, "There that will look beautiful with the dark green of that dress."

Sharing in the excitement of her sisters, as the outfit they are building for Eliza begins to fill out, Anastasia kneels down and without even giving Eliza a chance to see what she brought, starts wedging Eliza's feet into a pair of sleek dark brown, nearly black, shoes, with a small, barely an inch, heel. The other sisters smile as Eliza looks down with worried surprise at the footwear when a knock on the door has Anderson's voice call in, "Miss Victoria, the alteration you requested has been made."

Opening the door only enough to grab the dress, Victoria relieves Anderson of his possession of the garment, and closing the door calls through the wood, "Thanks Anderson." The sisters buzz with anticipation as they all stand with Victoria gesturing for Eliza to stand as well saying, "Come on, stand up and raise your arms."

Nervously Eliza follows the direction given, standing, and raising her arms, while closing her eyes, pressing down feelings of guilt that fill her for some reason for being treated so nicely, and remembering Val. The cloth of the dress is pulled forcefully down over her to get its waist to rest loosely on hers. Her hair is freed only to be pushed over her shoulder as someone tightens new lace in the dress' back. Letting the hair fall back into place where its hangs nicely covering the seam, the sisters release a combined high-pitched sound of excitement as Anastasia says, "Eliza, sweetie, open your eyes."

With the gentle command Eliza lets her eyes slowly open and before her stands Victoria and Liliana holding a mirror which shows in its frame, herself. Her mouth gapes open and she quickly covers it with a hand as she gasps with surprise at her appearance. Overwhelmed, not having expected that having her hair brushed, her clothes changed, and a small amount of makeup applied to her face, tears begin to well in her eyes from happiness and gratitude for those who made her so beautiful.

Seeing the glisten of Eliza's eyes becoming watery Victoria grabs a small cloth and jumping to Eliza, presses the rag nearly into one of the eyes saying, "Hey. Hey, there, don't do that, you'll make the makeup run."

Taking the rag from Victoria, Eliza lunges forward ensnaring the middle sister in a hug exclaiming, "Thank you."

Pushing Eliza away enough to look into her eyes, but maintaining the embrace Victoria responds, "I told you as long as our brother is in your company we shall be like sisters, just keep him safe ok?"

"Ok."

21

Elven High Council

Flame-Tender stands outside the room Eliza stayed in the night before, having just knocked, awaiting a response. When the door finally opens his shoulders drop to see floating in the freshly opened doorway, Boop, blinking heavily to get the sleep out of his eyes. With a sigh, Flame-Tender asks, "Well, at least unlike a cat or a dog you can talk a little. Is Eliza, in here?"

"No," Boop responds with a tone of curiosity.

"Do you know where she is?"

"In this house."

Pressing his hand to his head Flame-Tender sighs begrudgingly continuing his line of questions, "Do you know where in the house she is?"

"No."

"Look we have to start heading over to the council hall, can you help me look for her?"

"No."

"Why not?"

Before Boop can respond, Victoria grabs her brother's sleeve saying, "Hey, you're looking for Eliza right?"

"Yeah, we need to... Woah," Flame-Tender is struck silent as he turns and his eyes meet Eliza's form standing with his sisters in the hall.

"Well, why didn't you come to my room? I told you I would get her taken care of when you told me about how sad she looked when you chose not to buy her a dress when she couldn't afford it after buying you that stringed thing," Victoria builds up her voice becoming increasingly flustered as she recounts the reason Flame-Tender asked her for help in the first place, not seeing Eliza, look to her to catch specifically that he asked his sisters for help because he saw how down hearted she had gotten when the dress was too much. Turning to Eliza and pressing down the sides of the skirt, she smiles saying, "Now you go get whatever it is you need from those old farts on the high council."

Eliza smiles and nods and with a gesture is joined quickly by Boop who says to Flame-Tender as he drifts past, "Because she is already right here," before the two leave the company of the sisters and make their way in the direction of the exit.

Flame-Tender having fallen into a slap from his own hand, with Boop's comment to him, straightens himself up and resting his hands on his sister's shoulders, regaining her attention from watching Eliza walk down the hall, and he says, "Thank you. By how she acted I knew Eliza, didn't want the dress for the dress, she wanted to be presentable and to feel pretty for this meeting, and I knew that to buy her that dress I would not have let her meet my sisters and have whatever experience she had with you that gave her that smile," and the four share a look at Eliza, whose head is turned explaining her experience to Boop. A truly soft smile that shows her actual age glistens through her words, and he continues, stepping past his sisters, "We'll be back later, I doubt that Eliza, or the others will want to start our journey through the forest to Ear'Falmar at night."

With a light jog, Flame-Tender rejoins Eliza and Boop, and the three find their way out of the manor and into the street. The sun still beats down hot, only about two hours after midday, and the light breeze continues to blow ruffling the bottom of Eliza's dress as well as the loose silk that covers her shoulders and her hair gently, only just revealing several laces tied into bows down her back ranging from using nearly all of the thread in the knot, to barely having any for it. The air remains filled with the smell of baked goods switching from the morning breads to the sweets that will be deserts for families in the city.

The walk is short as the streets seem less crowded than they were earlier in the day, and waiting at the bottom of the stairs stand Nakhal and Bellar. With the crowd parting the two have their attention drawn with the attention of the shifting crowd around them to the three approaching them, and Bellar's eyes widen as he catches Eliza in his gaze. Double taking to make sure he isn't seeing things, he greets his companions, "Wow. Hello again."

"Are we ready to go in?" Flame-Tender asks pointing up to the waiting open doors and taking a single step up the stairs.

Regaining his focus, Bellar turns to Flame-Tender, responding, "Yeah, sorry, we might have to wait another few minutes, but we can go inside."

A juxtaposition of the city sits within the presence council building. Large, rigid, and looming almost oppressively over the stairs that lead into it. The heavy wooden doors to the entrance are held open to let the nice breeze of the city's fresh air attempt to breathe life into the hot, uncaring space. The imposing presence remains through the threshold, with the large space made claustrophobic from the dark stains that color almost every surface of the carved and crafted decorative wood work that presses down from the walls and ceiling. Even the furnishings which sit as a heavy monolith curve, hold similar embellishment as the columns and molding of the front chamber, and plain slabs of cold, unforgiving, stone, hold the silent menace of the building's nature.

The air is dry, hot, and musky with an almost unnatural silence as the walls muffle even the clamor from the street to the volume of a whisper muting those whispers of nervous groups waiting for their turn to be heard by the governmental leadership. The smell of sweat congeals with the toxic scent of aging wood stain and the grime of centuries of dust ignored in crevasses to inconvenient to bother someone to clean, and it permeates with the heat and tension of the room. Even the breeze fails to uplift the oppressive odor that presses into the lungs of those within this waiting area, making the wait insufferable.

The attention of the filled benches of huddled families, friends, and lawyers, worried about their clusters turn, for a split moment turns to see the new arrivals who step through the door to join them in the pressure cooker of bureaucratic anticipation. Each of the groups return to their own muffled conversations as they formulate their intentions for their upcoming turn to pass through the doors at the far end of the room. Eliza feels out of place, as scanning over the other groups she finds the outfits drab and plan, either intentionally or not, becoming almost part of the old imposing design of the interior, and the dress she is wearing becomes for the room almost like a single flower blooming through the ash left in the wake of a great forest fire.

The emotionless pit that is the room, though hot and uncomfortable in temperature, is cold in its silence as the doors at the far end slowly grind open. A group of three step from within, their faces filled with a look that is a mixture of sorrow, confusion, and disbelief, leaving a single person, distinctly lacking in any revealing trait to make them recognizable, standing in the now open door way, and turning to a group sitting on one of the benches, the man gestures into the chamber beyond addressing them in a monotone, indistinct voice, "The party of Fer'Anture, the Council will hear you know."

The group stands and clutching the documents they have brought with them, step past the individual into the waiting chamber. Before the door is closed the strange person makes eye contact with Eliza and her companions and gestures to the desk. With a turn and not a single word further the stranger closes the large doors leaving the room again silent.

Bellar steps to the desk at which no one is sitting, and taking a quill from a provided inkwell signs on a blank sheet of parchment left upon it, "Eliza and Company, on the matters discussed in the port liberated." After which the quill is replaced in the inkwell and the ink vanishes from the page. The dwarf steps ushering the others to the seats that had been emptied by the other group who stepped from the room.

The door into the next room opens again, and the last group to enter, exits, with another group being beckoned in. A few minutes pass and again, the group that entered last exits, and another is taken in. Each time a group leaves the expression they hold is never one that would show a success in what they wished to achieve with their turn to be heard. Instead the expressions tend toward contemplation, overwhelmed and baffled by information presented to them.

Finally, Eliza's group remains as the only group not yet called into the chamber beyond, and Eliza's nerves and anticipation culminate in a jittering uneasy energy that makes it difficult for her to remain seated. The door opens again, but the group that entered the room last are not the only ones who exit, as more than a dozen others join them. The attendant who has ushered each group into the room gives a nod and a gesture in saying, "Eliza and company the council will hear you in private now."

Standing and feeling her hands shaking, not knowing what will happen or what she is going to say or ask, Eliza leads the small group through the doors which are closed behind them with the attendant remaining outside. The air is cooler in the large chamber which, even though having the same aesthetics in the imposing wood work that makes the space almost feel as though it is pressing down upon those within, dwarfs the room prior. Along the chamber's outer edge run raised bench areas large enough to seat hundreds for the observation of the proceedings, now empty. In the room's center a platform nearly ten feet long and wide, and a meager three feet raised from the ground, stands waiting for Eliza and the others, opposite eight towering podiums that stand twenty feet above the platform. At each podium is a robed figure, except one, who wears her heavy metal armor, Ava, and one which remains empty.

Cordian and Ortidan are seated and robed in the same purple and blue robes they had worn when Eliza met them in Blackgate, along with one wearing red, one in green, one in yellow, and one in white. Eliza steps onto the small platform and by design is forced to look up to see the council looking down upon her, Boop, Bellar, Flame-Tender, and Nakhal. From above the commanding voice of the Commander of the Elven military calls down, "Eliza Black of the liberators of Blackgate, do you remember why you are here?"

Being addressed finally calms Eliza's nerves just enough to where she can respond. While though still nervous she is able to muster an audible, "Yes."

Then watching the high commander rise from her seat, Eliza's eyes widen when a pointed finger and glare focus down onto the low platform, "Then why is it that there are two others with you that are not part to your purpose."

Bellar steps forward responding for Eliza, saying, "This is my doing. I did not break the terms of agreement by recommending specific additions to their team, but with Commander Ironskin of Blackgate, unable to join them any further, I recommended to the remaining three that they look into increasing their numbers with others they can trust."

Ava's glare maintains itself as she sits back down, leaving an opening for Ortidan to rise and speak explaining, "It was not thought of in the conversation that your group would have autonomy of those who join and leave. Though the logic for these additions is strong, and there is not an evil intent about them at this moment, I will recommend that this council look past this overstep this time as to express a desire to aid and not hinder this group's progress."

The red robed figure, who at the moment is wearing a mask rises, her voice calm and smooth, sounding almost even further into old age than Ortidan, responds, "I second this motion."

The red robed figure sits again and Ortidan continues, "Then it is carried. This is not a motion that holds sway further, discussion will be had at a later point after this meeting to the extent of agreeance to the council. Now onto the matter at hand. To the company's request of the return of the dimensional anchor to the now owners of the Island of Negmor," Eliza prepares herself to need to respond and to debate the need for the anchor, "The request is granted, a guard will escort you to the port of Ear'Falmar first thing in the morning, and a ship readied to take you out to the point from which it was seized."

Eliza just freezes, her mouth agape, her heart stopping mid beat with surprise, and she can't help herself from asking, "That's it?"

A look of curiosity forms on the old mages face as he leans over his podium to ask, "Is there more you would request?"

"No, I just didn't..."

"Didn't think that the motion would pass without your need of defending your reasoning. Child, your case was made in Blackgate, and the impression you left us liaisons carried into our continued debate here, the motion passed with only one of the eight members refusing. Good luck in your mission. We hope to hear of progress soon. Please let Bethany know to step back in."

Flame-Tender, Eliza, and Bellar share the same look of shock and bewilderment as groups they have seen leave this room begin to reenter, and together they step from the platform and to the door. From the outer room they continue from the building and into the street. The sun is just beginning to set while remaining bright overhead as they walk back to the manor only just shaking out of their surprise at the ease at which the meeting went in their favor.

Over the course of the next few hours, Eliza returns the borrowed outfit's parts to the sisters, and joins the others for an evening meal before settling in for sleep. Eliza though lays awake with night having taken the sky above. Her head spins with what is to come next. A journey to the coast, to Ear'Falmar, she was planning on meeting with Alfredo. She wants to beg him to help prevent the side effects Alex had told her about, but now as she thinks to the time table ticking away to have something to show the council who even expedited returning a device to allow her and Pearl to traverse the globe more quickly, she isn't sure she will have time. She has noticed that her hair is still growing faster than it should, as are her nails, and the worry what else might be going on with her keeps her awake, even as Boop rests in her arms, with the knowledge that she will soon be rejoining Pearl.

22

Back to the Coast

Morning comes slowly, as the rising sun barely releases its rays through the window of Eliza's room. With the sounds of morning birds singing, the smell of breakfast seeps in from the hall, tickling Eliza's nose. Gently rubbing Boop to wake him, she stands, covered in her illusory dress once more, and grabbing her new bag steps from the room and through the hall to the dining room. There she finds the chairs that had consistently been empty, filled, with more than twenty individuals in military uniforms eating their fill of the morning meal.

With Eliza and Boop stepping into the room one of the uniformed individuals stands and steps to her. Stopping and giving a salute to Eliza, she is taken off guard as he addresses her with a strong commanding voice, "Miss Black, I am Captain Ferrandon, we will be your escort to Ear'Falmar. Once you and your companions have eaten we will take you to the vault so that you can claim that which you have been permitted by the council."

Slowly nodding, Eliza pulls away from the intensity radiating from the soldier, and taking a seat she waits for a plate to be brought to her, which arrives only a moment later. While she and Boop eat, Bellar and Nakhal arrive at the table. Finally, Flame-Tender enters the room and finds a seat. In near silence, the group eat their breakfast, with Bellar and Flame-Tender both taking note of the bags under their youngest companion's eyes, without grabbing her attention.

As it was explained to Eliza, the instant the last morsel finds its way from her plate, with her being the last one to finish her morning meal, the soldiers stand in almost perfect unison and turn, stepping through the door and out of the house. Five of the nearly twenty wait in the room to take the rear of the marching formation, and mildly off put by the strict nature of the military formality of motions Eliza slowly steps with the others at the soldiers' request. Leaving the room the group watch Ferrandon bow to Lady Izhutin as his large mass of people step into the streets from her home and form into rank and file with the small cluster of non-militants within.

The streets clear as would be expected with a military troop marching through and quickly they find their way back at the council building. Instead of the obvious official structure though, Eliza and her companions are ushered through the door of building to the council building's side. There they are lead down a secret staircase by Captain Ferrandon and a stranger who was sat behind the building's counter. The stairs lead down four flights before finally reaching the hidden basement's level, which opens as an expansive hidden warehouse that stretches in all directions, with dim lights floating above what seems to be miles of filled shelving units, cluttered with a plethora of objects that would seem to have no connection with the items next to them.

The stranger shuffles forward through the path between the shelves several yards before making a fast turn down another aisle, disappearing from view behind the towers of shelves. Captain Ferrandon gestures for the group to follow, and complying they make their way to the point the man turned from. Turning, they find him another many yards away staring down at a small leaf of parchment mumbling to himself before suddenly stepping into motion again down another path once more disappearing. Again, the group follows, reaching the point they lost view of the man, and there they see him only feet away inspecting a black object shaped like a literal anchor, inscribed with arcane script on all sides. With an open palmed gesture the man explains, "This is the device that the acquisition notice from the council states is for you to withdraw. I ask that you inspect it, and the team of contractors will be notified to begin the excavation as to begin its move."

Eliza is immediately confused asking, "Wait excavation?"

"Yes ma'am, the device here took a team of more than one hundred to transport from the location it was initially located."

"But, Bellar you said it shouldn't be difficult. How long did it take to get it here from where it was?"

"Three years."

Bellar smirks almost laughing as he responds to the man, "Serves you right for having relocated a dwarven archmage's craft from its intended place of rest," then turning to Eliza and nodding to her he asks, "Do you have the master's cane I said to bring with you?"

"Yeah," Eliza responds pulling the rod from her bag.

"Well Nakhal, you are by far the strongest person here, try picking the dimensional anchor up." Nakhal attempts the feat finding it impossible with the entirety of the force he can produce. "Now Eliza tap the head of the cane to the anchor and pronounce that you wish to relocate it with the dwarven word for move, gluais."

As she is told, Eliza brings the rod's end to contact with the metal of the anchor and mimics the word, "Glauis!"

Following the pronouncement Bellar looks to Nakhal and with a smile gestures to attempt lifting the anchor again, and doubting the possibility of a change Nakhal glares at the dwarf feeling as though he is the tail end of a joke. To his surprise, and the surprise of the man who explained that it took three years to move the anchor to the city from its place off the coast, the anchor lifts light in Nakhals grasp, barely feeling to weigh more than eighty pounds. Not necessarily a light load, the immense change in apparent weight means that the giant of a man can carry it rather easily, with its size and shape becoming, for him, the more encumbering properties.

"There," Bellar chimes, "I don't think we will need that excavation team, and I hope your soldiers will accept getting early leave when this mission takes a week instead of three years," as he looks at the man and the military captain who both look to each other with surprise.

With that the group is lead up and out of the secret basement, with Captain Ferrandon explaining as they climb the stairs, "Understand, if it is learned that any information about the contents of that warehouse are exposed and you turn out to be the source, that you will find execution by this nation."

Dishearteningly, for the captain that wished to impose some level of dominance over the individuals he is to escort, he turns in time to see them disinterested as Eliza yawns and Flame-Tender asks her, "It looks like you didn't get much sleep last night."

Rubbing her eyes Eliza lazily looks in his direction, "Not really."

"Do you want to talk about it?"

"Not really," Eliza responds with a pause for another yawn continuing, "But have you ever felt like there is no chance you can live up to expectations that are being put on you?"

"All the time, but what do you mean for you?"

"Well the quest we are on. The council gave us three months to produce some form of evidence that we are making progress toward finding what we are seeking to protect, and this anchor is supposed to help with that. I don't know if we should ever report any success, part of the reason we are the group and there isn't a group for each nation, is because even the leaders of each nation shouldn't know our end result. I really just don't know if I should be a part of this."

"Now wait a minute that is crazy talk."

"I'm only fourteen, and yes I can produce some magic, but Bellar is an exceptional mage. Pearl is agile, Umbra has some form of divine favor while being skilled with a sword, and you can make magic happen with just your voice."

"What are you saying? You are extremely capable, I have seen your magic with my own eyes, and it is impressive what you can do at your age."

"But that is the point! The magic I cast has a source that I have been told all of my life is evil. I believe it's evil. I have used it because I wanted to not be a burden on those who helped get me back to this plane of existence. I don't think what we are looking to find should ever be near someone like me. Someone who is connected to a source of magic like the one I am."

"Hold on, this is the first I'm hearing of you being connected to an evil source of magic. Are you sure it's evil? Can you be certain about that?"

"Well, I..."

"If the source of magic is a being, is it contacting you? Asking you to do evil deeds in order to have your magic?"

"No."

"Has it ever contacted you at all?"

"No."

"And you are saying it is evil? Says who?"

"Bartholomeus, the priest who raised me."

"Well, no disrespect to Bartholomeus, but my experience with priests, is that anything they can't explain with their religious doctrine immediately becomes evil. Did he know the source of your magic? Did he tell you its name?"

"No."

"Look Eliza, your relationship with Pearl seems strong enough that in the time you have known her if these doubts ever rose before within you, she would have said what I am about to say to you. You are not evil if you use a tool, unless you use that tool for evil. You have an amazing magical ability and if it is not hurting you or having others hurt you, and if you are doing good deeds with it, I don't think it matters that you are fourteen. I can without a doubt say you are stronger and braver than my sisters, my brother, or most anyone I know. So, don't let worries like you are not the right person for this cloud your mind. If you weren't I am sure a powerful wizard like Negmor wouldn't have chosen you."

"The spirits where very clear that I was to join you, and the blue one," Nakhal's voice adds as he looms over Flame-Tender, carrying the anchor across his back.

"Besides I can't be a part of this, first I have strong loyalties to a nation, secondly I have duties I must return to in that nation. I have done everything I can at your palace for now, so I will depart from this group when we are back on the ground below the city," Bellar adds bringing his presence back into the conversation.

Eliza, on the verge of tears from sleep deprivation and the conversation filled with only good words for her, turns to Bellar asking, "You're leaving?"

"Yes, but only for a short time. I have to take what I have learned thus far and try to research how master Negmor has set up his labyrinth of arcane inscriptions."

Suddenly from the side Boop gives Eliza a big slobbery canine kiss, saying, "Is ok we still have others."

Her vision becoming still, her fists loosening, and her head turning to nod at Boop, Eliza responds, "Your right Boop," then turning back to Flame-Tender says, "Thank you. I feel better now. You're right, I can do this especially since I am not alone, you, and Pearl will be there."

By this point in the conversation light from the morning sun shines down again on the group as they reach the top of the stairs. The man who showed them to the anchor returns to his station at the desk within the small shop, and Captain Ferrandon leads the group back into the ranks of his platoon explaining, "We are going to have to go down a different way than you came up through as that thing proved incapable of teleporting, due to the enchantment on it."

Bellar nods with a smirk replying, "It is called a dimensional anchor for a reason."

Rolling his eyes Ferrandon, continues his lead retorting, "Well, we were uncertain of what the device's name or properties were when transporting, it was after a mage identified it for us that we figured that out. The way we are going to take you is a mechanical lift, installed in case the gateway up and down ceases to function."

Explanation understood the group remains quiet as they are walked to the outer wall of the flying city and into a large structure that looks almost like the barracks they entered beneath the city, completely out of place amongst the rest of the city's architecture. Inside, the majority of the large space is open with two large, yard wide cables strung to the corner between the wall and the ceiling of the entrance running down and away. The far wall of the building is nonexistent, and the center of the room, a majority of the floor space, is disconnected from the rest of the building instead suspended by two struts which rise from the space's sides to cling to the massive cables.

Captain Ferrandon leads his soldiers and the group onto the massive platform. Once everyone is on he gestures to a uniformed soldier at the side of the room, who salutes before pulling a lever that he is standing next to. A loud click of large gears being released resonates for the connecting point of the supports struts and the cables, accompanied with a jarring thrust that nearly knocks Eliza from her feet. The jolt is the precursor of the entire floor beneath the group's feet beginning to descend along the cables, slowly inching its way down.

Several minutes pass before the upper structure disappears from view in the distance with the platform falling to just be within the clouds before Ferrandon turns to those with him commanding, "It is going to be some time before we reach the ground. Company at ease!"

With the command, the twenty other uniformed individuals drop from their stoic postures, becoming significantly more laxed. Several of the soldiers form into small groups, and begin to sit to play dice, while others find themselves opening books to read as they continue to lower through the many layers of vaporous expectant precipitant. Taking the example from some of the armed escorts, Eliza also finds a place to sit and read more of her ritual book finally making headway on another of the rituals presented to her within its pages, while Boop takes to playing fetch off the edge of the platform with a handful of the guards.

Two hours pass with the sun visibly moving overhead. The clouds give cover enough from the harsh rays of light to allow Eliza to avoid another painful sunburn as the group edges ever nearer to the ground. There the large wedge of the flying city finds home within a waiting structure with a missing section exactly the size of the piece coming down.

There is a heavy rush of what sounds like steam being released from a piston as the platform comes to a rest and Captain Ferrandon turns to his soldiers, who, realizing they have reached a destination, run back into their formation. With his command filling his voice Captain Ferrandon shouts, "Attention!" The sound or steel-chain-shirts shifting under the green tabards decorated with a single marking of the elven national crest on the chest, thunders with even only the twenty participants snapping to the command. Turning to face his soldiers, Ferrandon continues, "Men, I know you have questions about why the escort of these strange people is so important that the High Council assigned our twenty-man platoon to the task, or why the assigned duration of the escort was for a three-year mission. The reason it was expected to take three years was the pre-assumed difficulty in transporting that anchor to a spot off the coast, as that is what it took to transport it from that spot. It doesn't appear that it will take nearly that long with the ease that these individuals have been able to bring it to this point. Beyond that I know as much as you. We have been told to protect these four as though they were an unconscious member of the council and know that if I knew any more I would tell you. That being said, let's not take any longer than necessary so that we can all get back to our families even quicker than what is now expected. Move out!"

The order passes over the soldiers and in simultaneous movement the entirety of their number turn and step from the platform filing from the structure. With a gesture to follow given to Eliza and the others from Ferrandon they join in stepping from the building. Outside the lone structure in its own private clearing, wait three carts each strapped to a large moose, who patiently wait to draw the loads. Pulling Eliza, Flame-Tender, and Nakhal to the side as they escape the structure, Bellar gives each a nod saying, "I am going to be going now. You are in professional hands. I will contact you when I have made preparations to continue my work in the palace, but until then if you need anything from me, here." Turning specifically to Eliza, the mage hands her a rolled up scroll tied to a jar of ink that seems to almost have glitter floating within it, and he explains, "This is a ritual for the contact spell, it is more powerful than one like it that allows a limit of twenty five words, this one allows a five minute conversation. I know you are learning rituals so I thought this would be a good farewell for now gift so that you can contact me if you need anything. Who knows, you might even learn to use your magic to cast it without the ritual. Most wizards learn spells in this way, and that is their test for truly learning a spell. Anyway, I will hopefully see you soon."

Eliza takes the scroll and specially prepared ink, and watches Bellar preform the rites for a spell unlike the teleportation that used the glyph on the ground, before rejoining the soldiers as the mage vanishes from sight. Tucking the gift in her bag, she is helped onto one of the carts, and watches Nakhal and Flame-Tender each get helped onto carts before the whole caravan sets into motion. Then to let her mind become distracted again, she opens her book of rituals and continues on the translation she has been working on, with specific increased intrigue, as from the little she has decoded, she believes the ritual is one that involves communication as well.

The forest is as Eliza remembered it. Trees rise all around towering hundreds of feet overhead filled with an ever-present abundance of life. The sound of marching steps and rolling wheels compete with the songs of the forest, distant birds, branches rustling in the wind, and the sense of being watched from the foliage by wary predators and prey alike. Over it all rests the gentle tones of Flame-Tender practicing on the lyre Eliza purchased for him, sending a relaxing tone over the traveling band.

In the course of a single day's march the soldiers extend their stamina by taking turns of rest, joining Eliza, Flame-Tender, and Nakhal, in the three carts, never snooping into Eliza's book, or even thinking of requesting a break from Flame-Tender's impromptu songs. Night comes, and with it the carts slow to a stop for the beasts of burden to rest as the soldiers establish a make shift encampment, before rest sets in for all but a rotating watch, which has no need for the escorted to aid. Day springs back with the group fully rested and the journey continues with another day of the same. The forest itself seems less hostile than Eliza remembers, thinking back to the fallen tree bridge in one of the gaps in thought that come from prolonged examination of a foreign document. Perhaps due to the number of people that are traveling together, perhaps the route, perhaps even just the gentle lyre that plays throughout each day, but Eliza does not let go unnoticed the lack of unease in air with every hour of the days' traveled.

Three days pass in this fashion when Eliza becomes excited with herself making some progress in the strange symbols she tries to discern meaning from, but not wanting to disturb the peace that seems to sit on the traveling group. She keeps the development to herself becoming eager to share the news with Pearl. After that Eliza relaxes herself wanting a break from the painstaking task of unwinding the alien language, she instead returns to reading from the third book of the ten-book series Alfredo had assigned her. The journey continues an additional four days through the forest, before finally a familiar image of the port city of Ear'Falmar becomes visible on the horizon at the end of the seventh day.

Early the next morning the caravan rolls ever forward finding their way into the city. The sights and the smells remain ever the same as Eliza remembered them, a clamoring of strange faces all with things to do. The thick smell of sea water and the fish in the market to be sold. The perfume scents that waft through the streets in hopes of covering the gaging fishy smell, and as with all bastions of civilization the aroma of freshly baked bread on stands to be sold.

The streets of people split before the parade of soldiers who march for the docks, and there the group are aided from their spots on the carts and escorted onto a readied ship. The sky is clear and there is only a faint breeze, strange for where ocean meets lands, but the ship unerringly pulls from the harbor and begins its way quietly out to sea. Low waves crest beneath, giving only a gentle sway with the slow creep of the ship which takes more than four hours to get into place before the crew drop its anchor and Captain Ferrandon comes to Eliza, stating to her, breaking her focus on the alchemy book in her hands, "Miss Eliza, we are at the chartered location the high council has marked for us to transport you to."

Not really sure what she is supposed to do, Eliza nods and having Nakhal bring the anchor to side of the ship turns to those around her asking, "Does anyone know the dwarven word that means, activate in common, and return?"

"Gniomhach for activate, and Thill for return," Flame-Tender responds, stepping to join the two at the side of the ship.

With an appreciative nod, not needing to explain further her need for the word Eliza draws the cane from her bag and presses it onto the anchor, repeating, "Gniomhach," which sends a blue spark through the engraved glyphs in the metal widening Eliza's eyes with the sudden magical response, before continuing, "Thill," and the word causes the lingering blue light to flash three times rapidly. Nakhal's eyes widen as the anchor becomes suddenly heavy, and he barely directs the iron over the ship's side before it sinks rapidly through the water almost unhindered by the ocean's presence. Immediately Eliza's mind jumps to a twisted mass of thoughts that constitutes her attempts at understanding the quantum and arcane mechanics of teleportation, and she turns to Ferrandon yelling, "We have to move the ship. Now!"

Looking confused with the sudden sure hearted command from the woman who has been silently reading the entire journey, the captain of the escorts asks in hesitant response, "Wait, why?"

"Pearl is likely waiting to activate the device the moment it is available to be activated, to bring the palace here, and if we are here when the palace attempts to become here, there are a handful of possibilities only one of which is not possibly life threatening."

"What, palace? Teleportation?"

"Just move the ship!"

"To where?"

"Back toward the shore as fast as possible."

A single gesture puts the crew who were listening to the exchange into high speed activity, desperately attempting to raise the anchor and lowering the sails to catch as much of the almost non-existent wind as they can. Ferrandon, now concerned, looks back to Eliza asking, "How long until what you are worried about happens?"

"Well, Pearl hasn't transported the palace back yet, so she probably won't be able to until the anchor has reached the lay line which runs through the crust of the planet in this case the sea floor. With the rate at which it is descending not long."

"And what is this that we are trying to dodge?"

"The teleportation of an island."

"How big?"

"Large enough to reach horizons if flattened."

"There is no way that we can get that far with this wind. Is there anything any of you can do? I know you have some magic to be in the favor of the high council. Please! If you are worried about your life then I am worried for mine and this crew's."

"I can try something," Flame-Tender responds brandishing the lyre and giving it a preparatory strum. Then with his fingers dancing across the strings he begins playing a series of chords, that accelerate before beginning to crescendo as a gust of sea air lifts and pushes on the sail, with the only explainable source being the music played. The song itself only amplifies the panicked hustle on the ships deck as the crew hurriedly compensate for the sudden breeze which with the continued accelerando and crescendo becomes a torrent of tropical storm force winds.

The small cresting waves are bore through by the ship as it accelerates with the magically created wind column, to a speed faster than it has ever been sailed before. Stepping to the rear of the ship the captain looks out, seeing that in less than a minute the ship has created a wake nearly a mile long. From that vantage point he can see the magically created beginning of the tunnel of gusting wind, which propels the ship ever forward.

The boost in speed proves to not be enough though as the sound of a large bell rings from deep below the water's surface, and a blue shockwave shoots out only just visible through the murky blue. The magic ring of light thrusts out past the ship before coming to a sudden stop. Worry insets itself in the passengers of the ship as it suddenly begins to tilt the moment after the ring of light, which is bright enough to be seen from its position on the ocean's floor, stops. The area within the ring becomes like a bowel as the water is magically drained away, and the ship, with those on it, is caught on the new incline.

Flame-Tender's song stops as the incline becomes steeper and he has to fight to try to maintain his footing on the ship's deck, and the magic wind simultaneously calms. A loud thrum like that of a large sheet being swung against a stone wall to dust it, cracks out from the center of the newly formed bowel in the midst of the ocean, as a small hole in reality forms at the source of the sound. Water pours out for a few seconds quickly beginning to fill the bowel before the strange loud sound cracks again and the hole expands as if to an infinite size, leaving in its wake the island, now with two ships within the private lake alcove.

The ship is left gently bobbing on surprisingly calm water. The crew and passengers moan as they stand from having fallen to the hard wood deck. The wood of the vessel even seems to join in the moans complaining about the experience no ship could be built in anticipation for.

23

A Fix Hastily Consumed

The ship Eliza is on drifts and joins the larger one at the stone dock. There Eliza, Boop, Flame-Tender, and Nakhal, let themselves off, waving farewells to Captain Ferrandon. With their task complete the soldiers and their captain set their sails once again for the port, in silent bewilderment of the sudden appearance of an island around their ship.

Stepping along the marble path into the palace, a smile takes to Eliza's face as Pearl turns the corner to be visible through the large front doors. Sprinting to her friend Eliza nearly tackles Pearl with a strong embrace, to which Pearl asks, "Hey, what's up? You aren't normally a hugger."

"I just missed you," Eliza responds before Boop finds a way to push himself in between the two, getting himself enveloped as Pearl reciprocates the embrace.

"Hey, you weren't gone for long, wait, are your nails painted?" Pearl asks breaking the hug and pulling away enough to pull Eliza's hand up to her face.

"Yea," Eliza responds confused, "Flame-Tender's sisters helped me dress up for the meeting with the council."

"What? Really?" Pearl's eyes widen, before shrinking with devious intent, "Did you learn his real name?"

"Well, yes it came up."

Pearl grasps onto Eliza's shoulders asking in a way that looks like she might try to shake the information out, "What is it? What is it? Is it Eric?"

"No. I don't think it would be right to tell you his name when he obviously hasn't been the one wanting to share it. I only learned because his family refused to call him by the name he has told us."

Rolling her eyes Pearl moans, "You're just no fun sometimes Lizzy. Aldrin really did rub off on you some," before her mind flips topics, "Wait! Come quick, I got the outfit, and that rope," and she grabs Eliza's wrist, pulling them both into a sprint disappearing into the palace.

From Pearl's ship, Devin leaps down to join Flame-Tender and Nakhal on the stone jettison. Flame-Tender turns to the devilish looking fellow and gives a nod, before Nakhal takes lead carrying his bag back into the palace. As they silently reach the overgrown fountain, Flame-Tender asks, looking over head, at the sun just passing its highest point, "Hey you think you will be able to take us back to port Devin?" Devin turns with a curious look to Flame-Tender at the question before the explanation continues, "I think Eliza, has some business she needs to attend to there."

"Yeah, that shouldn't be a problem. It's Pearl's ship anyway. I am just here to give her a first mate and to pay off a debt I have with the person who gave her the ship."

Pearl, Eliza, and Boop arrive at their rooms in record time. Breathing heavy from the run, Pearl pulls Eliza into her room, before with a deep swallow to steady her breath, even slightly, she extends her arms to present lain out, three piles of folded fabric which can only be assumed to be

the clothes she had purchased for Eliza. Still heaving in a desperate attempt
to calm herself from the run Pearl steps to the piles explaining, "I had a few
extra things made. First, and most importantly, these should help you feel
more confident in yourself. There is something about having undergarments
on, that is comforting," she says tossing one of the piles Eliza's way. Two
garments fall from each other in their flight to Eliza, revealing themselves to
be the same articles Liliana had leant her. Both pieces are black, the top is the
only half that is interesting out of the two with more straps than the one she
was lent.

Looking confused that the spaghetti of cloth Eliza asks, "Where do
my arms go?"

With a snicker Pearl helps Eliza with the labyrinth of seemingly
unnecessary ribbon like straps, that form a make the shape of a five-pointed
star with one of the points pointed downward, when the brazier is worn.
Returning to the remaining two piles Pearl starts tossing articles of clothing
from the larger one at Eliza explaining, "Now for the main of it. He made
your outfits to have many parts, so no matter where we go you can take a
few pieces off to cool down or put more on to warm up. First let's see what it
looks like all together, then I won't stop you from mix matching pieces."

Quickly, Pearl helps Eliza into the many layers of the outfit, before
drawing back to get a good look. A tall pair of heavy purple stained leather
boots, purchased specifically to go with the rest of the new outfit, and to
replace Pearl's old boots, which were too small for Eliza's feet, encase most of
the way up the shins with thick leather, reinforced with studded straps.
Tucked into the boots is a pair of long pants made of a durable, but
breathable, nearly black, purple material. There are decorative belt like straps
on both legs or the paints, just above each boot, and another just a third the
way up Eliza's thigh, all four having silvery shining buckles, that hold the two
ends of the straps together. Two lines of vibrant purple almost pink thread
run around the pant legs at the top of each knee, where hidden in a clever
fold of the fabric there are two almost unperceivable seams that can be used

to separate the lower and upper halves of the garment. The leggings hold form fittingly to Eliza disappearing under a loose short skirt. The pleated four layers of the almost laces waves of skirt bounce off of each other as they fall from Eliza's hips, each layer is only just longer than the one on top of it showing the reinforced edges of silvery lavender-cream-colored fabric, which sit bright against the midnight blue of the rest of the article.

Covering the top of the skirt, appearing rigged, while simultaneously not interfering with Eliza's range of motion is a beautifully designed corset of a deep, while still lighter than the boots, purple amethyst color. Up the stomach runs a lighter mauve, on which is embroidered an intricate and eye-catching design that is like a jumble of vines or wrapping tentacles. Three vertical seams run up either side, equally distanced from each other, holding the wire used to make the article of clothing appear rigid even will being easily altered by movement. The top and bottom seam as well as the borders of the six horizontal straps that are latched with gold buttons, three on each side, are bordered with a rich blue reinforcing fabric that rounds the edges.

From beneath the corset a comfortable loose muted-hyacinth-purple silky tunic with a wide collar that doesn't cover most of the star, made with the brazier's straps, rests beneath a strange pseudo-jacket top. With sleeves long enough to cover Eliza's arms and most of her hands, rolled up to above the elbow and held that way with straps like those on the corset, the thick vibrant blue material, a color only just lighter than Pearl's hair, otherwise only covers Eliza's shoulder's and to just meets the corsets top on her back. A single strap spans the gap between the two halves of the minute amount of fabric that makes the jackets front, holding them together. Like the corset the outer edges of the jacket are reinforced, but with a fabric the same green as the embroidery instead of more blue.

Covering Eliza's forearms are individual black sleeves of fabric each, separate from the other pieces of the full ensemble, with a thin see through lace loosely covering her hands and elbows. Over all of Eliza's form, hangs, heavy and hot, a thick hooded cloak, of a blue, nearly black, fabric. From within, only the lower half of her face can be easily seen when she lets the cloak fall closed around her. With a twirl Eliza, asks Pearl cautiously, "So?"

Pearl just grins responding, "Oh yeah. That looks amazing on you," and picking up the third pile of cloth, she excitedly presses it toward Eliza saying, "I said I got you some extra things and, well, I have been teaching you how to swim, and I kind of thought you should have something specifically for that."

Taking the bundle from Pearl, Eliza lets the article of clothing unfold through gravity revealing it to be a single piece open back outfit, made with a single-color cloth that has an unnatural texture to it in her hands, and she responds halfheartedly, "Thanks."

"Oh, and Marcus told me that apparently he used a special thread gifted to him some time ago that makes all of our clothes from this set of work from him magical. I asked what he meant by that and apparently these clothes should clean themselves, repair minor damage, such as tears made by suddenly growing wings, and apparently resize to perfectly fit the wearer. Apparently, he hadn't use this thread before because he felt it was like cheating, but because of our special circumstances he used it for us."

"Oh, that reminds me, Pearl, I got a bag like yours in the elven capital."

"I saw you got a new bag, but you're saying it's magical too?"

"Yeah, so I can go ahead and carry those books Alfredo gave me now."

"You got your nails painted, had a meeting with the high elven council, got a magic bag, what else did you do while we were separated."

"Well there was the shaved ice made with sweet cream, and I got Flame-Tender a lyre, that supposedly has magic properties, and he showed me this fun thing to do of jumping off the flying city, where magic lifts you back up safely to the road."

Pearl's face contorts into a forced pout responding, "Man, you got to do so many fun things. Well with the clothes I also got this," she states drawing a sky-blue rope from her bag.

"Cool, so this is the rope that was made with my hair?"

"Yup. Well, most of it, I offered a length of it to the maker, and he took that to sell instead of payment, apparently he tested it and this stuff is really strong for its weight."

Pulling the tomes of alchemy from Pearl's bag and placing them in hers Eliza asks, in an attempt to not be too obvious in her intended course of actions with what she asks, "Hey, I know we just got back together, but do you mind sailing us back to port, I have something I want to do there."

"What?"

"Oh, just something, I don't think should wait."

"Alright," Pearl responds hesitantly, "let's go then."

Taking her bag from Eliza who transfers the last of the books from one bag to the other, Pearl steps to the door and gestures to be followed as she continues down the hall. Pressing the heavy cloak into her bag, Eliza joins and the two quickly make their way out to their dock passing Devin, Nakhal, Umbra, and Flame-Tender on the way, who turn and join them back to the black ship. Without any trouble the journey to port only takes another two hours from the day, letting the afternoon sun begin to wain into the evening and getting Eliza and her companions back to the port before the soldiers, who must rely on the natural winds to slowly push them back.

Pearl, doesn't press any further into Eliza to know what she intends to do in Ear'Falmar but having grown worried about the effects Alfredo's potions may have on her young friend in the long term, she trails behind as the group exits the ship. Not to Pearl's surprise, and almost to her disappointment, Eliza and Boop find their way to the alchemist's shop and enter. Pearl doesn't want to lose Eliza's trust in her by being discovered having followed her to this place when she obviously was trying to not let Pearl know, so she only creeps to the slightly open window to listen to any conversation that may be had in the store's front.

The conversation begins with Alfredo's voice, as calculated as ever addressing his visitor calmly but with surprise, "Eliza, interesting seeing you here, last we spoke you were in Blackgate, I wouldn't expect to see you for at least two more weeks if you were headed directly this way after the conversation we had."

"Never mind that, there was teleportation involved," Eliza's voice responds with a twinge of panic in it, "What we talked about. Please, help me create a counter formula to it, something to fix it permanently."

Boop drifts over to the window and sees Pearl who gestures with a single finger crossing her lips, before he turns back to the room slowly and quietly drifting away. In that same time Alfredo responds, with a tone that exerts his raised brow expression in his voice, "Have you finished the books I have assigned to you?"

"No, not yet, but why does that matter, if anything Alex said was true at all then I could be losing years off my life span every day."

"I told you Alex was a liar who would willingly say anything to discredit me to anyone he meets who has done business with me, and that blasted tattoo of his makes sure you can't even magically perceive his lies from his truths," Pearl just barely peaks into the window with worried eyes having heard for the first time a plight Eliza has been hiding from her, and finds Eliza's shoulders slumping with defeat with Alfredo's response.

"So, you haven't even looked into if any of what he said was true," Eliza says, her hand falling to her stomach which growls with what has become a hunger which no amount of food has been able to satisfy for more than a few minutes.

"Now, I didn't say that," Alfredo responds sending excited light into Eliza's eyes, "I looked into what you explained Alex's claim was, and it turns out there were some flaws in the structure of the molecules within the elixir. Learning that I did have the time to perform some experiments with the samples of your blood that I had kept after your departure. I believe this," and Alfredo brandishes a bottle with nearly the volume of an apple, filled with an opaque, non-bubbling liquid, "should be able to revert the increased cellular degeneration that peaked your worry, and possibly even undo any damage that has already been done. Just," before he can continue in giving Elia instructions on how take the elixir she swipes the bottle from his hand and chugs its entire contents. His voice becomes a mumble forcing him to finish what he was going to say, but only reluctantly as a pointless explanation of the intended dosage, "Drink an ounce of this a day with a meal, for a week or until gone. Oh, dear."

"What," Eliza's voice cracks as her eyes widen with fear of what may happen to her. Then the hunger that she has grown used to curdles in her stomach becoming infinitely more vast and morphing into something debilitatingly painful. The hand with the empty bottle finds its way to her stomach as she drops to her knees in pain, while Alfredo leaps over his counter disappearing into the back of his shop.

Boop looks down in terror at Eliza who begins to feel a piercing pain in every cell of her body, and rushing to the window he calls, "Pearl!"

Alfredo returns from the back with seven vials of the white cream that he uses as a meal substitute and kneeling down at Eliza's side, offers one to her saying, "Drink this, quick, the process that elixir is going to put your body through is extremely nutrient intensive." Eliza takes then first vial and downs it looking back to Alfredo who hands her a second saying, "It may feel uncomfortable in your stomach but you need to provide your body a week's worth of nutrition now," and Eliza drinks the second and third.

Before she reaches for the fourth vial offered to her Eliza hesitates her stomach feeling full for the first time since she consumed the first of the two replicatory elixirs. Another hand comes into view forcing the vial to Eliza's lips, and Pearl's voice speaks as an arm wraps around Eliza's shoulders, "You heard him Lizzy, you are going to need those vitamins and minerals for whatever that stuff is going to do to you. You didn't wait for instructions, now you have to do this fix. I know it won't feel good to have a week of food, or food replacement, in your stomach at one time, but that is the prescription. Now, bottoms up."

With Pearl's forceful help Eliza, finishes all seven of the meal supplement mixtures. Feeling overly bloated, as though needing to vomit, Eliza's looks into Pearl's eyes, and whispers, "Pearl, I'm," before her eyes roll back and shut.

Pearl, looks up to Alfredo with a glare, demanding, "What's going on? She finished that strange cream. Why did she pass out? What is happening."

Arms spread eyes wide and worry in his face that he hasn't shown to anyone in years, Alfredo responds, "I don't know, I never tested that formula for mass consumption, or potential effects of overdose. In the experiments I have run there is a brief period after the formula, nutrients, and cellular structures meet that the cells stop. Basically, resetting themselves with the formula aiding in the coding of the new DNA and RNA. I thought that might mean she would become drowsy, but that was with the recommended dosage I was going to have her take. She took far more than that, and even I don't know what will happen now."

Boop and Pearl look down with Alfredo at Eliza in Pearl's lap, when suddenly the three of them recoil away, as Eliza's hair begins to move on its own. Pearl lays Eliza down as gently as she can, before taking a step away while pulling herself free of the sky-blue tendrils that form and begin entangling her young friend. The hair grows, stretching and twisting around its producer, until a shell nearly a foot thick of it covers her entirely, before hardening.

Pearl watches as an unconscious Eliza is swallowed by her own hair, unable to do anything to stop it, and as the movement slows and the room becomes still again she trembles not being able to help. In a fit of emotion driven need to want to try anything, she draws a dagger and falling to her knees by the new ovoid shell that holds Eliza within, she begins to slam the point against the outer edge. Not a single strand is broken by the sharp blade, before Alfredo pulls Pearl away saying, "Stop, you might hurt Eliza."

Tears in her eyes, Pearl throws Alfredo's hand frm her shoulder exclaiming in return, "What do you care? She was only a test subject of yours. She's moy friend, my best friend. She doesn't see me as a lucky klutz, or a dumb flirt. She saw me as me, more than anyone I have ever known, and looked past my flaws."

"If you think she was merely a test subject, like a rat to me, then you are entirely wrong," Alfredo responds stopping Pearl before she could let herself fall into sobbing within her own hands, "if she were that, I wouldn't have cared to make this formula specifically for her, I would still be working on an umbrella prevention for what she was worried about. I haven't known you two long, but I was eagerly hoping to use that natural curiosity of hers to finally have a student who could surpass me. But right now, we have to hope that this is all part of my formula, and that she is recovering as we speak, we don't want to inadvertently injure her while this is happening."

Pearl looks into Alfredo's eyes, which close and turn away in shame, and standing she steps to him and takes him in an embrace saying, "If you have done everything you can, then it is my turn. We can't stay here and be a disruption for you. I will get Eliza to a safe place and we will make sure no harm befalls our mutual friend." Alfredo's eyes open and look to Pearl, before turning to Boop who returns a nod. Then releasing the alchemist Pearl turns to Boop, and with determination in her voice and posture says, "Alright, let's go find Nakhal, and get Lizzy home."

With another nod and a smile Boop responds, "Yes," in exclamation before turning and shooting at top speed through the door.

24

Proceeding Forward

The group stand around the entrapped Eliza within the room they use for dinning in the palace. It is quiet and has been since Nakhal pulled her from the alchemist's shop. No one dares say a word or has a word to say as they stare at the ovoid as they had on the short voyage from the port, contemplating what could have happened, if Eliza is alright within the shell, what drove her to that place for this. Finally Flame-Tender breaks the silence with a question, seemingly unrelated to what rests in the space before them, "So, what's next?"

Looking hard at the shell of hair in front of her Pearl looks up to find Flame-Tender still staring down at the strange object, "We head north, I have to find a ring on a sunken vessel off the southern coast of the gnomish continent, and then our quest takes us to the northern most coast."

"But what about this? What about her?"

"We take her with us. We protect her. Alfredo said she should be fine. While he doesn't know for certain, he examined Eliza before we got back to her, and told me that she is basically in a cocoon, as the over-dosage of what she took is now altering her drastically quicker than intended."

"What did she take? Why?"

"I don't know."

"You would think that being blessed with looks like hers she wouldn't need anything from an alchemist."

Pearl's fist balls tight, her knuckles turning white through the seafoam green slimy fish scales, "That doesn't matter right now. Right now, we just need to help keep her safe, and proceed forward."

Flame-Tender turns to Pearl and sees her tense from what he had said. Instead of saying anything further, he just nods and the group return to their silent stares at the cocoon. It is dark, and hours have passed before Nakhal, steps from the room. He heads out to find himself a place to rest, followed by Umbra, and Flame-Tender, but Pearl and Boop stay, and fall asleep in that room with Eliza, when they become too tired to keep their eyes open.

Morning comes and preparations are made as the group load their equipment onto Pearl's ship, before they all gather again around Eliza. Boop remains resting on top of the shell of hair, where he had fallen asleep the night before. His eye stalks as always remain active even in his sleep. There Flame-Tender asks, "Are we sure we want to be taking her? It is becoming winter in the north, and if childhood lepidoptery taught me anything about cocoons, they tend to be moist inside."

"Lepidopto-what," Pearl asks turning to Flame-Tender.

"Lepidoptery, the study of butterflies. You know those things that mutate from caterpillars with the use of a cocoon. My point is that if we are going to be on the continent that includes the north pole during the winter. It might turn out to be deadly if Eliza were to emerge from this dripping wet."

"We have to take her. There is no telling what is happening to her and what if anything she will remember, or do when she wakes. We can't just leave her here."

"Then we should wait for that to happen."

"She wouldn't want that. She, more than any one I have ever met wants to help people, even at the risk of getting injured or killed herself. We are on a deadline to prevent the elves from forming their own search party. We can't just wait for who knows how long, and let that time fall away."

Flame-Tender sighs, knowing his words won't let Pearl see sense, so with Nakhal's help, Eliza is transported as well onto the ship. Then, with the group ready as they will ever be for the cold of the north, the arcane dial is turned, and the sun slides along the horizon southward. Looking out of the widows of the high room, the group see where there was ocean around the island, now there is only ice.

Stepping out to witness if they will even be able to sail out of their personal lake with the ship, the group find their way to the front entrance. They instantly stop and ready themselves, as standing by the overgrown fountain are small figures only just about three feet in height, wrapped in heavy clothing, that hides every millimeter of skin. Seeing the weapons drawn in their direction, the small figures pull away, arms raised, exclaiming in nasal voices, "Don't attack!"

Then one at the front of the group, continues, "We were sent to escort the liberators of Blackgate into our city."

"How are you here?" Pearl asks stepping forward with her rapier drawn.

"Negmor was a good friend to our city, when it was mentioned in the meeting of the Lords, our leaders made note that a meeting party should be ready at the palace's anchor spot at all times until the group in possession of the palace can be shown the way to the nearest city. They despised the thought of you arriving and getting lost on the snow drift lake."

With a sigh of relief, Pearl sheaths her blade, and steps in the direction of the ship continuing as she walks, "Well we were expecting to be able to sail to a port, so all of our supplies are on our ship. How do you get around this far north, where your lakes are permanently frozen?"

"You will have options of transportation presented to you once we get to the city, but we have ample space for anything you want to bring with you. It is best to make as few trips as possible in this season."

With the other three letting the hilts of their weapons free from their grasp, the gathering of small individuals simultaneously sigh with relief before turning to the ship and rushing to help Pearl begin unloading. Quickly the ship is unloaded of all of the supplies Pearl had scrapped together from Blackgate and Dru'heim while she was waiting for the anchor to Ear'Falmar to be returned to its place. Their supplies are carried along a thin hidden path that skirts the edge of the island's mountains. At the small path's end, the solid foundation of the ice, which is more than two meters thick, waits with five snow sleds leashed to teams of eight dogs a piece ready to go. The gear that was on the sleds that the welcoming party was using to sustain themselves while they were waiting, is quickly removed from the carts and replaced with the supplies from the ship, including the encased Eliza.

With everything strapped in place to the sleds, the group is told to lay amongst the supplies, and once they comply the sleds begin forward. The sky is dark with the sun dipping under the horizon into an early night, with black clouds overhead. Snow seems to endlessly sprinkle down onto the group now also wrapped in their thick winter outfits, and the snow only adds to the endless white landscape which looks almost like a sandy dessert made of ice and snow.

After some time, which feels almost to have been just under two hours, the sleds slow as they approach a large mound, more than forty feet tall, and nearly twice as large around. There, one of the small figures driving one of the sleds pulls a small metal device from beneath his heavy clothing. Pointing it up into the dark of the sky he releases from it a spark which shoots up to twice the height of the mound. The orb of light glows a bright green light as it peaks in its ark and begins to descend, far slower than it should.

The ground suddenly begins to shake as one of the sides of the mound away from the group appears to explode sending out a wave of snow. The ground settles and the dogs, who seem unaffected by the sudden loud noise, mush over to the point of the burst. There the group find a monolithic iron door that is nearly as tall as the stone that makes the base for the snow mound.

From a smaller door in the immense barrier another small silhouette emerges and approaches the group. From behind Pearl one of the members of the greeting party steps from the sled, toward the approaching figure, saying, in a quickly spoken language, "Hälsningar! Vi laget tilldelade hälsning befriarna av Blackgate, återvända med dem, låt oss återvända till staden."

The other figure doesn't respond instead looking to the sleds for a split second he stares at each of the three larger humanoids, with Boop hiding within Pearl's cloak, before turning back to the door where several others wait staring from beyond. A finger to the sky spun counterclockwise, sends the waiting group into motion, and the ground begins to shake again as the doors slowly begin to force themselves open. The two walls each as thick as the ice of the lake swing slowly out toward the sleds releasing the groaning pained sound of grinding steel.

As soon as the doors are open wide enough the sleds move again and pass into the waiting area beyond. A warm red glow radiates from down a tunnel which waits as the only way forward and leads downward into the icy stone of the continent. Confusion takes the air, as the large steel doors begin to close and the group is ushered off the sleds and their equipment is piled on the cold floor.

Left standing by the pile of supplies and the ovoid that contains Eliza, Pearl's arms extend in questioning frustration as the sled runners mush their dogs to leave, headed below. The small figure, that had approached the sleds from within and signaled for the passageway to be opened approaches Pearl hoping to explain, "The job they were contracted to perform was to show you the way here from the great Negmor's palace. I will be taking over at this point your introduction to this city, and to the gnomish people," he says in a voice that is nasal in a similar way as the other's had been.

Umbra, Flame-Tender, Nakhal, and Pearl look at each other in suspicion of the gnome, as Boop visibly vibrates, free from Pearl's cloak, as he feels the freezing cold air against his naturally moist skin. Taking off her cloak, Pearl throws it over Boop forcing him to only use his central eye, and turning to the gnome asks, "What is going on here, why didn't they at least take our gear to an inn or something?"

"Rest easy, we did not intend you carry everything you might bring upon your person. You wish to search our continent and we wish to aid you however possible," the gnome explains removing his heavy cloak and handing it to another of his kin. In the same motion he extends his arm to point as a cart is rolled from a room on the side of the tunnel in the direction of the equipment pile.

The other gnomes around the group immediately begin loading, the equipment with haste, causing Pearl to shout at them in worry as they reach the point of loading the hair encased Eliza, "Be careful with that! We can't let anything happen to her," before turning to the obvious leader helping her group and asks, "So, what now?"

The gnome smirks, responding, "Now? A tour of course. We don't often have outsiders come to our city. We are too out of the way for general traffic, which is good and bad. Our security doesn't have to constantly work very hard at vetting people coming in, but we also don't have any form of revenue from tourism, like the elves and the dwarves do. At least they can attract outsiders to see what they build and enchant."

"Well," Flame-Tender asks as he climbs onto the cart, "Dwarven craft is known as the finest craftmanship for everything from plows to swords to structures, and the elves have mastered enchantment to a level to where the capital flies. What is it that the gnomes are masters of at that level?"

The smile only widens as the strange object Eliza is contained within is secured in the cart, and the gnome takes the driver's seat, "That is exactly what I want to show you on the grand tour. It is in fact our engineering. People often take for granted the work we do for other nations in laying out their streets to be optimal, to making a tram that can safely run underground without needing to be hand cranked, to even failsafe measures in case one day magic fails."

The grinning gnome gives a whip to the horses, giving only enough time for Nakhal and Umbra to begrudgingly climb onto the cart, with Pearl bounding for the passenger seat. Securely sitting next to the gnome as the cart pulls away from the steal barrier down the sloped path toward the warmth and red glow emanating from bellow, she turns asking, "We actually can't waste too much time, we have to search the southernmost and northernmost coasts as soon as possible."

"No worries. You will find if you take the time to slow down and prepare your equipment for your plans, that you will succeed in your expeditions not only more often but often more quickly. So, takes some time with me. Please allow me to show you around our city and then utilize what we have available to make your journey upon our continent easier upon yourself."

Pearl turns to the others in the back of the cart with the mound of supplies and gives them a shrug before turning back to the driver saying, "Alright then, if that is our only option let's do this thing."

A smile still on the driver's face grows somehow larger, as finally making it around a corner and past the last bit of wall concealing the red glow. He gestures into a vast chamber that, like a silo, is immensely deeper than it is wide, with the thirty-foot-wide road continuing around the edge of the depth of the complex. The clamor a city normally holds is quiet in the cacophony of air being released, with the spinning and grinding of gears, and clang of metal striking metal. Looking over the railing on the edge of the road, Pearl jumps in her seat as suddenly a platform shoots into place, adding to a chorus of pipes releasing sudden bursts of pressurized steam.

Looking back over the edge Pearl's eyes become wide with surprise at just how deep the central section of the city is. The red glow radiates up from the depths of the chamber, through a mass of pipes that rise from the bottom and disperse like branches into each level. Pearl and the others, quickly find the need to shed their warm clothes, as even the smells that normally fill a city's streets instead are suffocated by the unnatural warmth they can see radiating from within the branching pipes. Pearl leans back from looking down and the cart driver explains, "You see when the worlds land masses were being divided, before any discussion could happen the dragonborn and the elves claimed their continents with call to ancient ties to the land with their bloodlines. The humans chose the land best established for trade and for military intervention at any other point in the world, the continent that was fractured in the shattering, and on which Blackgate is now the hub. The Dwarves claimed the land most rich in resources and we gnomes were left with the continent that is basically one big desert or the continent we are on. With their minds set on prolonged prosperity for their people the leaders at the time chose for us the continent of cold, with the logic that you can always make things hotter, you can't always cool things down. Their first order of business was constructing a city that would allow for the most hospitable conditions for the average gnome, and so we dug down, through layers of permafrost, deep into the ground, until we were deep enough that the heat of the planet was close enough to the surface we had made, that we could use it. We found a source of heat that did not require us to add fuel, and from there we began to thrive. We are currently in the third complex, something most closely related to a city. There are several parts that you will find in our complexes. First, there is the part we are in the silo, also the city center, the heated water for the city it sent through that column of pipes and distributed throughout in the forms of steam and hot drinking water. Also running up and down that central space is the primary form of transportation between levels the lifts in this complex are able to take you from the heating rooms to the top level in only a handful of seconds. If you look to our left you will see lining this road the many stores and shops that we utilize in our day to day lives as well as thinner streets that lead out to residential areas, which are the second part of our complex. Much like a dwarven city, we, out of necessity, dig through the stone and dirt to make living space, and then send electricity and heated water out to these new dwellings, to make life sustainable. Unfortunately, if a tunnel is extended too far, the water cools to much before it reaches the domiciles, in one case even freezing to the point of causing pipes to burst."

"Wait, wait," Pearl interrupts, "Electricity? You mean like what is in a lightning bolt? What could you possibly be doing sending that at peoples' homes?"

"Ah, you see, while we gnomes have been generous in the engineering we have provided to other nations, we keep a great deal to ourselves. Here we have devices that can harness small amounts of the energy that would, yes, be in a lightning bolt, to do day to day things for us. Things such as flameless fireplaces, and stoves, lighting for our streets, like the elves have, but without any need of magic, and even some things I can't tell you about that are in development."

"Alright, alright, but you don't function completely without magic up here. We saw a wand get used to signal to have the gate opened."

"Oh? I am sorry you are mistaken. That was no wand. It isn't that we don't allow the use of magic. Our race is actually acutely more attuned to the use of it than humans or dwarves, it is just that magic is difficult to control. You can't use it for day to day life to make others have a better life, without having an outrageous expense in trial and error in every single enchantment. Our engineering comes with similar expenses, but because it doesn't involve the chaotic nature of magic once we find a method to reproduce what we want, we can quickly and accurately craft as much of the effect as we need. Take the flare you saw for example. We have seen the elven military use wands of a similar spell to be able to signal for formation changes and to signal their location to others around them. Wanting to achieve something similar we knew we needed a projectile, a long burning substance that shines brightly, and a way to allow the substance to burn while only falling slowly so as to provide a greater time for the signal to be seen. So, we started with a capsule filled with some long burn time nitrates, which seemed to work, and a timed-release parachute with metal wires so that they wouldn't be burnt, and then we used our rifles to shoot them, but..."

Pearl interrupts again slamming her hands on the seat by the driver, "Wait you have rifles? I thought Aldrin invented those."

The driver turns to face Pearl with a single brow raised and stroking the stubble on his chin responds, "You met someone with a rifle? Was he a gnome by chance?"

"No, Aldrin was definitely not a gnome."

"Interesting. I can tell you that if he was not a gnome there is a good chance that he had invented the rifle in his own way. It has been against the law for gnomes to share that technology with any non-gnomish citizen. I will have to tell this to my supervisor. In any case, yes, we have rifles here, devices that shoot."

He is interrupted again, "But if it is illegal to share information about that technology with outsiders why are you telling us about your rifle technology?"

Worry suddenly fills the gnomes expression as he stammers, "B-b-but your group has to be the exception, you are here through Negmor's palace, that has to mean you are alright to not have information withheld from," his hands grab his head and the horses slow with the reins being pulled gently back as he continues saying to himself, "Oh no, no, no, no. This isn't good. Don't tell anyone I have told you anything."

Pearl becomes concerned and tries to console the gnome saying, "Ok, easy there, I didn't mean to give you a panic attack. How's about we just get back to the tour. Um, so, you told us about residential areas. How about these horses, difficult animals to keep in healthy condition in a cramped environment."

No response.

"So where is it that we can find a good meal and a bed to rest in," Flame-Tender asks noticing the mortified gnome, trying to help Pearl change the topic, but still no response.

Rolling his eyes Nakhal gets off the cart which has come to a stop, and untying the horses removes the stammering gnome from his seat and sets him on the side of the road with the reins still in hand. Then pressing on the yoke, the large man's strength seems to even dwarf the two horses as the cart swiftly begins to move once more. Pearl slides into the drives seat to control the breaks and prevent the cart from gaining to much speed on the downward spiraling road. They stop once to get directions to an inn within the city and make their way there.

Mostly used for gnomes who travel between the three major cities the inn is as regrettably small as would be expected from an establishment not often used by outside visitors. All four of the group have to duck to find their way into the front room where they are greeted, and Nakhal finds that he annoyingly has to remain bent over the entire time they are within. Luckily, the reality is that the man at the front entrance has prepared for and wished that there would more out of nation visitors as he shows the group back out to the street they have parked the cart in and to another door which is of an appropriate height for human sized individuals. Through that door the group is told in the same accented type of voice, though with a bit more grizzle from age, "Make yourselves at home. The overhead is three coins of copper any print, if there is a discrepancy in mass we will be able to talk that out I hope, and I will bring a breakfast over to here in the morning."

Before the old inn keeper can turn and leave having said everything important to be said from his perspective Pearl asks, "Um, so, what time is it exactly at the moment, we haven't really adjusted to the time shift sense getting here."

"Five hours after this place's noon," Umbra says not turning to face

Pearl.

The old man turns and holding a small disk like device in one hand nods saying, "He is right. Turns out you have no need to worry. At least one of you has their bearings. Good morrow."

Letting the inn keeper leave Pearl turns to Umbra, who begins setting his bag down in a corner, and asks, "How did you know what time it was?"

Flame-Tender responds, not even giving Umbra a chance to if he wanted, "Remember when we were waiting for the sun to rise to take care of the monster in Dur'heim," Pearl nods, "Well, Umbra's divine magic connection is through a curse that the moon goddess placed on him. When you are cursed by the moon you can know by how oppressive that curse is on you at any given moment what time it is."

"Hmm, I mean I asked him but I guess you would know."

"He told me while we were traveling to Dur'heim, also said he doesn't like talking so, I try to help where I can."

"Alright. Well, I am going to go explore the city see if there is anything else, I can get to make this trip easier."

"Wait," Flame-Tender calls to Pearl but too late as the door closes behind her and she jogs down the street deeper into the city.

25

Pearl's Quest

Two hours pass before Pearl returns to the inn. When she does she slams open the doors exclaiming excitedly, "I am awesome!"

The room goes silent, interrupting a game of dice the three men had been playing in Pearl's absence. Boop is stirred from a vigilant nap he had drifted into on Eliza's entrapment. All eyes on her, Pearl stands in the door in a confident proud pose. She stays that way until Flame-Tender asks, "Why is it that you're awesome?"

"Only that I have gathered absolutely everything we need for the time we will be up here," Pearl responds stepping from the doorway revealing eighteen dogs tide six apiece to three sleds. The three sled all rest on retractable wheels for use in the warmed city, so that they are easily converted for the snowy wastes outside, and each of the carts is packed with mounds of supplies.

The men in the rented room look to the sleds, then to the supplies that they had unloaded into the room then back at the sleds and Pearl. Finally needing the question to be presented Flame-Tender looks Pearl in the eyes and asks, "So what made you purchase more supplies than what we had already brought with us?"

Immediately getting defensive, Pearl's hands go up toward Flame-Tender, as she responds, "Hey, I know what it seems like but seriously hear me out. Not everything we brought with us is good in this climate, not to mention we didn't even think to have dogs, and they need food. So, what we can do is go through both sets of equipment and decide what we take and what we leave back at the Palace."

All three of the other's sigh and feeling as though their ability to have an opinion on the matter has been taken from them before they even were allowed to have it. They begin unloading the sleds into the house. While carrying in a box of dry dog feed Flame-Tender asks Pearl, "You and Eliza explained that you believe this is the right continent. Anymore you know about our target?"

"Technically, we are supposed to be headed to the northern most cost, but with Lizzy in her current condition, we need to buy time until she can emerge a beautiful Lizzy-fly."

Curiosity in his brow Flame-Tender asks, "Lizzy-fly?"

Before Nakhal leans in asking, "Buy time?"

Flame-Tender nods and agrees, "That is a better question, buy time, why buy time?"

"You all haven't seen what one of these people from the other group searching for the same thing we are, can do. They are monsters that make that vampire we took on, look like a weakling. Trust me when I tell you we want Lizzy to be able to help us. That and, well, the curse that made me the part fish I am before you, kind of is bound to searching for something that just happens to be off the southernmost coast. Don't worry, I already looked into it. They are not technically on complete opposite sides of the continent, the north pole being within the land up here and all."

Flame-Tender's eyes roll as he turns to Nakhal asking, "What's your opinion, on this?"

"The spirits told me to follow the lady of the sea and the one with hair like the sky," Nakhal responds his deep voice thrumming with his lack of interest, already set to follow Eliza and Pearl where ever they go.

"That is all you ever have to say on it, the spirits said follow. Will you ever have something else to say? Perhaps your opinion not the spirits'.'"

"When the spirits choose to tell me of a new path then I shall change to follow them. My opinion is irrelevant in the works of the spirits."

"Whatever. What hurry do I need to feel like I should be in any way? It's not like when you were explaining this thing we are after, you made it out to be the fate of the world or anything," Flame-Tender shrugs goading with sarcasm.

Before Pearl can respond getting heated at Flame-Tender for not understanding that she is worried more about Eliza, being alright than simply pressing onward, Umbra's hand falls on the well-dressed man's shoulder. The voice again youthful but cold in a way that presses upon Flame-Tender for his comments, "Enough. Foes should never be sought out when you are weakened, or unnecessarily from within. We are weakened without that one. We should seek out this other quest while we wait her return to health."

Flame-Tender turns his eyes wide, "Umbra? What in the?"

"You are concerned with how much I have spoken. You have not heard my voice so much at one time. I don't waste breath. You needed to hear what needed to be said."

Flame-Tender's head falls forward as he sighs with defeat and understanding, before lifting it back to ask Pearl, "Alright, how do we get to the southernmost coast?"

Pearl having turned away, not wanting to punch Flame-Tender, turns back, a big smile having grown on her face that presses itself into her tone of voice as she responds, "I thought of that too. We leave in the morning to help a guy deliver mail, who is headed that way."

"Wait, tomorrow? Morning?" the question is harsh in the words that escape Flame-Tender's mouth. Pearl nods and Flame-Tender's words only become more aggressive, "How are we supposed to be ready to go by the morning? What are we supposed to do with the excess supplies? We won't have time to make the two trips it will take to get all of this to the island."

Pearl's face turns into a forced pout as she grabs the box of kibble from Flame-Tender responding, "If you don't want to help, fine! I am not asking you to do all of the supply's management yourself. On how, once we figure out what we need for the two and a bit weeks we need to get to and from that coast, I will take the rest to the palace, tonight, so that we only have here what we are taking with us in the morning."

Wanting to help, Boop has been carrying bundles of wrapped supplies into the rented space with the energy of his eye that grants him limited telekinesis. As Pearl and Flame-Tender are having their disagreement, and it comes to its end, the floating orb's voice calls out questioningly, "Aldrin?"

Looking back around and out the door, Pearl hastily puts the box down, and runs to Boop's side, as he begins looking around frantically after pulling from the sled a long slender tube of metal affixed to heavy wooden stalk. Grabbing Boop by his sides and turning him to face her, Pearl explains, "No Boop, Aldrin isn't here bud, he is still in Blackgate taking care of the people there, this is just a rifle. I always wanted him to make me one but he refused so I decided since we are in a place that has them, might as well. I am sorry for confusing you."

Boop just turns to look through the doorway to where Eliza lays encased in her hair cocoon, and with a whimper in his voice like that of a sad puppy, he responds, "Missing Aldrin. Still."

"I know bud, I do too, but we've got these guys now, and they are being just as stubborn as he was, so let's not worry about that right now," Pearl continues not catching Boop's meaning in looking toward Eliza to express the feelings that could just as easily be coming from her. Then an idea leaps into Pearl's head causing her to nearly shout, "Hey, you act pretty much like a dog. I've got some dog treats you want to try one? You might like it."

Opening one of the bags, Pearl pulls from within a small brown biscuit and offers it to Boop. Curious he drifts to her open hand and with his tongue, he lifts the treat into his mouth before beginning to chew. That is when it hits, a taste that for Boop is awful, dry, and has a strong herbal presence. As quick as the treat enters his mouth it finds its way on to the ground with him spitting it out.

The four burst into a much needed laughter at the exaggerated reaction to the disgusting taste, as Boop begins running his tongue against the stone wall of the structure in hopes of resetting his pallet. With a shrug, Pearl maintains her smirk and returns to the task of categorizing the supplies, and as she focuses diligently on the task the others, simply fall in around her quietly helping how they can. To the truth in her words, Pearl organizes the supplies, runs a nearly four our trip to the palace and back to deliver the supplies that are to wait for the group's return and settles in for her own rest as the city she returns to quiets and is allowed to cool for the night.

The group find only a few hours of rest when they return before they are awoken by a knock at the door. As Pearl rubs her eyes to press out the sleep she can, she opens the door to find within the crowd of still sleeping canines in the street, a small clean-shaven gnome wrapped in heavy clothes and holding on his back a bag that is larger than he is. Looking up to the person responding to his knock, the gnome is quick to ask, his voice higher pitched than those of the gnomes that Pearl has met thus far, "Are you the ones who are taking me to Revest?"

Yawning Pearl nods responding, "I think so. You are the mail runner?"

"Yes, I am told you spoke with my boss to ask to take me so that you can have a way to get there. Well come along we can't dally here all morning the sun is about to rise."

Turning back into the room Pearl tries to wave off the gnome saying, "We can wait until the sun's up at least."

Before she can take a single step away Pearl feels her arm pulled back through the door, as the gnome, getting irritated, responds, "Are you a moron, we are only going to just have enough time in the light to get to the first way marker before the sun goes down again at this time of the year."

"Fine," Pearl groans, before cupping one hand over her mouth to yell at the others, "Alright everyone, time to get up!"

Heads shoot from their pillows. Boop rockets up nearly to the ceiling from his position on the hair cocoon and groans fill the room in opposition to the command. Begrudging movement does fill the space and within a few minutes the remaining supplies and Eliza are loaded onto and strapped to the sleds. With a small amount of protest from the dogs, the group make their way up to the gateway out of the city. A hand flare is given to them to get them back in, they are let out into the cold, windswept, snow covered wastes which immediately strike the group with chill accurately allowing them to pinpoint any part on their bodies not total covered by their heavy clothing.

Boop slams full force into Pearl knocking her from her sled as the icy air blasts down the city street over them, and he burrows with no avail into her clothes trying to find warmth. Her boots, holding a magical enchantment of winter, warm Pearl allowing her to feel comfortable in any naturally cold weather. Boop is unable to hide beneath her cloak for warmth and begins to let out a whimper as the cold continues to make him shiver. Seeing this, a caring smile takes Flame-Tender's face as he steps to the pinkish-purple orb and pulling a small red ribbon from his hip pouch which he ties around one of Boop's eyestalks he says, "There, that should help you out."

"What is," Boop asks, as three of his four eyestalks contort the look at the ribbon on which is painted yellow letters, from a script that isn't used with the common tongue.

"I saw how little Pearl's cloak was keeping you warm and that was with her being able to focus on keeping you covered, with her driving one of the carts I knew that wouldn't be possible so I did a little shopping of my own. My family has a ritual that we do to help teach us when we are young about the shard of fire. We make ribbons like that one for festivals. There are two ways they can be used. They can either ignite become a mini explosion which is amusing to children," Boop's eyes all stop on Flame-Tender and fill with worry, "Or you can make the enchantment have a prolonged effect which can keep anyone warm at any cold temperature as long as it is natural to our world, and not from magic. That should last a couple of hours and then we will need to tie another one on."

Boop sighs, relieved that he isn't going to be turned into an explosive, and lunges for Flame-Tender giving an appreciative lick to his face. With that Boop rushes out into the blistering cold wind, as the gate keepers start moving over to the group angry that they have been standing in the gateway for so long. He grabs the lead of one of the sleds and begins pulling. Pearl, who just got back to her sled, nearly falls off as it is pulled and the dogs take to Boop's lead. Rushing back to the sled with Umbra, Flame-Tender give a whip of the reins to mush his dogs, and Nakhal follows with the gnome and mail on his.

The three sleds whip onto the snow and into the wind that blows against their path. Behind them they hear the heavy grinding of metal as the gate closes and is sealed once more and they become emboldened to move forward. Nakhal's sled takes the lead as the mail runner points the group in the general direction they need to be moving. As Pearl was told, the sun rises only a few minutes after they set out and sets within only two hours of having risen. By that time, still in accordance with what Pearl had been told, the group find a small pole that flickers to life with a soft blue light at its tip as the sun disappears.

The gnome's voice calls over the group saying, "We can keep going, just follow the lights now," as he points to another pole which flickers to life.

They continue like this moving from one pole tipped with a soft blue light to another for some time before Flame-Tender calls for the group to stop. He takes a moment to replace the ribbon of warmth protecting Boop from hypothermia. While he does this before taking the old ribbon off Pearl asks Boop, "Why don't you just go obsidian Boop? We would look after you, and you wouldn't feel the cold that way."

Looking to Pearl, Boop responds, "Eliza is only able to, not me."

"Oh."

From there the group continues another few hours in their south-westerly direction, following the way markers, and pressing forward, and again stopping. Boop gets a new ribbon and they continue again until the gnome calls out, "Stop at the next marker!"

They do, and Flame-Tender asks, "Why? What's wrong?"

Umbra responds as he steps off the cart, "It is time to sleep."

Pearl looks to the sky asking, "What? How do you know?" then remembering the conversation from the day before she answers herself, "Oh yeah, your special ability is to know the time."

"That alone isn't it," Umbra responds grabbing Pearl's attention to him pointing to the dogs, who breath heavily, with several of them also yawning in unison.

Camp is made by the way marker as the gnome mail runner unclasps flexible metal rods from around his person that were concealed under his cloak, and he stretches a large sheet of a strange material over them making a tent. No heat seems to escape the portable structure through the material as entering it at the gnome's request the group find themselves comfortably warm after only a few seconds. With no need to worry about replacing Boop's warming ribbons every few hours a watch is set, and the group begin their night's rest.

The waking for morning comes with a swift chill blasting into the tent as the gnome mail runner begins packing it away while the others strain to remain resting. The attempt to get even a moments extra sleep is futile for everyone but Pearl who wore her boots to bed. Boop rushes quickly to Flame-Tender who smirks and ties another ribbon to the small friend and again the group sets off. After, of course, Boop wakes Pearl by launching her a few feet into a mound of snow.

This process repeats for four more days. On the sixth, finally the group finds in their view a small ordinary looking town, with its streets empty of snow, and strange red lamps glowing along their lengths. As the group get within the town itself there is a small amount of movement, enough for what would be expect in a small out country town, and while cold winds whip through the streets, the strange lamps radiate a heat that fills the town making it comfortable in lighter clothing.

There the mail runner leaps from Nakhal's sled, and pointing to a building he explains, "That is the town's tavern, it has rooms for travelers. You can probably get some for yourselves and meet whoever you will need for the next neck of whatever you are doing here."

Pearl stops her sled, which now has its wheels extended to roll across the stone road, and asks back to the gnome as he turns and begins walking away, "Wait, you're not joining us?"

"Nope, I run this route often. I have a place to stay the night here, and unless you are headed back to Silo Three tomorrow this is where we part ways. Don't worry. Getting to and from that first marker is the hard part. I will leave you my tent. I have a second in my home here, just wait until sunrise after getting to that marker, and you should be able to find your way back," he responds all while continuing to walk away with his short gnomish legs.

Driving their carts over to the building they were pointed to the group park their carts outside. Stepping through the door the atmosphere is what they would expect from a small-town tavern. The room is fairly clean, with a settled aroma of roasted meats resting to be inhaled. There is no fire place, instead more of the red lamps that heat the street are spread sporadically through the main floor of the mostly empty establishment. The only souls within are the barkeep, a cook, a young woman who has a stature about her that imposes her as being above the other two, and a drunk man laying mostly on a table with a half-filled mug of mead. What makes the scene strange for the group that enters, though they should have expected it to be the case, is that all of the people already in the tavern are gnomes. All barely three feet in height, with heads nearly one and a half the proportional size they should be for their bodies and noses over proportion to their heads.

Walking in with panache that only she possesses, Pearl finds herself at the bar while bending to avoid hitting her head against the low crossbeams, and leaning on to it with her elbow she asks, "So where is it in this town that I could find someone to show us to the southernmost shore."

The man withdraws his arms raising defensively at the sudden questioning of the people of his town, and he stammers in his reply, "S-southernmost shore? I don't really know. We're a small town but it ain't our way to pry into each other's goings on."

Pearl leans in closer her eyes now affixed to the man's saying through a smirk, "That would be a problem if I were asking you, but I was asking the lady," and she turns to the well-dressed gnomish female gesturing with a finger and a wink before turning back to the man continuing, "You could be a help and get me a glass of something sweet."

The man steps slowly away feeling uncomfortable as his personal space is interfered with, and the woman, blushing, waves Pearl's gesture to her away, saying, "Now, you are a lady who knows who's in charge. You hear that Irving? She was asking me you old fool! The name's Esmirline Clatterpot, don't blame me for the name that was my parents' doin'. What was your question again? Oh, right, you're lookin' for a fella to take you south to the shore line. Hmm, I'd like to ask what for but I'm not gonna be rude, so I 'll just point ya to him. You see that drunk over there? The one wasting away at a normally decent person's hours of sobriety. He's a diver, or at least that's what he says he is. He's been goin' through a dry spell, in terms of his hall, can't stay dry in his profession, I guess."

"Thanks," Pearl responds flipping a coin from her pocket to the woman, while simultaneously swiping the mug of mead the barkeep returns with at the exact same moment. Flame-Tender smirks as he, Umbra, Nakhal, and Boop watch Pearl saunter back from the bar in their direction to take a seat across from the man stuck in a drunken daze. Setting her glass down and striking as natural of a pose as she can in the chair made for a person half her size she addresses her target, "So," but she doesn't even get a groan for a response, which causes her to lean in and shake the man's shoulder, "Hey old man."

Immediately the man throws himself back in his chair away from Pearl. His bald head is glistening with the soft auburn from the lamps of the bar revealing his salt and pepper grey hair facial hair, which protrudes out and wafts in the fall, one either side from his stash and the third down and out from his chin. With the sudden jerking motion away from Pearl the man cries out in a slurred old gnomish accent, "Assault! Don't touch me fiend! You all saw it! This woman has battered me and molested me. I demand restitutions! You saw it Esmirline," he exclaims, looking to the woman behind the bar and pointing to her before pointing to and facing up to the ceiling continuing his exclamation, "I have witnesses of your act against me. I demand to be refurbished for the harm ye have caused me emotionally and physically."

"Be quite you old drunk she was going to ask you a question. There is no way you've been hurt by her, at least not yet," Esmirline calls from the bar.

"I demand ten coins of gold!"

"Hush up, she doesn't owe you a..." Esmirline calls over but stops, interrupted by the sound of coins being place forcefully down on the table.

The old man also becomes silent as his eyes widen from the permanent squint of age, to stare at the specie placed before him. Blinking several times his hand shoots back up as he shouts again, "Did I say ten I meant twenty!" Pearl's hand draws another ten coins from her bag and she adds them to the others. The man is stunned again and looking up hopefully he mumbles knowing he may be pushing the bounds of generosity as he asks, "And your drink?"

Pearl's eyes roll and she slides the mug over to the old gnome who swipes it before bursting into happy laughter. Leaning in and catching the man's eyes with hers, she asks with a seriousness that she doesn't normally let her traveling companions see from her which she uses for gathering information, and she asks, "Can we talk now?"

"Of course, we can," the man says swaying in his seat, nearly bumping into Umbra as he and the others walk past toward the bar, "Whadya wants to talk aboot."

"My companions and I are looking for a shipwreck off the southernmost coast of this continent. We want someone to show us the way."

The man squints at the mention of a shipwreck before asking over the edge of the mug in a surprisingly sober tone, "What is your purpose for searching for a ship out there?"

"We are looking for a specific item that should still be on the ship. If you help us anything else we find is yours."

"Well then I guess I can't say no to that," the old gnome responds leaning back in his chair, forgetting that it doesn't have a backrest. He falls, slamming hard on the floor, knocking himself unconscious from a mixture of his intoxication and the trauma of striking his head against another chair.

Pearl leaps to the old gnome and lifting his head up turns the bar asking, "Um, I need some help over here. He just, fell over."

The woman, in the process of handing Flame-Tender four keys to rooms upstairs, stops what she is doing and rushes to Pearl's side. Grabbing the old man's sides, she puts her ear to his chest to check his heart and his breathing. Then feeling the back of his head, she searches for any bleeding or sign of fracture in his skull. Finding nothing she sighs with some relief, before standing and pulling out a chunk of graphite and small pad of parchment leaflets, on which she rights something down addressing Pearl, "Alright, his chest is actin' normal, and his head isn't bleedin'. Should probably get him to his home," and she tears the piece of parchment she has writing on free. She hands it to Pearl revealing an address scrawled on it continuing, "Here's the address, and let me gets you a small bottle of booze. His head 'ill be poundin' in the mornin' and you'll need a drink if you plan on workin' with him."

Looking down at the writing, then back up to the woman, Pearl sees the hostess return with a small half litter of a starch based clear alcohol. They share a nod as she stands back up lifting the unconscious man. Pearl gets to the door when she remembers and calls back to the others of her group, "Guys, don't forget to find a place we can let the dogs sleep," before she ducks from the building and past their sleds in search of an address in an unfamiliar town.

Eventually Pearl finds her way to a small building, near the center of the small town, that bears the address given to her on a placard hung from its side. It is a rundown old building, with significantly less care in how it has been maintained showing through the siding boards that fall lopsided into each other leaving holes for the elements to seep through. The door seems even worse off than the rest of the building that seems small, even for gnomish standards, as it leans warped and jammed in the doorway missing its lower hinge.

Stepping to the door, Pearl tests the handle and finds the door not locked, but also that she is unable to open it easily. The sole remaining hinge nearly breaks as Pearl gets the slab of wood free from the doorway with a forceful shove, and it screams angrily unoiled as she pushes it completely open. Through the low passage, Pearl finds a single room that takes up the whole of the building' square footage, filled claustrophobically with mounds of seemingly useless nick-knacks, old letters, and broken bottles. Attempting to light the oil lamp that hangs out of place from the ceiling, in a town where they have harnessed the ability to use electricity for oil-less heating and lighting, but she finds no success as the lamp hangs empty. With no heating lights, and not even a lamp for warmth the house is cold, even with the street just outside's unnatural warmth.

Pearl finds a bed hidden under a pile of old parchment on which gnomish script is printed, each with a date written at the page's top right. Digging the bed free she lays the unconscious man on his side and pulls the old quilt, that covers the bed, over him. The quilt is thin and riddled with holes, but it is something.

Finally, finding a small open space in the corner between two piles Pearl eases herself down avoiding any broken glass, and lets her eyes close. Sleep comes over her, and hours pass without her knowing. Suddenly her rest is broken when an old man's voice yells piercing into her ears, a split second before she is struck by something thrown at her, "Intruder! Get out of my house you fiend! Intruder, someone help, there is an Intruder in my house!"

Throwing her hands up to hopefully deflect any more projectiles launched at her, Pearl yells back, "Wait! Wait. We spoke last night, but you were intoxicated and fell off your chair. You hit your head and went unconscious. Esmirline gave me the address to this place and I brought you here, I stayed because if you started vomiting I wanted to make sure you wouldn't drown yourself in it."

Easing himself and stepping from his bed to the pile of bottles to try to find one with liquid still in it the old gnome growls, suspicious of Pearl, "Why would you do something like that?"

"Because when you knocked yourself out we had come to an agreement about you showing us to the southernmost coast, so that we can search for a sunken ship."

"No."

"What? But you agreed to it when I said we only wanted a specific item, and you could have everything else."

"I won't dive off that shore anymore there is nothing left down there."

"Are you sure? I am certain if you take us we will find the ship."

"You'll find many ships all picked clean by myself and the people who established this town. The only thing left down there is my pride, which kept me out there until I no longer had the ability to jump into a new trade."

"Come on. What do you have to lose but a few days. I already offered you those twenty gold coins. That should be more than enough to fix this place up," Pearl says fingering through the pile of letters which sits intermingling with a pile of envelopes.

"I like my home how it is," the gnome responds turning to the seemingly human woman in his house

"Alright, sorry. Geez. But you can't say that you would lose anything at this point. At least show us to the coast that is absolutely the furthest point south."

"Tch. I guess you're right," the gnome turns to Pearl with a glare, "But I don't like wasting my time."

"You mean like getting blackout drunk in a tavern by yourself with a homestead like this to return to? Don't get me wrong but wasting your time seems to be your norm."

"Why you!"

"It's fine I'll leave. You said that this town was established by divers, right? I'll just find someone else."

Pearl steps from the small house and makes her way back along the path she took to get to there from the tavern. A few minutes pass in the journey before she turns a corner to see the waiting door, with Boop looking for something next to a heat lamp. The few people not already entrenched in their days work that are walking the street, see Boop, and cautiously and purposefully go out of their way to avoid getting within ten feet of him crossing the street if necessary. It is the instant that Pearl comes around the corner and sees Boop looking around that one of his eyestalks locks onto her and he rushes to her side. Upon making impact his voice whimpers, "Pearl."

Wrapping Boop with an arm Pearl is curious about his reaction to seeing her so she asks, "Hey, bud, what's with the greeting, did something happen to Lizzy?"

"Master still wrapped up. Why you leave? Don't do that."

"I'm sorry I was trying to get the escort we need to get rid of my curse," Pearl explains as she gives Boop a pat and notices him beginning to shiver, "How about we get you back into the warm inn? Get me some food, and start looking for someone else."

Boop nods before turning and rocketing into the warmth of the ever-glowing red lights in the inn. Pearl joins him with a slow walk entering the gnome sized tavern. The woman sits in a different dress from before, in the chair she occupied when last Pearl saw her, and the others, Flame-Tender, Umbra, and Nakhal sit with plates of food on a table between them. Stepping to the bar Pearl is quickly addressed by Esmirline saying, "So you're back. Oh, and Gilly isn't with you, what a shame. Well, have some breakfast sweetie, I'll try to think up someone else I could introduce you to for your problems."

A voice calls in from the entrance, the old man's, "Don't worry yourself. I'm going with them."

Pearl smirks without turning to the man, saying to Esmirline, "Two plates of your morning special please, we need our strength before we head out."

The group gather around the one small table and have their breakfast. Flame-Tender gives Pearl an approving nod as she smiles at the man named Gilly, who looks away not wanting to admit any form of defeat between them. Umbra's mask is only lifted enough for each bite to be taken in, Nakhal radiates an odor of strong incense, and Boop wears a smile while constantly peaking away to look in the direction of the room within which Eliza's cocoon is being stored.

Their stomachs satiated, the group and their escort make their way out and around the tavern to a kennel in the back, and retrieve their dogs who appear to also be happy and rested. Hooking their canines to the sleds, they load their equipment again onto them. After that they finally set off, just as the sun begins to rise.

As expected the path Gilly directs the group along is not directly southward, instead tapering some degrees to the east. The sun sets after its only few hours of being in the sky, and the old gnome demands the carts stopped explaining, "It's not my fault you came in the season were there is little time in the day. I need to be able to see my landmarks."

"Landmarks," Pearl exclaims questioning the gnomes sanity, "What landmarks? There is only snow for miles."

"I don't care what you think. If you want my help, then you will make camp here."

Begrudgingly the group complies and the tent is set out to keep them warm as the darkness sets them into their watch order which they have to pass through more than twice before the gnome allows them to pack up and prepare to leave again. They repeat this three times, traveling as far south as they can in the limited time they have light, before stopping and setting up a prolonged camp. Finally, in the light of the fifth sunrise the sounds of a tide can be heard and the ocean seen and relief comes for a hopeful end of the forced monotony.

Only as the sun begins setting Pearl sighs, "Finally here," before looking to the cocoon holding Eliza, "Hey, when you get out of there I might not be a fish anymore."

"Set up camp," the gnome demands stepping from the cart to a pile of large stones westward down the shoreline.

In protest Pearl asks, "Wait, what? We're at the shore, right?"

"Not even close we are just at the point I store my diving equipment. We should be there half way through tomorrow's light."

"So, we're an hour or so away, why don't we just head there, we don't need to camp for more than twenty hours. Look there are other things we need to do on this continent. We were going to do this quick while Lizzy remains trapped in that cocoon of hair."

"Fine, do what you want. The southernmost shoreline is that way. Wait, there is a person in there?"

"Yes, there is a person in there. What? Did you think that we were just lugging around a wad of hair because it was soft and smelt nice?"

"Possibly."

"That just happens to have my best friend in it. She has made some bad decisions, but that cocoon of hair is part of the solution."

"Look, I am sorry. I didn't mean to upset you. We can head done the shoreline, I should be able to see where my marker is even in the night."

Pulling a tarp out of the way, which had blended perfectly with the snow, Gilly reveals hidden within the rocks a strange device. Like a large barrel made out of metal with four legs, two claws, and a see-through pane on one end which shows inside ample space for a gnome to sit and operate the many levers within. Surprised and curious about the device revealed, Pearl asks, "What's that?"

"Like I said this is my diving gear. You go ahead and head out I will stop you when you get to the right point. This thing can go pretty fast once I get it in the water."

"Alright," Pearl responds with doubt in her voice.

With a spin Pearl returns to the others at the cart who nearly began unpacking the tent before Pearl stormed off to say what she said and pointing down the shore they return to their positions, mushing the dogs to pull them along the snow-covered beach. Behind them as they pull away, the group hears a loud pop followed by a grinding noise like stones being tumbled together to polish each other. Turning to see the source they watch the strange contraption's legs jerk and twitch, in a way that moves it forward. The moment it is submerged in the water enough that the legs can no longer carry it forward the device picks up considerable speed, and jets along the coastline past the running sleds.

As explained only about two extra hours of running bring the group to a point on the shore where the strange device is waiting for them, having left them behind as it propelled itself through the cold ocean waters. Without any further argument even necessary the group once again set up the tent and settle into their shifts of watch. The night passes.

Sleep is ended again by a gust of icy air let into the tent, and Pearl is roused with a forceful nudge of her shoulder. Gilly stands arms crossed in the tents opening, from where he asks, "So, as I explained to you I have picked pretty much everything of value clean from all of the discoverable ships off this coast. I am anxious to hear your plan to find a ship I haven't already scoured."

"Finding something isn't an issue. Tell me the name of what you seek and I can pinpoint it for you," Umbra explains stretching his shoulders, "There is nothing that can hide from the moon, or her shadows."

Everyone looks at Umbra with confusion for his comment's suddenness and phrasing, before finally Pearl breaks the awkward silence that formed, saying, "The ship we are looking for is the Free Traders' Esperago, specifically I need to retrieve the ring off of the captain's finger, who I was told went down with his ship off the southernmost coast of the continent of the gnomes."

Raising his hand to pull attention to himself Flame-Tender asks, "That is great and all, and I am sure you can do what you say Umbra, but we over looked one small detail. There isn't a boat for us to go out searching in."

Hands find chins as the conundrum is made evident to the group, but answer comes quickly as Gilly turns, "I guess I will have to loan you mine."

The proposal seems absurd causing Pearl to turn and ask, "What? You can't be serious even if one of us could fit in that thing we wouldn't know how to control it."

"Not my artificial subaquatic search support system, I have a boat stashed somewhere around here. You don't think I cleared out all of the ships sunk around here by making trips back to shore with that thing every time its graspers picked anything up, did you? That would be like collecting eggs from a chicken coup and only using your hands. Sure, you can do it, but wouldn't it make your life all the easier to have a basket."

"Then where is this boat?"

"I don't remember. You need to help me look for it."

"You don't know where your own boat is?"

"Look on my last run it was the fifth time I went out to come back with nothing. I may have had a bit too much to drink before hiding my equipment. I don't remember where I dug its hole last time."

Packing the tent and sparking torches to provide even a minute amount of flickering light in the icy wind, the group begins their search in the dark. It is only a minute though, far shorter than expected, for Umbra to press his sword through feet of snow to find wood below. The minutes drag on as in the whipping wind as they drive through the snow until the group pulls a small boat across the shore and into the water.

"Now then, we only have as long as we have sun light," Gilly explains, climbing into his vessel finishing with, "So lead the way," Before closing and sealing the hatch in its tail end that he entered through.

The same pop followed by the growl of gears grinding like stones being tumbled together escapes the contraption again as it starts rumbling, and its legs step it into the water where it begins to bob softly. The tent is left up with Eliza, Boop and Nakhal, remaining behind, and into the darkness, eager for the sunrise, Pearl presses the small boat forward with strong determined rows. Her determination offset by the frustration of the starting and stopping motion of Gilly's vessel behind them.

While the boat bounces on waves beneath him, Umbra crosses his legs and centers himself. Even with the chaos around him and the darkness that envelopes him, he enters a meditative trance which for him expands his senses. Through his breathes he releases, "Esperago," and unseen by anyone but him, across the ocean floor, a wave of white radiates out from a single source.

After a minute another wave of white expands for Umbra to feel, runs across the ocean's floor. Again, and again, every minute they press further out to sea, the edge of the ring becomes more and more rounded, as they approach the source. It is still before the sun has a chance to rise when Umbra puts his hand up and says calmly, "Stop. The ship Esperago is beneath us."

"Seriously?" Pearl questions surprised how little they had to actually go out.

"There is no reason for me to lie."

"Alright then," Pearl exclaims, as she begins to take off her clothes.

Immediately, Flame-Tender averts his eyes asking, "What are you doing?"

"Look, my boots are keeping me warm and comfortable, but if I come out dripping wet I don't know if I will become frozen solid or not. I don't have to worry about the cold with my boots on, but that doesn't mean I can't be comfortable and incased in ice."

"Well I doubt that will be," Flame-Tender tries to respond before there is a splash from the side of the ship. Leaving only Pearl's boot covered feet and the tip of her blue cat tail visible for a split second before vanishing with a kick.

Pearl's gills flare revealing themselves from the camouflaged state they normally remain in. Her eyes adjust to the water as she blinks and a separate pair of eye lids from the ones she has always had close and open over them. That is when her heritage activates, and the darkness becomes clear, with faint auras of magic radiating off everything thing, enough to where she can see almost anything within sixty feet of her.

Watching Pearl strip and then dive through the water's surface, Gilly gives chase in his sub-aquatic machine. Astonishment comes over him as the contraption which was able to out run the dog sleds, struggles to keep pace with Pearl as she swims down. Looking at the woman he can't help but be concerned as he calculates in his head that even the strange webbing on her hands can't account entirely for her speed.

As luck would have it, as Pearl disappears into the darkness beneath where Gilly is able to see, the slight golden light of the sun beginning to rise begins to beam through the crystalline surface of the cold northern waters. Deeper and deeper the two dive, further down than Gilly believed the floor had been, as they continue into a crevasse that he had overlooked. Down and down they continue to a point where the pressure begins to make the Iron haul of the gnome's vessel groan in discomfort.

Finally, down to nearly twice the depth of the sea floor around the crevasse, the two reach the bottom. The way there has light of the sun fade from view and lights on the diving device flicker on revealing to them a sunken ship, one that Gilly had never seen before. Quickly, Pearl darts through the water over to the drowned ship and finds her way through a door into what could only be the captain's quarters. There sitting in a chair facing the door, stoically having remained still even in the loss of his last breath is what can only be assumed to be the captain, and on his right hand, around one of his decomposed fingers, is a small golden band.

Grabbing it Pearl pulls only for the entire arm to break apart at every joint, leaving a finger in her hand with the ring around it. Slightly disgusted, but also amused at the pirate's stubbornness to let his treasure go, she gives a bow to the waterlogged skeleton as she slides the ring finally free. A thought enters her mind in that instant and fills her with worry, what if she stops being able to breath underwater this instant because she has recovered the ring.

Panic takes Pearl and she rushes as fast from the ship and up toward the surface as she can. She emerges, from the water and takes a deep breath of air, having held her breath in fear of losing the ability to breath mid inhale, and she notices that nothing about her has changed, remaining distinctly part fish. More importantly a voice only becomes audible as her head is freed from the water calls, a panicked Boop who turns to her and nearly yells, "Pearl! Master!"

Worry fills Pearl's eyes as she asks, "What's wrong with Lizzy," before turning and swimming as fast as she can back toward the shore.

26

Butterfly

At the shore in the tent Nakhal sits, eyes closed, burning incense. The cocoon of hair tilts and shakes in the place it was set like an egg about to hatch. Smoke leaks out from the small warm space extending as a thin trail into the sky that can be seen from where Umbra and Flame-Tender are.

Getting to the ice and rock covered shore Pearl's worry for Eliza nearly causes her to overlook the sudden appearance of a pumpkin next to the large rock face that Gill had told them represented the southernmost shores exact location. Not giving it much thought beyond recognizing that it hadn't been there before they set out to sea, she and Boop burst into the tent, where she demands, "What's wrong?"

Nakhal calmly turns to Pearl and with one hand gestures toward Eliza explaining, "She is making her way free."

"Lizzy," Pearl calls, throwing herself to the side of the hardened hair, "Lizzy can you hear me?"

Eliza tries to call back, but through the more than a foot of hair, is unintelligibly muffled. At that moment the flap into the tent flips as though someone is entering though no one is there, and a cloud of incense seems to press itself in from the column over the tent onto Nakhal. With the motion of the shell around Eliza, as she tries to escape, becoming more frantic, the hair itself seems to grow again, increasing the thickness of the barrier between her and the world.

Seeing the growth and feeling worry that Eliza could be suffering, Pearl pulls a dagger and goes to slice the hair shell open. Her hand is stopped though by Nakhal whose position hasn't changed except to out stretch his arm. Releasing a deep breath, which he had taken when the incense suddenly rushed onto him, he tells Pearl, "Don't interfere."

"What? You can't be serious. She struggling, that means she is conscious. We need to help her get out," Pearl responds franticly trying to free her wrist from the large man's grasp.

"A baby bird released from its egg by power not its own, even if it is ready to be free, will not survive, when it must fly on its own."

"What's that supposed to mean? Let me go, we need to let her out."

Boop is rushing around the tent still panicked and not knowing what to do as Nakhal's hand grabs him, stopping him. His eyes still closed and a calm tone in his voice Nakhal continues, "The spirits have spoken to me again. The one with sky hair has been in turmoil spiritually for a long time. The alchemically induced metamorphosis she has been enduring for the past week and a half has unleashed that struggle. She has had nothing but herself and her thoughts this entire time. If she can find peace with herself now that her body is ready, then like a bird she will be free of her shell."

"What if she can't though."

"Trust that she can."

Pearl looks at Nakhal's stony expression, and her arm falls limb in his grasp. She stands trembling and looking over Eliza wanting to help. Sitting down with Nakhal in the smoke of his incense she wraps her arms around her knees and between them buries her chin just staring and the shaking object that is imprisoning her friend. Boop joins her and floats to rest between her and Nakhal watching and hoping his Eliza will be alright.

In the time it takes for Flame-Tender and Umbra to return with the row boat, the ovoid releases an incredibly quiet muffled scream. Eliza, within the confines of the shell, slams her fists against the inner walls. Unable to break free, she grabs the side of her head as the thoughts rush back in. The torture she endured as a child at the hands of monsters in human skin that would call themselves her parents, who somehow still live, press on her mind. What they would say to her, that she was the bridge, that she would learn to enjoy her suffering in service to their master digs like talons into her brain. The knife she still carries that she used to saw the head from the man who showed her what a father's love should be saws at her sanity. She watches Boop get taken as he saves her from the Plane of Undeath. Finally, she watches, an out of body perspective of herself walking past Aldrin and refusing to acknowledge him as her friend.

Then everything begins to repeat as it had for a week to this point, the only change being that feeling has returned to her appendages now, and she can writhe now in the torment. Each image flashes in her head and she slams her fist against the wall of her prison. Each slam pushes her to utter, "What could have been different? Why wasn't I safe? Archangel, why wouldn't you defend me? Was I not beautiful enough for your protection?" Her mind shifts to the mirror in Alfredo's room as the effects of the first elixir are revealed to her, and she tries to take that image of herself and impose it on the other memories. Each one she attempts to make change but her fist slams against the wall of her cell as they continue to proceed as normal, "I wasn't beautiful enough," the image of her after the many more potions she has consumed appears before her. She tries to change it, tries to make it more beautiful, mutating it, miss proportioning it as an adolescent who just has begun puberty would, trying to create her perfect body. Still the images pass through her mind and she finds no comfort. None of them pass any differently than they had, and her heart sinks. Alex reenters her mind, his warning about a shortened life.

It is that moment that Eliza's hand finds the amulet around her neck. The crystal that had been spreading on it, infecting it, nowhere to be found, and images flood into her head. Glimmering juxtapositions of those that have plagued her the time she has been sealed away. Radiant days in the temple's courtyard, running with Boop as Bartholomeus sat reading a novel. Pearl's sword shimmering as she makes Eliza laugh with her reaction to being startled by Boop. Vall outlined by the light passing through her room's window as she offered Eliza something to wear to replace the torn and stained nightdress. Every time Pearl has laughed. All shining over the darkness.

Clutching the amulet, Eliza takes in a deep breath and releasing the air through her nose lets a smile only just grow on her face. In that moment, when the struggling comes to an end, Eliza comes to a form of peace with all the numerous thoughts still spiraling through her head, but none overshadowing the memories of the good times she has had in her life to this point. The strong hold her hair interlocks with to give it strength, a shell from the world, loosens and suddenly begins to retract.

Flame-Tender and Umbra make it to shore, and to the tent just in time to watch in astonishment with Pearl, Boop, and Nakhal as the coils of hair move on their own in a reverse of how the sky-blue locks had when Eliza consumed the elixir that caused the transformation. The shell thins with each passing moment quickly becoming porous allowing only glimpses in to Eliza who lies still, her eyes closed, releasing trickling streams of tears clutching the medallion of Archangel in her hands. The cold finally makes its way through the holes in the hair ovoid, and Eliza's eyes open before she releases the medallion to recoil away from even the tinyest amount of light that fills the tent, and she begins to shiver. Recognizing Eliza's chill as she wraps her arms around herself looking around the small smoke-filled tent, Flame-Tender realizes he is the one standing in the tent's entrance holding the flap open and letting the warmth, that had built up from body heat, out.

As Flame-Tender slides into the small space and the flap closes behind him, Eliza's hair ends its existence as a shell, showing that the entire time the encasing was decaying it was simply shrinking, with it becoming only the length Eliza had cut it to. Eliza stares mystified by everyone gazing down at her before. In an overflow of happiness Pearl leaps forward tackling her and enwrapping her in strong embrace. Simultaneously Boop joins in rushing to Eliza's side to give her cheek a lick and snuggling close in against her.

With the cloths doing as they were said to be able to do in resizing themselves, Eliza's outfit covers her how it did before, fitting her form perfectly. To everyone in the tent she doesn't seem to have changed at first glance, in any way since she consumed the potions, except her figure perhaps may be minutely less exaggerated. With Pearl's embrace though the others are able to see that some changes have taken place, as she is smaller in comparison than she was before, and upon further examination they realize that her face no longer resembles that of an adult. Beyond her figure's proportions which remain about the same and about as developed as they were, she actually appears fourteen, her age, in most other aspects, and something about that is uplifting to the group as they look upon Pearl's embrace with her.

"You had all of us scared silly, Lizzy," Pearl sobs through tears of joy.

"I'm fine now Pearl," Eliza responds, grabbing Pearl's shoulders and pushing her out to arm's length to look into her friend's eyes, before looking around the tent again, "By the way where are we and why is it so cold?"

Flame-Tender responds as Pearl presses again into the embrace, "It was suggested that you would prefer we didn't just wait and do nothing, while you recovered from what we were told was a bad reaction with a potion."

"So, we are up North. Which coast are we nearest to, northern or southern?"

"Southern. It was also a point of contention that we shouldn't try to go to where we believe the shard to be, with you in the state you were in."

"That means. Pearl, have you gotten what you needed?"

Pearl wipes tears away nodding, "Mhm," and taking a swallow to clear her throat continues, "But nothing's happened," and she produce the ring for Eliza to see.

"Maybe you have to take it somewhere," Eliza responds before putting her hand on Pearl's shoulder again, "We'll figure it out. Anyways, I am not trapped anymore, so should we start heading Northward?" With Eliza's question the whole group nods in agreeance. Pulling the heavy cloak from her bag which had been sealed in with her, she wraps herself saying to the others, "Lead the way."

"Yes!" Pearl exclaims turning to the tent flap, and raising a determined fist.

"Oh, and Pearl."

"Yeah?"

"Maybe you should put some clothes on."

An expression of suddenly remembering who else is around strikes Pearl, and taking a second to contemplate the comment, and shrugging she responds simply, "I guess you're right." Stepping out to the row boat she puts her outfit back on and returning to the tent asks, "Why aren't you guys packing up? We shouldn't waste any more time than we need to here."

Everyone quickly agrees and they begin collapsing the tent and tying it again to the sled, as Gilly finally returns to the land. Seeing Eliza for the first time he looks to the other four asking, "So, um, who's this?"

Her joy that Eliza is alright, still hardly able to be contained, Pearl throws her arm around the back of the girl in the blue heavy cloak nearly throwing both forward, and makes the introduction, "This is the person that was in that orb of hair. Eliza, this is the person who showed us how to get to the absolute Southernmost coast, Gilly."

"Thank you for helping my friends," Eliza says giving a short bow to the gnome. As she stands back up it becomes all the more obvious that she is now nearly a foot shorter than Pearl again.

Only just catching a glimpse of Eliza's face, Gilly waves off the gratitude responding, "No, no, it was my pleasure, besides, I now know where that ship is so I can make my way back here in the summer, when there is more light for excavating. As it appears you all want to head back to town, would you mind helping me bury my boat? Oh, and let me return my equipment back to where I store it as well?"

"Sure," Pearl responds before reaching deep into her bag. After a moment she draws from within an old, dirtied shovel whose head is bent and damaged.

The remaining smidgen of time with the sun's light is spent burying the small boat, and the group make their way back along the shoreline to the place where Gilly stores the strange metal device. After that, with Gilly's approval, they begin heading back in the direction they came, with the notion that the landmarks he looks out for are easier to see on the way to the town. They arrive in the warmth of the glowing street lamps without any further stops there they find their way to the inn.

Bursting through the door, still in lifted spirits having been shown a ship he can scavenge, Gilly calls to Esmirline, "Hey, I need a round of mead for my friends here! They're heading back to Silo Three tomorrow and I want to send them off in good spirits."

Seeing the smile that holds itself on the old gnome's face, Esmirline laughs responding, "Well, I'll be. You're in good spirits Gilly."

"This lot helped me find something to look forward to is all."

The round is had and the group disperses into rooms they rent. Morning comes with Umbra waking everyone while the sky, as it has every day, remains dark. They hook up their sleds and finding the blue marker waiting outside the town, with another waiting further in the distance, they set off.

27

Armor

The monotony returns of running the sleds, until the dogs tire out, setting a camp, then repeating, along the route marked with the blue glowing lights. In these four days Eliza sits where she had been secured to the sled when she was wrapped by her hair, and reads one of the alchemy textbooks from Alfredo. When the camp is set up for the first time, after leaving the small town, Eliza's quick return to reading into alchemy spurs Flame-Tender to ask her, before taking over the watch, "So, what exactly happened?"

Eliza, who only just noticing Flame-Tender's presence with his words, closes her book and looks to him asking, "What do you mean?"

"Pearl, told us you had a bad reaction to an experimental potion."

"That's true."

"What is a person your age doing drinking potions? Let alone experimental ones."

"It was to help cure me of something."

"Hmm, cure you of something? What was that?"

"I don't know what it would be called, but the cells in a living things body have a maximum number of times they can replicate naturally, and that replication is what gives us our life spans. My cells began losing from the number of times they could divide, shortening how long my life could be."

Flame-Tender turns to Eliza recognizing that she must have had that on her mind while he was trying to be carefree while showing her around the elven capital, "What? Are you ok now? Do we know if what you took did what is was supposed to while you were wrapped up? What caused the degeneration?"

"I don't know, I will have to return to Alfredo to see."

"Well, Pearl and I are glad you are feeling better, and I know Boop is happy you are back in action."

Being told that the others had worried about her and knowing they had done everything they could to make sure she was safe, Eliza forces a smile and turns to the tent responding, "Thank you."

Not sure if he had said something wrong Flame-Tender avoids speaking to Eliza for the next few days unless spoken to. The group continues and they find no difficulty rise before them as they reach the mound of stone they remember as the entrance to the city. Pearl ignites the flare she had been given and the gates open.

Making their way down the group return to the inn they had stayed at before, and Pearl procures the key to the room they had used before. In the exchange that earns her the key, Pearl asks the inn keep about who they should talk to for heading north, instead to be pointed in the direction of a tram that runs between the city silos of the gnomish continent. After unloading their gear into the room, she and Eliza, investigate the information and find that, Silo Two is the furthest north of the silo cities, and probably the group's best bet to find a person to take them to the northernmost coast. They also learn that the tram takes two days to get from Silo Three to Silo two and two more to get back, and that it had just left the day before.

"We have three days to kill," Pearl exclaims opening the door to find the guys playing dice again, in the same position they were in when she made an announcement to them the last time they were in the rented house.

"What do you mean," Flame-Tender asks, standing and stepping from his last roll which would have without a doubt lost for him.

"It means the fastest way to go north is the tram, which according to the lady at the station won't be back for three days."

The thought crossing her mind Eliza grabs Pearl's arm asking, "Can we go to Ear'falmar in the meantime then? I want Alfredo to make sure I am alright now."

"I was already thinking the same thing," Pearl responds with a smile. Turning back to the room she asks, "Anyone else want to come along," to which Nakhal stands and steps to the door.

As the large man leaves the room, Flame-Tender responds from behind him, "I think Umbra and I will stay here. You go ahead."

"Fine then," Pearl calls back with a wave, and turning back to the street sees Eliza sitting on the sled with Boop in her grasp, both waiting for her. Nakhal steps to the sled he has been mushing as Pearl steps to hers, and they set off back to the palace on the frozen lake.

There, they turn the dial on the arcane device and the sky above them becomes clear of the clouds that sat overhead in the north, and they step to Pearl's ship to find Devin only just waking up and coming out of his quarters when they arrive. The horned individual groans as Pearl steps onto the deck asking, "What's going on?"

"Relax, D, we just have some time we need to let pass so we are going into Ear'falmar to have Lizzy get a checkup," Pearl explains stepping to the crew urn.

Devin rubs his eyes groggily opening to see Eliza step onto the ship which prompts him to ask, "Eliza, when did you get back?"

"She's been with us the whole time silly," Pearl laughs, "That big thing of hair that just happened to be the same color as her hair. Duh. Raise the anchor set the sails to your stations sunken crew."

No further conversation is needed as Devin goes about trying to wake up and perform his tasks on the ship for the short two hours it takes to get to the port. There he is left again with the ship and returns to his quarters to continue his rest, only after having the crew return into the urn.

Pearl, Nakhal, and Eliza, step into the streets that are as they remember them, oozing with the salty sea air, and busy as ever. The morning air only just has begun to fade taking with it the smells of fresh bread, while the sun begins to approach its midday peak. Eliza in particular walks with a joy in her step, with no worry or pressure of impending events weighing on her in the slightest. She instead seeks to enjoy the moment she is in, even keeping Boop in his active form, regardless of the strange looks sent the group's way at his mere presence.

Shock comes though, when Eliza turns the corner onto the street of Alfredo's shop bringing it into view. She stops still, causing Pearl to accidentally run into her from behind, before looking to what caused the freeze. Alfredo's front door is missing leaving an open passage in. The points where its hinges had been are broken with damaged wood remaining as a scare from the door bursting out from within.

Concern takes Eliza and she runs from Pearl's side to the door only to see devastation waiting. Everything within lays mostly destroyed, as rubble on the floor with a pinpointable epicenter from where the damage came being obvious, Alfredo's desk. From there everything is destroyed radially away from its point on the back-right wall. The structure still stands with the two other rooms still holding their shape, but the rest of the area is filled with rubble.

At that moment, as Pearl runs to be at Eliza's side, a figure emerges from the back room. Alfredo, slowly meanders to a wheelbarrow and goes to begin loading it, with only one arm as the other is held up with a sling and wrapped in a cast. Bandages cover the man's face, and he seems focused on trying to clean the result of whatever has happened within his shop.

Only as he bends down to pick up the first bit of what remains of his lively hood, does he notice Eliza staring in from the doorway. Immediately his expression changes from downtrodden defeat of repairing a mistake, to one that is an indescribable mix of concern and curiosity. The few bits of rubble fall from his grasp and stepping onto the splintered wood he calls to the door, "Eliza? You returned, I wasn't expecting to see you for some time."

Eliza, shocked at the state of the alchemist's shop, is wide eyed as she responds, "We have to wait a couple days for a tram. I got out of that hair shell, and wanted to see if you think I should be alright now. What happened here?"

"Oh this? Well, one of the risks of testing fields not yet explored means that you will be surprised from time to time. That doesn't matter," Alfredo waves off a thought, and grabbing a chair that somehow survived in the front of the shop he pulls it to Eliza saying, "Now I need you to sit here."

"What, why? I mean you have a lot to do I don't want to be any bother."

"You not letting me perform this examination now that you are here, would be a bother to me. Please have a seat."

Eliza complies, looking to Pearl who moves into the room's corner. Then looking back at Alfredo she asks, "So, you're going to need more blood? Do you have what you need still to run tests?"

"Yes, yes, a new sample should allow me to confirm what I was able to ascertain before the incident that destroyed my shop, but right now I want to test the quandary that was the cause," Alfredo explains, picking a small plank of wood from the ground. Worry fills Eliza and Pearl's eyes, to which he continues to explain, "After mapping your cellular structure out from a strand of hair that was left behind after you too eagerly consumed all of the elixir. I ran into a curiosity. When let near a magnetic field, or something that produces a static charge, the cell structures in the hair seem to rapidly mutate. Don't worry if this goes how I think it will, none of us will be in any danger. Eliza, I want you to reach out and grasp for this piece of wood, but don't move from the seat."

Confused still about the state of the store, and now by the request from Alfredo, Eliza asks, "Why?"

"Just do it."

"Alright," she responds and reaching a single arm in the direction of the piece of wood, she tries to grasp at it without moving. Her arm strains and she can feel the struggling stretch of her muscles for a few split seconds, before suddenly a bundle of hair, her hair, whips out and ensnares the splinter of lumber.

The appendage made of hair which suddenly grew to grasp the wood that was beyond Eliza's reach retracts bringing her the splinter. Surprise strikes Pearl and Eliza, at what just happened, Alfredo nods, putting a hand to his chin contemplatively, before muttering, "Precisely what I thought."

"What? You expected that to happen!" Pearl asks her voice raised from the surprise that fills her.

"Yes, at least that was my most hopeful hypothesis seeing you enter my door. Like I said. When I was examining the effects the elixir would be having on Eliza's cellular structure, I managed to witness strange mutations occur when electric imbalance was introduced to the strand of hair that was in my possession. My shop is currently in ruin because in my research I introduced a strong electrical current to the strand and what resulted was comparable to an explosion where the hair rapidly expanded and multiplied filling the room. I believe that this is an additional side effect from the other elixirs you have consumed before the one to revert any progressive deterioration of your cellular structure. It was a theory of mine, which I now believe to be proved accurate, that it could be possible that your hair had developed in a way that it would now respond and act in accordance to your brain waves. In short, your hair now should be able to grow and shrink and even manipulate objects in a similar way as pseudopods. To what extent? I am sure you will test that in your travels, but I can tell you from what I have observed this should not impact your physicality in any way. By that I mean it did not show any effect on the rate of cellular breakdown, in fact from my observations your lifespan may have been extended through these experiments at this point, but I can't confirm that. You need not worry any further about your life span being shortened by your helping me. Now, I am not going to ask you to stick around and help me clean up so why don't you go ahead and see the extent to which you can utilize this side effect. Oh, and finish those books."

Eliza stands and with a smirk, and tears of joy having been told that she will be alright, she and Pearl leave Alfredo to clean his shop and join Nakhal once more in the street. They make their way back to the ship and to the palace in silence, just letting the news of good health rest amongst them. In her room Eliza begins to practice her new found ability setting out books and attempting to lift them, open them and hold them.

When the ship comes to rest, docked in the Palace's lake, Eliza emerges from her room, and steps onto deck and toward the gangplank with three outstretched appendages of hair each holding two of the large textbooks as she attempts to find the limit of the new ability she has been given. Before she can step to the stone dock Pearl catches her saying, "Lizzy wait."

Stopping and turning Eliza asks back, "What is it Pearl?"

"I just wanted to let you know that I was really worried about you when you were trapped in your hair, and that I am glad you are ok."

"Thanks Pearl," Eliza returns a smile, and reaching out to rest a hand on Pearl's shoulder continues, "Don't worry, we will figure out how to remove your curse."

"I think it may have something to do with a pumpkin."

"A pumpkin?"

"I only just saw it, before getting into the tent after hearing that there was motion from you."

"You don't think you might have to take that ring to that guy Pumpkin-head do you? I mean he is supposedly a magic user pirate, perhaps he gets his power from the god that cursed you?"

"That doesn't matter right now," Pearl grabs Eliza's shoulders, "What matters is I need to tell you, never do that to me again."

"Do what? Oh," Eliza thinks back to the peace that freed her from the binding of her hair, and with a smile she looks into Pearl's eyes responding, "Pearl, I am glad I met you, and you don't have to worry, I won't be taking any more experimental potions."

Pearl throws herself into an embrace encompassing Eliza, saying, "I don't care about that. Don't scare me into thinking I might lose you."

The surprise of the sudden hug causes Eliza to lose focus and her hair to drop the books it was holding and recoils, returning to its normal mid back length. Boop only just manages to catch one of the books before it would have hit the water, as Eliza returns the embrace to Pearl. Pulling away she smiles, saying, "Well, we have to know that what we are meant to do is not a safe life. There is a good chance there are more people like that Domavir that we will have to encounter. Hey, but if it will give you some peace of mind I have been learning another ritual that may help me not get hurt if things get too dicey. Come on I will show you inside."

The three gather the books and return them into Eliza's bag, and they step from the boat into their palace. Eliza leads the way, into the central garden which remains in disrepair and, like the fountain out front, is overgrown with its foliage. Curious Pearl asks, "So what is it you wanted to show me?"

"Well I haven't tested it yet, but one of the rituals in the book this Victor guy left for me in Blackgate, is meant to be a protective spell. Each section in here has the main bits of the different spells that I am trying to translate, and in the same script are notes all around them to help me learn what the intended use of each is, and some other information. This one is said to have been adapted from a spell used by druids to give them armor when they think they may have to face foes. The notes say that when they would perform the ritual the environment they are guardians for would form into armor stronger than steel for them. Usually this must have been leaves and branches, so our garden has to be a good place to try to cast it for the first time."

Pearl smiles at Eliza, accepting the palace as their home, and gesturing with both hands open to her young friend she responds, "Well let's see it then," before sitting on a nearby stone, "I would love to know that your well protected before we venture any further."

With a smile Eliza centers herself, in the small clearing within the garden that has become a forest, within view of Pearl's perching stone. Pulling out the small ritual book she opens it and her hair extends to be a third hand for her to hold it on the page turned to. Taking a deep breath, she begins. With one of her feet she draws a circle in the underbrush and grass, turning up loose soil. Then dropping to her knees, she digs small trenches that extend into symbols each with a single line originating within the initial circle, the whole time she regularly double checks the tome to ensure that she is creating the ritual circle exactly as the book explains how to.

Pearl watches with a smile from being as impressed as ever at the ease in which Eliza utilizes her talent, that she never was able to achieve herself, to be able to understand any arcane script and be able to use that information at all. She watches Eliza finish the glyphs and prepare for the next step of the ritual by stepping back into the circles center. Checking the book one last time Eliza turns again to Pearl with a smile, and then putting her hands together begins.

"Mgah'ehye frn ahnythor ah mgepnnn llll ya bthnknahor nng nnn ya," sounds meant to be words from an alien and ancient language that Eliza somehow finds herself able to understand, escape her mouth as the utterance to summon the energies to perform the ritual. Pearl continues to be in awe as a torrent of wind picks up around her friend with the magic beginning to concentrate as she focuses on the spell. Then the effect finally becomes visibly as threads form into existence, black ribbons from the shadows of the trees of the garden and golden lace from the light that pierces through the canopy. Pulling themselves into reality the threads stretch and wrap themselves around Eliza who, repeats the incantation, and keeps her eyes shut, only knowing that the magic is working as the wind tosses around her.

After nearly ten minutes from the point Eliza drew the circle with her foot, the wind fades, and she opens her eyes only for the armor that forms around her, woven from the light and shadows, to vanish from sight in the same instant. Pearl runs to Eliza, and having watched the armor be woven and suddenly disappear, she asks, "Wait, where'd it go?"

"Where did what go?"

"The armor, for a moment, it looked like the spell you were casting was working. It created what looked like a beautiful suit of a knight's plate made out of threads of shadows and light, but when you stopped, when you opened your eye it vanished. Wait when you opened your eyes! Lizzy close your eyes," Pearl says looking with eager anticipation at her young friend. Eliza complies, but nothing about her visibly changes. Pearl's shoulders drop into a pout, as she groans, "Dang it, and it looked so cool to. You really had my hopes up that you were finally going to be in an almost acceptable level of protection from the things that try to hurt us."

"I did it right. I know I did. Here how about," Eliza looks around her, and grabbing a stick offers it to Pearl, "You try to hit me with this, if the spell is actually in effect, you won't be able to, and if you do at least we will know I messed up with only a stick striking me, and not say a sword or an arrow."

Pearl squints not wanting to hit Eliza, but also being appreciative of the attempt being made to help give her peace of mind. Giving in she takes the stick responding, "Fine, at least you still have that ability to heal small wounds, so the worst we will have to worry about is a splinter," and pulling the stick back she brings it down, toward Eliza's shoulder.

Eliza's eyes close in anticipation of the impact, but when the sound of the stick cracking into a spray of splinters snaping into the air, she feels nothing. Opening her eyes again she looks to her shoulder and finds a mystical barrier, holding the shape of ornate plates of metal fashioned as armor, formed from a magical mix between shadows and light, floating an inch from the surface of her jacket. The barrier remains for only a split second before become dark and vanishing again from sight. Eliza's eyes widen having seen only a trace amount of the what Pearl had explained, then turning back to Pearl she goes to ask something, starting, "What do you," but is interrupted as she recoils in a flinch as Pearl brings the stick down again toward her.

Again, another portion of the branch is released into the air as a shower of splinters, as the visage of the magical protection appears at Eliza's wrists which rise to block the wooden weapon. Realizing Eliza was about to say or ask something, Pearl withdraws what remains of the twig and rubbing the back of her head with her open hand laughs, "Ha, sorry about that, you said you were hoping this would make me feel better about you being safe moving forward as we get closer to whatever this shard of prime has guarding it, or in a fight against the others who might be seeking it. I had to make sure this spell of yours wasn't a onetime thing. I mean that would seem like a waste, ten minutes, a show of shadows and light making a full suit of armor for you and then it goes and only blocks one attack made in your general direction," then with an apologetic smile that could have been produced by a child, she gestures back to Eliza with the open hand, "You were saying?"

A glaring squint pierces through Pearl's expression from Eliza's eyes, who responds, "I was about to ask what you thought it means that the spell is making armor from what it is. The notes on the page I think said that the spell the druids use, creates armor from sticks and leaves."

"Well you said that the spell, was based on that, maybe this version was a modified version that instead uses light and shadows. I mean, it would look weird for you to be walking around in a tree trench coat," Pearl responds, before pulling the stick back one more time, and swinging it into the armor which appears again to block the blow, "With it like this you don't have to worry about covering up your outfit, and it still protects you."

Pearl doesn't even make contact with what remains of the stick against the mystical shielding around Eliza when her hand is stopped. Instead with Eliza's glare intensifying, a cluster of her hair whips out and grabs the fishy hand stopping it, "Pearl you can stop trying to hit me now."

"Look, I am just trying to be made satisfied that it will keep protecting you."

"Fine then go for it," Eliza explains spreading her arms and releasing her hair's grasp on Pearl's wrist. Pearl grabs a new stick and begins swinging, and after a minute or so of striking the glowing protective shield tears begin to form in her eyes, causing some of her swings to not even strike the armor, but miss entirely. Letting her head drop recognizing the situation to its fullest, Eliza asks Pearl, "This isn't about testing the armor anymore is it?"

Stopping for only a moment to let Eliza's words process in her head, Pearl realizes how tight her grip on the stub of wood has gotten, and letting it loosen asks back, "What do you mean? Of course it is. We need to know how many times we can rely on this magic to stop attacks made against you."

"Then how many times have you struck the spell."

"Thirty-four?"

"Eighty-one. Pearl you're mad at me."

Finally breaking, Pearl drops to her knees sobbing, and the back of her fists just slam themselves toward Eliza, striking the magic, "How could you do something so stupid? I have never been able to comprehend using magic, or engineering, or anything very complicated at all, but you and Aldrin make it all look so easy when you do it."

"Pearl."

"Why? Why couldn't he see that you needed him to come with us, that I needed him to come with us?"

"Pearl, you said it yourself, he needed to help there, we have each other."

"Then, why would you be so stupid," Pearl's fists slam against Eliza's shielding with enough force that the blow causes its target to stumble away leaving Pearl's hands planted on the ground, and her staring at the dirt of the overgrown garden, "Why would you not even wait to hear what you are supposed to do with an experimental drug? I get that you needed it to counteract something you had taken before, but why were you in that position to begin with."

Silence, for only a second takes the garden with the question cast upon Eliza, who only just realizes the pain her actions have caused Pearl who has been watching over her. Then the silence is broken by the sound knees hitting the dirt as Eliza falls down and throws herself into Pearl in a way to pull them both up into a hug. Her eyes now watery as well, Eliza's voice softly escapes into Pearl's ear, "I'm sorry."

The two sit in that embrace for several minutes, before the mood is broken by Eliza's stomach growling. Pearl snickers and wiping their faces the two step down to grab some of the food from the ice creatures' storage space, and settle into their rooms for the night to take them. The entire time, Boop has remained in Eliza's room gnawing on the master's cane.

In her room, alone after Boop has fallen asleep, Eliza pulls from her bag the blade that she had been forced to use in executing Bartholomeus, and she sets it down in front of her, in the moon light that passes in through the window. Putting her hand to her chest she feels the amulet she had been given by him, the gold it is cast from, shaped to be a symbol of the faithful to the deity, Archangel, it is smooth and blemish less, without even a trace of the dark crystal that had been forming on it since some time ago, as she takes it off and lays it down next to the evil knife.

Pulling out the leather-bound book that holds the ritual spells Eliza is learning to cast, she grips it tight and lays it down next to the dagger and the amulet. Finally looking to Boop, who rests in the corner of the room, she remembers every single moment she has been with Pearl, and tightening balled fists in her lap says to herself, "I am sorry Pearl, but now that I know that my looks aren't my beauty I have to know if I can ever be. I have to contact Archangel with this ritual, if I can, and ask." In a burst of rapid movements, she slams open the ritual book to the page she had been working on for a spell to contact a being on another plane of existence, and she lifts the dagger from its spot by the amulet. Grasping her hand around the curved serrated blade she takes a deep breath and pulls tearing the metal through her flesh, immediately releasing a gout of blood into her fist. Quickly, with the blood as her ink she inscribes a glyphic circle on the floor around the amulet following a pattern shown in the line layout on the open page of the ritual book. "*Alright, an. a few .rops of bloo. to the object of importance,*" her voice passes through her head as she squeezes her hand closed to let a few more drops fall onto the amulet before she takes to silently waiting, "*Contact Archangel. Let me speak to him. Let me ask my questions.*"

After a minute more of waiting a voice responds, deep and malignant, like wrapping tendrils around Eliza's brain, "Archangel is but a child. You contacted me, disturbed my watching, do not do it again!"

Eliza is thrown from the spot in the room she was performing the ritual. Her back slams against the wall, and her eyes are filled with panic not knowing what she had contacted, or if she had woken Pearl or Boop. To her relief both remain sleeping and no further communication occurs as she cleans up the blood of the ritual circle. The last thing she does is focus and heal the wound on her hand so as to not let it be obvious to Pearl in the morning.

28

Beginning North

Morning comes and Eliza, Pearl, Boop and Nakhal, convene in the upper room to transport the island back to the Gnomish continent. After doing so they find their way back to the mound which holds the entrance to Silo Three, the city Flame-Tender and Umbra have stayed in. There they present the others with Eliza's new control over her hair, and the spell which allows her to protect herself. After which they relax and wait for the rest of the time they need to, before the tram returns to allow them to begin their trip to the northernmost coast.

As it was told to them the tram's journey takes nearly a full two days to traverse the subterranean passage way between the city called Silo Three, and the city called Silo Two. There the group find an underground city like that of Silo Three, but with one major difference. The people of Silo Two have no trust of outsiders, and expressive disgust at non-gnomes walking through their streets. This is made apparent from the grumbling welcome given to them from the attendant at one of the stands at the tram station, which they go through to enter the city, to the sudden silence that is overtaken by grumbling as they enter a tavern they are pointed to by a begrudging gnome who they have to present two golden coins to for his time.

The room, like the Silo, is not nearly as warm or as brightly glowing red as the tavern they had been within in Silo Three. A thick musk fills the air with the familiar smell of old beer, and vomit, that they have grown to recognize as a common thread between the seedier of bars. Stepping past the looks of distrust, and disgust, most of which seem actually pointed toward Nakhal in particular, and strangely not toward Boop, the group find themselves to the bar counter.

An old portly female gnome finishes filling a flagon with a frothing beverage, and before a single word can escape Pearl's mouth after she opens it, the woman's arm extends in their direction with a single finger raised. This stops Pearl short from being able to speak and the gnome explains, in what must be a more back country accent for gnomish accents, "We don't serve his kind here."

Confused Pearl gestures to Boop pointing at him with her thumb and asks, "Boop?"

"That floating dog thing isn't the problem, the one with giant's blood in his veins is."

Without even waiting for Pearl to clarify the comment's direction toward him, Nakhal turns and without a word steps from the establishment. The woman watches as he leaves, holding her finger up to prevent any conversation until the very instant the door closes behind his stepping into the street. Confused and a little angry by the actions that just transpired Pearl asks, "What's with that?"

To which Eliza adds, "Why would you refuse service to him? Because of giant's blood? What does that even mean?"

Frustrated that she needs to explain, the woman sighs, "Like I am a gnome, and you can easily know me as such, that man is what is called a goliath. You are all outsiders, so I wouldn't expect you to understand the pains and hardships put on gnomes by giants and their off spring. Like how you can get people who are of human and elven heritage simultaneously, you can have a person who is basically the same thing with giants, they are goliaths."

"But why would you refuse to serve him, you don't even know him."

"Like I said I wouldn't expect an outsider to know the hardships that us gnomes have been put through at the hands of things like him. Now you can order something or you can join him outside."

Eliza immediately turns from the bar and with Boop mimicking her motions, to a more greatly exaggerated effect, joining her, the two storm out. The woman behind the bar, shifts her weight from one foot to the other and crosses her arms as Pearl turns to Flame-Tender saying in a hushed voice, "I need to go after Eliza, we need an escort to the northernmost coast, can you handle that, please?"

With a head nod toward the door Eliza is nearly stepping through Flame-Tender turns to the gnome behind the bar, leans down with a halfcocked smile saying, "Hey there, sorry about my companions. Your astute observation was entirely spot on, we are from out of town and it seems like a bit of culture shock for them. You'll have to excuse them for not being familiar with proper etiquette around a beautiful young gnome like yourself."

Weaving her way through the maze of chairs, tables, and patrons of the tavern, Pearl escapes through the swinging door to find Eliza, Boop, and Nakhal, moving somberly up the corkscrew street. Running to catch them she asks, "And where do you think you three are going."

"Well, with how abrasive that woman was we aren't thinking that we will even be allowed to rent a room. We were just going to go ahead of you guys and set up camp outside the city," Eliza responds.

"You know what, that's a good idea, but we shouldn't leave the sleds with just those two back there, and we should let them know what we are doing."

With a one-eighty, the small group of outsiders make their way again back to the tavern Flame-Tender and Umbra are in. Eliza, Boop and Nakhal wait with the groups sleds as Pearl returns inside. There she finds Flame-Tender, recoiling in terror from an equally stout gnome as the woman running the bar male gnome, who wields a large knife, and who pulls the fancily dressed human from the gnomish establishment, with Flame-Tender stammering, "Look, look, I am sorry. I didn't know she was married. Look, I wasn't honestly hitting on her, I just needed information. She provided it now my friend and we will be on our way."

Taking action to fit the moment, Pearl storms into the room, and exclaiming loudly toward Flame-Tender, "So your flirting with women here too," she broadcasts her intent to him in a split second as she brings her arm around as though to slap him.

The sound of her ever-wet fish hand striking flesh rings out silencing the tavern atmosphere, drawing all attention to the confrontation. Feigning having been struck to the ground with the force of the strike, Flame-Tender acts as though recoiling in pain from the blow, begging, "Pearl, please, no, don't get the wrong idea."

"And what would that wrong idea be that this man is coming at you with a butcher's knife," she responds before acting out another hard slap hitting him. Then turning to the man with the knife she bows, apologizing, "I am extremely sorry, my group has been so much trouble for you and your establishment. First, we break an unspoken rule by bringing our large companion in here, and I understand ignorance of a rule doesn't grant amnesty for breaking it. Then our companion here, was overly entranced by the woman behind the bar. I am greatly sorry."

The man with the knife, having seen, and fully believing that Pearl slapped the man he was upset with, forceful enough to send him to the ground, twice, waves off the apology responding, "No, no, you seem to have things handled."

Raising her head with an intentionally flamboyant whip of her hair, she turns with a stern look in her eye to Flame-Tender, who only just has begun acting as though he is struggling to get to his feet. Stepping to his side, she grabs his earlobe and begins to pull dragging him toward the door. Eliza only just looks in to see what the commotion is about, when in his acting with Pearl to get out of the dicey situation Flame-Tender exclaims, "Ouch! Pearl, please have mercy. I didn't mean to do anything wrong. Pearl, please!"

Subtly Pearl's eyes interlock with Eliza's and she mouths, "Outside. Back outside," and Eliza complies stepping back out through the door where she is quickly joined by Pearl, Umbra, and feigning being painfully dragged out, Flame-Tender.

Eyes wide with concern of what could have possibly provoked Pearl to drag Flame-Tender out by the ear Eliza asks, "What's going on? What'd he do?"

Finally getting around the corner out of view from the swinging door, Pearl releases Flame-Tender who explains, rubbing his ear, "Pearl, got me out of a tricky situation," then turning to Pearl still rubbing the earlobe which had legitimately been pulled pretty forcefully he says, "I had no idea you could put on such a good performance."

"You have only barely been able to see my skills in the time we've been together," Pearl responds with a prideful grin, "Now please tell me you at least got a lead on where we might find someone to show us the way."

"Yea, she told me about a guy. Come on."

Mounting their sleds, the group let Flame-Tender take the lead as he drives his dogs back down the corkscrew in the direction of the tram branch. When they come to it though, the group continue even deeper, and the heat of the depth begins to become intense, but they keep descending. Finally, after the heat has become enough to where everyone has broken out in a sweat Flame-Tender turns at the sight of a street sign down one of the passage ways.

Down that road the group continue a few blocks before finally coming to a stop outside a small building with a sign hung from the door that reads, "Northern Explorers Guild."

The paint on the structures outer walls is old and has begun to peel in the overabundance of heat. The door is solid and opens with little complaint from its hinges, revealing the small space inside. The one room building is nearly empty with rolls of papers sitting on shelves on the side walls. A single enormous axe with a blade nearly as large as one of the sleds, sits on hooks spanning the back wall, behind a counter. In the center of the room a small table with a tea set, that seems to be steeping, rests with a large plush chair facing the hanging axe.

From the chair a voice that seems to almost have no accent compared to the other voices the group have heard in the city speaks as the door is opened and closed by the group entering, "I have told you the payment is in the post, you needn't come attempt to procure it in my residence and place of business." From the other side of the chair the head of an old gnome peaks around the side looking to the group standing at his door. A common appearance seems to be true about old gnomish men with the top of the man's head shines to a polish in how bald he has become, with thick tufts of white and grey protruding from the sides and back of his head, which continues down onto his face in bushy mutton chops. Sun leathered skin, pocked with years of damage and age, pulls into a grateful smile as the man's eyes focus and fall upon his visitors. His voice equally fitting the scar that runs through his right eye, which an old eye patch covers, a sign of an adventurous past, rolls out again as he stands from the chair and approaches the strangers, "What a relief," before getting completely around his chair he takes a moment to lay something across it, "You aren't the collection agencies goons."

Wanting desperately to be sarcastic, Pearl refuses to contain herself, raising a brow, and leaning into as tough of a pose as she can muster, responding, "How would you know?"

"Pearl," Eliza complains about the bad joke she is trying to play.

Pointing to Nakhal the gnome rolls his eyes, "The agency has used outsider's before to collect on debts but never would they use a man whose heritage lies with the giants."

Immediately Pearl slumps, defeated, responding, "Yea, you got us we aren't with this agency. Actually, we came here because we were told you could take us along the fastest path to the northern most coast of the continent."

The man pulls away, "Are you crazy? Not only do you have to go through frost giant hunting grounds during the summer to get there, and if you go during the winter you can't rely on landmarks because you won't likely have any daylight at all. If you want I can help chart a voyage for you from one of the coast towns, but I would still recommend waiting until the summer."

Eliza for the first time in a conversation like this one speaks up, "It can't wait."

Seeing that building the nerve to interrupt with just those few words was difficult for her friend Pearl continues in her stead, "We are looking for something, and we are on a timeline that cannot wait until summer. We are lucky that we have the lead that we do pointing us to this coast in particular."

"Fine I'll take you," the gnome responds.

"Wait you will."

Scratching the back of his head nervously the man continues his response, "Well as you could probably tell on your way down here, this map store isn't really in the best location, nor is it really relevant for the people here. As you probably figured out by the start of our interaction, I am in a smidge of a predicament, financially, so I honestly can't afford to deny work. So, I will cut you a deal. If you can pay me five hundred unitary coins of gold, I could care less about their mint, for the whole journey, half up front, I will make arrangement to be ready to leave whenever it is that you wish to depart."

"Are you ready now?" Pearl asks pulling a bag of coins from within her satchel.

The gnome's jaw drops and he blinks several times before pinching himself, thinking that he is in a dream. Then looking in the bag and giving it a rough estimated count based on its weight, he looks at Pearl to stammer, "S-sure. I mean I could use the rest of the evening to gather my own rations, I assume you are handling the mode of transportation," he begins hastily pulling up various floor boards within the building revealing stashes of adventuring equipment, and shoving it all into a single bag he looks to the group to continue, "Honestly I've been in a bind financially and was prepared to accept my fate. I was simply saying a number expecting that you would leave and not be able to return until after I was no longer, but the fact that you have the money on you, and seem to be in a bind for time yourselves, I am saved. You are saved. We are saved. Alright, where are you staying within the city? I will join you, and purchase my rations on the way."

"Well actually as you pointed out, our companion here isn't really well accepted in this city, so we were going to go outside the gates and camp there."

Suddenly breaking the conversation heavy fist falls slam through the establishment's door. A voice deep and angry for a gnome's calls in, "Bedeguar you better be haven' our money!"

Hearing the voice, the gnome the group has been talking to becomes suddenly panicked and puts a finger to his lips. He explains in a whisper, "That shouldn't be a problem, quickly we'll leave through the back," and quickly scrawling something on a piece of parchment he grabs the strange antique rifle that he had laid across the arm rests of his chair while simultaneously leaving the note and bag of coins in the seat. He then pulls a panel out of the back wall and ushers everyone through resealing the secret exit only just before the front door cracks and two gnomes charge it and burst in.

From there the group sneak quietly around the building and from down the street they whistle for the dogs. With Boop's help as pack leader the sleds suddenly whip off from in front of the building. The collectors within only just see the commotion to recognize that their quarry is escaping as the sleds turn around a corner, but they don't give chase. The one that poses as the most in charge, stops her compatriots before they can give chase showing them the note Bedeguar left, which explains how the sum left, while only part of the amount he owes, was just the beginning of Bedeguar's repayment, with more to come shortly.

Reaching the city gates, the group are begrudgingly given a flare to signal for reentry while simultaneously being encouraged out. Beyond the gate Eliza asks the man who is going to escort them, "You said that during the winter there isn't light to see land marks. What do you mean?"

Turning to the now heavily robed young teen Bedeguar responds simply, "Well, since you've been on this continent, you've noticed the shortened time that you get to see the sun, right? Well that gets worse the deeper into winter and the further north you go."

"Then when should we leave? We will be relying on you to tell us the way."

"Well, really we should head out whenever you think the dogs are ready. We should keep going as long as they can."

From the side Nakhal's voice reaches into the conversation, "Then we can go now."

The gnome and Eliza turn to the large man who has knelt down amongst the dogs, and who with the things he has been doing with them has earned their admiration. Even Boop seems oddly friendlier to Nakhal than to Umbra or Flame-Tender. Having become the pack's alpha by sheer personality, Boop turns and agrees, "Yeah, we ready."

With no other reason to set up camp near the city the group take to their sleds and set out. They travel as far as they can with the dogs and when their canine companions tire, they stop and set up the warm tent. During the nearly eight hours of travel the group comes to know that the northern icy desert is not as barren as they would have thought with large boulders, and cliffs that they have to be ever ready to avoid at Bedeguars command.

The tent set, the group settle in to prepare their watches and cycle their rest. During her turn Eliza, still intrigued and finally with an opportunity, wants to investigate who or what the voice was that she heard when she was trying to contact Archangel. She pulls out the ritual book, and the blade, and pulling it along her hand draws the circle in the snow. Sitting down and chanting the phrase quietly so no one is woken, "Mgah'ehye frn ahnythor ah mgepnnn llll ya bthnknahor nng nnn ya," she readies herself to ask a question.

The instant the magic takes hold the same deep menacing voice from before echoes in her mind, "Begone annoyance!"

The magic breaks. A backlash of energy is thrust into the circle from beyond and is released in an explosive shockwave, with a loud pop. Eliza's head is thrown back hard into the snow, and the blood ritual circle is cast away, scattered into nothingness within the powdery white ice. There she lays, spread to the elements, for Pearl, who had just traded watch with her to discover in a panic from the sudden sound.

"Lizzy," Pearl calls, running to Eliza's side and lifting her head from the snow. Eliza simply slumps in Pearl's arms as if lifeless. Still breathing Eliza's eyes force themselves unnaturally wide, and she gasps like a fish out of water, all while folding to the will of gravity like a doll made of rags. Seeing the black dagger, and the spreading patch of red growing around Eliza's left hand, Pearl sighs saying to herself, "Lizzy what are you doing?"

Putting Eliza's ritual book back in the purple bag and taking the dagger in to her own bag, Pearl pulls Eliza, who seems simultaneously conscious and unconscious, back into the tent where the others begin to stir from the loud noise and commotion of Pearl springing from the tent. The first to speak is Flame-Tender who groans, "What's going on Pearl?"

"I don't know Lizzy and I just traded off watch and I was nearly asleep when there was a pop outside the tent, and what seemed like a single strong wave of wind. When I checked outside to see if anything was wrong she was nearly buried in the snow and hasn't been responding."

"Well, let's lay her down, maybe she'll go to sleep and be fine before we set off."

In the moments that this is happening Eliza's eyes water, as locked in a familiar prison within her own mind, she finds herself unable to control her body. She watches Pearl lie her down, with a look of worry and disappointment, and step from the tent to resume watch for a second shift. The entire time, Eliza screams, but her voice is unable to escapes, "I'm sorry Pearl! I just, I just need to know if it is actually evil or not."

Inevitably Eliza, drifts to sleep, and Pearl trades off watch with the others, until Nakhal, who has some skill managing the animals, confirms that the dogs are ready to go again. At that point Pearl kneels by Eliza, and with a nudge to the shoulder, Eliza's eyes flicker open. In control of her body again Eliza sits up with a smile for Pearl and goes to say, "Hey, Pearl, so…" but she's cut off before the word sorry can be formed.

Then in a single swift motion, releasing a loud high pitch pop of wet skin striking soft dry skin, Pearl's hand swings in a slap across Eliza's cheek. Pearl holds her head low, her eyes concealed by her bangs as they fall forward. Eliza in unable to comprehend what just occurred. Her face sits facing away as her pale skin begins to redden, releasing into her a slight stinging sensation. Pearl's hands fall into her lap tightening into balled fists as Eliza slowly turns to face her. With a few tears falling from Pearl's eyes, she asks in a soft determined, voice, "Why?"

"Pearl."

"Why would you lie to me? You told me you would stay safe. You made me think you were done doing things that were causing you to hurt yourself," she begins to yell, but she stops herself. Standing she pulls from her bag the knife, and she throws it down next to Eliza's hand which had been bandaged sometime in the night. Without another word, and without even giving Eliza a chance to respond Pearl steps from the tent.

Putting her bandaged hand to the cheek that was struck Eliza steels herself and leaps from the tent. Springing from within she throws herself at Pearl saying nothing. Pearl turns but doesn't have a chance to dodge before Eliza makes impact and the two fall into the snow. There, having stopped Pearl, Eliza lifts her head, looking into Pearl's eyes, and says with full certainty, "I tried what I did to become more sure of my safety, for you."

Pearl's eyes, still dripping with tears from her having instinctively stricken Eliza widen and shake with fear and lack of understanding, "What?" is all that is able to escape her lungs.

"I wanted to know if the thing that my power comes from is actually evil, or not. I tried to contact Archangel with that ritual to ask if I could truly be good, but something else answered, I think I contacted the thing my magic comes from. I did the ritual for the second time last night, and it back fired. I must have done something wrong but I have to know if using this magic is only going to put you at greater risk, or if I can delve into it deeper, safely, without putting either of us at risk of being lost." After saying this Eliza, pushes herself from Pearl and looking down and away finishes, "I understand if you still want to be mad at me, but I wanted you to at least know why I was doing it."

Eliza honestly is expecting Pearl to continue to step away, agreeing with the feelings of betrayal she thinks Pearl might have, but she is caught completely by surprise when she is suddenly wrapped in Pearl's arms. Pearl's voice finally becoming shaky with the emotions that have brought her to tears. Softly she says, only for Eliza to hear, "It isn't about you doing things that could be dangerous. Heck that is the life we live. It is that you try to do it alone. That's what hurts."

"Hey you two, are you coming? I thought you said we didn't have much time to waste," Flame-Tender's voice calls to the embrace that becomes shared, and after but a moment more, the two step back to their sled.

"Your right let's go."

29

Contact

The sleds whip quickly over the vast icy northern wasteland for several hours, but the day's progress ends swiftly when in the distance an orange glow begins to grow. His hand extended upward, Bedeguar calls to the other two sleds, "Stop, stop. That's a fire's glow, there shouldn't be anyone this far north to start one. Not a gnome at least."

"Who could it be then," Flame-Tender asks as Umbra pulls the sled he is on, to a stop next to Nakhal's.

"Well let's hope that it isn't giants."

No sooner does the comment leave the gnome guide's mouth when a boulder, twice the size of one of the sleds, crashes down only a few yards from Nakhal. Turning to see the large mass made mostly of ice, Nakhal's expression curls into something of anger. Grabbing the gnome by the caller and tossing him into the snow behind the impacted boulder projectile, Nakhal turns back to his group commanding, "Lights out."

The gnome lands, and lifting his head sees the mountainous chunk of ice and stone in front of him and immediately recoils pushing himself away exclaiming in a shaky panicked voice, "Ahh! it's giants!" only just before the last of the lanterns is extinguished casting him and the sleds into the black of the thick cloud covered winter north.

With the lights that illuminated the sleds, no longer shinning, they become nigh impossible to be seen by what ever is launching boulders in their direction only just in time for another heavy crunching impact to touch down to the other side of them as the first. With half of the group having some ability to see, even in pitch black darkness, Nakhal points toward the distant glow commanding, "If this is a giant, then they die or we do. Aim for the fire and try not to run into each other," and with that he mushes his sled team.

Quickly after Nakhal begins away, a distant sound erupts from the direction of the fire. Like an immense war-horn the sound is quickly joined by three others, as in the dark around the glow, four wolf silhouettes spark into existence with an icy blue outline. The forms in the darkness each are large enough to appear as though next to the group even though their actual forms are near the fire, and after their howl the quartet turn in the direction of the sleds, vanishing, the magic blue light going dark. The wolves charge into the darkness for the carts, causing another silhouette to form casting a shadow from the fire behind him, a form with the proportions of a man, but significantly larger stand with two enormous axes drawn glaring into the dark of the direction presumably he threw the stones.

With the terrifying titanous howl of the wolf like monsters coming for the carts, the dogs get spooked. Going against the command of their drivers all three teams turn and begin running in the opposite direction. In the split second that he recognizes that he is losing control of the animals, Umbra, leaps from the cart yelling, "One person go after the animals, the rest of us need to deal with the threat," before disappearing from where he was.

"Leave to me," Boop shouts, releasing himself from the lead of Pearl's sled, in the same moment that everyone else leaps into the snow and begin to make their way toward the fire and the waiting giant.

In the darkness Nakhal is able to hear the large impacts of a massive wolf creature only just in time for him to leap out of the way of its snapping maw. In the same instant, the shadow figure shifts as another form appears next to him. Out of the shadows, swinging one of his swords for the giant, as the others are still only half way to the fire, Umbra begins the melee.

With speed that is impressive for his size, the giant turns and deflects the blow, with one of his axes, giving Umbra a good look at the whole of his visage. Built like a muscular man the figure is more than twenty feet tall. His skin is an icy blue that is almost white, which must have been an adaptation to deal with the extreme cold. All he wears is a loin cloth, a set of boots, and a cloak all made out of the same leathery pelts of an animal of an equally great size as himself. Snow-white hair, segmented and frozen with crystals of ice, protrudes from the being's face and head, long and unkempt. The most terrifying thing that Umbra sees about the massive figure is the glare of hatred that he sends the small man's direction for having to exert the effort he did to avoid getting cut.

As Umbra falls from above the shoulder height of the giant, the other axe is brought up in his direction. An opening is made, and Eliza takes it, stopping and creating the small glyph in front of herself she presses out a blasting beam of the black and purple, which strikes the giant's sides sending waves of pain into him. Then as Umbra vanishes into the shadows again like a puff of smoke, the giant turns to face the source of the pain, and Eliza releases the last of the energy that the glyph holds sending another beam which strikes his chest.

The conversation from the start of the day still on her mind causes Pearl to trace the line of dark magical energy from the giant back to see Eliza's visage, which is illuminated, but only barely by the glow of the floating glyph releasing its power. Knowing a fight like this to not be the time or place to worry, she shakes her head and returns her focus to the approaching battle just in time to notice one of the monstrous wolves pouncing toward her.

The white fur of the beast like the beard of the giant, clumps of jagged icy crystals. The large form is heavy as it lands behind Pearl and she rolls beneath its pounce. The weight of its impact makes Nakhal's strength more impressive as Pearl watches from the side the wolf that pounced on him get flipped onto its back with the grey man wrapped around its neck.

Again, Umbra appears in the fire's light bringing his sword into the ankle of the giant, who spins around with the intent of bringing both of his blades onto the small foe, but the sound of a lyre begins to dance through the air and he becomes suddenly dizzy. His vision blurs and he sways before digging both large sheets of metal that are his blades, into the snow beside Umbra where an image of him was standing. Giving a nod to a spot on the side of the hill, Flame-Tender ducks out of view, and Umbra vanishes.

Another beam of dark magical power leaps out from Eliza striking the giant as he begins to get his bearings, hitting him in the back, nearly toppling him over. Angry and seeing the barely glowing source the giant throws himself forward, digs a hand into the snow next to him, and pulling up another icy stone he launches it in Eliza's direction.

"Look out," Pearl calls as she notices the projectiles trajectory, and Eliza looks up to see the descent of the stone speeding toward her. Raising her hands, and with them the glyph that had shot the first beam, she presses into the magic. The beam leaps out, and while the physical push the magic normally strikes its targets with is minute, most of the damage coming from the forceful presence of the strange magical energy, the boulder's path is altered, only just enough to have it strike the ground to her side.

The impact sends a burst of snow out with force that causes Eliza to stumble away. Steadying herself she takes only a moment to look out and retake the events of the conflict. She counts the one giant, and only two wolves, and becomes worried. The thought comes into her mind and festers that Boop and the group's guide are in danger, as two wolves that are unaccounted for may be after them. Looking to Pearl, who leaps over the wolf she is occupying, while leaving a cut in its pelt with her rapier as she goes, she sighs. Knowing that no spell that she has produced with her power could help both encounters, the one with her companions, and the one that Boop is likely engaged in, simultaneously, she feels torn.

A desperate want to see none of those she cares for hurt presses on Eliza, and she takes it in with a deep breath. Directing herself away from the panic she would normally be swallowed by, she inhales, and remembering that the strength of her magic seemingly increases when the wings within her are extended, she attempts for the first time to force them out intentionally. Gritting her teeth and pressing on the muscles in her back she prepares herself for the pain she is used to feeling from their expulsion from within her.

A wave pulses out as the flesh of Eliza's back tears, like a sonic wave but filled with dark magic energy. As the fire is struck it turns black and the world is cast into a reality without color. The fire's dance slows, while the struggles of the many conflicts continue in their natural speed.

A strange feeling rests upon Eliza. Still gritting waiting for the pain to strike her, she opens her eyes feeling the weight of the wings fully extended. Looking over her shoulder, the sight of them stretching from her back, straining as though trying to press out further, strikes her numb. Her muscles instinctively relax from her confusion, and in the same instant the black bones that make her wings pull in and fold into a relaxed position. They are not frayed with splinters as they had been the last time Eliza had seen them. Instead they are smooth with an ancient type of script carved into them that glows pulsing with black and purple.

Looking up to the thick clouds above her, Eliza calls out as the world regains its color, "Archangel, help me defend my friends. While the magic I use is from a source of unknown intent, please direct it."

Eliza feels the magic form to her hands, and they dance to draw a symbol within a circle in front of her. Letting her body work on its own as she has learned to do in the moments she has called upon her magic, she presses the seal down on the ground dropping to a knee. The moment her hands touch the snow the seal vanishes and the white snow becomes black in a circle around her.

There is a pulse that causes a piercing pain to form in the center of Eliza's chest when the black circle is created beneath her. With the pulse, a vision flashes in Eliza's head of the space she went, where she thought was within herself, before becoming able to polymorph herself. Another pulse, and she feels pain in the bones of her wings as they instantly splinter, back to how they had been before, and she sees again in her head the visage of the expanse beyond the barrier within her.

Time seems to freeze as a third pulse of pain washes over Eliza. In that instant large, thick, otherworldly tentacles burst from the ground around her, from the tips of the out stretching black, beneath each of the wolves, and the giant. With time frozen, Eliza's consciousness is transported away.

Around her is a vast expanse. She merely floats with no control of how she drifts. She feels her body relax as it comes to rest floating through infinity.

Slowly, small orbs of light form like eyes opening, becoming a galaxy of stars. The faint glow they emit illuminate's stalks of something moist slowly shifting in a fathomlessly large mass that surrounds Eliza. In the darkness, a bellowing voice, the same one she had heard with the ritual she had performed, radiates through the drifting teen's very being, sounding as if always a millimeter behind her ears.

The sounds that are made are alien, even more so than the ones used in the rituals Eliza has been learning, but somehow Eliza finds herself with understanding. Her mind alters the sounds for her allowing her to hear within the chorus of discordance, "Unknown quantity, your persistence is vexing."

Eliza attempts to respond but feels no breath in her lungs. She doesn't gasp for air, she feels no need for it. Her voice echoes instead in her mind, "What is going on? Who or what are you?"

"As said, in every timeline, across every plain of existence, everything is exactly as it should be. Everything exists in its present as I have seen for all of this eternity. Everything except you," the ominous tones relay to Eliza, who feels at the stop every one of the countless orbs of light turn and direct themselves to her. "You who should be no more to me than a single atomic quark. You have drawn my attention. You are disorder. A thing that has altered reality to be. The space around you alters, the time line changes, the ends of some become the midpoint, while others find their end. I, who am time, who holds all knowledge of the ever, has been, is, and will be, am intrigued, for even in the split microcosm between realities, I am uttering to a nothing, your existence at no point in any timeline, should be."

"Please let me go, my friends are in danger. Boop is in danger. Pearl is in danger."

"Know that as I commune with you, that you are not part of any timeline, I will return you to the moment I summoned you from, when I am done with you, as it is not my way to remove from the realities, merely bare witness."

"What do you want from me?"

"I wanted to observe you, who would draw power from me. I wanted to see how a being so insignificant could do so. I have witnessed what I wanted."

"What? Wait you are the thing my blood parents bound me to?"

"That is probable. I mask my expanse across time, but there are some perceptive enough to witness me in flashes of what they call divine inspiration. To those, I do not smite them upon their drawing of my power, they are but mites consuming the dead flesh that has already begun to fall from me. These you call your parents may have been such people, but you are different. Your existence shouldn't be. You, somehow like myself, exist nowhere on any timeline, except in the wake of your presence sending waves of disorder through it."

"What will you do to me? That which alters what you know."

"Nothing. Your presence alters the timeline, it presents me with more to observe."

Suddenly Eliza is thrust back into her body pressing down into the snow. Around her the tentacles lay prone the wolves and restrain the giant. The fire has returned to glowing red and orange. Mimicking the sound of a trumpet Boop appears from the darkness the sleds in tow, and he pulls next to Eliza. She quickly boards and is whisked in Pearl's direction.

The giant falls to a knee as Nakhal's sword splits open the back of his leg. From behind him Nakhal calls to the others, "Leave the wolves," before moving to stare into the giant's eyes from bellow becoming menacing, "This is the enemy for them as well." One swift slash brings Nakhal's blade through the giant's abdomen, and he steps out of the way for it to fall into the snow.

The sleds pull up to Nakhal with Pearl and Eliza stepping off, Umbra and Flame-Tender remain in the dim of the fire, weapons drawn and pointed at the restrained prone wolves. Returning his sword to its sheath Nakhal turns, and begins drudging through the snow, which is shallow on the fire lit hill, toward the largest of the white beasts. Running to his side Pearl asks, "What do you mean 'Leave the wolves' they attacked us too."

"They were commanded to. These are North wolves, or Winter wolves as you may know them. They are loyal to a pack leader determined by strength, as long as that leader provides," Nakhal explains. Reaching the largest of the wolves he glares down at it asking, "Am I correct?"

Looking up the wolf responds, "You are correct, Alpha."

Pearl leaps back almost tackling Eliza in the process and pointing at the beast asks, "Did, uh, did it just talk? Like, in common?"

"We north wolves are no mere beasts. We are born within magic, translating for an alpha that is not our kin is the task of the beta," the wolf responds, directing his gaze to Pearl, who feigns having already known the information given to her. Then turning back to look up at Nakhal, the wolf asks, "You killed the one who was our alpha, what would you have of us?"

Looking down upon the wolf for only a moment, Nakhal turns away responding with a cast-off manner, "Do what you want, we are going north," and stepping to Eliza, he places a hand on her shoulder saying, "Release them, they are no longer a threat."

Looking to the epicenter of the spell that has summoned the tendrils forth Eliza, extends a hand and wills the magic cease. She feels another pain on her sternum, like that of a bee sting, and the tentacles begin to recoil. After a second the visible effects of the magic are completely gone and the wolves rise from the snow and move quickly away together.

30

Northernmost Coast

The group return to the sleds and they collect their guide who in panic had hid behind one of the boulders that had already landed. In setting up their camp, Eliza pulls Pearl to the side to talk. Quiet, so to not let the others hear, Eliza starts by asking, "Pearl, you remember the conversation we had when you slapped me?"

Immediately worried where Eliza may be going with the conversation Pearl responds wearily, "Yeah..."

"Well just now, in that fight when I created those tentacles..."

"That was pretty cool, I thought you weren't going to delve into your power anymore, at least not until... Wait you didn't do that ritual behind my back again, did you?"

"No, no. Actually, when I extended these," Eliza says gesturing to her wings that fold behind her, the black bones still jagged as Pearl had last seen them, "I prayed for Archangel to direct my magic, but the instant it took effect, I was contacted by that being again; the one my blood parents connected me to." Pearl's eyes fill with worry and immediately Eliza tries to ease her continuing, "I am telling you because of what you said to me. How you don't want me be to alone in this. I can say that based on what it said, I don't think it is evil. It is more of a watcher. It doesn't prevent those who seek it out from using a miniscule amount of its power but it doesn't seem to care who uses it or what is done with it. What was weird, it said that it knows everything in reality, down to the life span of individual flies, it said that it exists outside of time, and that I was an anomaly. That it couldn't see me, my past, present, or future. It seemed to see me as something amusing for it to watch."

"Wow, that is a lot," Pearl says stepping away, and pressing her hand to the back of her head with a squish.

"Hey, at least now I know that the magic I use really is like a sword. Some would use it to do evil, but it in itself doesn't seem to be evil. I can actually use it to do good, and to protect."

"Let's get back to helping set up the camp."

The next seven cycles of travel are unextraordinary. Eliza doesn't attempt the ritual to contact a being on another plane of existence again, but she does continue eagerly again reading the books from Alfredo and translating the book of rituals. The entire time she is cautiously thinking about her conversation with the being and Pearl's seeming withdrawal reaction.

It is at the point that the ocean's salty air begins to waft over them and that the group find themselves at the continent's shore. Before the group, as they crest over a hill's edge while they travel along the icy coast, a sight befalls them that is a complete juxtaposition of the wastes they have run through. Before them waiting at the mouth of a river is a field of overgrown grass that seems to have infectiously spread from down the stream.

Flame-Tender's head shoots up from his lazy lyre strumming and rubbing his eyes he asks, "What in the…?"

The sleds slow to a stop, breaking Eliza's attention on her book, and Boop releases his lead of her sled, rushing into the green brush. Above the river which runs from within the folds of two mountains in the distance, the thick clouds that have remained overhead, are broken leaving just enough space to see the stars through them. Eliza folds the book of rituals, and standing from the sled she looks over the wellspring of life in a desert of ice before turning to Bedeguar asking, "Is this normal?"

Equally awestruck as the people he is escorting the gnome responds, "No. I mean, I have never been to this place exactly. Since we got through livestock country I had as much bearings on our location as you all."

Turning to the others, eyes wide, Eliza says with realization, "This has to be a side effect of the," she stops herself, to not say exactly what they are after for Bedeguar to hear, "The thing we are looking for."

"Well there is only way to check," Pearl says, as she finishes lowering her sled's wheels for the snowless terrain, "Let's look for a shipwreck," and with a crack of the reigns her dogs mush forward into the green along the coast. Eliza's arm reaches out as Pearl whips past quickly traveling only a few hundred feet before stopping. Turning back to the group she calls, "Yep, there is a ship run aground up here!"

"That means we are close," Flame-Tender says looking up to the break in the clouds, "and if the abundance of green and the unnatural break in the clouds are a sign, looks like we are headed up stream."

Pearl brings her sled back around to the group who finish extending the wheels of their sleds, and together they begin their way up stream. They travel for what feels like two hours before their dogs tire out. They set up their camp on the side of the river. The night is quiet but not silent like those of the journey to this point on this continent. Instead the gentle trickle of the stream mixes with a chirping of insects that for all normalcy should not be able to survive in the northern climate.

The group wake as Nakhal confirms the dogs are rested enough to continue, and in the dark of the endless night that takes the north in winter, the group set off again. As they continue they find themselves on a thin path which leads up the mountainous cliff faces of the fjord that the stream ushers them into. In the course of traveling the group find themselves removing their cloaks as the air around them, warming them unnaturally.

The change in the climate around them is almost comforting, but the good feeling is ruined when the path they are on bends into a small rocky clearing with three houses protruding slightly from the far cliff's face. The thing that is startling and off putting is the presence of four bodies lying within the clearing, motionless. Upon approach it becomes apparent that the bodies are of the same race as the giant the group had encountered before. Each is covered with a myriad of strange wounds and marks not from normal weaponry.

The sleds come to a stop and the group ready themselves for a potential conflict when a growling voice rolls out from within the house on the far left of the clearing, saying, "Har du Hort noe?"

"Nei," a second, deep, voice responds.

Quickly Nakhal gestures to the others and he directs them to move their sleds back away. They round the corner onto the path that brought them here just in time to be out of sight as a the flicker of torch light glows to life in the clearing with the sound of a heavy foot fall. Looking to the others Nakhal whispers to them, "Giants."

To which Pearl responds, "So? If that last one was any indicator, they aren't that tough."

"Don't underestimate giants," Nakhal's eyes become deadly serious. Then, gesturing up he explains, "If the clouds are what we follow, then this is our destination."

The others look up to see the hole through the sheet of clouds above them is larger over them and doesn't continue any further upstream. Panic nearly enwraps the group as the light of the torch swings with movement, as worry about their conversation strikes them. The panic passes as the light fades with the heavy footsteps growing distant. With this added information

Flame-Tender chimes in, "I think Nakhal is correct. First, we don't know how many of them there are, and second, we don't know how well they know this place. Home territory advantage should not be underestimated."

"They have not been here long," Nakhal responds, "The faces of these structures are far too small for them, and they haven't been made into large passageways yet. Which means they haven't made this a permanent residence."

"Well that is one thing in our favor then. If the environment is not in their favor then it is in ours. That still doesn't mean we should even attempt to fight them. We know from experience that these people have considerable strength to match their considerable sizes and without a clear count of how many there are we could still find ourselves overwhelmed even with Eliza and my magic. Keep in mind that whoever lived here before was able to take out several of them but was still runout or killed."

Taking in Flame-Tenders comments, Pearl turns to Eliza, whose face is morphed into a contemplative scrunch. Seeing the expression of thought, she asks, "What are you thinking, Lizzy?"

Eliza looks to Pearl her face remaining tense, and shifting into a look of worry, "If this is the place why are giants here? Could we be too late?"

"Their presence may be coincidence," Nakhal explains, "The giants of the north are nomadic, and while not unsophisticated in their inner social structure, they are not treasure hunters."

"But, that doesn't mean they haven't been hired," Flame-Tender adds, rebirthing Eliza's worry.

"Their kin are a proud people. They wouldn't do work for an outsider."

"What if it wasn't an outsider," Eliza asks looking to Pearl, before turning to the others continuing. "When we fought a member of the group looking for the shard before, they were giant, at least in size. What if they are all like that."

Before anyone else can say anything further, Umbra's voice, soft but distinct enough to grab attention when used, utters, "We don't have time for this worry. If they have found the shard, with the power it is said to have, why are there some that are still here? If they haven't found it are they even looking for it? Chatting about what might be won't answer these questions."

"Umbra's right," Pearl says going to acknowledge him by placing a hand on his shoulder, but in that instant he vanishes and her hand passes through where he had been to the dirt below. Dusting her hands off, she continues, "What we need to do is get information."

31

Another Deal

Through the door of the leftmost structure of the clearing there is not the normal makings of a home, which is the visage it presents with its front. Instead, immediately through the door, which is twice the size of a normal set of double doors, in both height and width, the cliff side opens into large cave tunnels, fifteen feet tall and wide. Three rooms spur off from the main tunnel with the largest being at the paths end and the other two off set from each other along the length. Each room is nearly seven feet larger in height than the tunnel, spanning between four hundred square feet of floorspace with the smallest, and sixteen hundred for the largest.

Unlike the clearing beyond its door, which is unlike how the northern environment should be, the structure is icy cold. The stone of the walls are nearly blue with chill and the edges of the ceiling hold icicles seemingly as decoration.

The only life within sits in the large back chamber, where two giants sit in the light of a single torch with expressions of having been wronged on their faces, both staring into the flickering light. With them, bound and gagged lays what looks to be an old wrinkled woman, with icy blue skin, a long, pointed nose, thin patchy white hair that may have never been washed and squinting angry black eyes with pupils that reflect green in the fires light, glaring at the giants. As for her size, she appears to be the original resident of the abode the three figures are within, seemingly able to straighten herself to be nearly fifteen feet in height herself, but with an ever-present bend in her back that would lean her forward, if she could stand.

A few minutes after returning to his seat with the torch the giant that was sent out to check if there was a sound stands, again saying, "Jeg gar pa tisse."

His companion squints frustratedly as the giant-sized torch is pulled from the floor, responding, "Vel vaere rask om det, du kommer til a vaere forste klokke."

Casting off of the comment, a groan escapes the first giant as he turns, giving a disgruntled swiping wave to the other, and he bends over and begins to shuffle his way out of the tunnels. Once outside the giant makes his way out of the clearing and dropping the waist of his leather trousers releases a stream into the river. A sudden noise rustles at his side, pulling his attention from his business, but the light of his torch doesn't reveal anything so he continues finishing up.

Inside, the tunnels are not completely black. From the smallest room a pulsing white light grows and fades in intervals that take eight seconds to repeat, and the ice of the walls allows that light to dimly fill the entire complex. The second giant sits staring at the entrance to the room he is in, one hand resting on a large sack, which in proportion is most likely his backpack, and in his other hand he holds an axe. Something is uneasy in the back of his mind about the present night.

The large door to the structure, closes. Nearly silently to the outside, the clasp of the latch is loud within as it rings off the smooth icy walls. The giant's squint turns into an eye roll as he growls, "Fikk du fakkelen i elven igjen, du var ubekymret. Vel kom inn her har jeg en annen." He leans forward pulling from his bag another of the giant-sized torches, and he stops as the heavy sound of his companion's footsteps doesn't fill the silence as he would expect. With a single strike of the steel of his axe against a stone he pulled from his bag, the torch ignites and the light reveals standing, weapons drawn in the entry way into the room, a group of five little people. Surprised, and angered, the giant yells as one of the figures creates a magic glyph in the air, "Hva har du gjort med Eric?" The question escapes an instant before Eliza presses into the glyph blasting the giant's shoulders with her magic.

Outside the first giant lays unconscious with two trees, that had not been there before, growing on either side of him their roots ensnaring him before making their way into the ground. Sat on top of him, Bedeguar, holding a long strange gnomish device, and Boop drifting in a small vigilant patrol of the area, both watch for movement. While the conflict begins inside the icy structure, the giant moves once, to find a beam of telekinetic energy thrusting his head hard into the ground from Boop, and a jolt of electricity applied to a vein in his neck from the gnome's device.

Eliza's magical attack causes a brief moment where the giant's body seizes up long enough for him to not be able to guard himself as Nakhal slices the backs of his legs deep enough to make standing excruciatingly painful, but shallow enough to not be the cause of him bleeding out. The cave quakes as the giant falls to his knees, while choosing not to brace himself with his hands, he instead swings at the strangers.

Pearl, running in his direction bends and jumps onto the axe's blade with enough force that it falls short of its intended target, digging into the stone a yard in front of Eliza. The sudden stop throws Pearl from the point she had planted herself on and for her young friend who, braces for the impact, and allows Pearl to swing around her with neither of them completely losing their footing. Pearl strikes a flourish of a pose with a smile acting as though the twirl was calculated, as she looks to Eliza who stares at the blade wide eyed and breathing heavy.

The other hand comes down hard for the center of the group, in hopes that it will hit something. Seeing the approaching burning log, Flame-Tender takes only a single step back in time for the burning end to impact the floor in front of him. He simply stands with his hands behind his back and looks up from the flame with a smirk.

The giant's eyes go wide in rage at being thwarted with such seeming ease of little people, as the dapper man in a suit who dodged the torch pulls from behind him a small handheld lyre and begins playing. The strumming chords fill the room and tunnels with an enchanting song that causes the giant's eyelids to become heavy and flutter, threatening to close. His head turns to face the woman to growl, "Dette gjor du ikke er heks," seeing, as his eyes force themselves closed, a small tree grows to the height of an average human.

The tree transforms into a beautiful young woman, who upon falling free of the magic that brought her into the room lands on her knees by the bound older woman. Grabbing the restraints, she looks the woman in the eyes saying something that sounds like the mixture of forest sounds and small ringing bells. Pearl hustles to the two woman and releasing the bonds with a dagger finds both turn to her with the youthful one saying in the common tongue, but with a strange accent from the other language being her primary one, "Thank you for saving my sister."

Flame-Tender's strumming quiets and comes to a stop as Pearl steps to the two women, saying with a smile, "Well, this is obviously not a giant's place of living so I am pretty sure you were attacked by them, so it was only our pleasure."

Free from her binding the old, icy, blue of the two women stands, and in a voice that is gnarled and haggard to the extent that would be expected to fit her appearance she expresses with what seems like contempt, "You can go now."

"Sister, they just freed us from those awful creatures. The least we can do is let them rest a short while," the other blurts out, standing to bring her eye to eye with the hunched over other.

Stepping past her sister the one which was bound brings herself, with shaking movements to the giant, who lays in a way that he takes up most of the rooms space. Out stretching a hand toward him, a black begins to spread in the ice of the floor like poison spreading through veins. The Instant the strange coloration touches even the slightest bit of shadow cast by the sleeping giant's form, a cluster of icicles shoot up like spears into his neck and across his body. Without turning from this the older looking of the two asks, "What are you doing here?"

"Sister," the young looking one, whose form still maintains the appearance of wood, snaps feeling insulted on behalf of the group.

Not insulted and understanding the one's caution Eliza responds, "We are here for probably the same reason they were."

"Lizzy," Pearl says leaping to Eliza's side and putting a hand over her mouth before whispering, "I thought we agreed that was a need to know thing where only we needed to know."

"She is right Pearl," Flame-Tender responds putting a hand on Pearl's shoulder.

Pearl removes her hand from Eliza's face, who has patiently waited, and her mouth free she continues, "These two and those who are dead outside are not the only ones who came here are they? They were looking for something. Where are they? You are alive, with guards, I know from experience that that means they still need you for something. Their group is after the Shard of Prime, we just want to keep it from them. They want to use it, we just don't want that to happen."

Squinting the decrepit looking woman stares at Eliza for a moment before stepping past into the hall saying, "Fine, follow me. Daedratta stop playing with your food. You five come."

Outside, Bedeguar and Boop leap from their spots as the tree roots shift, piercing and crushing the giant causing a spray of gore to escape in a burst before it is completely entombed within the wood. Witnessing the anomaly, the two take a moment to stare wide eyed at that tumor of wood that protrudes from the ground in front of them which they just watched eat a giant whole. Panic takes them as they look to each to confirm what the other saw, and immediately they run for the door of the cave.

Licking her lips, Daedratta smiles before skipping to her sister's side. Leading the group toward the pulsating light, she shares her smile to those following, and explains, "You are correct. There were more of these, led by a woman who only in appearance was one of their kin. You are also correct in your assumption that my sister and I were at one point made responsible for guarding access to the shard. That was after our eldest sister was taken by her age."

"Hush up," the elder in appearance snaps with a swift strike of her hand, contacting the back of Daedratta's head.

The group comes to a quick stop when Daedratta turns to her sister in response to the strike, and the upper half of her body suddenly transforms into what looks like a giant snapping fly trap made of wood releasing a hiss like that of a serpent ready to strike. The transformation quickly reverts though when the serious look in her sister's eyes somehow intensifies, and she pulls away sheepishly. That instant Boop and Bedeguar run up to the group, from the side. Breathing heavy the gnome points back the direction he and Boop had come from and tries to say something which comes out unintelligible through his heavy breaths. Noticing Bedeguar's struggle Boop instead blurbs, "The tree's, they eat giant!"

Flame-Tender's eye open with sudden understanding as he puts together the information he has absorbed about the sisters standing before them, and instinctively he lungs out pulling the group away from them, saying, "Everyone keep your distance. These two are Fae."

Both of the sister turn to Flame-Tender with glaring eyes, and the elder responds, "So you figured that out. It isn't like we were hiding it from you."

"We have to go, now."

"Hold on young man, we wouldn't have if we were not so overpowered as to get captured, but those you want to stop have stepped through the gateway and are one step closer to finding what you want to prevent them from finding. It isn't on this plane of existence anymore, but a plane of radiance near the boundaries of time's pull."

"We will find another way."

Stepping from behind Flame-Tender and turning to face him, Eliza asks, "And how long will that take? This is exactly what we didn't want to learn. Not only is one of the group we want to stop on the right trail, but they are further along than we are."

"You don't understand, Fae are worse than devils, when a contract is struck with one there isn't even a way in Hell to escape it and they are far more devious in the construction of their contracts than even devils."

The old hag rolls her shoulders, responding to the claims made, "You are not wrong, but something you are not considering is that we share a similar goal at the current point in time."

"Would you grant us aid without striking a contract with us, then," Flame-Tender asks with a discerning look in his eyes.

Daedratta breaks into laughter for a moment, quickly quieting for her sister to respond, "So all you know about Fae like my sister and I is that we bind people with our contracts, then you know very little. The prime reason contracts are created the way they are with our kind as you put it, is because there is always risk on behalf of our entering them with mortals. That and the magic of binding a contract allows our kind to produce greater power than we would normally be able to for the purpose of completing our end of the bargain."

"Look, we need to go after the shard," Eliza interrupts looking at both the woman and Flame-Tender, then looking back to the old woman she asks, "What bargain would you present?"

Flame-Tender throws his hands up and he steps away in protest, at the same moment the woman responds to Eliza, "I shall open the gateway to the plane of existence the shard of prime you seek is on, and in exchange, upon finding those who embarrassed my sister and I, you will do everything in your power to kill them."

The hag extends her hand to seal the deal, but Eliza stops responding, "Not good enough. You explained that you want us to succeed as much as we do, so how about…" she taps her chin in thought, "You open the gateway, guarantee that you will open it for us to return, provide us with as much information as you can to expedite our locating the shard, and then in exchange for that upon finding those who embarrassed you and your sister we will do everything in our power to serve them just retribution." With that Eliza extends her hand, but the hag withdraws hers, causing Eliza to ask, "What's wrong? Did I over extend with that?"

"It isn't your contract constructing skill child, I am impressed at your wit to formulate what you did so quickly, but you are currently in a contract with another, I cannot enter a contract with you."

Flame-Tender's voice comes from the back of the group, "What?"

"But you are not bound to a contract currently," the hag continues, ignoring Flame-Tender and turning to Pearl, "How about we strike the contract that I offered her?"

Pearl goes to extend her hand and Eliza knocks it away, as Flame-Tender's voice continues, "Wait, wait," and he grabs Eliza by the shoulders, and turning her to look her in the eyes, he asks, almost as though scolding her, "Eliza is she lying? You never said you had made a contract with a Fae being before."

A smile grows on the hag's face as she extends her hand, boney, gnarled, with a wart on the knuckle of her index finger, she asks, "The deal your friend presented then?"

"The deal Eliza Black, presented," Pearl returns the grin, presenting her hand forward.

Breaking away from Flame-Tender, Eliza responds to him, "Pearl and I told you. Protection was 'offered' to us for the palace, and I was the only one of our group at the time given a reasonable offer, I had to let my name be changed across reality. I don't remember what the name I go by used to be but that is why it's now Eliza."

The hag returns an appreciative nod to Pearl for being quick enough to make the clarification and reaching, grasps Pearl's hand. Releasing she turns from where the gathering had stopped in the tunnel and continues to the room from which the pulsing light glows, and the group follows, giving Eliza a reason to not subjugate herself to Flame-Tenders overbearing superstition any further. As they walk the hag's voice speaks without her turning to face the group, "The plane you will be transported to is between the prime plane of water and the prime plane of light. As I said, it sits near the edge of time's pull on reality. This means that when you go in, there is no telling when you will return, or if it will be before or after the time you left. All I know about the place the shard is, is that on this plane our elder sister explained it was at the radiance tower. I don't know of where that is or how you will get there. Take this," she points to a small stone, "When you are ready to return from that plane, press the heel of your boot onto it."

Finally, the women come to a stop before the group facing into a small room with a crystal in the center, the source of the light they have been approaching. Beneath it engraved into the stone is a symbol which at first glance looks almost like the bloom of a flower. Beyond those two noticeable aspects, the room is empty, but is quickly filled with the forms, of the group.

The younger sister, smiles as even Flame-Tender begrudgingly steps into the room, and with a quick clap she extends her hands toward two of the points of the glyph. Branches begins to grow and twist around each other from both of her outstretched hands before driving into and seemingly fusing with the ground. Her sister, rolling her hunched shoulders again, extends her hands to two other points and black ice does as the branches had. With both connecting themselves to the magic circle, the sisters moan in unison, a phrase again in the language that sounds like echoes of a forest, and there is a flash from the crystal.

Looking up from having turned away in reaction to the sudden bright light the group see through the crystal as though it were a doorway, an ocean, brightly lit, with waves cresting and crashing onto a shore of waiting sand. The smell of warm salty air returns to their noses as the sound of the waves makes everything real. Intrigued Pearl leaps for the image shoulder first, prepared to have been fooled into tackling hard crystal, but she passes through and finds herself falling into the sand of the beach.

One by one the others follow, with Nakhal and Bedeguar being the last in the room with the Fae women. Turning and kneeling Nakhal rests one of his hands, titanic in comparison to the gnome's shoulder where if lands, and explains, "You have done your part, please care for the canines until we return," before standing and stepping through the portal.

32

Vincent Jay

The sky is filled with a blinding light that is without source in juxtaposition to the seemingly endless winter's night that consumes the northern continent of the group's home plane. The passageway they step through remains open and throbbing in its existence for only a moment more after Nakhal joins the others, before snapping shut with a pop. It isn't long for the six to notice that in having been teleported to another plane of existence, they have been marooned on a small island within a seemingly endless ocean.

Slowly Pearl stands dusting off the sand that clots to her moist mucus covered skin. Quickly she joins the others in looking in angered disbelief at the nature of their stranding. In frustration, she pulls from her side pouch the stone that is intended to allow them to return to the hag's hideaway and throws it into the sand. She is about to bring the heel of her boot down on it when she is stopped by Flame-Tender asking with squinted eyes, "Is that a ship?"

The question draws everyone's attention, to him and then to the horizon where, through the clear wavy warping of heat radiating off the ocean, a spec that appears black against the bright blue of the sky and ocean meeting. Eliza turns with a smile to Boop laughing, "Well that's a stroke of luck, they seem to be coming this way."

Nakhal shakes his head to the comment responding, "Not luck. The spirits destined this."

With the dot on the horizon growing ever slowly, minutes pass into hours as the group waits, knowing that their calls would be purposeless at the current distance. Nakhal sits, with his sword, in its scabbard, laying across his lap, almost meditatively basking in the sun. Umbra finds comfort, in the shade of one of the three solitary palm trees on the small island. Eliza, also sits within the shade reading, and throwing a small stone for Boop to fetch at almost regular intervals, and Pearl paces impatiently along the edge of the island so that she can regularly check the progress of the dot's approach. Above all of the patience, and lack thereof, Flame-Tender plays a gentle resting toon with his lyre.

The small amount of peace that the group found for themselves in waiting, ends abruptly when Pearl comes to the belief that the vague shape, which has grown to look more and more like a ship as time has passed, has come close enough for her to begin yelling and waving her arms to signal to whom ever might be piloting the vessel. What is unexpected is that to Pearl's call there is a response, as a voice, unnaturally amplified but not deep like a giant's, calls back from over the ocean, loud enough to be heard, "Ahoy, ahoy! Ye, are unfamiliar to mine eyes. Yet ye stand on me island. Prepare for parlay."

Hesitantly watching the still distant vessel slow to a stop in the wavy mirage of heat rising from the ocean, the group gathers with Pearl, not sure what they should be expecting from the source of the voice. From the main blob that is the vessel in the distance a small object is hoisted from the side, and begins to approach. Several uneasy minutes draw the group's weapons from their hilts as they wait for the side vessel to grow near enough for the visage of its passengers to become clear.

Standing on the point of the boat is a picturesque man dressed in an outfit strangely similar to Pearl's. A blue tri-brimmed hat covers a head of short blonde hair over a sea tanned clean shaven face. The most impressive aspect of his appearance is the confidence in his pose as he approaches, one foot on the point of the boat, a hand on his hip, and the other on his brow.

After several minutes of waiting, the group finally meet the person approaching as his small boat, with just himself and a single other person, run aground allowing him to leap off into the sand. He steps to the group, who in anticipation of possible hostility point their drawn blades in his direction. Culminating the group's confusion Pearl asks, "Who are you?"

Raising his hands empty in front of himself the stranger responds, "Hey, hey, I don't mean to fight, besides you are the ones on my island, so I should be asking you the same question."

Gesturing to the others to put down their arms, Pearl explains, "He did call for parlay, so he wasn't calling for a fight. You will answer first though, then we will explain our being here, and perhaps we will request your help, if you accept gold coinage as payment at least."

"I don't know a man who wouldn't. But if talks would be halted by stubbornness then I shall oblige, I am the great and magnificent Vincent Jay," the man says with pride filling his voice. Eliza watches Pearl's hands immediately clench into fists to which the man calling himself Vincent Jay is oblivious as he continues, "Great captain and explorer extraordinaire, known for thousands of exploits thought impossible by most common folk," before he can say anymore, the man is stopped when Pearl, who had stepped to him in his gloating, brings her hand across his face in a powerful angry slap. He recoils bringing his hand to the stricken cheek, and yells in response to the pain, "Ow! Hey, what was that for."

"Bellathona Sarya, do you know that name," Pearl nearly yells holding back her emotions.

Recollection opens Vincent's eyes, and almost wistfully he looks up and away in memory, responding, "Aw, Bellathona, how long has it been? Yes, I know," but again his speech is cut off by a heavy slap across the same cheek.

"Pearl!" Eliza exclaims stepping to Pearl pulling her away before she can bring another slap for the man's face.

"Twenty-six years you mule faced swine!"

Vincent recollects himself from the debilitating blow, and keeping his head down raises an open hand toward Pearl shouting back, "Wait! Twenty-six years? I could have sworn would have been longer by now," Eliza has to hold Pearl back from bringing a fist at the man, who stands and continues, "What I might ask, is how you know that name, or how long it has been since my last opportunity to visit my home plane?"

"I am Bellathona's daughter. She only ever loved one man, and from that love, I was born. But he left to never return."

"Bella had a daughter? That is fantastic," Vincent responds stepping close to Pearl as he begins to look her over, "Are you sure you are her."

"You! I am currently cursed you jerk!"

"Oh, that explains it. Last I remembered Belly was a beautiful elven woman, and I am not a fish person obviously, so for an appearance like yours this would be an awkward meeting. Here, let's do something about that," Vincent explains before releasing a single snap of his fingers.

The instant after the sound cracks out, Pearl's appearance suddenly transforms. Her hair, while maintaining the look and feel of being permanently wet, becomes once again blonde. Her skin, while retaining the glisten of a thin layer of protective mucus, returns to its sun-tanned appearance that only Eliza and Boop of the group's members have seen before. Her hands take on the look of no longer having webbing between them, and her teeth, while remaining sharp and pointed to the touch of her tongue, outwardly become a normal straight toothed smile. With this, her eyes stay green, slightly glowing, with vertical cat like pupils, and still from her coccyx extends the long slender cat tail, now covered with fur that is blonde, nearly white.

"Woah," escapes Flame-Tender's mouth instinctively seeing Pearl in a more human appearance for the first time.

At the same moment of Flame-Tender's exhalation, Vincent's face contorts, curious of an oddity of the transformation. Looking at Pearl's eyes and then down and around at her tail he mumbles only just louder than to himself, "Now that doesn't make sense," and then looking up to Pearl's face which has turned to look over her shoulder down at him, he apologizes, "Well, I created an image of you free of the effects of another being's curse, but you seem to have retained some mutation if you are the daughter of Bellathona Sarya and myself."

"Um, that is actually from an encounter with an alchemist's experimental elixir, but I would very much like to know what magic you used to free her of her curse," Eliza explains leaning forward with her hands hiding the instructional book of alchemy behind her back.

Vincent turns to the voice, and almost as if seeing Eliza for the first time widens his eyes and blinks them heavily to attempt remove any potential illusion from them. With her still in front of him as he had first seen her, he straightens himself up and with a punkish smile he leans in and with a flirtatious nature in his voice says, "Hello there, who are we that I may make acquaintanceship with such a fair lass."

Immediately Pearl slides herself between the two as Eliza pulls away, slightly creeped out by the man she knows to be Pearl's father expressing attraction to her. Breaking the line of sight Vincent looks up to Pearl's eyes which are almost angry as she says, in a near growl, "She is fourteen, and my friend. How about you focus on the daughter of yours standing in front of you?"

Feigning having been broken from an enchantment, Vincent responds, "Your right, your right. I don't normally have an opportunity to meet my lineage. I just have spent every moment of the past twenty some ought years on a ship of barnacle coated men and was overcome with the first woman my eyes fell upon, beyond my daughter, being so intoxicatingly beautiful, I lost my bearing and I apologize." Looking past Pearl, he nods, with an earnest smile, and continues, "You are a very attractive young woman. I am sorry for my advance. I have not relieved the curse from her, but in this realm, I have provided her the appearance of being free of it."

"Wait, in this realm, are you some kind of god?" Pearl asks leaning to block her father's line of sight with her face.

Realizing he will not be allowed to continue creepily staring at the beautiful young woman that has appeared on his island with his supposed daughter, Vincent straightens himself again and denies the claim, responding, "No, no, far from it. Well, how to I explain this? Are the books about my exploits still popular? I wasn't on my home plane for long before having to return."

"Yeah, they were my favorite books, before I learned you were my father."

"Oh," Vincent seems hurt by the latter end of Pearl's comment, "So Bella, doesn't speak well of me then?"

"I don't know, she never spoke of you to me at all."

"Wait, then how did you learn about me?"

"A guy named Negmor. It was this whole thing, regardless about that, what does the popularity of your books matter?"

"The popularity thing was just to know if you had read or been read them."

"Well, yeah, I just."

"Well think back to the one about my journey with Gretchen Hubblestump. Remember that one?"

"Yeah," Pearl responds becoming concerned.

"Well on that voyage I was wounded searching for, I don't remember what, but what is important is that I was wounded. I met

Gretchen, and she lead me to something to heal my wounds. It worked. I was no longer dying. In fact I became effectively immortal, but I was bound away on this plane of existence, for the rest of eternity. Lucky for me I found that I could escape once every few decades, to visit my home and enjoy the pleasures that I am otherwise sealed from. I was bound to this plane, and in the millennia or so I have been here I have learned to manipulate it to my will, slightly. Basically, the long way of saying, not a god just a guy who will live forever."

"Why?"

"I'm sorry, did I not just explain that?"

"Why, would you be so selfish as to let a woman fall in love with you, enough to have your baby, while knowing you would have to leave her?" Pearl asks, her fists tightening again.

"You don't know what you are talking about here."

"You don't know how hard it was for her, for me, alone how we were."

For the first time Vincent's boisterous demeanor shakes, and he turns responding, "You really weren't listening. I can't control when I return. Bella, knew the entire time that I wouldn't be able to stay with her. She is the one who insisted on our relationship. I have every intent of returning to her when I can escape again. I wish so much that I could have been there for her, for you, all this time. I am sorry."

From behind, Pearl feels a gentle nudge toward her father. Looking over her shoulder she finds Eliza the source of the nudge, and in her head, she hears Eliza's voice, "*He is being earnest Pearl, he is as hurt as you are that you ha* to grow up without him.*"

Awkwardly, Pearl steps forward and is about to hug the man she had always admired as a fictional character, which has turned out to be her absentee father, when he turns, unintentionally preventing the embrace, to exclaim, "I know! Let me help you. It is the least I can do for not being there for you all this time. I know, I know, I can never make up for the, twenty-six you said, years I haven't been there for you, but I can at least be there for you now."

Pearl pulls away slightly, experiencing for the first time a dose of a personality as forward and over bearing in optimism as her own. Hesitatively she responds, "Uh, well we could use it. We would be stuck on this island otherwise."

"Good, good, let's get going then. We can talk about the details more on my ship," he says turning away and stepping to the edge of the water. Then beginning to stretch his shoulders he asks, "Hey, Pearl, that is your name, right? I'm sorry, you are my daughter, but we did just meet. That fishy curse of yours, does it help with swimming?"

The air, beginning to uplift from the dower turn it had taken, lets Pearl smirk at the question, responding, "You can say that. Why?"

"Let's race. From the low tide line to my ship."

Flame-Tender, quietly letting the father daughter issues work themselves out, speaks up at the proposition, "That's crazy, that thing is so far out at sea, you'll die of exhaustion."

Pearl shrugs, "You know I'll be fine."

"And I told you, I'm immortal here," Vincent adds, "You lot will be coming in with George on the landing boat, so if either of us find ourselves unable to make it all the way just pick us up as you pass us."

Without even a moment of delay further, the two, father and daughter, look into each other's eyes and with a synchronized nod they take off into the ocean and begin swimming for the ship. Watching the two begin to pull away from the shore, Flame-Tender sighs, and the group left behind begin slowly stepping into the dingy. Once fully loaded, the crewmember, who had brought his captain to shore, a man with barnacles growing on his moist darkened skin, nods and with a single thrust of the oars the boat is pushed out.

The curse from the sunken god of death on Pearl, propels her faster through water than she would naturally swim even considering the webbing that has grown between her fingers after receiving it. So, at the start of the race she expects to greatly outpace her father, who seems more or less human, but after a few seconds, when she looks over her shoulder to confirm him falling behind, she instead finds that he is handily keeping pace with her. Dangerously competitive Pearl pushes herself and begins to swim as fast as she can, with results bearing themselves after a few more seconds when the man does begin to lag behind.

Swimming at a normal human's speed would take next to an hour to reach the ship from the shore. For Pearl this time is drastically reduced to nearly a handful of minutes. Reaching the ship, she slaps its side proud of a hard-fought victory. Breathing heavy and looking back to see how much of lead she had achieved, she smirks to herself not seeing any sign of Vincent between her and the boat Eliza is on.

The proud feeling of victory doesn't last, as a rope ladder is rolled down to her and Vincent's voice follows from above, "You're fast, good race. Climb on up and let's see if we can set a course for where you need to go on this plane."

Pearl looks up to see Vincent turn from looking down at her and step toward the center of the deck, causing her to gasp, "Who the... how the..." as she double takes the path they swam and the edge of the waiting ship deck. She slams an arm down against the water's surface in frustration of having lost and specifically for not knowing how. Then, with a sigh she climbs the ladder.

Reaching the deck of the ship, Pearl glances back in the direction of her friends, and seeing them still only a short distance off the far coast she turns back to step to her father, asking, "How did you? You've even dried off."

With a smile the target of inquiry responds, "I told you I can alter reality slightly in this realm. If I couldn't you surely would have beaten me," and he claps his hands together eagerly, "Now, where do you need to get to? I know this realm better than the back of my hand so name a land mark and I will get you there."

"Well," Pearl responds still hesitant to trust the person, her father, and for the first time takes in notice the members of Vincent's crew. Like the one that had taken him to the shore, the rest of the crew shamble slowly through the tasks of maintaining a ship. Their bodies, bulbous and waterlogged with seaweed and barnacles clinging to their flesh concerns Pearl. She explains, "We need to find a place called the Radiance Tower. There are others that we need to beat in getting there."

"A race then," Vincent exclaims, "Worry not my daughter. You can have faith in your father, Vincent Jay. I shall get you to the Tower of Radiance faster than those you face."

Jumping to the side of the ship closest to the approaching dingy, Vincent raises his hands. Through a blur like a mirage the distance between the two vessels shrinks rapidly until they are touching. This in itself fills the group with worry similar to that which Pearl has begun to feel toward this man.

Pearl and her father help the others onto the ship, and the boat is quickly drawn up. Pulling her companions to the side away from Vincent she whispers to them so that only they can hear, "I don't trust this guy."

"Follow the light boys! Turn her around, we're sailin' to the tower," Vincent's voice calls to his crew.

"Pearl, he's your dad," Eliza retorts in the whisper of the group.

Checking over her shoulder to ensure her father still can't hear Pearl explains, "We don't know that. What we know is that he is a being who can alter reality in this place. That without him we would still be stuck on that island, and that he claims to be Vincent Jay. I just think he seems to have lost his marbles. Have you seen his crew?"

"So? Your crew are ghosts," Flame-Tender asserts.

"Look, just lay low out of the way until we get to where ever he is taking us," Pearl says, as the ship leers to one side in a sharp turn to point it in the opposite direction it was headed.

Trusting Pearl's judgment in this instance, the group go about settling themselves into the ships environment as unobtrusively as they can. There is no need for them to lend aid to any of the sodden crewmen, so they stay out of the way, and return to doing what they had relinquished themselves to when they believed themselves stranded and in need of ideas to escape the island. Pearl isn't as lucky as to be allowed to fade into the boarding of the ship and remain simply a passenger. Vincent pulls her along, testing her knowledge of the sea, and of being a captain as her outfit presents.

The ship itself is larger than Pearl's by a fair margin, with three decks below, one of cabins, one of cannons, and one of storage. The captain's chamber is garishly furnished with golds and velvets of all kinds of craft, from all types of cultures, filling a space nearly twice the size of the four small rooms on Pearl's ship combined. The thing that catches Pearl's eyes in her father's quarters, is a small wooden figurine, held in place on a mantle with a sticky resin; an open clam.

Slowly, Vincent steps to the small object, peels it from the adhesive holding it in place, and with a gentle smile he offers it to Pearl, saying, "I wanted to give it to you, but before it was finished the ship, crew, and myself were banished back to this existence."

The small trinket isn't carved with great detail, the old wood that it is made from is frayed with splinters. Pearl looks intently over the object finding a hinge where the shell's two parts meet, there carved into the upper shell is simply, "Bella & Vincent Jay."

"I did know about you Pearl. I knew Bella was pregnant, and I wanted to be there for you. I wanted to be there, with your mother for our Pearl. I am sorry I couldn't have been."

Pearl doesn't say another word instead stepping to the man and wrapping him in a hug that actually feels natural. An embrace that only a father and daughter can know.

33

Poratan

The journey feels long for the group, as they sail on seas that are free of waves, as if taking them several days if not weeks, but as the light never sets, or even dims, they continue without any concept of the passing of time. They eat when they get hungry, drink when they get thirsty, and oddly enough never tire or need of rest. Eliza finishes two of the tomes of introductions to alchemy. Flame-Tender ends up needing to retune his Lyre from having played if for so long. Umbra, and Nakhal relocate their places of meditation a fair deal more often to remove themselves from the way of the crew at work, and Pearl plays a seemingly endless game of fetch with Boop to the point that even he becomes tired of it.

The meals had, account for at least seven days of uninterrupted, uninteresting travel on the quite seas. This is before Vincent approaches Pearl after the twenty first meal saying in a hush, "We should be at the tower within the next few hours."

"That's great," Pearl responds causing Vincent's hands to gesture for her to keep quiet.

"Not so loud. Do you really trust these people?"

"What do you mean? Of course, I do."

"Well, I just feel that the entire time they have been on my ship they have been shady and have kept almost exclusively to themselves."

"That's because I told them to. Keep in mind, my father or not, compared to them you are the stranger, the unknown quantity."

"What? Pearl, that is hurtful, but I understand where it is coming from. Let your friends know that we will be at your destination soon," saying this Vincent turns to step away but with a thought entering his mind he turns back to look to Pearl asking, "Why are you going to the Tower of Radiance anyway?"

"There is something inside we need to protect."

"You aren't likely going to get to whatever it is. The Guardian of the Tower doesn't take kindly to people. Learned that from experience."

"We still have to try. You don't understand."

"Just be careful alright, for your mother's sake," Vincent finishes stepping up onto the main deck.

Pearl nudges the others, and they begin preparing themselves for what could be waiting for them, gathering anything they had taken out of their bags, and stretching the muscles that had stiffened in the time they were traveling. From the main deck, as they gather in wait, the group can see out on the horizon a point of light, blinding like the sun, but distant and small. With each passing moment that they sail toward it, it grows rising into the sky.

Exactly as Captain Jay had said, beneath the blinding orb of light grows an island, from which rises an enormous tower, the base of which, looking to have a radius of at least a mile, covers most of the land that extends from the sea. Only just as the base of the tower comes into view so does a struggle being fought in front of the door. An angelic figure, taller than Nakhal with white feathered wings that span only about half the span of Eliza's, struggles to fly as he is pulled down by ensnaring chains around his arms and legs, held by his attackers. Four giants like the ones the group have fought up until this point, nearly twice the size of their quarry, hold a chain each as a woman, larger than all of them, commands them to bring the angel down.

Seeing this immediately sparks the group into action. Without hesitation Pearl leaps over the side of the ship and begins swimming faster than it is moving for the shore. Flame-Tender strums a chord on his lyre, before striking into the tune that summons wind to fill the sails. The others run to the front of the ship wanting desperately to help without being able to because of how far away they are.

Each of the four giants release with the hand lower on the chain and using their immense weight advantage over the flying form pull it down several feet while moving their free hands to be higher on the chain. With the panic taking his daughter, and her companions, Vincent calls, out, "What's going on, what are you doing?"

To which Eliza turns from the front of the ship, the wind catching her skirt and hair, responding, "Those are the people we have to stop. We need to protect that angel."

"Say no more," Vincent calls back through the howl of Flame-Tenders wind, and finally proving the reason he is known as a legendary captain, and leader, he takes charge commanding, "You four, get on the dingy and start rowing for shore," and facing Flame-Tender continues, "Use that magic of your to help my daughter as soon as you are close enough to," then yelling to his crew he commands, "Port to starboard! Prepare the cannons!"

Thinking quickly, as the ship begins to lean into its turn Eliza, calls to Boop, "Hey, get them to Pearl as fast as you can." To which Boop responds with an eye stalk performing a salute, before flying down with the landing boat, and forcing it forward with his telekinetic ray.

Captain Jay sees Eliza still on the ship as the others begin quickly away and he calls, "Aren't you going to help?" Ignoring him Eliza takes a deep breath, and out stretching her hands begins the casting of her spell of polymorphing.

The angel is drawn down another few feet, and the enormous woman notices the ship in the distance and the approaching parties. Rolling her eyes, she raises a hand in the direction of the small boat. Quickly and precisely a glyph is drawn in the air of icy blue energy, but before whatever spell was being cast finds its completion Flame-Tender strums a discordant chord, which rings out unnaturally loud into the woman's ears, and the spells shatters.

From the ship a blast of black and purple erupt from a sphere and rising up in the stunned vision of Vincent, Eliza bears the powerful form that she has become before. Pearl gets onto the shore, and ducks down to avoid immediate detection while her companions have the enemies' focus. Seeing the blast of energy from Eliza's direction she can't help let a smile take her face while she slinks around into the small amount of beach foliage she can hide in.

The huge woman looks at her hand having had her spell dispersed before its casting, and looking again to the small boat, with her expression shifting from annoyance to anger, she extends both hands and begins carving glyphs into the air with the same arcane energy. Again, another discordant chord is produced from the lyre, which sounds almost pleasant following the first, and again the magic the giant woman attempts to prepare is broken. Angered even further she stares at her hands for a split moment and stomps to one of her underlings before taking from him a spear, the size of a ballista bolt, but twice as long.

With a hefting throw, the projectile takes flight. The same instant the shaft leaves the giant woman's hand the ship in the distance releases a powerful, loud explosion, followed by the side facing the island releasing a column of grey smoke. A split-second passes before, six mango sized metal slugs impact the island and those standing on it.

Something that would kill someone of a smaller race, the direct impact of a cannon ball with the abdomen, merely winds the woman, dropping her to her knees. From the ship following the explosion of cannon fire Eliza, rushes over the water, only just soon enough to blast the giant spear away, with her telekinetic eye ray, saving the small boat from its piercing power. With her friends protected, she joins Boop in propelling them for the shore.

The woman's large fist strikes down onto the sand of the beach, as she turns to the four giants, who, in their confusion of whether to continue their task or help their leader, have lost some of their progress pulling down the angelic form. Pointing to them and then to the approaching party the woman commands, "Slutte a kaste bort tid, drep disse gnagere!"

Two of the underlings hand off their chains to the other two who begin to strain in holding down the flying form when the small boat is pushed up onto the sand. They charge for the small creatures. Nakhal and Umbra draw their blade, as Flame-Tender escapes the boat to run away down the shore.

The clash of steel rings out, Nakhal and Umbra both deflect blows enough away that they are unscathed by the giants' initial strikes. That act gives Eliza and Boop enough time to find the figures with their eye rays and almost in unison blast forth with a total of five beams. Eliza releases a beam of fire, a beam of black, and one of a white that produces a trail of cloud like fog. Boop releases, his ray of frost, and the disorienting yellow ray, and all five rays hit, impacting both of the giants, causing them to stumble back.

With attention on her companions, Pearl creeps from the foliage, out in the direction of the two holding the chains. Rapier in hand, she looks up to the giant's back and bouncing a few times in place to get her adrenalin flowing, she runs and jumps. One hand grabbing the back of the giant's shirt, she pulls herself up and drives her blade into her target's spine.

He feels a needle like pain. Then he stops being able to feel his legs. Unable to hold himself up or plant his feet to pull against the angel, the giant and his companion begin to be dragged forward.

The giant still holding chains and able to stand on his own power, looks over desperately wanting to help the other, but looking back to the chains he is holding, knows he can't. He looks twice more though, and on the third glance as he watches Pearl climbing up his companion's back, toward the neck, he is unable to stop himself. He releases the chains, and with a single swipe launches Pearl off into the distance.

Eliza, releasing another ray of fire to scald the flesh of the giants, but watches with one of the eyes that she is not using, Pearl's form get flung thirty feet before colliding with a tree. Eliza hears the crack of the impact, and her brow furls. Pearl's body shifts, as she tries to push herself up, but she collapses under her own weight unable to move. In the midst of a confrontation, this is more than Eliza can handle, and she becomes furious. She lets out a scream and abandoning the fight with the others she charges at the giant who struck Pearl.

Above the beach, the angelic figure feels the slack in the chains that bound his arms and drawing his hand around in an arc, a sword of light forms and breaks the remaining chains. Bindings broken, the angle squints down at his attackers, and sees the group fighting them. Angling himself down the angel readies himself to join the fray, and with a single thrust of his wings launches himself downward.

Nakhal and Umbra land as the two giants fall motionless into the sand beneath their feet, and Flame-Tender maintains a phrase of music in dal segno which has summoned a torrent of wind now holding the leader of the four giants aloft. That is when down the beach there is an explosion. Eliza goes to release a barrage of attacks on the giant but is stopped as the angelic figure slams into the beach sending out a shockwave of sand. The figure grips a sword made entirely of radiant energy and looking over his shoulder says without moving his lips, but also not telepathically, in a voice that booms with regal authority, "Go tend to your friend, I will have this fight."

Stunned and confused, Eliza has to shake herself back into reality with the command, and returning a nod, she begins around toward Pearl. Seeing the creature with many eyestalks trying to get past him the standing giant moves in Eliza's direction. Immediately after taking a step, he feels a divine presence behind him as the angel, flying nearly ten feet of the ground to have an even head level with him, rushes forward and grabbing the back of the giant's head slams it down into the ground.

Having dispatched the other two giants, and believing the leader handled by Flame-Tender's magic, Umbra, Nakhal, and Boop move to assist the angel. They are stopped short, before they are able to move more than a few feet, by an outstretched open hand, from the angel. Behind them Flame-Tender calls out, "Hey, I can't hold this forever!"

Eliza, slows, and reverts to her natural form, landing beside Pearl. On her knees she pulls Pearl into her lap and forces back her tears that try to break free seeing Pearl in the mangled state she is. Pulling the amulet from her neck Eliza, presses it onto Pearl's chest and focuses on health, on healing, and her hands begin glowing the golden light.

The standing giant pulls back several steps. Pulling an axe from his hip, he and the angel prepare to charge. Both glare at the other, waiting for the other to make the first move.

A scream echoes over the field. The leader of the giants begins to mutate. Her face elongates into a maw. Her flesh loses its color, splinters, and hardens into a hide of scales. Her fingers extend and grow talons from their tips. From her back burst a pair of draconic wings that force themselves out into the arcane torrent of wind and as her eyes begins to glow the icy blue of her magic, her scream echoes and morphs into a rasping monstrous roar.

The giant and the angel throw themselves forward into a charge for each other. Both swing for the other and their weapons collide releasing an explosive ringing clash of metal that rivals the roar, and a bouquet of sparks explode from the collision. The angel casts the giant's axe down to the side and pulling his blade back slices his opponent's thigh.

The glow of Eliza's hands intensifies, to the point of the two becoming a radiance that competes with the blinding light thousands of feet above them. It becomes as though the two are cast into a realm of their own. Cloaked in light as Pearl looks up to Eliza and moans, "Lizzy," and she coughs, continuing, "You don't like that name. I'm sorry. I wasn't quick enough."

Eliza can't hold her tears back as she presses the symbol of Archangel even more powerfully into Pearl's chest. Ethereal golden wings unfurl from her back as she looks down at her injured friend, only a quarter the size of her wings of bone. With the appearance of the illusory wings, Pearl is cast within a separate aura of gold from Eliza's magic, only moments before she resides herself to a fate from her injuries.

The torrent around the giant half dragon destabilizes, and in an explosive burst she frees herself. Flame-Tender, is thrown away to the water's edge as she drifts back down onto the sand. Boop, Nakhal, and Umbra turn in time to jump out of the way as the woman exhales a large blast, of icy breath that freezes the moisture in the air instantly causing it to become a torrent of sleet in the group's direction.

The angel pulls away as the giant falls to his knee, unable to support his own weight. Stepping to his side, the angel rolls his shoulders exclaiming in the booming regal voice, "You are among those who would seek the prime constructor's fragment for your own gain, you are sentenced to death." Stepping to the giant, the angel draws his radiant blade across the intruder's chest, casting him down motionless into the sand.

Eliza falls onto Pearl and suddenly a breath fills Pearl's lungs, and Eliza pulls back. Pearl reaches up and feeling her bones setting themselves, succumbs to the pain, that she can only imagine Eliza suffers from her wings and polymorphing, before her eyes close and she passes from consciousness.

Nakhal charges for the giant woman, and Umbra darts to the side around to find the flank. Boop ascends up releasing down a barrage of eye rays onto the woman forcing her to raise her arm to block it, opening her to Nakhal's assault. His blade connects and drags across her groin. The material of her padded leggings tears away leaving her scaly flesh exposed and undamaged.

The angel steps to the other giant, who, still unable to feel his legs, has been crawling away. A single motion pierces the radiant sword into the laying giant's back, pressing it down into motionlessness. The angel sees Eliza and Pearl and turning to the confrontation he leaps to join the continued fight.

The woman draws several glyphs in the air around her and dragging a claw through the four symbols she releases a wave of magic that manifests in a storm of sleet, which contains itself in a sixty-foot-wide, one-hundred-eighty-foot-high column. Boop is struck by a sheet of icy precipitant falling painfully into the sand. The others around the woman, duck in a feeble attempt to avoid the downfall. Unphased the angel continues his charge, where his blade swings and is caught in a clash against his foe's claws.

The part dragon, giant woman throws the angel back, away from her to the edge of the concentrated sleet storm. The downfall is unrelenting preventing flight and hampering movement, but still, the angel charges back for his target. He drives his blade into the woman's lower leg. She screams out ferociously, swinging her claw across his chest.

The freshly wounded angel falls away, placing one hand to the source of his new-found pain. Looking again to the monolithic foe, he charges, and pulls the radiant blade through the gash that has been made in her armor. The blow causes her to fall to a knee, yelling her way down in pain. She throws both of her claws for her attacker but finds difficulty as one is blocked by Nakhal's blade and might, and the other is deflected into the chilled sand at the angel's feet.

Another roar releases another cone of icy artic air, and the three in front of her are consumed by the blast. The angle turns as the blast escapes the woman's maw, and his wings expand out blocking the majority of the blast from Umbra and Nakhal. Ice shards form hanging onto the wings as they block the wave of frost that would kill mortals. The shards of ice fall from the wings, and into the sleet on sand at his feet. His wings flex and in a single motion he turns removing the woman's head.

34

The Shard

A thump of the head hitting the sand silences the movement on the island. The angel steps to the side, out of the way of the body as it falls, and without turning to the group that came to his aid, his voice calmly echoes to them, "You have my gratitude. Now explain your purpose for being here."

Taking charge, Flame-Tender begins stepping in the angel's direction responding, "We were looking to stop these people and the group they are a part of from claiming what I am sure you are protecting."

"The shard," he interrupts, before turning to face Flame-Tender continuing, "How have you come to know of this."

"Well," Flame-Tender responds before Eliza's voice calls to them.

"A man by the name Negmor," she says gaining the gatherings attention.

The angel turns and begins stepping in Eliza's direction. Returning their swords into the holsters Umbra and Nakhal join Flame-Tender, in following the eleven-foot tall radiant titan. Getting to Eliza the angel looks down at the unconscious Pearl in the young girl's lap and kneels down with an emotionless cold expression on his face as he examines them both. Placing a hand on Pearl's forehead, his hand begins to glow, with a radiant magic like that which Eliza used to stabilize Pearl, but his thrums with an intensity in its power that far exceeds what Eliza was able to produce.

After merely a second, the radiant energy fades, and the angel stands. Suddenly, Pearl's eyes flicker open and a smile takes her face and Eliza's. Straining she attempts to sit up, and as Boop cautiously joins them she throws her arms over him using him for leverage moaning, "That hurt. I hate to say it Nakhal but you were right. They have some muscle."

"You explained that you are here through the instruction of the one known as Negmor. Is that correct," the angel's voice reverberates in the air around the group.

Free from under Pearl, who with Boop's assistance has found her feet beneath herself, Eliza stands responding, "Yes sir. Specifically, he told Pearl and I, and that we needed to prevent it from falling into the hands of those people and those they work with."

"Then it is that time. My guard has come to its end. Come with me," the angel says before stepping for the tower.

Free from the chaos of combat, the group finally take a moment to bear witness to what is around them. The island is unspectacular in every aspect except that it serves as the base for the enormous tower. Huge twenty-foot-wide cubic bricks of polished white stone are stacked together to form the structure that extends so far upward that its form fades into the blue of the sky before its pinnacle, the source of the blinding light above.

Running to the angel's side, looking like a child in proportion to the large form, Flame-Tender asks, "What do you mean your guard has come to an end? We need all the help we can have protecting this thing."

"That being true, I cannot assist you. The holy man in the company of the one known as Negmor summoned me here, and as soon as I pass the mantle onto your company, so to will the magic that permits me to be the guardian of this artifact fade."

The towering angel steps up to the mammoth forty-foot-tall set of doors which lead into the waiting tower, and in a motion that seems effortless, for him, he pushes one of them open. Through the passageway is a vast black empty chamber. Far from the door, in the center of it, levitating several feet up, is something glowing a gold and red light. Surrounding the distant glowing object is an almost invisible spherical shell, that is only able to be witnessed as the ring it creates in the inch of water that covers the floor.

Pearl leans on Eliza and Boop as they join the angel in the doorway. With a smirk she asks, "So, that's it? All of this fuss for a tiny floating, glowing stone?"

"Do not jest about the significance of your new purpose. That is a fragment of the very thing that was used by the gods to solidify reality," the angel quickly scolds Pearl for her sarcasm.

Mesmerized by the distant shard, Eliza's breath escapes her saying, "Wow. It's beautiful," and looking up to the angel she asks, "What are we supposed to do?"

"Protect it, however you see best, you were chosen because the mage saw something in you, I am sure. That will mean that you will be able to succeed in this task until you choose those who will replace yourselves."

Stepping to the water's edge, Flame-Tender says abruptly to the others, "Well regardless of what we want to do from this point on, we can't keep it here. Not only could the others of that person's company find them through many forms of magical detection, but I don't see any food or water around here."

Eliza, eyes locked on the distant glowing shard, not even hearing Flame-Tender through the trance she has fallen into, releases Pearl, leaving her to lean on Boop, and takes a single step forward placing her foot into the water, sending a single ripple cascading across the chamber's floor. From behind, Pearl's voice breaks Eliza free from the trance, "Lizzy?"

Eliza turns to face Pearl as her other foot joins the first in the water. At that instant there is a loud crack from the shard and Eliza's head snaps to face it. Her body stiffens and she feels a pain in her chest. Her arms extend, out and down to her sides as a ghostly gaseous black and purple aura explodes visibly into existence around her. Panic fills her as she strains against the magic controlling her and she calls out, "Pearl! I don't know what's happening."

Flame-Tender, having stepped with Eliza through the threshold, recoils as the aura radiates with an energy that becomes painful to him for his proximity. This only lasts a moment before he is thrust through the water along the edge of the chamber that spans the entire base of the tower more than thirty feet away from her. As he slides away he calls to the angel asking, "Angel what is happening!"

For the first time the angel's expression mutates from stern indifference to confusion as he tries to respond but before sound can escape him a burst of light surrounds his form and he vanishes. Watching this Pearl reaches out wanting to help Eliza, only a few feet away through the door, but unable to support herself she falls as Boop frees himself from her weight. He shoots forward wanting to help but as he reaches the precipice of the doorway where it transitions from outside to in, he is struck and thrown away with same raw power that launched Flame-Tender away. He throws himself into the seemingly impenetrable barrier several times, and tears forming in all of his eyes he cries out, "Master! Master! Mother!"

"I don't know what is going on Boop," Eliza calls back, "It will be alright! Just, don't watch ok."

The floating orb creature tries one last time, throwing himself into the force preventing him from reaching Eliza's side. The others stand watching, helplessly not knowing what they could do. Striking the barrier, the one final time, Boop freezes and suddenly transforms into the obsidian orb, falling to the ground by Pearl with a thud.

At the epicenter of the pain in Eliza's chest a black crystal pierces free from her flesh, extending as a pointed cluster for the thing in the center of the chamber. The aura around the young girl explodes and expands five feet in all directions, but not blocking the group's ability to see her, only ever appearing as an outline. Concentrating, the aura shrinks again and begins extending out as a needle toward the shard of prime, which reaches out with its own funnel of otherworldly magic.

The two cones of power meet each other, and the magic of each begins to seep along the other like infectious veins spreading. Eliza feels a connection form almost as though she is in more than one place at the same time. That moment Eliza's eyes widen as she begins to be pulled forward toward the shard.

The others watch helplessly as Eliza is lifted from the water, the crystal in her chest pulls her along the path of the connected magic funnels. Seconds pass as the slow progression continues, and the center of the two funnels' connection shifts remaining perfectly between the two sources as Eliza drifts closer. After nearly a minute she reaches the edge of the undulating shell around the shard, and suddenly she is thrust forward. The crystal protruding from her chest and the waiting shard collide, a wave, a combination of the two colors of magic, explodes out; filling the room. A half second later it collapses with a low thump.

Pearl, hoisted up with Nakhal's help, reaches out calling as the eruption collapses, "Eliza," and the magic releases its sound. In the wake of the collapse the center of the room is empty. Eliza and the glowing crystal are gone, missing from where they were, and Pearl looks down to where Boop had been, finding an empty divot in the sand.

About D. B.

I am a nobody, who has stories to tell. I am a person who when young and was introduced to the idea of writing would never have thought myself looking to even dream of being published or publishing myself. Dyslexia, literature always seemed distant from me something that I would never be able to connect to or fully understand the enjoyment others gain from it. I still don't. For me I can not find pleasure in reading, a task which when set to gives me headaches, something that I had to deal with even trying to edit my own work, but I can understand a want for a good story with strong characters that you as the one experiencing it through any medium can feel an attachment to, a want to see them succeed and a sorrow if you see them fail.

I feel this way not because of the great stories I feined reading in grade school, or because of a great epiphany I had as I got older. It was there ever since I can remember when my brothers and I would stay up far past our bedtime creating stories and games to play with one another, and it was fortified when my father introduced us to Dungeons and Dragons. I was 8 at the time and my Half-orc barbarian met the craft of storytelling when the day turned into a dark and stormy night while he was in a field and instead of seeking shelter he sat on the nearest rock to wait out the storm. To get me to move, my dad had me struck by lightning, at that moment I was entrenched and I knew that telling stories would be a part of my life. I just didn't know how much it would be.

As every kid I had dreams of what I wanted to be growing up, whether it be a star athlete, a video game designer, a trumpet player, a tech at Google, I never had the dream to be a writer. Not until recently, when going through a wave of depression, whose reason for being is no longer important now what is important is how I coped, I locked myself in my room and I started to write. When my brothers and I were young our mother had us keep a journal sometimes during some of our summers off from school, and we learned that putting words to paper could be a way of working things out in our heads even if the words don't match what we are thinking. So, I wrote, a book that will never see the light of day, for trademarked things were used in the book and the one publisher who would be able to publish it has denied it as a work for them to take on. What I learned though, was a great passion I felt creating a story, something I do all the time normally, down onto paper, with the hope of sharing it.

I sign here now at the mercy of the subjective world of literature, prostrating myself with all I present, as my work, to speak for itself, and pray that I have done well, in providing a story, that will hopefully bring readers back for more from me and that they will share with their friends and families, as I continue to write.

Acknowledgments

This book would not have been possible without: My family, who inspired me and even when disparaging me were pushing me to be strong in my own convictions, and to see through what I start. My friends who laid the ground work for this story in the D&D game we played. Lastly the few in number who got themselves a copy of **Black: The Name** for making it feel less like I was squandering my time and life putting these words to these pages.

Thanks for joining Eliza on her journey to find where she belongs! Please, if you are so inclined, let me know what you thought with a review! If you enjoyed, please let your friends know about our young Eliza, and follow me on Twitter to see what projects I am working on and hear about progress on Eliza's continuing journey!